HOME SONG

Also by LaVyrle Spencer

Family Blessings

November of the Heart

Bygones

Forgiving

Bitter Sweet

Spring Fancy

Morning Glory

The Hellion

Vows

The Gamble

A Heart Speaks

Years

Separate Beds

Twice Loved

Sweet Memories

Hummingbird

The Endearment

The Fulfillment

HOME SONG

LaVyrle Spencer

G. P. PUTNAM'S SONS
NEW YORK

G. P. Putnam's Sons
Publishers Since 1838
200 Madison Avenue
New York, NY 10016

Library of Congress Cataloging-in-Publication Data

Spencer, LaVyrle.
    Home song / LaVyrle Spencer.
        p.   cm.
    ISBN 0-399-14014-X (alk. paper)
    1. High school principals—Minnesota—Fiction. 2. Family—
    Minnesota—Fiction. I. Title.
    PS3569.P4534H66 1995   94-24852 CIP
    813'.54—dc20

Book design and composition by The Sarabande Press
Printed in the United States of America
1 2 3 4 5 6 7 8 9 10

This book is printed on acid-free paper.

To
Deborah Raffin Viner
and
Michael Viner
I love you both
for bringing so much into my life,
not the least of which
is a friendship I treasure

I wish to thank Tom Cole, his wife, Joanne, and daughter, Jennifer, for their help with this book. Also, thanks to Marcia Aubineau, and Jon and Julene Swenson. Tom's help was especially valuable, and his willingness to read partial drafts of the manuscript and to offer suggestions was truly appreciated. It's absolutely an accident that I'd chosen the name Tom for my protagonist long before I'd met Tom Cole. My hero, along with his family, his school, and his past, are strictly fictitious.

Home Song
by Henry Wadsworth Longfellow

Stay, stay at home, my heart, and rest;
Home-keeping hearts are happiest,
For those that wander they know not where
Are full of trouble and full of care;
To stay at home is best.

Weary and homesick and distressed,
They wander east, they wander west,
And are baffled and beaten and blown about
By the winds of the wilderness of doubt;
To stay at home is best.

Then stay at home, my heart, and rest;
The bird is safest in its nest;
O'er all that flutter their wings and fly
A hawk is hovering in the sky;
To stay at home is best.

HOME SONG

One

Minnesota lay green and vibrant, freshened by a night's rain that rinsed the late August sky to a watercolor blue. East of St. Paul, where the suburbs nudged the Washington County line, fingers of new streets flexed into the expanses of ripe grain, new houses sprouting where only fields and forests had lain before.

There, where the city met the farmland, a modern brick school building spread its U-shaped wings, bordered by blacktop parking lots on the north and east, and an athletic field on the south. Beyond the spectator stands a stretch of whispering cornfield still held its own against the urban sprawl that threatened it, but its plight was clear: more development could be seen on the distant hills.

Across the highway, a small section of older homes, built in the fifties and sixties, straggled within shouting distance of the county road, where the speed limit had been lowered when the school went up five years earlier. Sidewalks had been installed then, too, though some taxpayers said they led to nowhere, petering out into sectors where tractors still worked the land. The school district was growing at an alarming rate, however, and had been for years.

That Wednesday morning, six days before the start of school, a vibrant aquamarine Lexus pulled into the visitors' parking lot on the north side of Hubert H. Humphrey High. A woman and a boy emerged and approached the building along a lengthy stretch of sidewalk. Already the eleven A.M. sun had heated the concrete, but the janitors had propped open the double front doors to let the breeze blow through.

The woman was dressed in a gray no-nonsense suit, paler gray silk blouse, matching pumps—simple, but expensive—and a subdued scarf in shades of burgundy. Her streaked blond hair was cut in a conservative ear-length bob, blown back from a side part. Her only jewelry, a pair of tiny gold stud earrings, seemed a mere concession to femininity, which her style downplayed in every other way.

The boy was taller than she by a head and a half, wide-topped, skinny-hipped, athletic, erect in stature, dressed in blue jeans and a T-shirt lauding the Texas Aggies. He had dark hair and stunning brown eyes in a face that would—his entire life long—make females turn for a second look. Two generations earlier teenage girls would have called him a heartthrob; his mother's generation would have said he was a fox. Today, a pair of sixteen-year-old girls came out of the school building just as he entered; one gazed back over her shoulder and exclaimed to her friend, "Wow, he's *hot!*"

The office of Humphrey High sat in the dead center of the building, sandwiched between walls of glass. The front looked out across the main hall at the visitors' parking lot and the huge brick planter showcasing the school colors—red and white—in a bed of petunias. The rear of the office overlooked a lovely arboretum cared for by Mr. Dorffmeier's horticulture students.

Kent Arens held open the office door.

"Smile," Monica Arens said pleasantly as she swung past him into the cool billow of air-conditioning.

"At what?" the boy replied, following her.

"You know how important first impressions are."

"Yes, Mother," he replied dryly as the door closed behind them.

Unlike the grounds, the office was in chaos: people were moving everywhere, dressed in blue jeans and T-shirts, collating papers, answering phones, using computers, clattering typewriters. Two janitors were painting the walls, while another wheeled in a dolly stacked with cardboard cartons. The blue carpet scarcely showed beneath the stacks of books, piles of stapled materials, and the general flotsam of maintenance work.

Monica and Kent picked their way through the commotion to a twelve-foot crescent-shaped counter that prevented all visitors from advancing further. From one of the numerous desks behind it, a secretary rose and came forward. She had a pudgy face, plump breasts, and short brown hair just beginning to gray.

"Hello. May I help you?"

"I'm Monica Arens, and this is my son, Kent. We've come to register him for school."

"Sorry about the mess in here, but it's always like this the last week before school. I'm Dora Mae Hudak. I answer to 'Dora Mae,' and I'm just the one to see." She smiled at the boy. "You're new here this year."

"Yes, ma'am. We just moved from Austin, Texas."

She assessed his height. "A senior, I'd guess."

"Yes, ma'am."

Dora Mae Hudak momentarily stalled in her tracks: she was unaccustomed to being called "ma'am" by high school seniors. Most called her Dora Mae. Some addressed her "Hey, lady," and occasionally one would break forth with "Yo! You . . . secretary!"

"Love those Southern manners," she remarked as she reached for an admissions form and a student introductory booklet. "Do you know what classes you want to take?"

"Pretty much. If you have them all."

"So you haven't seen our list of electives yet?"

"No, ma'am."

She placed a pamphlet and a sheet of blue paper on the counter. "Classes are listed in here, and this is the admissions form, but we like all new students to talk to a counselor before registering. Our seniors are counseled by Mrs. Berlatsky. Hang on a second while I see if she's in."

Dora Mae poked her head into one of the side offices and returned with a fortyish woman dressed in a thigh-length blue knit pullover and stirrup pants.

"Hi. I'm Joan Berlatsky." She extended her hand. "Kent, welcome to Minnesota. Ms. Arens, hello. Want to come into my office where we can talk?"

They followed Joan Berlatsky into her office while she apologized for the mess. "It's like this every year, the custodians trying to finish up everything after the summer-school people finally clear out. It never seems like the building will be ready in time, but somehow, as if by magic, it always is. Please . . . sit down."

They had a friendly talk, during which the counselor learned that Kent had a 3.8 grade-point average and was college-bound, and that he was concentrating on science and math and wanted to take as many honors classes as possible. His mother had already made arrangements for his records to be forwarded from his former high school, but they hadn't arrived yet. Joan pulled up class lists on a green computer screen, and within thirty minutes they had settled on Kent's senior class schedule.

Everything went smoothly until Monica Arens said, "Oh, and who should we see about signing Kent up for football?"

Joan turned from her computer screen and said, "There might be a problem with that. The team has already been working out for two weeks, and it's possible Coach Gorman has the team roster all set."

Kent's eyebrows beetled. He leaned forward anxiously. "But I've already lettered in both my sophomore and junior years. I was counting on playing my senior year, too."

"As I said, the team has been working out since mid-August, but . . ." Joan frowned thoughtfully before reaching for her phone. "Just a minute. Let me call down there and see if Coach Gorman is in." While the phone rang in the locker room, she said, "You probably already know that sports are really big here. Our football team took second at state last year, and our basketball team was the double-A state champion. Shoot, it doesn't sound like he's going to answer." She hung up. "Just a minute. Let me go ask Mr. Gardner, our principal. He likes to meet all the new kids personally anyway. Be right back." She had barely whisked around the corner before her head reappeared. "Want to ask Dora Mae for the computer printout of your schedule while I'm gone? It'll come up on the printer out here."

The pair followed her to the outer office, where they stood before the crescent-shaped counter while a printer clacked and spewed forth Kent's class schedule.

Tom Gardner sat at his desk, facing his open office doorway with a phone at his ear, trying to reason with a textbook sales rep: only three business days to go before school started, and his new tenth-grade English textbooks were nowhere to be found.

At Joan's appearance, he gestured for her to stay, holding up one index finger while continuing his conversation. "Our purchasing agent ordered them in January of last year. . . . Are you sure? . . . When? . . . In July! But how could that many textbooks just disappear? . . . Mr. Travis, my problem is that next Tuesday I'm going to have five hundred and ninety tenth-grade students coming through these doors, and English is a required course for every one of them." After a lengthy pause he wrote down a bill-of-lading number. "To the loading dock? How big were the cartons?" He dropped the pencil, rubbed his forehead, and said, "I see. Yes, thank you, I'll check at my end. If they can't be located, do you have more in stock? . . . Yes, I will, thank you. Goodbye."

Tom hung up and expelled a breath that puffed out his cheeks. "Missing textbooks. What can I do for you, Joan?"

"I've got a new transfer student out here you'll want to meet. He's a senior and he wants to play football. Will you handle it?"

"Sure," he said, rolling back his chair and rising. As much as he loved his job as principal of HHH, Tom hated this last week before school. During these crazy days he became primarily a problem solver, working in the chaos left behind by the summer-school staff, who moved things they weren't supposed to move, hid equipment that was in their way, and stuffed incoming supplies into the most unlikely of places. Electricians were installing a new overhead lighting system, and some snafu had held up a batch of the fixtures, so there were no lights in the home economics department. A physics teacher he'd hired way back last May had called the day before and said she'd accepted a better offer from another district and wouldn't be coming to work here after all. And now the textbook people claimed a trucking company had delivered thirty cartons of books onto a loading dock at the district warehouse on July 15, but nobody at this end had ever seen them.

Tom Gardner stuffed it all behind a calm exterior and focused on the facet of his job that he considered most important: the students.

This new one was waiting with his mother on the opposite side of the counter—a tall, dark, good-looking kid with an athlete's build who wanted to play football.

Joan led the way and made introductions.

"This is Kent Arens. He'll be a senior with us this year. Kent, our principal, Mr. Gardner."

Tom shook hands with the boy and felt a hard paw with plenty of muscle behind it.

"And this is Kent's mother, Monica."

The two began shaking hands as automatically as any strangers, but midway through the introduction a sixth sense buzzed through Tom.

"Monica?" He said, peering at her more closely. "Monica Arens?"

Disbelief widened her eyes.

"Tom?" she said. "Tom Gardner?"

"Well, for heaven's sake, this is a surprise."

"That's you? Mr. Gardner . . . the principal here?" Her gaze shot to the brass name plate beside his office door.

"That's me. I've been here for eighteen years, first as a teacher, then as principal." He dropped her hand, for it was awkward holding it above the elbow-high counter. "Obviously you live in this school district."

"I . . . yes . . . we . . ." She had grown flustered and her face began flushing. "I've just been transferred here. I'm an engineer for 3M. I never would have . . . I mean, I had no idea you lived anywhere near here. I didn't even know what the principal's name was until Mrs. Berlatsky said it a minute ago."

"Well, that's how it goes," he said with an easygoing grin. "Paths cross, don't they?" He hooked his hands on his hips, letting his gaze linger on her affectionately. She remained flustered and offered no smile, only the impression that she was struggling to overcome some gross embarrassment. "And you have a family now . . ." He turned his attention back to the boy.

"Just one. Just Kent."

He was truly a handsome young man, as tall as Tom himself.

"You know my mother?" Kent asked, surprised by the discovery.

"Way back when," Tom replied. "In nineteen seventy-five."

"But we haven't seen each other since," Monica hastened to add.

"Well, enough about us. We've sort of left you out of the conversation here, haven't we, Kent? Listen, why don't the two of you come into my office, where there's less confusion and noise. We can talk in there."

In his office, with its view of the arboretum and the football field beyond, they sat facing each other across his desk. The late-morning sun angled above the east wing of the school building and spread across the south windowsill, where a gallery of Gardner family photographs faced Tom's desk.

Tom Gardner tipped back in his swivel chair, loosely steepled his hands, and said to the boy, "So you want to play football, I'm told."

"Yes, sir."

The kid looked familiar. "You've played before? In your last school?"

"Yes, sir. I lettered in both my sophomore and junior years, and last year I was all-conference."

"What position did you play?"

"Running back."

Tom had been a coach himself; he knew what questions to ask to determine if the kid was a team man or a *me* man.

"What was your team like?"

"Just great. I had some really good blockers who were smart, and they really understood the game. It made it easy to play, because we sort of . . . well, you know, we understood what each other was doing."

Tom liked the kid's answer. "How about your coach?"

Kent answered simply, "I'm going to miss him," impressing Tom further. Once again, he had the strong impression he knew the boy from somewhere. Not only his facial features but his expressions looked awfully familiar.

"So tell me about your goals," Tom said, feeling the boy out further.

"Short-term or long-term?"

"Both."

"Well . . ." Kent rested his elbows on the arms of his chair, joined his hands, and cleared his throat, thinking over his answer. "Short term . . . I'd like to bench-press three hundred pounds." He sent Tom a mini-grin, half shy, half proud. "I'm up to two-seventy now."

Tom said, "Wow," returning a pleased grin. "And your long-term goals?"

"I want to be an engineer like my mom." Kent glanced at his mother, throwing the front of his face momentarily into direct sunlight. Something caught Tom's eye, something he hadn't paid any attention to before, something that clicked in his brain and sent a sizzle of warning through him: a tiny cowlick right at the center front of Kent Arens's black crew-cut hair, the smallest wedge, which made it look as if no hair grew at the very tip of his widow's peak.

Just like his own.

The recognition came and kicked Tom Gardner in the gut while the boy went on speaking.

"I'd like to go to Stanford because they've got a great engineering program and a super football team, too. I think I'm good enough to maybe go on a football scholarship . . . that is, if I can play again this year so the scouts can see me."

The boy looked back at Tom, full-face. The similarity was uncanny. Startling!

Tom glanced away to disabuse himself of the preposterous notion. He reached across the desk. "Mind if I take a look at your class schedule?"

Concentrating on the blue paper, he hoped that when he looked back up he'd believe he was mistaken. The boy had chosen a very heavy load: calculus, advanced chemistry, advanced physics, social studies, weight training, and honors English.

Honors English . . . taught by Tom's wife, Claire.

His gaze remained lowered longer than necessary. *It can't be, it can't be.* But raising his eyes once again, he saw features too much like those he encountered in the mirror every morning—a long swarthy face wearing a deep summer tan, brown eyes with dark brows curving much like his own, an aquiline nose, a good, solid chin—faintly dimpled—and that tiny wedge of a cowlick he'd hated his whole life long.

He shifted his attention to Monica, but she was studying her knees, her mouth drawn tight. He remembered how flustered she'd acted when they were introduced in the outer office, how she'd blushed. Sweet Jesus, if it was true, why wouldn't she have told him seventeen, eighteen years ago?

"Well, this . . ." Tom began, but his voice cracked and he had to clear his throat. "This is an impressive schedule . . . tough courses. And football on top of that. Are you sure you can handle it all?"

"I think so. I've always taken a heavy class load, and I've always been in sports."

"What kind of grades do you get?"

"I have a three-point-eight average. Mom's already told my old school to send my records, but I guess they haven't gotten here yet."

Queer, zingy rivers were whizzing through Tom's bloodstream as he rocked forward in his chair and spoke, hoping nothing showed on his face.

"I like what I see, and I like what I hear, Kent. I think I want you to talk to Coach Gorman. The team has been practicing for two weeks already, but this should be the coach's decision."

Monica spoke up, meeting Tom's eyes directly for the first time since entering his office. She had regained her composure but her face remained impassive. If she had truly blushed before, she now exemplified a woman in control.

"He's college-bound, one way or another," she stated, "but if he doesn't get a chance to play his senior year, you know what happens to his chances of getting a scholarship."

"I understand, and I'll speak to Coach Gorman myself and ask that he get a tryout. Kent, do you think you could come down to the football field this afternoon at three? The team will be working out then and I can introduce you to the coach."

Kent glanced at his mother. She said, "I don't see why not. You can take me back home and use the car."

"Good," Tom said.

At that moment Joan Berlatsky interrupted, thrusting her head around the doorway. "Excuse me, Tom. I forgot to tell Kent . . . we have a newcomers' group that meets every week, Thursday morning before school. Nice way to get to know the kids, if you're interested in joining it."

"Thanks, I might."

When Joan disappeared, Tom rose, and the other two followed suit. "Well, Kent . . ." He extended his hand across the desk and Kent returned the handshake. At close range, appraising his dark good looks, touching him, Tom's suspicion seemed even more believable. "Welcome to HHH. If there's anything I can do to make your transition here easier, just let me know. I'm here for the students anytime. Even if you just need to talk . . . well, I'm available for that, too."

Tom went around the desk and shook Monica's hand. "Monica, it was nice to see you again." He searched her eyes for a clue, but she gave away nothing.

She fixed her gaze on something behind his left shoulder and remained coolly distant. "Nice to see you, too."

"Same goes for you. If you need any help getting him settled in here, just give a call. Mrs. Berlatsky or I will be glad to help however we can."

"Thank you."

They parted at his door, and he watched them walk away through the messy outer office, where someone had propped open the hall doors to dilute the strong paint smell. A radio was playing a Rod Stewart song. A copy machine set up a rhythmic *shd-shd-shd* while yellow papers flapped from it. Secretaries typed at their desks while a trio of teachers checked their mailboxes and chatted—everybody going about their business and not one of them suspecting what a life-altering shock had just befallen the man who led them all. He watched as Monica Arens and her son walked out of the office, crossed the hall, and exited through the set of propped-open outer doors into the sunny August day. He could tell they were talking as they strode down the sidewalk, stepped off the curb, and continued toward a new Lexus of a piercing aquamarine blue. The boy got behind the wheel, the engine started, and the sun glinted off the car's clean, luminescent paint as it backed up, turned, and disappeared from his view.

Only then did Tom Gardner move.

"I don't want to be disturbed for a while," he told Dora Mae, as he entered his office. He closed the door, which was normally left open unless he was with a student. Alone, he flattened his vertebrae against the windowless door and let his head drop back against it. He felt all cinched up inside, as if a tree had fallen across his chest. His stomach quivered and held a knot of impending fear. He closed his eyes, trying to force the fear into submission.

It didn't work.

Pulling away from the door, opening his eyes, he actually felt dizzy.

He went to the window and stood in the slanting rays of late morning, one hand covering his mouth, the other wrapped across his ribs. Outside, in the arboretum, the sun striped the manicured grass, dappled the pruned trees, and faded the old-fashioned wooden picnic tables; in the distance it sketched a second, fallen chain-link fence at the foot of the one delineating the perimeter of the tennis courts; it whacked out large trapezoids of shadow from the visible half of the spectator stands; it lustered the cornfields behind them.

Tom Gardner's gaze registered none of it.

Instead, he saw the handsome face of Kent Arens and the stricken, blushing one of Kent's mother. Then later her closed expression and the air of detachment as she carefully avoided Tom's eyes.

God in heaven, could the boy be his?

The dates matched.

The third week of June 1975, the week of his marriage to Claire, who had been pregnant with Robby at the time. Staring sightlessly, he regretted that one breach of good sense eighteen years before, that single infidelity on the eve of his wedding, that sin for which he'd done silent penance earlier in his marriage but which had faded gradually as the years of absolute fidelity had built between himself and Claire.

He dropped his hand from the heat of his own blush and felt a wad in his throat that stuck there like a piece of hard candy each time he swallowed. Maybe the boy wasn't seventeen. Maybe he was sixteen . . . or eighteen! After all, not every senior was seventeen!

But most were, and common sense told him Kent Arens was too tall and well developed to be only sixteen. It appeared he shaved every day, and his shoulders and chest muscles were those of a young man. Furthermore, the startling physical resemblance to himself seemed to bear out Tom's awful suspicion.

He stood over the photographs of his family. He touched the frames. His family: Claire, Chelsea, and Robby.

None of them knew a thing about the night of his bachelor party.

Oh, please, let this kid not be mine.

Abruptly he spun and opened his door. "Dora Mae, did you file Kent Arens's registration card?"

"Not yet, it's right here." She picked it up from her desk and handed it to him. He took it back into his office, dropped to his desk chair, and read every word.

Kent was seventeen, all right: birthdate 3-22-76, exactly nine months after Tom Gardner's irresponsible act of rebellion against a marriage for which he wasn't ready.

Parents' name: Monica J. Arens; no father listed.

He searched his dim memory of that night, but it had been so long before and he'd been drinking—a lot—and she'd been nothing more than this girl who showed up at a party delivering pizza. Had either one of them used any birth control? He had no idea if she had. Had he?

Probably not, because at that time Claire was already pregnant, so no birth control was necessary. Before that she'd been on birth control pills, but she had forgotten to take them along on a weekend ski trip to Colorado, and like most randy young whelps, they'd thought themselves invulnerable, and that's when she'd gotten pregnant.

Irresponsible? Yes, of course, but that entire night of his bachelor party had been irresponsible, from the amount of alcohol he'd consumed, to the porn movies his fraternity brothers had shown, to his indiscriminate sex with some girl he scarcely knew.

All because he was being rushed into a marriage that had—in the long run—turned out to be the best thing that ever happened to him.

Sitting in his office holding Kent Arens's registration card in his hand, Tom sighed and rocked forward in his chair. Could the kid look that much like him and not be his? Given the circumstances, he doubted it. And if he had so easily spotted the resemblance, anybody could: the office staff, Chelsea, Robby . . . Claire.

The thought of his wife threw him into a tailspin of panic, and he rocketed from his chair, leaving the card behind, instinct driving him straight to her to protect whatever might possibly be in jeopardy.

"I'll be up in room two-thirty-two," he told Dora Mae, striding past her desk.

Like the main office, the long halls leading to the classrooms were a mess, piled with study materials, covered with drop cloths, smelling of paint. From some of the classrooms came the sound of radios, the volume turned low while teachers, dressed in work clothing, put their rooms in order. The audiovisual director came trudging toward Tom, pushing a cart piled with tape recorders, having trouble negotiating the junk-filled hall.

"Hi, Tom," she said.

"Hi, Denise."

"I need to talk to you sometime about the new photography class I'll be teaching. We'll have to work out a darkroom schedule between us and the school paper staff."

"See me in my office and we'll set something up." Already he resented the intrusion of school business and felt a pang of guilt for letting his personal concerns eclipse the importance of the job he was paid to do. But at that moment nothing mattered as much as his relationship with Claire.

Approaching her room he felt a touch of contained terror, as if his indiscretion of eighteen years ago would somehow show on his face and she might look at him and say, *How could you, Tom? Two women at once?*

Her room faced south, like his office. A name plate beside her door read MRS. GARDNER. Though there was no school policy on students, using teachers' first names, she held that the respect inherent in their using the more formal term of address carried over into their respect for her in the classroom. And she realized plenty of it from her students.

Tom stopped in her open doorway and found his wife bent over a cardboard box, removing an armload of portfolios. Her backside was pointed in his direction; she was clad in blue denim stirrup pants and a red football jersey that nearly reached her knees. The sun fell in slices across her blond hair and her shoulders as she grunted and set the heavy stack of paper on a table. She pushed her hair back, jammed both fists into the hollows of her waist, and stretched backward. Observing her so—unaware she was being studied, working at the job she did better than any other teacher he knew, still trim, stylish, and pretty after eighteen years of marriage and two children—Tom experienced a sudden stab of fear that he might lose her.

"Claire?" he said, and she turned, smiling, at the sound of his voice. She was tan from a summer of golf. A pair of twisted gold earrings appeared richer for swaying against her golden skin.

"Oh, hi. How are things downstairs?"

"Still crazy."

"Did you find the new English books yet?"

"Not yet. I'm still working on it."

"They'll show up someplace. They always do."

The missing textbooks had lost all importance as Tom entered the room and shuffled to a halt before her.

"Claire, I've been thinking . . ."

Her face clouded. "Tom, what's wrong?"

He took her in his arms.

"What is it, Tom?"

"Let's go out Saturday night, maybe even stay somewhere, just the two of us. Maybe we can get Dad to come over and stay with the kids."

"Something *is* wrong!"

He could hear in her voice the sudden worry, feel a faint stiffness in her shoulders.

"I just needed this"—he drew back to see her face, holding her loosely by the sides of her neck—"and I think we both could use one night to ourselves before school starts and things get even crazier."

"I thought we had an agreement—nothing personal in the school building."

"We did, but I'm the principal and I can break the rules now and then if I choose." He bent his head and kissed her with a more overt show of feeling than he sometimes displayed in their bedroom at home. He loved this woman in a way in which he'd at one time thought himself incapable of loving. Yes, he'd married her under duress and had harbored some deep resentment at that time, a young man fresh out of college with some footholds he'd wanted to gain before saddling himself with a wife and children. But she'd gotten pregnant and he'd done what at that time had been touted as "the honorable thing." Love for him came only afterward, after she'd had Robby and he'd seen her mother him, then a year later Chelsea, and when, within two years, she'd returned to work and juggled both careers so admirably.

She was bright and hardworking, and they shared so much common ground—both of them being educators—that he couldn't imagine being married to anyone else. They were good parents, too, having seen so many disastrous results of bad parenting right here in their own school. Divorce, abuse, alcoholism, neglect—they frequently sat in on conferences with parents of children who suffered because of such home situations. Consequently, Tom and Claire knew what built strong families; they talked about it, kept their own relationship strong and loving, and presented a unified front before their children in their decision making. They counted themselves lucky that so far, their methods and their overt love for their children had worked beautifully. The kids had turned out great.

Love Claire? Hell yes, he loved her. After all these years, and all their building, their relationship had become the fastness from which both of them operated their busy, rewarding lives.

A girl with long blond hair came around the doorway and stopped dead still at the sight of her principal kissing one of the English teachers. She smiled, dropped a shoulder against the door frame, crossed her arms and ankles, and rested the toe of one worn-out athletic shoe on the floor. Chelsea Gardner watched her mother's hands spread on her father's back and felt flooded by a sense of security and happiness. Though they openly showed affection at home, she'd never seen them do it here.

"I thought this school had a rule about necking in the halls."

Their heads snapped around, but Tom's hands remained at Claire's back.

"Oh, Chelsea . . . hi," he said.

Chelsea peeled herself away from the door frame and approached them, grinning. "You could get a pink slip for that, you know. And haven't I heard a thousand complaints about stuff like this, around the supper table? About all the *gropers* who push each other against the lockers and corner each other under the stairs?"

Tom cleared his throat. "I was inviting your mother away for the weekend. What would you think about that?"

"Away where?"

"I don't know. Maybe to a bed-and-breakfast somewhere."

Claire exclaimed, "A bed-and-breakfast! Oh, Tom, do you really mean it?"

Chelsea said, "I thought you didn't go for that frilly stuff, Dad."

"So did I," Claire added, studying him curiously.

"Well, I just thought . . ." Tom shrugged and released Claire. "I don't know, you're always after me. Maybe it's time I tried it for once, because after this weekend, you know how crazy my schedule gets. Both of our schedules."

Chelsea grinned. "Well, I think it's a good idea."

"I'll ask Grandpa if he can stay at the house Saturday night."

"Grandpa! Oh, come on, Dad, please . . . we're old enough to stay alone."

"You know my feelings about parents' leaving kids alone."

She did. She'd heard about that around the supper table, too. Monday mornings at school were the busiest for police traffic, and much of it resulted from kids' being left alone by their parents over the weekend. Besides, her grandpa was really okay.

"Yeah, I know," Chelsea conceded. "Well, listen, whatever you decide about Grandpa is okay, I guess. But listen, you guys, I'm in sort of a hurry. I just stopped by here to get some money for a new pair of tennis shoes. These are fried."

"How much?" Claire asked, heading for her desk to find her purse.

"Fifty dollars?" Chelsea asked hopefully, screwing up her face.

"Fifty dollars!"

"All of us cheerleaders are getting the same kind."

It turned out both Tom and Claire had to pool their cash to come up with what Chelsea needed, but she left with the full fifty for which she'd asked.

At the door she brought herself up short, spun to face her parents, and said, smiling, "You know what? When I walked in here and found you two kissing, I had this really sensational feeling, like—wow, you know?— I'm the luckiest kid in the world because my mom and dad have really got it together, and nothing can ever go wrong with our family."

Her words pierced Tom like a hot wire. He stared at the empty doorway after she'd gone. *Let it be true,* he thought, *let nothing ever go wrong with our family.*

But even as he willed it, he realized their troubles had already begun.

Two

At three o'clock that afternoon Tom walked onto the football field where the team was warming up. Kent Arens—prompt, Tom observed —was waiting on one of the lower bleacher seats.

Even before his suspicions were confirmed, Tom felt a rush of emotion at the sight of the boy rising—straight, sturdy, and strong—from the metal bench. It swept down upon him with a force he had not expected as he found himself unconsciously assessing the quality of Monica Arens's parenting. First impressions indicated she'd done one hell of a job.

"Hello, Mr. Gardner," Kent said.

"Hi, Kent." It took an effort to speak and act calmly when his heart was clubbing so. "Did you talk to Coach Gorman yet?"

"No, sir, I just got here."

"Well, come on . . . let's go flag him down." They walked the sideline together, Tom captivated by the boy's nearness, by Kent's bare arm so close to his own, by his vitality and honed young body. Merely walking beside him brought a rush of physical response not unlike that accompanying his earliest awareness of girls as sexual beings, though this was paternal, pure and simple. It had a wrenching pathos, being close to Kent, believing he was his son, convinced he was right when Kent had no idea about their relationship. *Are you? Are you?* The question battered his mind, relentless as a litany, along with others he'd want to ask if this turned out to be true.

What were you like as a child? Did you resent having no father? Did you ever wonder what I looked like? Where I lived? What I did? Did you have any father figure in your life? Did you wish for brothers and sisters? Were you always so polite and serious?

The repressed questions formed an ache in Tom's throat as he spoke dutifully of other things.

"Pretty hard to make a move like this at the start of your senior year."

"Yes, sir. But we've moved before, so I know I can adjust. Anyway, when you go to a new school you find out people are pretty nice about helping you out."

"And going out for sports is certainly a good way to start looking for new friends. You mentioned other sports besides football."

"Basketball and track in school. Tennis and golf away from school. In Austin we lived on a golf course, so it was pretty natural for me to give it a try."

All were sports Tom himself had pursued at one time or another, though his life now left little time for leisure. He noted the mention of the golf course and concluded that Monica must have done quite well to provide them with an upper-class home. He found himself seized by a peculiar greed to learn all he could about the boy, and to find parallels between Kent and himself.

"Did you letter in basketball and track, too?"

"Yes, sir."

"I used to coach when I first started teaching," he told Kent. "I think I have a pretty good eye for an above-average athlete. I'd be awfully surprised if Coach Gorman doesn't give you a uniform."

"I hope so."

The truth was that as principal Tom had only to give the word that he wanted a student on a team for the deed to be done. In this case, the boy's record, goals, and personality seemed to speak for themselves; he had little doubt Gorman would see that too.

They approached mid-field and watched the team doing ten-yard sprints combined with high knee lifts. Out among the red practice jerseys, the player wearing number twenty-two raised his arm and waved. Tom waved back and said, "My son, Robby." The head coach caught sight of the principal and left the team to join him.

Bob Gorman was shaped like a butcher block with arms. He wore gray sweatpants, a white T-shirt, and a red baseball cap bearing the school initials, *HHH*, in white. When he stopped at the sideline he did so in a James Cagney stance, feet wide-set, his cannon-shaped arms arching away from his sides, too muscular to hang easy.

"Tom," he said in greeting, simultaneously nodding at the boy and giving the bill of his cap an unnecessary reset.

"Coach, how's it going?"

"Not so bad. They're a little rusty after vacation, but a few of them worked out all summer and really kept in shape."

"Coach, this is a new transfer student, Kent Arens. He's a senior this year and he wants to play football. I told him I'd bring him down and put the two of you together and let you take it from there. He's lettered the last two years in Austin, Texas, and last year he made all-state. He wants to attend Stanford and study engineering, maybe on a football scholarship."

The coach took a good look at the six-foot-two boy who towered over him. "Kent," he said, extending his beefy hand.

"How do you do, sir."

The assessment continued while the handshake ended.

"What do you play?"

"Running back."

While the coach went on asking Kent questions, number twenty-two came jogging off the field and panted to a halt at the sideline.

"Hey, Dad," Robby Gardner said breathlessly.

"Hi, Robby."

"You gonna be around after practice? Chelsea took the car out shopping, so I haven't got a ride home."

"Sorry, I won't be. I've ah"—Tom rubbed the underside of his nose with a knuckle—"I've got an errand to run." He told himself it was an evasion, not a lie. Until he knew the truth about Kent Arens, some caution was necessary. "What about the school bus?"

"The dreaded school bus? No thanks. I'll find a ride."

As Robby headed away Tom called, "Oh, Robby, just a minute." It was a queer moment of muddled emotions, one in which Tom Gardner wondered if he was introducing his two sons to each other. Given the choice, he would have forgone the introduction altogether, but protocol demanded that as principal he make every effort to ease the incoming student into this new society in whatever way possible. "I want you to meet Kent Arens. He's a senior, too, and he's new here this year. Maybe you can introduce him around to some of your friends."

"Sure, Dad," Robby said, turning to assess the newcomer.

"Kent, this is my son, Robby."

The two boys exchanged a self-conscious handshake.

One was blond, the other dark. Tom resisted the temptation to stick around and compare them further. If his suspicion proved true, he'd undoubtedly spend too much time doing that in the future. "Well, Kent, I'll leave you to the coach. Good luck."

He gave the boy a smile, which was returned, before he left the field and headed for his car, passing on the way the aquamarine Lexus owned by Monica Arens. Its presence gave him a jolt not unlike that he'd experienced as a teenager when some girl he had a crush on would cruise past his house in her daddy's car. But this jolt had nothing to do with crushes. It had to do with guilt over a boy who might possibly be his, and uncertainty about how to handle the situation if it was true.

The windows of his red Taurus had been rolled up in the warm August sun. He sat for a minute with the doors open and the engine running, wondering what to do next. The picture of those two boys shaking hands kept playing inside his head as he wondered, *Are they? Are they? And will I find out soon?*

When the air conditioner started blowing cool, he slammed the doors and pulled Kent's green school registration card out of his breast pocket. The address was there, printed in careful draftsman-style letters that resembled Tom's own printing somewhat: 1500 Curve Summit Drive. It was an area of new construction, a subdivision of affluent homes in the hills above the west shore of Lake Haviland in the western suburb of St. Paul Heights, Minnesota. After eighteen years, Tom knew the addresses in his school district almost as well as the police did.

He felt like a damned philanderer as he drove out to find it, his emotional side wishing Monica Arens wouldn't be home after all, his more rational self realizing there was no advantage in delaying the inevitable: whatever the truth, he had to know, and the sooner the better.

The house was impressive, a two-story walk-out, built of eggshell and gray brick with an irregular roof line and a triple garage. It sat on a crest of land, with the driveway climbing at a rather steep angle.

Tom parked at the bottom of the drive and got out slowly, pausing with his hand on the open car door, looking up at the house. The lot had not been sodded yet, but the finish grading was done and already new trees and shrubbery had been planted—a lot of good-sized trees and shrubbery that cost dearly to have brought in. The driveway was made of concrete and shone white in the sun while a freshly laid sidewalk curved upward, connecting it to the front door.

Monica Arens did very well indeed.

He slammed the car door and approached her house with his every instinct urging him to return to his car, drive away, and leave well enough alone.

But he could not.

He rang the doorbell instead, waiting with his key ring caught over an index finger, dreading the moment when she'd open the door, realizing that the next hour could change his life forever.

She opened the door and stared at Tom in stunned surprise. She was dressed in canvas shoes and a loose-fitting jumper-style dress clear down to mid-calf, a shapeless style he'd never learned to like, one that Claire had bypassed not because of his dislike, but because of her own.

"Hello, Monica," he said at last.

"I'm not sure you should be here."

"I thought we should talk." He kept his keys handy in case she slammed the door in his face. She looked less than pleased by his appearance, and stood with her hand on the doorknob, moving not a muscle, her face devoid of anything resembling welcome.

"Don't you think we should?" he asked, the words nearly snagging on the lump of apprehension in his throat.

She released a breath and said, "Yes, I suppose so." When she stepped back he knew she resented having to do so.

He entered her house and heard the door close behind him, sealing him into a foyer that segued into a vast combination living room/dining room. The west wall was dominated by a center fireplace flanked by two sets of French doors, which were thrown open onto a redwood deck spanning the entire sunset side of the house. The place smelled of fresh paint and new carpet, and though its windows were bare, it held the promise of future richness. North American Van Lines boxes filled much of the space between the furniture. Monica led the way to the left end of the room, where a dining room table and chairs created the largest island of cleared space. The table appeared to have been freshly polished, for the lemony scent of furniture wax lingered in the room, and the faint swirl of rag marks was exposed at an oblique angle by the light cascading through the nearest pair of French doors. Beyond them, the deck overlooked the unsodded backyard and a new house still under construction a good acre away.

"Sit down," she said.

He pulled out a chair and waited. She moved around the corner of the table and took a place, leaving plenty of distance between them. When she sat, he did the same.

Tension pervaded the room. He felt himself struggling to frame the correct words, to suppress his embarrassment at even being here.

Monica—it appeared—had her mind made up to fix her eyes on the bare tabletop and leave them there.

"Well . . ." he said. "I guess I'll just ask it straight out. . . . Is Kent my son?"

She turned her head away. Staring across her tightly joined hands at the rolling backyard, she offset her jaw, righted it again, and answered quietly, "Yes, he is."

He let his breath out in a ragged gust and whispered, "Oh, God." With his elbows propped on the table, he covered his face with both hands. Adrenaline shot through him like an electric current, leaving his skull and armpits damp with sweat. He made a ball-and-socket of his hands and pressed his thumb knuckles hard against his mouth. Studying her, sealed within her armor of indifference, he wondered how to proceed. Life, it seemed, set no precedent for a situation such as this—sitting with a belligerent woman, a veritable stranger, discussing the son you never knew existed.

"I was . . ." He had to clear his throat and start again. "I was afraid so. It doesn't take a genealogist to spot the likeness between us."

She said nothing.

"Why didn't you tell me?"

She rolled her eyes and said, "Isn't that obvious?"

"No, I guess it isn't. Not to me. Why?"

She flashed him an angry glance. "By the time I found out, you were already married to her. What good would it have done to tell you?"

"But I'm his father! Don't you think I should have known?"

"And if you had, what would you have done—just what?"

He replied honestly, "I don't know. But I'm not the kind of man who would have left his care entirely up to you. I would have helped however I could, even if it was only financially."

She let out a disdainful huff. "Would you? If I remember right, your fiancée was already expecting a baby when you got married. I was no more a part of your future plans than you were a part of mine. I didn't see what good would come of telling you, so I didn't."

"But didn't you . . . didn't you think that was deceitful?"

36

"Oh, please . . ." She pushed back her chair and rose with reproof in the trim of her shoulders. Moving away, she stationed herself amid the boxes in the living room behind him. He pivoted on his chair seat and followed with his eyes, crooking an armpit and wrist over the chair back. "We had already made one mistake," she went on. "What good would two have done? You told me that night of your bachelor party that you were marrying her under duress, but you were marrying her nevertheless. If I'd found you afterwards and told you I was pregnant, I might have broken up your marriage, and what purpose would that have served?" She clapped a hand to her chest. "*I* certainly didn't want to marry you."

"No," he replied, coloring faintly. "No, of course not."

"We were just . . . that night was just . . ." She shrugged and fell silent.

Just a hot-blooded June night that never should have happened. Eighteen years later they both knew it and were suffering the repercussions.

She admitted, "It was as much my fault as yours. Maybe more, because I wasn't on any kind of birth control, and I should have insisted on you using something. But you know how you are at that age—you think, 'Oh, it'll never happen to me. Not from just one time.' And when I went there, I never dreamed anything like that would happen. Like I said, we were both equally to blame."

"But you weren't the one getting married the next weekend."

"Maybe not, but I knew you were, so which of us is more guilty?"

"Me." He got up and followed her to the living room, where he propped his hips against a stack of cardboard boxes facing her, a goodly distance away. "It was an act of rebellion, plain and simple. She was pregnant and I was being forced into this wedding I wasn't ready for. Hell, the ink wasn't even dry on my college diploma yet! I wanted to teach for a while, have a few years of freedom, buy a new car and rent an apartment with a swimming pool, live with the guys. Instead I was visiting gynecologists with her and trying to scrape together enough money for the rental deposit on a one-bedroom apartment. Getting outfitted for a tuxedo I didn't even want to wear, for heaven's sake! I just . . . I just wasn't ready for it."

"I know," she replied calmly. "I knew all that before you and I slept together that night, so you don't have to plead your case with me."

"All right, then you plead yours with me. Tell me why *you* went to bed with *me?*"

"Who knows?" She wandered away from him to stand looking out the open French doors, her arms crossed defensively beneath her breasts. "Temporary insanity. The opportunity was there. I was never what you'd call an armpiece, so I hadn't had a lot of attention from men. You were a good-looking guy I'd talked to at a couple of parties, enjoyed a few laughs with . . . and then I delivered those pizzas to that hotel suite and there you were with all your crazy friends . . . I don't know. Why does anybody do anything?"

He sat on the stack of boxes regretting that night afresh.

"It bothered my conscience for a long time after I got married . . . what I'd done with you."

Over her shoulder, she looked back at him. "But you never told her?"

He took some time gnashing through more present guilt before giving a hoarse reply. "N . . ." He cleared his throat. "No."

Their gazes held, hers passive, his troubled.

"And the marriage—did it last?"

He nodded slowly. "Eighteen years, every one of them a little better than the last. I love her very much."

"And the baby she was expecting?"

"Robby. He's a senior at HHH."

The full implications registered on her face before she breathed quietly, "Oh, boy."

"Yeah. Oh, boy." Tom rose from the boxes and wandered to another spot in the room. "The two of them are out on the football field together right now. And Claire . . . well, Claire teaches twelfth-grade honors English, for which, it seems, your son—ah, our son—has registered."

"Oh, boy," Monica repeated. Her crossed arms actually loosened slightly for the first time.

"Claire and I have a daughter, too. Chelsea. She's a junior. Our family is very happy." He paused a beat, then said, "Your registration card doesn't list a husband's name, so I take it you're single."

"Yes."

"Never been married?"

"No."

"So who does Kent think his father is?"

"I told him the truth, that you were someone I met at a party one night and had a brief affair with, but that you were no one I ever considered marrying. I made a good life for him, Tom. I got my degree and provided a solid home with all the support a child could ask for."

"I can see that."

"I didn't need a man. I didn't want one."

"I'm sorry if I did that to you, made you bitter."

"I'm not bitter."

"You sound bitter. You act bitter."

"Keep your speculations to yourself," she snapped. "You don't know me. You don't know anything about me. I'm an achiever, and that's always been enough for me. That and Kent. I work hard at my job and at being a good mother, and the two of us have gotten along very well."

"I'm sorry. I didn't mean to sound critical, and believe me, in my occupation I'd be the last one to criticize any single parent who's single by choice, not when she's raised the kind of kid you've raised. I see so many dysfunctional families where the parents stay together for the kids' sake. Those kids are in and out of my office every day, and the counselors and police and I are always trying to straighten them out . . . mostly without success. If I sounded as though I thought you haven't done a good job, I didn't mean to. He's . . ." Tom ran a hand over the side of his neck, stirred anew by the little he knew of Kent Arens. He looked at her and gave a flourish of one hand. "He's an educator's dream. Good grades, goals, college plans, a wide variety of extracurricular interests—I imagine he must be a parent's dream as well."

"He is."

He still stood by one stack of boxes. She still stood by another. Her antipathy had waned considerably during the course of their dialogue, but neither of them had grown more comfortable with the other.

"I sent him to a Catholic grade school."

"Catholic," he said, absently touching his chest as if straightening a tie.

"It gave him a good solid beginning."

"Yes . . . yes, of course it did."

"And the sports helped, too . . . and his high school in Austin was very highly regarded."

He stared at her awhile, realizing she was defending herself when she had no reason to. A question came to him, pertinent to so much, though he hesitated awhile before posing it.

"What about grandparents?" he said, unable to stop himself.

"There was only my dad, but he died nine years ago and he lived here in Minnesota, so Kent never knew him well. Why do you ask?"

"I have a father who's still alive. He lives less than ten miles from here."

A moment of silence, then, "Oh, I see." Her arms dropped to her sides and her eyes remained on his while she inquired, "Aunts? Uncles?"

"One of each, plus three cousins. And on your side?"

"I have one sister here. He barely knows her either. My family didn't exactly send up flares when I announced that I was having a baby out of wedlock and intended to raise it on my own."

The tension was taking its toll. Tom felt an ache across his back and shoulders, and returned to the dining room, dropping wearily onto a chair, one hand thrown across the polished walnut. While Monica remained standing, he sat silently; each of them was locked in solitary rumination. After a while she, too, sighed and came back to the table to sit.

"I don't know what's the right thing to do," she admitted.

"Neither do I."

From a distant construction site came the sound of carpenters hammering and saws whining while the pair at the table sat silently, trying to piece together some sensible conclusion to this meeting.

"For myself," she said, "I'd like everything to stay as it is. He doesn't need you . . . really, he doesn't."

"I'd like the same thing, but I keep asking myself what's fair to him."

"Yes, I know."

More silence, then she showed an unexpected burst of emotion, covering her face with both hands and propping her elbows on the tabletop. "If only I'd called your school and checked first!" She flung her hands wide. "But how in the world was I supposed to know you'd be working there? I didn't even know you wanted to be a teacher, much less a principal! I mean, we didn't exactly trade life histories in the few hours we were together, did we?"

For the duration of a sigh he let his eyes close and his shoulders curl backward around the chair. Then he sat erect and made a decision.

"For now, let's let it ride. He's got all he can handle adjusting to a new school, making new friends. If a situation arises where we have to tell him, we will. In the meantime, I'll do what I can for him. I'll make sure he gets on the football team, though my guess is that's already settled. When it comes time to apply to Stanford, I'll write a letter of recommendation for him, and as far as scholarships are concerned, he won't need any. That much I intend to do—pay for his college education."

"You don't know him, Tom. I could pay for his tuition, too, but he doesn't want me to. He wants the scholarship just to prove to himself that he can get it, so I want to let him try."

"Well, there's time to discuss that later in the school year. But listen . . . if there's anything that comes up, anything you need, anything he needs . . . whatever . . . you come and see me, okay? Just come to my office at school. Parents do that all the time, so nobody will think a thing of it."

"Thanks, but I can't imagine why I'd need to."

"Well, then . . ." He laid his palms flat on the table as if to push himself up, but changed his mind, experiencing a welter of emotions, and none of them settling. "I feel so . . ."

"So what?"

"I don't know."

"Guilty?"

"Yes, that, too, but—it's hard to describe—disjointed, I guess. As if there's something else I should do, only I don't know what. I walk out of here and watch him at school every day and don't tell anybody he's my son? Is that what I'm supposed to do? Hell, Monica, that's a sentence! I earned it, I know, but it's still a sentence."

"I don't want him to know. I really don't."

"The miracle is that he didn't already guess. When he walked into my office and I studied him point-blank, the resemblance almost knocked me off my chair."

"He has no reason to suspect, so why should he guess?"

"Let's hope you're right." Tom pushed himself up and Monica rose to accompany him toward the front door. There, they paused uneasily, as if obligated to exchange a few friendly words to mitigate their sense of distance. Their total strangeness to one another felt misplaced in light of the fact that they were linked by a seventeen-year-old son.

"So you're an engineer at 3M."

"Yes, in research and development. I'm working on improving an electronic connector for the Bell telephone system. The prototype is being produced now, and we'll be testing it here, then I'll follow the project right through to the end, until the production tooling is designed and we're turning out marketable pieces."

"Well . . . I'm impressed. It's obvious Kent gets his math and science skills from you."

"You're not good at math?" she inquired.

"I couldn't design an electronic connector, if that's what you're asking. I'm a people person, a communicator. It's the kids I love, working with them, watching them during the three years they're in high school turn from stumbling adolescents into bright, well-educated young adults ready to face the world and challenge it. That's what I like about my job."

"Well," she said, "I think he got some of your communications skills as well. He does very well around people."

"Yes, I could see that."

They stood groping for more polite niceties, but none surfaced.

She opened the door. He turned and shook her hand. "Well, good luck," he said.

"You too."

They dropped hands. He felt an almost unreasonable reluctance to walk out of this house with the knowledge he had gained in it. Once he did there'd be no one with whom he could discuss this traumatic day in his life.

"I'm sorry," he told her.

She shrugged. "I'll make sure he's at the new-student orientation tomorrow. Who speaks to them?"

"Among others, me."

"Then you will need luck, won't you?"

They stood in the doorway, unable to find an apt parting remark. "Well, I've got to go."

"Yes, me too. I've got a lot of unpacking to do."

"You have a nice house. It makes me feel good to know he lives here."

"Thanks."

He turned and descended the curl of concrete steps that took him down to his car. When he reached it and opened the driver's door, he glanced back up to see she had already closed the door and returned inside.

He was too agitated to go straight home. Instead, he drove over to school and parked close to the front door, where a small metal sign said MR. GARDNER. Football practice had ended at 5:30, and the afternoon activities bus had already left the grounds. He wondered if Robby had been forced to ride it. Since buying the car for the kids, Tom and Claire had been amused at how put-upon they acted when forced to ride a bus as they'd done for years.

The main front doors were unlocked. As he stepped through, they closed behind him with their familiar hiss and clack. Inside, the building smelled of fresh paint, reminding him of how little attention he'd paid today to the affairs of a school year that would officially begin next Tuesday. Somewhere in the distance the custodians—Tom's greatest blessing—were still painting the halls and would work uncomplainingly till eleven or twelve P.M., as they would do every day from now through Labor Day. One of them was whistling "You Light Up My Life." It echoed through the halls and brought a curiously calming effect to Tom.

He took out his key and unlocked the plate-glass doors to the deserted main office. Inside, it was blissfully quiet. The secretaries were gone. The phones were still. All the lights were off but the usual one, in the far corner. The walls were spotless and a lot of the boxes gone. Someone had even vacuumed the hard-surfaced blue carpeting.

In his office he snapped on the ceiling lights, laid Kent Arens's registration card on his desk, and dialed the athletic office.

The coach picked up and said, "Yuh. Gorman here."

"Bob, it's Tom Gardner. What'd you think of the new kid?"

"Are you kidding?" Tom heard the twang of Gorman's desk chair as he tilted it back. "He makes me ask myself what I'm doing wrong with my own."

"You questioned him?"

"Of course I questioned him. The kid's got his head on so straight I almost wanted to hear something foolish come out of his mouth just so I'd know he was for real."

"Can he play?"

"Can he *play? Boy*, can he play!"

"So he's on the team?"

"Not only on it, I have the feeling he could be the spark that makes it happen for us this year. He knows how to follow orders, how to handle a ball and avoid tacklers. He's a real team man, plus he's in great shape. I'm glad you had the good sense to bring him down to talk to me."

"Well, that's good news. A boy like that with college goals and plenty of gray matter between his ears, he's the kind that makes our whole school system look good. I'm glad you put him on the team. Thanks."

"I'm glad you brought him down, Tom."

After he'd hung up, Tom sat at his desk, wondering what would happen during this school year, what changes his life would undergo because of all he'd learned today.

He had another son. A smart, athletic, bright, polite, seemingly happy seventeen-year-old son. What a discovery to make at mid-life.

The phone rang and he jumped guiltily, as if the caller could divine his thoughts.

It was Claire. "Hi, Tom. Coming home for supper?"

He forced brightness into his voice. "Yup. I'll head out now. Did you pick up Robby?"

"He caught a ride home with Jeff." Jeff Morehouse was Robby's best friend and a fellow football player.

"Okay. I told him I wouldn't be around when practice ended but it turns out I had to stop back at school anyway. See you in a few minutes."

On his way out of the office, Tom left Kent Arens's green registration card on Dora Mae's desk for filing.

Tom and Claire Gardner lived in the same two-story colonial they'd bought when the children were three and four. The trees had grown a lot since then, and when the senior class decided to TP them, the cleanup was horrendous. The yard looked nice today, however, still wearing its summer green, with Claire's impatiens blooming in the redwood tubs beside the front step.

Her car was in the garage, and the kids' junker—an ancient, rusted-out silver Chevy Nova—parked right behind it. Tom pulled into his customary stall on the left, got out, and skirted the rear of Claire's car on his way to the back door.

He put his hand on the knob, but delayed turning it and facing his family with all this new knowledge of which they had no idea.

He had an illegitimate son.

His children had a half brother.

Eighteen years ago his pregnant wife-to-be had been betrayed by her intended one week before the wedding.

What would happen to his happy family if they ever learned the truth?

He entered the family room and walked through it into the kitchen, where the homey scene suddenly clutched him with love—his wife and children in a room that smelled like supper cooking, waiting for him to join them and round out the family.

Chelsea was setting the table. Robby stood by the open refrigerator door eating a cold wiener, and Claire was at the stove filling buns with barbecued hamburger.

"Put on some pickles, too, will you, Chels? And Robby, stop eating those wieners! I've got supper all ready." She glanced over her shoulder, smiled, and kept on working. "Oh, hi, Tom."

He shuffled to a stop behind her, slid an arm around her ribs, and kissed her neck. It was warm and smelled like onions, Passion perfume, and schoolteacher. She paused, the spoon in one hand and a bun in the other, craning to see him behind her.

"My goodness," she said quietly, giving him a private smile. "Twice in one day?"

He kissed her lingeringly on the mouth while Robby said, "What's that supposed to mean?"

Chelsea said, "I caught them mashing face in Mom's classroom this morning. And it wasn't just a mini-mashing either. He had her in a full-body press. And guess what—they're going away for the weekend and leaving Grandpa with us."

"Grandpa!"

"Sit down, you two," Claire ordered, escaping Tom's embrace, carrying a plate of steaming sandwiches to the table. "Your father suggested that maybe we should get away before school starts and things get crazy. You don't mind, do you?"

"Why can't we stay by ourselves?"

"Because we have a rule about that. Tom, would you get those carrots and celery sticks from the refrigerator?"

Tom found them and they all got seated at the table. Robby put three burgers on his plate before passing the platter to his sister.

"What a pig," she said.

"Hey, listen, you didn't bust your butt on a football field all afternoon."

"No, I did it over at Erin's house. We were practicing our cheerleading over there."

"Big deal," he said disparagingly.

"Whoa, aren't *we* in a surly mood."

"Just lay off, huh? Maybe I've got a reason."

"Oh, yeah—what reason?"

"Dad knows, don't you, Dad? Some new kid moves into town, doesn't even show up for football practice till *after* we've been through hell week, bustin' our butts in the eighty-degree heat, and he just saunters onto the field and says, 'Yessir, nossir' to the coach a few times with this fakey Southern drawl, and the coach says, 'You're on the team.'"

Tom and Claire exchanged quick glances before he asked, "Have you got trouble with that, Robby?"

"Well, jeez, Coach Gorman is letting him play running back!"

"Any reason he shouldn't?"

Robby stared at his father as if he couldn't believe his ears. Then he blurted, "Yeah, *Jeff plays running back!*"

Tom helped himself to a hamburger. "Then Jeff will just have to play better than Arens, right?"

"Aw, come on, Dad! Jeff's been here since he was in first grade!"

"Giving him the automatic right to play running back, even if somebody else might play it better?"

Robby rolled his eyes. "Jeez, I don't believe this."

"And I don't know what's gotten into you, Robby. You've always been a team man before. If the new guy is good, he makes you all look better, you know that."

Robby quit chewing and stared at his father. The corners of his mouth were orange with barbecue sauce. Two spots of red appeared on his clean, shiny cheeks, which had just been showered at school. Chelsea's eyes swerved from her brother to her dad. She picked up her glass of milk, took a swallow, and asked, "Who is this new kid anyway?"

Tom laid down his sandwich and said, "His name is Kent Arens. He just transferred in from Austin, Texas."

"Is he cute?" she asked.

Adrenaline rushed through Tom, lighting his face while he grappled for an honest answer. Claire, meanwhile, was sitting back and letting the whole conversation roll on without her, but observing carefully.

"Yeah, pretty cute," Tom said, as if it had taken some forethought to reply.

In rampant disgust, Robby muttered, "Jeez," and hid behind his glass of milk. Slamming his glass down, he said, "I hope you don't expect me to drag him around every place I go with my friends, Dad."

"Not at all. I just expect you to be polite to him, treat him the way you'd want to be treated if you were the new kid in school."

Robby wiped his mouth on a napkin, pushed his chair back, and got up with his dirty dishes. The set of his shoulders told the whole family he was disgusted with the table conversation tonight. "You know, sometimes I really hate being the principal's son." He rinsed his plate and glass and put them in the dishwasher, then left the room.

When he was gone, Claire said, "Tom, what's going on here?"

"Nothing. I took the new boy down to the football field to introduce him to Bob Gorman, and I asked Robby to introduce him around, that's all. But apparently a bit of jealousy has reared its ugly head."

She said, "That's not like Robby at all."

"I know. But Jeff Morehouse has always been top man in the backfield, and you know who's always handed off to him. This new kid, I think, will present a threat to Jeff. It's natural that Robby would resent him if he comes in and bumps his best friend."

"Might be good for Robby. Teach him a thing or two."

"I think so, too. Listen, about the weekend . . . I'll take care of calling Dad, and you see if you can find a nice place you want to go, okay?"

They both got up and headed for the sink. "I thought I'd talk to Ruth," Claire said. "She and Dean used to go to inns all the time."

"Good idea."

They each rinsed their plates and Claire put them in the dishwasher.

Standing above her, studying her curved back, Tom was struck by a tidal wave of panic. Nothing had ever threatened his marriage before, but suddenly the worry was there, hanging over his head, and it terrified him.

"Claire?" he said as she straightened.

"Hm?" She was busy doing three things at once: reaching for the dishcloth, turning on the tap, sloshing hot water around the sink. He curled a hand around her neck and made her stop moving. She turned and looked up at him, her wet hands still trailing over the edge of the sink. He wanted to say, *I love you*, but his reason for doing so seemed suddenly prompted by panic and less than honorable. He wanted to kiss her passionately, make up for the times he maybe should have done so in the past, mark his indelible possession of her as the wife he loved and would always love.

But Chelsea was rising from the table now, too, bringing her dirty dishes to the sink.

"What, Tom?" Claire whispered, searching his troubled eyes.

He put his lips by Claire's ear and whispered words that were far from what he meant. "Take something sexy to wear on Saturday night, okay?"

When Tom walked from the room, Claire's eyes followed him. Her lips wore a transient smile, for inside, a disquieting voice was calling after him, *What's wrong, Tom? What's wrong?*

Three

Ruth Bishop's front door was open when Claire crossed the yard to the house next door. She knocked on the screen door and called, "Ruth, are you there?" After half a minute, she peered into the entry and called again, "Ruth?" No voices, clinking dishes, or signs of supper. The double garage door was open, and Ruth's car was there, although her husband Dean's was gone.

Claire knocked again.

"Ruth?" she called.

Finally Ruth appeared from Claire's left—the direction of the bedrooms—shuffling to the door and opening it spiritlessly. She looked crumpled and crestfallen. Her long, thick brown hair, always unmanageable, stuck out like grape tendrils in every direction. Her red-rimmed eyes had violet pillows beneath them. Her voice was coarser than usual. "Hi, Claire."

Claire took one look at Ruth and said, "What's the matter?"

"I don't know for sure."

"But you've been crying."

"Come on in."

Claire followed Ruth into the kitchen.

"Do you have time to sit for a while?" Ruth asked.

"Of course. Just tell me what's wrong."

Ruth got out two glasses and filled them with ice and 7-Up without asking what Claire wanted. She carried the drinks to the table, then sat down with her shoulders slumped. "I think Dean is messing around."

"Oh, Ruth, no." On the tabletop Claire covered the back of her friend's hand and gave it a squeeze.

The sliding glass door was open and Ruth stared disconsolately at the redwood deck, which had been built around a mature maple tree. Her blue eyes filled with tears, and she ran her fingers back through her tangled hair. She sniffed and looked down into her glass. "Something's going on. I just know it. It started last spring right after I made that trip out to Mother's with Sarah." Ruth and her sister, Sarah, had taken a trip out to Phoenix to spend a week with their parents, who were buying a home in Sun City.

"What started?"

"Little things . . . changes in routine, new clothes, even a new after-shave. Sometimes I'd come to the door of our bedroom and he'd be on the phone with somebody and say goodbye right away. When I'd ask who it was, he'd just say, 'Somebody from the office.' At first I didn't think much of it, but this week I've answered two telephone calls that were hang-ups, and both times I knew somebody was there because I could hear music in the background. Then last night he said he was just going to run up to the store for a battery for his watch, and when he came back I checked the odometer on the car. He went twenty-five miles and was gone for nearly an hour and a half."

"But did you *ask* him where he went?"

"No."

"Well, don't you think you should, before you jump to conclusions?"

"I don't think I'm jumping to conclusions. It didn't just happen overnight, it's been happening all summer. He's *different*."

"Oh, Ruth, come on, this is some pretty circumstantial evidence. I think you should just ask him where he was last night."

"But what if he *was* with somebody else?"

Claire, who had never doubted her husband a moment in their marriage, felt great empathy for her friend. "You really don't want to know, is that what you're saying?"

"Would you?"

Would she? The question bore some impact, when considered fully. Ruth and Dean had been married even longer than she and Tom. They had two children in college, a house nearly paid for, retirement in the offing, a marriage that had—to the best of Claire's knowledge—no overt problems. Their situation was much like Claire and Tom's. The mere idea that such a stable marriage could be fraying at the seams unsettled Claire. She could imagine how it must terrify Ruth, and how strong was her friend's inclination to abstain from further investigation. Yet Claire worked in an atmosphere that valued communication and counseling as the means toward problem solving.

"I think I would," she answered. "I think I'd want to know the truth so we could work at the problems."

"No, you wouldn't." Ruth's firm rebuttal startled Claire. "You just think you would, because it isn't happening to you. But if it ever happens to you, you'll feel differently. You'll hope that if there's anything to it he'll just come to his senses and break it off with her so that it'll never have to be brought out in the open."

"So that's what you intend to do? Pretend you aren't worried and say nothing?"

"Oh, God, Claire, I don't know." Ruth let her forehead drop onto her hands, driving her fingertips into her disorderly hair. "He dyed his hair. Do you realize that?" She lifted her head and repeated belligerently, "He dyed his hair, and we all joked about it with him, but what made him do it? I certainly didn't mind the gray starting, and I told him so. Doesn't it seem out of character for him to do a thing like that?"

It did, but Claire decided agreeing would only deplete Ruth further.

"I think this last year has been hard for both of you with Chad leaving for college. No kids left at home, getting on toward middle age—it's a difficult transition to make."

"But other men make it without taking mistresses."

"Now, Ruth, don't say that. You don't know it's true."

"Last week one night he didn't come home for supper."

"So what else is new? If I accused Tom of cheating every time he didn't make it home for supper, our marriage would have been over years ago."

"That's different. His job keeps him at school, and you know it's a legitimate reason."

"But I still have to trust him a lot, don't I?"

"Well, I don't feel like I can trust Dean anymore. Too many things don't add up."

"Have you talked to anybody else about this? Your mom? Sarah?"

"No, just you. I don't want my family to know anything. You know how they love Dean."

"I have a suggestion."

"What?"

"Plan a weekend away. Take him to somewhere romantic where it'll be only the two of you and you can concentrate on . . . well, on renewal."

"We used to do that a lot, but that's sort of fallen by the wayside, too."

"Because he always planned it as a surprise for you. Maybe he got tired of planning all the surprises and it's your turn."

"Are you blaming me for—"

"No, I'm not. I'm just saying that it takes work. The longer you're married, the more work it takes, for all of us. The same old face on the opposite pillow in the morning, the same old bodies starting to sag here and there, same routine when you make love—or worse, don't make it. How have things been in that department?"

"Crappy, especially since the kids moved away."

"See?"

"It's not me. It's him."

"Are you sure?" Claire raised her palms as Ruth began to bristle. "Now don't get so defensive. Just think about it, that's all I'm saying, and for heaven's sake, talk to him. Where is he now?"

"He joined a sports and health club—and that's another thing! Out of the blue he says he has to shape up and gets this membership to a club. Now he's going to be over there several nights a week. At least that's where he says he's going."

"Why didn't you join it with him?"

"Because I don't want to. I'm tired when I come home from work. I don't want to go to some damned gym and walk on a treadmill for an hour after I've been on my feet all day."

Though Claire and Ruth were good friends, Claire was far from blind to Ruth's faults. The woman was stubborn and often refused to accept the truth when it was right before her eyes. She was complacent as a wife, and Claire had long thought she took her husband for granted. She was argumentative at many times when Claire believed she needed to listen, as now.

"Ruth, listen to me. This is a time you need to work *with* Dean, not against him. Be with him every chance you get, and—who knows?—working out at the club together could bring a fresh, new vigor to your relationship, to say nothing of the obvious health benefits it will bring."

Ruth sighed and slumped her shoulders. "Oh, I don't know . . ."

"Just think about it." Claire rose to leave, and Ruth accompanied her to the door, where they hugged. "Who knows? You could be totally wrong about Dean. He loves you, you know that." In the end, Claire hadn't the heartlessness to bring up the subject she had come here to discuss. How could she ask Ruth to recommend a weekend getaway when Ruth's marriage was on a downslide? She decided she'd call one of her co-workers instead.

Tom was gone when she got back home, having returned to school at the request of the janitorial staff, who thought they might have solved the mystery of the missing English textbooks.

Shortly after ten P.M. Claire was stripping off her clothes and preparing to take a shower when Tom entered the bedroom, closed the door, and leaned back against it, watching her with lazy interest.

"Hi . . . you're back," she said, without even turning around. "Did you find the missing books?"

"Nope. We think they were thrown away directly from a loading dock where they were delivered."

"Oh no, Tom. What are you going to do?" When no reply came, she paused with her thumbs hooked inside the waistband of her stirrup pants and looked back over her shoulder. He remained as he was, leaning against the door. Softer, she asked, "What are you going to do?"

"Use last year's." He sounded uninterested in the subject of lost books.

Their gazes held, and even across the room she could sense a stirring within him. "What?" she said, with a smile starting to pull at her mouth. "You've been watching me that way ever since you got home from work."

"What way?"

"The way you used to when we were dating."

He grinned, pulled his hips away from the door, sucked in his belly, and began tugging his shirt out of his waistband. "You gonna take a shower?" he asked, just before his head disappeared inside the pullover.

"I need one," she answered, while continuing to undress. "It was so hot in my room today, and I hate unpacking. It's such dirty work."

He threw the shirt aside and freed his belt buckle while watching her bend over, naked, scooping her dirty clothes into her arms, heading for the hamper in the bathroom. He sauntered after her, unbuttoning, unzipping, catching her in the act of turning on the shower with one leg protruding from behind the open door and the rest of her turned opaque by its textured glass.

The shower pattered and spat for half a minute before she stepped inside and closed the door. He observed her through the streaming glass, her figure a flickery pastel ghost that lifted its face, its arms, turned a slow circle, and ran its hands across its chest, revering the water.

He finished undressing and joined her.

Claire's eyes flew open at his touch. "Well . . . hi there, big boy," she said in a sultry voice, catching his mood with an immediacy he loved.

"Hi there." Their joined stomachs made the water branch into a Y below. "Haven't we met somewhere before?"

"Mmm . . . this morning, at Hubert H. Humphrey High School, in room two-thirty-two?"

"Oh yeah, that's where it was."

"Then again at the kitchen sink, around six-thirty tonight."

"Then it *was* you?" His hips moved in a figure eight against hers.

"Yes, it was . . . the one you French-kissed on two very peculiar occasions today."

"Peculiar?"

"Well, maybe one peculiar occasion. You have to admit, turning a woman on in the middle of a workday in the middle of the workplace is very peculiar for a responsible person like you."

"Just warming up for the weekend, that's all." He reached out blindly, felt for the soap, and started using it on her back and buttocks. She grew still, closing her eyes and humming a note of pleasure.

He soaped her breasts and pulled her into a kiss that became as sleek as the fit of their bodies. When it ended, he was touching her inside, where he'd touched her a thousand times and had grown to know her intimate preferences.

"Did you find a place for the weekend?" he murmured.

"Yes. Did you call your dad?"

"Yes. He'll come."

He pushed the wet hair back from her face and bit the edge of her left nostril, her upper lip, then her lower lip. Holding her slick neck in one hand, he kissed her as if licking a honey jar clean while the hot water hammered their necks and put a flush on their skin.

Against her mouth, he asked, "So where are we going?"

She drew back, doubled her arms behind his neck, and nestled the curve of her stomach just below the curve of his. "I called Linda

Wanamaker, and she told me about one up in Duluth. Do you want to drive to Duluth?"

"Hell, I'd drive to Hawaii right now if you asked me to."

They laughed together, comfortable with that laughter after years of it at times such as these, bonded by it even before they moved to the bedroom.

"Let's get out of here and dry off," he said.

As they stood outside the shower, four feet apart, drying their backs and bellies, legs and toes, their expectant gazes met, parted, and met again. In unison they chuckled—impatient and knowing— traversing the familiar terrain of precoital loveplay that told them very clearly: *This will be a good one.*

It was.

It satisfied them both, sexually and emotionally, for they'd worked diligently in the early years of their marriage at learning how to achieve such satisfaction. They'd talked. They'd read. They'd failed at times, and fought at others. But they'd come through to the point where they knew that every sexual encounter wasn't going to be as wholly satisfying as the one they'd had tonight.

"Mine was really dynamite tonight," she said afterward, sighing, rolling back, closing her eyes.

"I could tell. The kids probably could, too."

Her eyes flew open. "I wasn't *that* loud, was I?"

"Only before I put the pillow over your mouth."

Once again they chuckled, then resumed a loose embrace that put her face against his chest and his chin on her hair.

"Well, you weren't so quiet yourself."

"I know, but at least I made the effort to time my outbursts with the beat from Robby's stereo." Through their common bedroom wall they could hear the faint thrum of a rock station, which played at Robby's bedtime every night.

Claire sighed and rubbed Tom's chest. "Do you ever think about how wonderful it's going to be when they're gone and we can have the house to ourselves?"

"Yeah . . . wonderful and awful."

"I know." They lay in silence, amazed at how fast that time was approaching.

"Two years," she said, with a wistful note of sadness, "less than two years."

He rubbed her arm and kissed the top of her hair. She heard his heart clunking along reassuringly beneath her ear.

"But at least we'll still have each other. Not everybody's that lucky."

"Oh?" He drew back to look into her face, warned by a note in her voice that she was troubled by something.

"Ruth thinks Dean is cheating on her."

"Oh, yeah?"

"She's collecting evidence. It's largely circumstantial, but she thinks she's right."

"I guess it wouldn't surprise me."

"It wouldn't?"

"Dean and I are pretty good friends, too. He's never said anything directly, but I've gathered from inferences that she sort of lost interest after the boys went to college."

A knock sounded on their bedroom door, and Tom pulled the covers up to their armpits. "Come on in," he said, leaving his arm around Claire.

"Hi." Chelsea poked her head into the room, took in their pose at a glance, and repeated self-consciously, "Oh . . . hi. Gosh . . . sorry to bother you."

"No, It's okay." Tom straightened up against the pillows. "Come on in, honey."

"I just wanted to tell you that Mrs. Berlatsky called, and they're short of kids to act as partners for the new students tomorrow, so she recruited me. But she forgot to say what time."

"Eleven-thirty in the library."

"Great. Well . . . g'night." She smiled at the two of them and was withdrawing when Tom called, "Hey, Chels?" Her face reemerged wearing an expectant expression. "Thanks for helping out, honey."

"Sure. G'night, Dad. G'night, Mom."

"Good night," they replied in unison, then exchanged a look of approval. "Pretty great kid, huh?" he said.

"You bet. We raised nothing but good kids."

In her own room, Chelsea pulled the puckered taffeta tiebacks from her twin ponytails. They'd been mounted one atop the other behind stiffened bangs that shot forth like fireworks above her face. She brushed her hair, dressed for bed, and climbed in to lie in the dark, smiling about her mom and dad. They did it yet—she was pretty sure. It wasn't the kind of thing she'd ever asked them about, but she didn't need to. There'd been a rule about entering their bedroom without knocking since Chelsea was in the first grade, and tonight Mom's shoulders had been bare, and they'd been snuggled up as if *something* was up.

She wondered about *the act*, about how it was possible to carry out such a thing gracefully. How often did married people do it, and how did they approach doing it? Did they just *say something*? Or did they automatically do it on days when they'd been flirting, like her parents had been today? She knew they sometimes took showers together and had caught them at it once when she was thirteen, but she'd been so scared of getting caught staring at the steamy shower door that she'd turned around and gotten out of there before she was discovered.

Sex . . . that awesome force. She'd been thinking more and more about it lately, especially since her best friend, Erin, had confided that she and Rick had gone all the way this summer. But Chelsea had never gone steady with anyone for the length of time Erin had gone with Rick. Oh, there had been boys she'd liked, and she'd been touched and tempted some. But never to the point where she'd even come close to considering doing the *Big Nasty* (as she and Erin had called it for years).

Lying in her bed on a pleasant August night with her brother in his room and the faint sound of his radio finally being turned off, and her parents across the hall, with a new pair of cheerleading tennies in her closet and the promise of a super school year ahead, Chelsea Gardner hoped that no boy would become so important to her that she lost her good sense, not while she was still in high school. She wanted to go to college, get a career, then have a marriage like her mother and father's, one where they were the only ones for each other and still in love after lots of years. She wanted a home and a family like this one where everybody loved and respected each other. Chelsea figured one sure way to risk losing all that was to get tangled up with some boy and get pregnant.

She could wait. She *would* wait.

And in the meantime she'd be grateful that she could go to bed every night feeling secure in the knowledge that she had the best family in the world.

The following morning Tom found himself distracted much of the time by thoughts of Kent Arens. Shaving, patting on after shave, combing his hair, he found himself studying his reflection in the mirror and recalling how much Kent resembled him. Things happened inside him whenever the boy came into his thoughts, a tightness around his heart, a prickle and flush fired partly by apprehension, partly by exhilaration. He had another child, a third child, a child different from the two he'd known, who would bring a different mix of genes into the future, would achieve different things, go different places, maybe have grandchildren someday. The fact that Kent didn't know him as a father brought added depth to Tom's anxieties over the boy. The knowledge had a preciousness to it while at the same time stirring alarm within him at the unknowns his future would undergo because of Kent's advent into his life.

By eleven-thirty, when the new students met in the library, Tom found himself approaching the meeting with such intense expectancy it had actually elevated his pulse. To walk into a room and cast your eyes on a young man of seventeen, knowing without question for the first time that he was your son . . .

Watch yourself, Tom. Don't go straight to him, or study him too much, or show overt favoritism to him; there'll be other faculty members in the room.

Indeed there were. A number of them were already assembled and greeting students near the door when Tom arrived. The school librarian, Mrs. Haff, was there, along with the vice-principal, Noreen Altman, three school counselors, including Joan Berlatsky, and a half dozen coaches. Some of the students who were acting as guides today were also near the door.

Tom greeted them but his attention veered immediately in search of Kent Arens.

He found him with no trouble, standing half a head taller than most around him. He had gone to a bookshelf and selected a volume, through which he paged, his dark head bent, his shoulders looking impressively broad in a blue plaid short-sleeved shirt with crisply creased sleeves.

My son, Tom thought, his heart racing, his face warming. *Holy Mary, mother of God . . . that boy is my son!* How long before he could look at him without all of these physical reactions? *My son, whose whole life I've missed until now.*

Kent looked up, caught himself being watched, and smiled.

Tom smiled, too, and started moving toward him as Kent replaced the book on the shelf.

"Hi, Mr. Gardner." He extended his hand.

"Hi, Kent. How did it go with Coach Gorman?" So grown up, Tom thought, marveling again at the manners this young man had been taught. Clasping his hand, Tom felt an undeniable rush. If there was such a thing as father love, he felt it at that moment when he touched his son's hand: the mindless thrust of emotion that accompanies the mere knowledge of paternity.

The handshake was brief.

"I made the team at running back."

"Good for you. I'm glad to hear it."

"Thanks a lot for taking me down and introducing me to the coach. It helped a lot."

The two were still talking when Chelsea Gardner entered the media center, smiled, and said hi to some of the faculty.

Mrs. Berlatsky said, "Hi, Chelsea. Thanks a lot for helping out today."

"Oh, sure. No problem."

"Help yourself to cookies and pop."

"Thanks, Mrs. Berlatsky." She eyed the refreshment table in the middle of the room and headed that way. Dressed in a short white split skirt and a hot-pink tank top, she looked as if she were heading for the tennis courts. Her skin was tan. Her makeup was simple. Her nails were unpolished. Her shoulder-length hair was pulled up high on the sides and secured with combs. Her bangs were standing at attention. She moved with the quickness and agility of a tennis player, too, taking a chilled can of orange soda and popping its top while she glanced over the crowd. She'd taken one sip when she saw her dad talking with a tall, dark, good-looking student she'd never seen before. The can lowered slowly from her lips.

Wow, she thought, and walked toward them immediately.

"Hi, Dad," she said with a big smile.

Tom turned, suppressing his dire anxiety at his daughter's arrival. When she'd stuck her head into their bedroom the night before and announced that she'd been recruited to be a partner here today, he could think of no logical excuse to ask her not to come. It would have been pointless anyway: He couldn't keep her from meeting Kent Arens indefinitely.

He dropped an arm around her shoulders and said, "Hi, honey." But she wasn't even looking at him. She was focused on Kent and offering him her usual bright, welcoming smile.

"This is my daughter, Chelsea. She's a junior here. Chelsea, this is Kent Arens."

Chelsea briskly offered her hand.

"Hi."

"Hi," he said, as they shook hands.

"Kent is from Austin, Texas," Tom put in.

"Oh, you're the one Dad was talking about at the supper table last night."

"I am?" Kent glanced at Tom, surprised that he'd been the subject of conversation at his principal's house.

"There's always a lot of school talk at our supper table," Tom replied. "You can imagine . . . with four of us here in the building."

"Four of you?"

"My wife teaches English here, too."

"Oh . . . sure, *that* Mrs. Gardner. She's going to be my teacher," Kent said.

"So you're an honors student," Chelsea put in.

At that moment Mrs. Berlatsky picked up a microphone and spoke into it. "Good morning, everybody! Feel free to help yourselves to cookies and pop, then take a seat so we can get started."

Tom said, "I'd better visit with some of the others," then moved on.

"Do you want a can of pop?" Chelsea asked Kent. "Or a cookie?"

"A can of pop, maybe."

"What kind? I'll get one for you."

"Oh, you don't have to do that."

"That's our job, to make the new students feel comfortable. I'm one of the official partners here today. What kind?" She was already heading away.

"Pepsi," he called after her.

She returned momentarily, handing him a chilled can.

"Thanks," he said.

"You're welcome. Let's sit."

They sat at a library table sipping, and before they could speak, Mrs. Berlatsky got on the mike again and started the program.

"I want to welcome all you new students to Hubert H. Humphrey High School, and to thank all of you old students who came today to act as partners. We really appreciate your help. To all of you who don't know me . . . I'm Joan Berlatsky, one of the school counselors." She introduced the rest of the faculty present, ending with Tom. ". . . And last, I want to introduce you all to Mr. Gardner, your principal, who's here to officially welcome you this morning."

Chelsea watched her father move toward the front of the library and take the mike. She felt a radiant pride, as she did whenever she witnessed him performing his duties as principal. Though there were plenty of kids who called him names and wrote nasty things about him on the restroom walls, they were primarily the geeks, the druggies, the law-breakers, the losers. Those in her circle pretty much agreed that her dad was a fair man, that he'd do anything he could for the students, and they liked him. And he hadn't grown fat or sloppy like some middle-age people did. He was still trim, and he was a really neat dresser, though today he wore only a yellow polo shirt and tan chinos—to put the new kids at ease, she knew. She thought surely he must be succeeding as he stood with one hand in his trouser pocket and spoke into the mike with a pleasant expression on his face, letting his eyes scan the room.

"Welcome, everyone. I'd guess there must be between fifty and sixty of you here who moved in from other districts and other states over the summer. I imagine you're all wondering what our school is like, what it'll be like for you coming here five days a week, and some of you a lot of evenings as well. This morning we're here to answer your questions, show you your building, tell you about our academic and sports pro-grams . . . give you a chance to get to know us a little and for us to get to know you."

Tom and others took turns filling in the new students on attendance policies, major activities of the year, lunch schedules, early-release forms, fire drills, study halls, student parking rules, and the sexual harassment policy. The coaches spoke about eligibility rules, the Minnesota State High School League, and the HHH sports program.

After a question-and-answer period, Mrs. Berlatsky said, "We're going to turn you loose now. Each of you here will be paired up with a student who'll act as your personal guide and will give you a tour of the building. We've established the partner program to help new students feel less like newcomers and more like a part of the school community right from the first day. Your partner will help you not only today, but throughout your first month. Could I ask all those who volunteered as partners to stand, please?"

Chelsea stood, glanced around at the others who'd risen to their feet, and discreetly wagged two fingers at some of Robby's friends.

Mrs. Berlatsky went on. "If all of you new students would pair up with one of the volunteers, we'll let you get on with the school tour. Now, all you guides, remember to make sure you give them a copy of the student handbook, and take special time acquainting them with the media center, though it'll be a little crowded if you all start here. So some of you go on out to other parts of the building first, then come back here."

Shuffling sounded in the room as students began rising. Tom took the microphone. "Kids, remember . . . Mrs. Altman's and my doors are always open. We're your principals, but that doesn't mean we're un-reachable. Feel free to come to us or your counselor with any concerns, at any time. Now, enjoy your tour and we'll see you bright and early on Tuesday morning."

When Kent Arens stood, Chelsea said, "Well, I know I'm not a senior, but I'll be your partner if you want." She rushed on. "I mean, most seniors want a senior, but not enough of them volunteered, so I was recruited. And I'm not a boy, so I can't take you into the locker rooms, but I can show you everything else."

"I've already had a tour of the locker rooms, so thanks. Lead the way."

Tom Gardner saw his daughter leading Kent Arens from the library and felt a ripple of panic. She waggled two fingers at Tom in goodbye, and he waved back. But his hand lowered slowly to his side as he watched them go out the door. *It's nothing,* he thought. *Joan recruited her, and she just happened to approach me when I was talking to him. And they just happened to sit together. She's always been school-minded, and this is just one more extracurricular duty she's taken on because she knows it pleases her mother and me.*

It's nothing.

But the panicky feeling persisted.

"Your dad is nice," Kent said as he followed Chelsea from the library.

"Thanks. I think so too."

"But it must be weird, having your father be the principal."

"Actually, I kind of like it. He's got a mirror inside a cupboard door in his office, and he lets me keep a can of hair spray in there and a curling iron, and I can go in there whenever I want and fix my hair. And we get refrigerator privileges in the kitchen for after-school activities. I mean, sometimes I might have practice for something right after school, then another activity in the evening, and I don't have time to go home between. So I bring a sack lunch and get to put it in the lunchroom cooler. But the neatest thing is, we always know what's going on around the school building because both Mom and Dad talk about it at home."

"Like you talked about me last night?"

She cast him a sideward glance as they walked down the hall. "It was all good, I assure you. Dad was very impressed by you."

"I was impressed by him, too." After a pause he added, "But don't tell him. I wouldn't want him to think I was brownnosing."

"I won't." She led him through a doorway. "Now this is your first-period classroom. Hi, Mr. Perry."

"Well, Chelsea . . . hello there."

As they went from room to room, Kent said, "Everybody knows you. You must do this kind of stuff often."

"I like doing it, and my parents like us to be really involved in school. We're not allowed to have jobs until after we graduate."

"Neither am I."

"Scholarship first."

"Yeah, that's pretty much what my mom says."

"So you like school too."

"Everything comes easy to me."

"Are you going to college?"

"Stanford, I hope."

"I haven't picked one yet, but I know I'll go."

"Mom says Stanford's got the best engineering program, and I want to play football, too, so it seems like a logical choice."

"You're going to be an engineer?"

"Yeah, same as my mom."

"How about your dad?"

Kent paused a beat before replying, "My mom's never been married."

"Oh." Chelsea tried not to show her surprise, but she felt it inside. She'd been hearing the term "nontraditional family" for years—her parents tended to talk in terms that the counselors used at school—but the idea of a mother who'd never been married sent a shock through her.

An awkward moment passed before Kent said, "She made sure I had everything I needed, though."

The reassurance left Chelsea with a heavy burden of pity: how awful it would be to have no father. She'd heard so many sad stories at home about various students whose broken or single-parent homes had torn them up or made their lives miserable; about how divorce had a negative effect on students' emotional and scholastic well-being; about how some kids cried in the counselors' offices about sad situations at home.

What could be sadder than a home without a father?

"Hey, listen," she said, stopping Kent with a light touch on his arm. "Maybe I shouldn't say this, but my dad meant what he said about his office door always being open. He's really a fair man, and he loves the students. If you ever need a guy to talk to, you can talk to him. And what I said before, about how he and Mom talk about school stuff at home— well, that doesn't mean they tell us confidential stuff. You could talk to him about anything personal and he'd keep any of that stuff just between you and him. My friends think he's just great."

She thought she saw a brief defensive expression touch Kent's dark eyebrows.

"I told you . . . my mom made sure that one parent was enough."

There was a change in his voice: she was right . . . he was naturally defensive about his family. As she looked up at him she had the oddest sensation that she was looking at someone she knew from long ago, someone she'd known very well. From elementary school, maybe. Yet no name came to mind. She'd never had any classmates who looked like him, never played with any boys who looked like him, not even when she was little. But she liked his looks a lot, and it sounded as if he really had his head on straight.

"Well, then you're lucky. Come on, I'll take you to my mother's room, and I'll warn you only one thing about her. Lots of the teachers don't care if you use their first names, but my mom does. She's Mrs. Gardner to all her students, and don't you ever forget it."

Claire Gardner looked up from her desk when Chelsea brought the new student in, and she was struck with the same thought: *Who is this boy? I've met him before.*

"Hi, Mom. This is one of your new fifth-period students, Kent Arens."

"Of course. Tom spoke about you at supper last night. Hello, Kent." She rose from her desk and came forward to shake his hand.

"How do you do," he said.

"You're a transfer student from Texas."

"Yes, ma'am, Austin."

"What a beautiful city. I've been down there to attend a seminar. I liked it a lot."

While they went on talking, Chelsea wandered away and walked the perimeter of her mother's classroom, stopping as she always did at the gallery of framed photos on a credenza just behind her desk. These were all her former students, some of them posing in their caps and gowns with their arms around her shoulders, some in costumes at class plays, some showing their college diplomas, others in their wedding gowns and tuxedos, some even holding babies. Her mom was one of those teachers kids loved and never forgot, and these photos—her prizes—she kept on display with a pride and love that went beyond teaching certificates and paychecks. Of all her accomplishments, these pictures rated right up there at the top, just as the photos of her own children were cause for pride at home.

Leaving her mother's room, Chelsea said, "Bye, Mom. See you at home."

In the hall, Kent said, "Well, hey . . . what can I say . . . your mom's nice, too."

"Yeah. I'm lucky," Chelsea replied. They walked for some time while she dwelled on their conversation of earlier. "Listen . . ." she said, "I think I upset you before when I asked about your father. I didn't mean to. I just assumed, you know? And if there's one thing I should know after living with parents who work in the school system, it's not to make assumptions about families, 'cause there are all kinds of families these days, and I know a lot of single-parent families work better than a lot of regular ones. I'm really sorry, okay?"

"It's all right," he said, "just forget it."

As they continued their tour, she felt better. She showed him the media center, the nurse's office, the lunchroom, and the arboretum, where students were allowed to eat at picnic tables on nice days.

When the tour was done they walked together to the front doors, which were propped open, letting a warm draft waft through the building. They stopped on a metal grid and stood with the incoming wind tugging at their clothing and riffling their hair.

"Well, listen . . ." she said. "I know it's tough changing schools, but I hope everything goes okay for you here."

"Thanks. And thanks for the tour."

"Oh, sure . . . no problem." A pause followed. The silence said quite clearly that they'd enjoyed being together. "Have you got a ride home?" she asked.

"Yeah. I took my mom to work, so I've got her car."

"Oh. Well then . . ." There was no reason to linger. "Where does she work?"

"3M."

"Where do you live?"

"A new subdivision called Haviland Hills."

"Oh, it's nice up there."

"Where do you live?"

"That way." She pointed. "A couple of miles. Same house I've lived in just about my whole life."

"Well . . ." He pointed out at the sunny parking lot. "Guess I better get going."

"Yeah, me too. I'm going to stop by Dad's office and say goodbye."

"Well . . . see ya Tuesday maybe."

"I'll come by your homeroom before first period and see if you need anything."

"Okay . . ." He smiled. "Yeah, that'd be great."

"Well, have a nice weekend."

"You too. And thanks again."

She watched him turn away, felt the vibrations from his heels as he crossed the metal grid and went out onto the sidewalk on the shaded side of the building. Her eyes followed his tall, sturdy form into the sunlight and way off into the parking lot, where he unlocked and got into a car of very bright aqua. She heard the engine start in the distance, then saw the car back out of its parking spot and head slowly away.

What was it about Kent Arens that kept her standing there watching him drive off? That face. What a face. She couldn't get it out of her mind, nor the ridiculous feeling that she'd known him before. What was she doing, standing here drooling over a boy she'd known exactly two hours and fifteen minutes when just last night she'd admitted how lucky she was to be free of teenage infatuations that could get in the way of her goals?

Putting Kent Arens from her mind, she turned toward the office to say goodbye to her dad.

Four

The image of Kent Arens walking away, immersed in conversation with his daughter, was fresh in Tom's mind when he returned from the library and walked into his office to find the boy's cumulative file lying on his desk.

He looked down at it, drew a huge breath, and let his cheeks puff out, feeling the emotional drain of the situation even before he opened the file. He rested four fingertips on the crisp manila cover, then glanced up and saw Dora Mae working at her typewriter within clear view of his desk.

He crossed his office and closed the door, then returned to his desk and, standing behind it, opened the file.

Lying on top of a thick stack of papers was his son's kindergarten picture. It caught him by the heart and squeezed, this color photo of a smiling little boy in a striped T-shirt, with tiny teeth, big brown eyes, and long bangs that twisted apart in the center, exposing the cowlick at the hairline.

Tom dropped into his desk chair as if he'd taken a load of buckshot in the knees. For a good thirty seconds he stared at the picture before finally picking it up. The face was so much like his own at that age. He tried to imagine the child charging into a kitchen to report that he'd found a caterpillar or picked a handful of dandelions. What had he been like then? He was so polite and directed now that Tom found it difficult to equate the child in the picture with the grown senior. Regret came, immense regret at never having known him as a little boy. Guilt, too, for having been an absentee father.

He turned the picture over to reveal some long-ago teacher's printing on the back: *Kent Arens, Grade K.*

Next came a sample of Kent's own printing, crooked but legible, done with a blunt lead pencil: *Kent Arens, Kent Arens, Kent Arens*—all the way down the left side of a blue-lined tablet sheet. It was followed by a sheet on which his kindergarten skills were listed in flawless printing, again by his teacher:

> Knows address
> Knows phone number
> Knows birth date
> Knows left and right
> Can name days of the week
> Can tie shoes
> Can recite Pledge of Allegiance
> Can print name: *Kent Arens*
> (This name was again written
> by Kent himself.)

Next came his kindergarten report card, whose header read: *Heritage Elementary School, Des Moines, Iowa.* A series of checkmarks were all entered under the "passing" column.

After that came a card showing remarks from his teacher/parent conferences—two of them that year. His mother had attended both. The remarks read: "Can recite the alphabet and print it. Printed numbers up to 42. Good number knowledge. Doesn't know an oval. Incident with chewing gum."

Tom wondered what the incident had been and felt cheated that he'd never know. It was probably forgotten by both Kent and his mother by now, as was much within this file.

There were other school pictures, and each time Tom came to one he felt a jolt of recognition, regret, and a paternal reaching within that closely resembled the love he'd felt for his legitimate children. He lingered longest over the photographs. The haircuts changed over the years, but the cowlick remained constant.

Throughout the file there were test results—the Otis Test in sixth grade, The California Achievement Test in seventh grade, a career test in ninth, clearly showing his interest in science and math. Also included were physical-fitness reports listing how many sit-ups and push-ups he'd done, the length of his long jump. His fifth-grade teacher had written: "Good sight reader," and at the end of the year, "May the Lord watch over you. We're all going to miss you." (He was in an elementary school called St. Scholastica by that time, and his teacher's name was Sister Margaret.)

His high school records showed the history of a student well liked by his teachers. The year-end remarks were all similar: "An exemplary student. A fine young man liked by his peers. A hard worker who is very goal- and task-oriented. Real college material."

His report card marks were consistently A's and B's. His sports record showed that he was a true competitor and had lettered the previous year in football, basketball, and track.

It was apparent, too, that not only was Kent an exemplary student, his mother was an exemplary parent. The file was peppered with verification that she'd attended parent/teacher conferences throughout his school career. Also, there was a photocopy of a note from her to a teacher named Mr. Monk that spoke volumes about the positive reinforcement she had given the school system.

Dear Mr. Monk,

As the school year ends, I thought you should know how much Kent has enjoyed having you as a teacher. He not only learned a lot from you about geometry, he also admired you as a person. Your handling of the situation regarding the Mexican boy who was consistently being discriminated against by the other track coach made you a hero in his eyes. Thank you for being the kind of role model young kids need in today's world of fading values.

Monica Arens

As an educator, Tom Gardner knew how rare such positive feedback was. Most times parents emitted a river of complaints against a slow trickle of compliments. It struck him again that Kent Arens had scored himself one darned fine mother.

The thought nevertheless did little to cheer him.

When he'd gone through the entire file, he returned to Kent's last class picture and sat for a long time staring at it, feeling increasingly forlorn, as if *he* had been an unclaimed parent rather than Kent an unclaimed child. He propped an elbow on the open file and stared out the window at the bright green grass in the arboretum.

I should tell Claire right now.

The thought terrified him. He'd taken another woman to bed one week before his wedding, while Claire was pregnant with their first child. It would decimate her to learn that, no matter how strong their marriage was now. And once revealed, the truth could never be retracted. Suppose she couldn't live with it, couldn't trust him again, what would happen to their marriage then? At the very least a period of great emotional stress would result, and how would he explain it to the kids? Admit his guilt and work through it: that was the logical answer, for he could tell already that his conscience would make him an emotional mess until he bared it.

On second thought, now was not the best time to tell Claire. He'd do so this weekend. What better time than when the two of them were off on a romantic getaway by themselves? Might she accept it better in a situation that reinforced the strength of their marriage, and how much he'd grown to love her?

Tom's gaze shifted from the grass to the framed photos on the windowsill. From this distance the images were indistinguishable, but he knew them so well, the details of the smiling faces were clear in his mind. He lingered over those of Claire, wondering—if she found out, was there even the slightest chance she'd be so hurt that he'd lose her?

Don't be silly, Gardner. Is that all the faith you have in your marriage? You tell her, and do it quick.

But what about the wishes of Monica Arens?

He stared at Kent's picture again. The boy deserved to know who his father was. There were dozens of reasons, ranging from practical to emotional, from future health questions to future children. Kent, after all, had two half siblings, and their relationship could extend for years. His children would be cousins to Robby's and Chelsea's. They'd have aunts and uncles. Kent himself had a grandfather, alive and well and with a lot to give *all* his grandchildren by way of friendship, the passing on of family lore, paternal support such as that he was giving this weekend by staying with the kids. And what about when Kent was an adult faced with losing his only acknowledged parent? At times like that the support of siblings mattered so much. Was it fair to rob him of the knowledge of the existence of a brother and sister when it appeared he had little chance of ever getting one through his mother?

While Tom was still doing inner battle, his telephone rang. It was Dora Mae.

"Someone from the Rotary Club is on the phone and wants to know if they can use the school gym next spring for a fundraiser."

"Doing what?" Tom asked.

"A celebrity donkey basketball game."

Tom withheld a sigh. Politics again. Saying no to the Rotary Club was courting criticism, yet the last time he'd allowed animals in the gym it had been the American Kennel Club, and the dogs had made a mess, leaving not only a bad smell but permanent raised spots on the wood floor that had brought complaints from the athletic director and custodians alike.

Tom closed Kent Arens's file and picked up his phone to handle one of the hundreds of administrative duties that sometimes tried his patience and had nothing whatsoever to do with education.

The new Arens home was slowly coming to surface beneath the boxes that had been piled shoulder high the day the moving van pulled away. On Thursday afternoon, after she and Kent arrived home, Monica set a sack of Chinese carry-out food on the kitchen counter and went to her bedroom to change clothes. When she returned to the kitchen dressed in a loose cotton peasant jumper, Kent was standing at the open French doors with his hands in the rear pockets of his jeans, staring out at the grassless backyard and the house under construction in the distance.

"Why didn't you get out some plates?" she asked, glancing through the doorway that connected the kitchen with the dining room.

He acted as if he hadn't heard. She opened cupboards and got out dishes, silverware, and two raffia place mats and set them on the dining room table, which held a new bouquet of cream silk flowers. In the living room, furniture was set in place and the labels had been removed from the new windows.

"The house is starting to get into shape, isn't it?" she remarked, returning to the kitchen for the white cardboard containers and taking them to the table. She flipped open the boxes, releasing the aroma of cooked meat and vegetables into the air. Still Kent stood with his back to her, staring outside.

"Kent?" she said, puzzled by his reticence.

He took some time before turning around, doing so slowly enough that she knew something was bothering him.

"What's wrong?"

"Nothing," he said, and sat down in the loose-jointed, dissociated, teenage way that often said, *Read my mind.*

"Something go wrong today?"

"No." He scooped out a mountain of lo mein, then handed her the container without meeting her eyes.

She helped herself and spoke again only when their plates were loaded and Kent was eating.

"You missing your friends?" she asked.

He shrugged in reply.

"You are, aren't you?"

"Just drop it, Mom."

"Drop what? I'm your mother. If you can't talk to me, who *can* you talk to?" When he went on eating without giving her so much as a glance, she reached out and covered his left hand on the tabletop. Quietly she said, "You know what the hardest thing is for a parent to hear? That answer—*nothing*—when I know perfectly well it's something. Now why don't you tell me?"

He got up abruptly, brushing around the back of his chair and heading for the kitchen to pour himself a glass of milk. "You want some?" he called.

"Yes, thanks."

Her eyes followed him while he brought back two glasses and sat down. He drank half his milk, then set the glass on the mat.

"I met this really nice girl today . . . actually it was Mr. Gardner's daughter. She acted as my guide for the school tour, and you know how it is when you meet somebody—you sort of ask each other questions to be polite. She asked if I was going to college and I said I wanted to be an engineer like my mother, and one thing led to another and pretty soon she asked about my dad."

Monica's fork paused in the air above her plate. She stopped chewing and fixed her eyes on Kent with a peculiar look of alarm. When she finally swallowed, the food seemed to have trouble going down.

He went on speaking while studying the lo mein on his plate. "It's been a long time since I went to a new school and had to make new friends. I sort of forgot how hard it is to answer kids when they ask me about my dad."

Monica began moving again, becoming immersed in her food. For a moment Kent wondered if she was trying to avoid the issue, then she spoke quite calmly. "What did she ask?"

"I don't even remember, just what my father did, I guess. But this time I found it really hard to say that I didn't have a father. And I could tell she felt like a jerk for asking."

Monica set down her fork, wiped her mouth, picked up her milk, but stared out the window instead of taking a drink.

Kent said, "I guess you don't want me to ask anything about him, do you?"

"No, I guess I don't."

"Why?"

Her gaze flashed back to him. "Why now?"

"I don't know. Lots of reasons. Because I'm seventeen, and all of a sudden it's starting to bother me. Because we're living back in Minnesota, where you were living when I was born. He's from here, isn't he?"

She sighed and turned her gaze out the French doors again but gave no answer.

"Isn't he?"

"Yes, but he's married and has a family."

"Does he know about me?"

Monica rose to her feet and carried her dishes away. Kent followed, continuing to pressure her. "Come on, Mom, I've got a right to know! Does he know about me?"

She was rinsing her plate under the running water as she answered. "I never told him when you were born."

"So if he found out now, I'd be an embarrassment to him, is that it?"

She swung around to face him. "Kent, I love you. I wanted you, I always wanted you from the time I found out I was pregnant. Getting pregnant never even slowed me down. I went on working toward my goals and I was happy that I had you to work for. Hasn't that been enough for you? Haven't I been a good mother?"

"That's not the point. The point is that if I have a father somewhere around this city, maybe it's time I got to know him."

"No!" she shouted.

Home Song

In the silence following her outburst, he stared at her while his cheeks grew pink.

Realizing her mistake, she covered her mouth tightly with one hand. Tears sprang to her eyes. "Please, Kent," she pleaded, much softer, "not now."

"Why not now?"

"Because."

"Mom, listen to yourself," he said reasonably, more quietly.

"It isn't a good time for either one of us. You're . . . well, look, this move to a new city, a new school, making new friends . . . it's all you can handle right now. Why load more onto yourself by bringing up this issue now?"

"Did you think I never would, Mother?"

"I don't know what I thought. I just . . . I guess I thought . . . well, when you were old enough to have children of your own, maybe then."

He looked at her with questioning brown eyes, then said, "Would you tell me something about him?"

"I don't know much."

"You never kept in touch after I was born?"

"No."

"But he lives here now?"

"I . . . I think so."

"Have you seen him since we moved back?"

She told her first lie ever to her son. "No."

He stared at her with a solemn expression on his face, his mind working and wondering.

Quietly, he told her, "Mom, I want to know him."

Above all, she realized he had that right. Beyond that, it seemed almost as if fate had placed him and his father in the same arena for the sole purpose of forcing their introduction. Was it possible that some ineluctable energy was at work when the two of them were together, mysteriously shifting protons and neutrons in the atmosphere and giving Kent some sixth sense about his father? Could the bond of blood be so powerful as to key some recondite thought transference between the two of them? If not, why had he asked now?

"Kent, I can't tell you now. Please accept that for the time being."

"But, Mom . . ."

"No! Not now! I'm not saying I won't ever tell you. I will, but you've got to trust me. This isn't the right time."

She watched his face turn hard, then he spun from the kitchen and headed for his room.

He slammed the door the way he'd been taught years ago he was *not* to slam doors, then flung himself onto his bed and clamped his hands beneath his head. Through a haze of angry tears he stared at the ceiling.

She didn't have any right to keep it from him! None! He was a person, wasn't he? And a person came from two people, and a lot of what that person was and felt and hoped and yearned for stemmed from who he came from. And everybody knew who they came from but him! Well, it wasn't fair! And she knew it, otherwise she would have stormed in here and chewed him out for slamming the door.

All his life she'd been doing extra things to make up to him for not having a dad, and all his life he'd pretended it didn't matter. But it did, and he wanted to know. She'd had a dad, so she didn't know what it felt like in elementary school when everybody drew pictures of their families and his just had two figures in it. She didn't know what it felt like to stand in a circle of boys and listen to one of them tell about how his dad had put a cool set of handlebars on his bike for him, or taken him out fishing or shown him how to use a soldering gun. When they'd lived in Iowa, he remembered a boy named Bobby Jankowski, whose dad did everything with him, taught Bobby how to pitch and hit a baseball, took him camping, helped him make a soapbox car and enter it in a race. And one sublimely wonderful day when the schools closed for a blizzard, Bobby's dad built a two-story snow fort with a stairway, windows made of hard plastic, and furniture made of packed snow. He took a lantern out and let the kids play in the fort after dark, and when they asked if they could sleep out in it in their sleeping bags, Mr. Jankowski said, "Sure." All the kids except Kent got to try sleeping in that fort. Sure, they were all back in their own houses after an hour, but Kent's mother gave an adamant "No!" right off the bat. Forever after, he'd been convinced that if he'd had a dad, he'd have gotten to try sleeping in that fort. He had never quite forgiven his mother for refusing to let him try it. Now that he was grown he realized that all those moms and dads knew perfectly well the boys wouldn't last out in that cold . . . but the chance to share the adventure for even one hour—that's what Kent had missed.

Bobby Jankowski: the luckiest kid Kent had ever known.

And now today, that girl, Chelsea . . .

When her dad had put his arm around her and introduced her, and later when she'd said how proud she was of him because all her friends thought he was a fair man—heck, Kent's mother couldn't begin to imagine the mix of emotions that caused in him. Uppermost was a sort of sick longing tinged with regret, followed today by anger and a strong resolve to find out who his father was and meet the man.

And no matter what, he was going to do that.

Wesley Gardner drove a nine-year-old Ford pickup with more than eighty thousand miles on it, wore styleless trousers with flappy legs and a dirty blue fishing cap. He lived largely on venison and walleyed pike, loved a beer before supper, and brought smiles to the faces of his grandchildren when he walked into their house late Friday afternoon.

"Hi, Grandpa!" Chelsea said enthusiastically as he gave her a hug.

"Hi, snookums."

She reached up to cock his silver-rimmed eyeglasses lower on the left side. "Your glasses are crooked again, Grandpa; what am I going to do with you?"

He took off his glasses and threw them onto the kitchen counter, where they ricocheted off the canisters and landed with the earpieces sticking up in the air. "Well, straighten the dang things then. They always bother you more than they do me. Robby, look what I brought for you and me." Into his grandson's hand Wesley thrust a plastic bag sealed with a Twist-Tie, holding a curl of white meat. "Walleye. We'll cook it in some beer batter the way you like it."

"Walleye. All *right*. They been bitin' out there?"

"Caught this one yesterday off the sandbar. A four-pounder. Thought you were gonna come out this week and go fishing with me."

"I wanted to, but I had football practice every afternoon except today."

"So are you gonna whup Blaine this year or not?" Blaine High School was the archrival of the HHH Senators.

"We're gonna give it a try."

"Well, you better, by gol, 'cause I got a bet on with Clyde." Clyde was Wesley's brother and next-door neighbor. They lived out on Eagle Lake, side by side, in a pair of cabins they'd built when they were young married men. Both were now widowers, content to sit on their front porches and look at the water when they weren't on it in their fishing boats.

"Chelsea, go out in my truck and get those tomatoes I brought, and there's some new potatoes too. I dug up the first hill this morning and, say, do they look good. We'll have us a supper fit for a king."

Tom came through the kitchen carrying a garment bag and an overnight case. "Hi, Dad."

"Well, if it isn't Romeo"—he smiled as Claire followed Tom into the room—"and here comes Juliet."

She kissed his cheek in passing. "Hi, Dad."

"Where are you two lovebirds going?"

"To Duluth."

"Well, you don't have to worry about a thing back here. I'll keep these two in line." To the kids he said, "I remember once when your grandma was alive, I took her up there just north of Duluth during smelting season, and, say, those smelt were running so thick we were scooping 'em out of the river by the washtubful. Never saw a year when the smelt ran like that. Well, your grandma, she never really liked smelt, hated cleaning 'em, but she was a good sport and went along just the same. We camped out in a tent that night, and next morning when I got up and stuck my foot into my boot, something wiggled in there. She'd stuck a couple smelt in each of my boots, and, say, when those fish started wiggling, I threw that boot so far the fish flew, and your grandma, she laaaaughed." He drew the word out in fond memory. "Yup, your grandma, she was a good sport. Knew how to make fun out of hard work, and let me tell you, that smelting was hard work."

Tom came back into the kitchen after taking the clothes to the car. "You telling that old smelt-in-the-boot story again, Dad?"

"Not to you, I'm not. You get on out of here and leave us three alone so we can fry fish. Robby, I got a six-pack of Schlitz in the truck. You go get it and put it in the refrigerator for me, but leave one can out so I can mix up that batter."

"Sure, Grandpa."

"Well, I guess Mom and I are packed," Tom said, leading the procession out to the driveway, where goodbye hugs were exchanged by all. Tom hugged his father last. It was a real hug, involving four strong arms and thumps on the back. "Thanks for staying with the kids."

"Are you kidding? I wish I could do it more often. Keeps me young. You just have a good time with your bride."

"I will."

"And, Claire," Wesley said, "if he doesn't do right, just put a fish in his boot. Man needs a fish in his boot every now and then to make him stop and appreciate what a good woman he's got."

Tom didn't need a fish in his boot. He realized what a good woman he had and performed the forgotten courtesy of holding the car door open for her.

"Woo," she said, slipping into her seat. "I like this already."

He slammed her door, got in, and they backed down the driveway waving goodbye. She waved for half a block down the street, then arched back against her seat and said to the roof, "I can't believe we're actually going!" Impulsively she caught Tom around the neck and planted a kiss on his cheek. "I've wanted to do this for so long. You're going to be *sooo* happy you got this idea."

She ran a finger down his Adam's apple into the open neck of his shirt, then smiled to herself and settled back for the ride.

They reached the port city an hour before sunset and found The Mansion with no trouble. It was located north of downtown on London Road, a wooded thoroughfare where the area's most elegant estates had been built in Duluth's golden days in the early part of the century. The twenty-five-room house, originally the home of a wealthy iron ore magnate, was perched high on a promontory above Lake Superior, surrounded by trees and lawns and separated from the road by a thickly wooded front lot and a pond populated by a flock of tame ducks. The ducks all came waddling and shaking off their wings, looking for handouts as Tom and Claire got out of their car.

Inside, they were shown to the immense south guest room, with a wide sweep of leaded windows set into solid brass casings, a step-down bathroom, and an antique bed so tall it could not have been housed beneath the ceilings of most contemporary homes. The view was awe-inspiring. It stretched east over six acres of emerald lawns, ending at the brink of the tall rocky cliffs overlooking the lake. Out on the water, incoming oil tankers and outgoing grain boats raised wisps of smoke on the horizon. The property was flanked by ancient pine trees, and off to the right the remains of a sixty-year-old garden led to terraced steps that dropped down to an aged orchard, then the hundred railed steps that clung to the rock wall leading down to the lakeshore far below.

When the innkeeper closed their door, Claire moved directly to the window, opened the casement, and breathed reverently, "Wow."

A landward breeze carried in the scent of pine and honeysuckle, which bloomed on the terrace below. The brass window casings were cool beneath her palms as she leaned on them and filled her senses with the serenity of the setting.

"Wow," she said again as Tom dropped his car keys on an ornate marble-topped dresser.

He moved up behind her and crooked his hands over her shoulders. *Tell her*, an inner voice chided. *Tell her and get it over with so you can enjoy the rest of your time here with her.* But once he told her, this almost mystical perfection would be shattered. She was so happy he didn't want to do that to her. Or to himself.

"Should I open the wine?" he asked, thinking maybe it would be easier with wine.

"Mmm . . . yes. Wine, give me wine," she said euphorically, flinging her arms around herself straitjacket style, whirling into his embrace. "But first kiss me."

She had been his only lover for eighteen years; how extraordinary that he could feel the charge still, after so long, but it returned in a glorious wave that carried them through a succession of kisses to the pouring and drinking of wine, to disrobing, and onto the bed within minutes of their arrival. What happened there rather stunned them both with its intensity and wiped from his mind the idea of baring his secret. When it ended, she said, "Did you ever think it would be this way after all these years?"

"No," he whispered, his voice nearly failing. "I never did."

"I love you."

"I love you too."

She touched his face. "So somber though. Tom . . . what is it? I just keep thinking something's wrong. You've been so preoccupied."

He smiled for her, caught her hand, and kissed the inner curl of her fingers, then left the bed to return a minute later with their wineglasses refilled. Stacking his pillows, he sat down beside her.

"Here's to you and me," he toasted, "and a good school year ahead."

They drank, then he rested his glass on an upraised knee and stared out the window beyond the foot of the bed, rehearsing various ways of telling her about Monica and Kent Arens, terrified of bringing it up, realizing he must.

She cuddled close and ran the foot of her wineglass across his chest. "You know what sounds good for supper? Chinese. Linda Wanamaker said she's eaten at a place called The Chinese Lantern and they do lobster some kind of exotic way that'll knock your socks off. You in the mood for lobster?"

When no answer came, she said, "Tom?" Then she pulled back and said, "Tom, are you listening to me?"

He cleared his throat and sat up straighter. "Sorry, honey."

"I was asking if you're in the mood for Chinese food tonight."

"Chinese food . . . ah, sure."

"So how does The Chinese Lantern sound?"

"Great!" he replied with synthetic brightness. "Just great."

But she was not fooled. He was worrying about something, and she was unsure whether to prod or let it be. She'd been snuggled close to him with her head against his chest for some time when he finally said, "Claire . . ."

A knock sounded at the door. "Afternoon tea," someone called. "I'll leave the basket out here."

Tom rolled out of bed and reached for his robe, and whatever he might have said was waylaid by the interruption.

They went to The Chinese Lantern and ate an exotic meal served in stupendous portions. Afterward they snapped open their fortune cookies. Tom half expected Claire's to read: *Your husband will be telling you a secret soon that will hurt you.* But he didn't tell her that night. He lay awake with the secret burning within, stealing all the joy he should have been having on this beautiful getaway with Claire. Fear was something new for him. Apart from the occasional near-traffic-accident, or the times when the children were babies and hurt themselves, his life had been relatively fearless. Procrastination, too, was alien to him. He was a man whose very position as the school principal forced him to make decisions daily, and he did so with wisdom and self-confidence. To find himself fearful and procrastinating revealed to Tom Gardner a side of himself he had not known before, one he did not like. No matter how many times an inner voice said, "Tell her," when he drew breath to do so some stronger force held him silent.

In the deep of night Claire rolled over and stretched an arm toward Tom. The sheet was cold on his half of the bed. She rolled onto her back and opened her eyes, realizing she was not at home, but in Duluth, at an inn. She saw his profile at the window and, startled, lifted her head from the pillow. "Tom?" she whispered, but he did not hear. All he needed was a cigarette to complete the picture of a tormented man, like a scene from some old Dana Andrews picture—his silhouette a black cutout against the moonlit sky beyond the open casements. She sat up, bracing on one hand, her heart suddenly racing as she watched him stand motionless, staring out at the night and the lake.

"Tom?" she said, "what's wrong?"

This time he heard her and spun. "Oh, Claire, sorry I woke you. I couldn't sleep. Must be the strange bed."

"You're sure that's all it is?"

He crossed the room into the shadows and got in beside her, drew her close, and wriggled himself into a comfortable position, flattening her hair so it wouldn't tickle his nose. "Go to sleep," he said, and sighed and kissed her hairline.

"What were you thinking about by the window?"

"Another woman," he answered, rubbing the base of her spine and fitting one of his legs between hers. "There, now are you satisfied?"

She'd have to be patient and hope he'd tell her in his own good time.

He said nothing the following morning when they made love again in the glow from the wide east windows, then ate breakfast in the spacious formal dining room, then walked the grounds and wended their way down the many steps to the overlook where the incoming waves off Lake Superior battered the shoreline and speckled the air with rainbows.

Nor did he tell her that afternoon, while they drove farther up the North Shore Drive, and stopped to admire rock-strewn rivers and gurgling waterfalls, wondering in which one his father had gone smelt fishing. They talked of other things, of how often they'd do this when the kids were gone from home. They speculated about which college Robby would choose, and how the new teachers would work out at their school. They both admitted how they were dreading Tuesday, that horrendous first day when the whole building turned to chaos.

But in between conversations Claire often found Tom distracted and off in a world of his own. At one point she said, "Tom, I wish you'd tell me what's bothering you."

He looked at her and she saw love in his eyes, but something else, too. Something that brought a sharp spike of fear as she added it up—his frequent distraction, his sleeplessness and outright worry, his opening the car door for her when he hadn't for so long, the way he'd kissed her in her classroom, this entire romantic weekend, which he'd suggested after so many years of being too busy for such a getaway. He acted like a man who felt guilty about something.

It was shortly before they headed home that the shattering thought hit her broadside: *Oh God, maybe it really is another woman.*

Five

$\maltese\maltese\maltese$

It rained the first day of school. Chelsea and Robby picked up Erin Gallagher, parked the Nova in the student parking lot, and ran through the downpour with portfolios over their heads. By the time they got inside, Chelsea's bangs had drooped, her chambray shirt was damp, and her white jeans were spattered at the hems.

"Oh, rats!" She stamped her feet on the metal grid inside the front door. "Look at my jeans! And my hair—ugh!" She plucked at her bangs and stomped further inside as students pushed in behind her. At the intersection of the corridors beside the front office her dad was standing in his usual spot, monitoring the halls as all the teachers did between classes. She barely paused as she passed him.

"Hi, Dad. Okay if I use the mirror in your office?"

"Sure, honey. Hi, Erin. Feel different coming in as a junior?"

"Sure does, Mr. Gardner. We're the big kids now."

Robby lifted his hand in greeting as he rounded the corner near his dad. The girls went into the office.

"Hi, Dora Mae. Hi, Mrs. Altman."

"Hi, Chelsea, Erin. Kind of wet out there, isn't it?"

"I'll say. We're going to fix our hair."

In Tom's office they plugged in a curling iron and opened his coat-closet door.

"Oh, look at this mess! I worked on it for forty-five minutes this morning!" Chelsea wailed.

"Well, at least you can put the curl back *into* yours. When it rains I can't get it *out* of mine."

They took turns before the mirror.

"Let's hurry and see if we can find Judy," Erin said. Judy Delisle was their mutual friend.

"Can't."

"Why not?"

"Something I've got to do."

"What?"

"You know that boy I told you about?"

"What boy?"

"The one I took on the orientation tour? I told him I'd stop by his homeroom this morning . . . just to say hi, see if there's anything he needs. I mean, there might be some . . . some questions he's got, or maybe he's feeling a little spooked being in this mob of strange kids or . . . or whatever."

Erin used one shoulder to butt her friend off-balance. "Chel-seeea! Is *that* why you're spraying about a ton of that hair spray on your hair and you're all bummed out about your jeans getting wet?"

"No, y' geek."

"C'mon. You can tell me."

"Nothing's going on, and I'm not bummed out. And they're more than wet." Chelsea cocked one knee and looked at the back of her pantleg. "They got mud splattered on them and it's going to leave spots." She unplugged the curling iron and they headed out.

"What's his last name again? Kent what?"

"Arens."

"Oh, yeah. Tell me about it at lunchtime. You got *A* lunch?"

"Yes, but I'm supposed to show him the routine in the lunchroom—part of my job, you know?"

"Which you don't mind a bit, I can tell." They parted in the hall, Erin walking backward, sing-songing, "Good lu-uck!"

The air in the halls was clammy and smelled of damp denim. The squeak of wet rubber soles on the freshly waxed floors punctuated the babble of young voices. A boy whistled through his teeth at his friend and yelled, "Hey, Troy, wait up!" The smell of perfume wafted from some girls who'd just run through the rain. About eighteen kids said hi to Chelsea on her way to Mr. Perry's room. She reached it in a state of anticipation.

In Mr. Perry's room half the desks were full while clusters of students stood talking in the aisles. One of Robby's friends, Roland Lostetter, spied Chelsea in the doorway and raised an oversized hand. He was a tall, burly guy with a baby face and springy brown curls cut close to his scalp. "Yo, Chelsea! You're in the wrong class, kid. This is *seniors* social studies."

"Hi, Pizza. Just passing through."

At the sound of Chelsea's name, Kent Arens swung around and found her in the doorway while Pizza Lostetter dropped a notebook on a vacant desk and sauntered toward her. "So, what're you doin' in here?" he asked, grinning—the upperclassman indulging his friend's little sister.

"I'm on the partners committee to help new students get acquainted with the school. And this is the one I'm helping. Hi, Kent." He, too, had moved to the door and stood by waiting.

"Hi, Chelsea."

"Have you two met?"

"Sort of," Pizza said, giving a half shrug. "On the football team."

"Kent Arens, meet Roland Lostetter, better known as Pizza."

One said, "How y' doin'," the other said, "Hello," and they shook hands.

"Excuse us, Pizz', I've got to talk to Kent."

"Sure."

When they were alone by the door she smiled and said, "So . . . how's it going?"

"Okay, I guess. I found my homeroom." He glanced at it over his shoulder then back at her.

She had to look up to meet his eyes. His shirt, like hers, showed damp spots, but his hair was too short to succumb to rain damage. It sprouted up from either side of a center cowlick and glistened, as if he'd spiked it with styling gel.

"Anything you need?"

"Yeah." He pulled a small blue card out of his shirt pocket and underlined a word with a cleanly groomed thumbnail. "Can you tell me how this teacher's name is pronounced again?"

"Bruhl," she answered, the name rhyming with *rule*.

"Oh, that's right, thanks." He slipped the schedule back in his pocket.

"You'll be getting assigned a locker here in homeroom today, and everybody has to buy their own locks. My first class is just around the corner in room one-ten. I can stop by after first period and help you find your locker if you want, then I'll meet you there at lunchtime. Part of my job is to show you the ropes in the lunchroom. It's all sort of automated here, so I guess you're stuck eating lunch with me today."

"Sounds all right to me," he said, giving a little half smile. "What time is lunch?"

"We're on *A* lunch—eleven forty-three. Makes for sort of a long afternoon, but at least the food is hot."

He had incredible brown eyes with thick, dark lashes that made her feel unsteady inside, yet she hid it well and put on a perky air for his benefit. "Well . . . guess you're okay for now. See you after first period."

"Yeah, see you. And thanks, Chelsea."

She turned away, then changed her mind. "Oh, by the way . . . Pizza Lostetter's an all-right guy. Anything you need to know you could ask him."

"Thanks, I'll remember that."

She signaled goodbye to Pizza, who bellowed "Yo!" as she left Mr. Perry's room.

When classes broke after first period Kent was waiting by the door of his homeroom. Working her way toward him she found she'd already grown familiar with his low-key form of greeting: nothing more than the suggestion of a smile while he fixed his eyes on her as she moved toward him. It wasn't intended to be sexy but it was. There was a way boys waited for girls in the hall that she'd witnessed many times: standing motionless and watching the girl approach, smiling as she reached him, then merely turning his shoulder just behind hers and looking down at her as they spoke for the first time and continued along together. Kent Arens did it just that way, the way steadies did with their girls. And she indulged in the momentary fantasy of going steady with him.

"So how was your first class?" he asked.

"Organized like a military drill. Mrs. Tomlinson is known for that. I'm going to like her a lot. How was yours?"

"All right. Sounds like we'll be reading lots of newspapers this year if we want to get good grades in there."

They shuffled along in an ocean of kids.

"What's your locker number?" she asked.

"Ten-eighty-eight."

"That's down here." She led the way, shouldering around a cluster of students moving toward her. Sophomores were running. Seniors were strolling. Teachers stood beside their open doors. Claire Gardner was in front of hers and smiled as they came into range.

"Hi, Kent. Hi, Chelsea."

"Hi, Mom."

"Morning, Mrs. Gardner."

"Is she taking good care of you, Kent?"

"Yes, ma'am."

"Good. See you fifth period." The kids moved past and Chelsea led Kent to his locker, located in the center of five long banks of lockers annexed in an 'L' off the main hall. At the end of each bank a tall, skinny window looked out over the cinder roof. Rain furrowed the exterior view. Overhead fluorescent lights put blue flecks in Kent's black hair.

He opened locker number 1088. "Empty." His voice echoed inside the metal cubicle as other students crowded in behind them. A girl came by,

turning sideways to squeeze past, nudging Chelsea— "Oops, sorry"—
and bumping her into Kent's back.

When her breasts hit him he peered over his shoulder.

"Sorry," she said, drawing away, embarrassed.

"Crowded in here," he remarked, closing his locker door while a
dozen others opened or closed around them.

Chelsea retreated without blushing, but he was hiding his face for the
same reason as she.

By lunch break the pattern was even more familiar—Kent looking
over heads, watching for her; Chelsea smiling in the crowd as she
approached him.

On their way to the cafeteria she asked, "Did you get your PIN
number?"

"My what?"

"Your personal identification number. You should have gotten it in
homeroom."

"Oh, that. Yes."

"And you brought a check from home?"

"Yes."

"Good, because everything's computerized in here." The cafeteria
smelled like spaghetti and swarmed like an anthill. "Today's the only day
you'll deposit your check at noon. After this you should bring it in in the
morning, before school. The cooks are here thirty minutes before the
first bell every day, and you give them your check and they'll deposit it in
your PIN account, then the computer keeps track of your purchases
every day and tells you how much you've got left. Hi, Mrs. Anderson,"
she said to a chubby strawberry-blond woman in a white uniform and
hairnet. "This is a new student, Kent Arens."

"Hi, Kent." Mrs. Anderson took his check and his PIN card and
punched buttons on her machine. "You're in good hands with Chelsea."

"Yes, ma'am," he said quietly, and once again Chelsea felt a flutter of
attraction for him.

She showed him the routine. "There are four serving lines and four
computers. Main serving line, à la carte line, malt and cookie bar, and

salad line. You can go through as many of them as you want, then after you've picked out your food the cook enters the amount of your lunch in the computer and you punch in your PIN number. That way nobody's got to handle any money."

They went their separate ways to pick up their lunches, then met in the middle of the noisy room, holding trays.

"Are you really going to eat all that?" The volume of food on his tray dwarfed hers.

"Are you really going to live on that?"

Someone called, "Hey, Chelsea, over here!"

"It's my friend Erin. Mind if we sit with her?"

"Fine with me."

Chelsea made introductions and sat down. To Chelsea's dismay, Erin ogled Kent with her mouth hanging open. She noticed other kids casting curious glances, too.

Erin started yakking. "I hear you're from Texas, and you play football, and you live in that swanky new addition out by Lake Haviland, and you've got Chelsea's mother for English, and you're in a lot of honors classes and want to go to Stanford on a football scholarship, and you drive a real cool aqua blue Lexus."

Kent stopped eating, a forkful of spaghetti two inches from his mouth. He looked from Erin to Chelsea, then back again.

Chelsea said, "Er-*in*!" and to Kent, "I didn't tell her all that, honest I didn't."

"Hey, he's a new kid, after all. The girls will be curious," Erin said.

"Erin, honestly, cool it."

Erin shrugged, dug into her lunch, and the meal proceeded under a mantle of tension. When Erin finally finished and left with her empty tray, Chelsea said, "I didn't tell her all that stuff, Kent, honest. I don't know who she heard it from."

"Don't let it bother you. What she said was true. New kids always get scrutinized at first, and what does it matter where she heard it?"

"But she embarrassed you. I'm sorry."

"No, she didn't."

"Well, she embarrassed *me!*"

"Forget it, Chelsea. It was her, not you."

"So you believe me?"

He tipped his head back finishing the last of his milk, then wiped his upper lip with the edge of one hand. "Sure," he replied, swiveling his head to meet her eyes while his hands were busy squashing the milk carton.

Across the room, Tom Gardner stood at one end of the salad bar, overlooking the lunchroom. He tried to spend two out of the three lunch periods in the cafeteria; it was his theory that in order to establish a good relationship with his students, a principal should be visible as much as possible. His hall and lunchroom monitoring were a big part of his visibility.

Here kids felt they could approach him.

Here they joshed with him the way they wouldn't at other times.

Here he overheard conversations that told him much about their home lives.

Here he often halted trouble before it started.

But the trouble he was watching today might have already gotten a jump on him. Chelsea and Kent Arens. They were sitting together already, though—thank heavens—they were with Chelsea's friend Erin. There wasn't much conversation going on at the table. Still, how in tarnation had she managed to double up with him in the first place? Out of all the new students in the library on orientation day, why him? There was no denying it: the boy was handsome, athletic, well proportioned, and neatly groomed and dressed. What girl wouldn't look twice? And Chelsea was cute, too. What boy wouldn't do the same?

When Erin finished her lunch and left them alone, sitting side by side at the long table, Tom immediately observed a shift in their demeanor. They looked at each other more openly. They began speaking, and by the looks of it they weren't discussing their afternoon classes.

Maybe his guilt was making him paranoid. After all, they'd only met last Thursday, and they'd seen each other exactly twice.

But if the chemistry was right, twice could do it.

As casually as possible, he walked over and stood behind them in his usual lunchroom stance, arms crossed and shoulders relaxed.

"Looks like you two enjoyed your lunches."

Like a mirror and its reflection, they shot glances back over their shoulders.

"Oh, hi, Mr. Gardner."

"Hi, Dad."

"How's your first day going, Kent?"

"Just fine, sir. Chelsea's keeping me from getting lost."

Chelsea explained, "They didn't have a computer system in his last lunchroom, so I showed him how it works."

Tom glanced at the wall clock. "Better get going, though. Classes start again in four minutes."

"Oh!" She leaped up and grabbed her tray. "I hadn't even noticed! Come on, Kent, I'll show you where to put your dirty dishes."

They went off without a goodbye, leaving Tom staring after them and wondering if he was being overanxious in worrying about any kind of teenage crush between them. Five days. They'd known each other five days, and Chelsea had never been the kind to get gaga over boys at the drop of a hat. If anything, she was more sensible than most of her classmates. Tom and Claire had discussed it often, how lucky they were that their daughter wasn't the kind who got boy crazy and let it affect her good judgment or her grades.

Still, when he'd walked up behind them and spoken, they'd both jumped.

Tom spent the remainder of his day settling a rash of early-school problems. He nailed down a short-term sub for the teacher who'd gotten the better job offer elsewhere and spoke to the district office about getting more desks for Mrs. Rose's room. He took a call from a reporter at the local newspaper, gave comments on the coming school year, and set up ongoing tracking between himself and the paper for the rest of the year. A police officer dropped by with complaints from the homeowners near school, who were upset about students ignoring parking restrictions on their street. And in between all these duties he managed to speak to eighteen students who were sent to his office for everything from getting caught smoking in the lavatories to requesting a student parking permit. At 3:02 P.M., when the seventh and last period ended, he did his stint in the hall, then returned to his office, where two sets of parents were waiting to speak to him. At 3:40 he arrived ten minutes late for a social studies department meeting, then afterward went back to his desk to return a half hour's worth of phone calls, including one from Coach Gorman about accessing the varsity football games on the local community cable channel.

At the end of the conversation Gorman remarked, "That new kid, Kent Arens? He's working out really fine, Tom. What a powerhouse! Must've been coached by somebody who knew his business because the kid's a real worker. Man, he lit a fire under the whole offensive line! Thanks for sending him down, Tom. He's going to make a major difference on our team."

"Well, Bob, I was a coach once myself. We can usually spot the good ones, can't we?"

When he'd hung up, Tom sat at his desk staring at the pictures on his window ledge, recalling Chelsea and Kent in the lunchroom in the middle of some intense discussion. Hell, the boy would probably turn out to be a hero on the football field, too, making him twice as attractive to Chelsea. And she was a cheerleader. How in the world could he keep the two of them apart if there really was a budding attraction between them?

He sighed and ran a hand over his face, tipping back in his chair, tired after the hectic day, worrying about this personal dilemma on top of all the snags and problems inherent in the *first week*.

He glanced at his watch, startled to discover it was already ten after six. He dialed home and Claire answered.

"Hi, it's me."

"Hi."

"Sorry, I just looked at my watch. Didn't realize it was so late."

"Are you leaving now?"

"Yup, be there in a few minutes, okay?"

"Okay, but . . . Tom?"

"Yes?"

"Can you stay home tonight?"

"Sorry, honey, I've got to be back at school at seven for a Parents' Advisory Committee meeting."

"Oh . . . well, then." He could hear the disappointment in her voice.

"I really am sorry, Claire."

"Oh, it's okay. I understand."

"See you in a few minutes."

He sighed, pushed back from the desk, snapped out the fluorescent lights, and headed home. She'd held supper for him and was scooping pasta into a serving bowl when he walked in the door. He hung his suit jacket over the back of his chair, moved close behind her, and pecked her on the neck. "Hey, darlin', what's for supper?"

"Chicken with fettuccine. Sit down." She raised her voice as she swung clear and carried the food to the table. "Kids! Supper's ready!"

He loosened his tie and took his customary place at one end of the table. When they were all seated and the bowls were being passed, Tom said cheerfully, "So . . . how was everybody's first day?"

"Mine was great!" Chelsea replied with enthusiasm.

"I got that spacehead Mr. Galliaupe for government class." Robby was going through a negative stage that was testing everybody's patience.

"Why do you say he's a spacehead?" Tom asked.

"Oh, jeez, Dad, everybody knows it but you! Look at the way he dresses! And he talks like a geek."

"Not every guy dresses cool like Dad," Chelsea put in. "Right, Mom?"

"Yeah, right." Claire's glance stopped on her husband. "So how was your day?" she asked.

Tom replied, "Busy, but okay, as opening days go. How about yours?"

"I had enough desks for everyone, nobody called me 'Yo,' and I think I'll have some fairly intelligent students in my classes."

Chelsea said, "So what do you think of Kent Arens?"

Robby interrupted. "Everybody knows what *you* think of him, don't they? I hear you're eating lunch with him already."

Some subtle change warned Claire to watch Tom—a barely perceptible squaring of his shoulders, a pause as he reached toward the butter dish with his knife, the quick glance at her, and the quicker glance away. In those two brief seconds she could have sworn what she sensed was fear, yet what could he possibly be afraid of? They'd only been talking about a new student whom Tom himself had been praising last week.

Claire filled her plate with pasta while pushing the subject of Kent Arens. "He's got wonderful manners, he seems very bright, and he's not afraid to participate in class. I found out that much already."

Chelsea couldn't resist badgering her brother, "So what if I ate lunch with him? I'm his official partner, you moron."

"Yeah, and pretty soon you'll probably be his unofficial partner. Better watch it, Chels."

"Dad, would you tell your son what it means to be a partner in this school? Not that he'd ever spend any time finding out for himself. He's too busy in the weight room, making his neck as thick as his head."

Once again Claire carefully watched her husband, surprised by his reaction. She knew Tom too well to mistake the fluster in his face, the telltale stretching of his jaw, as if his shirt collar didn't fit correctly. He always did that when he was feeling guilty about something. When he caught her studying him, he focused on his plate and spoke to the children. "All right, you two. That's enough. Chelsea, it *is* a little early in the school year for . . . well, for pairing up. Your mom and I have always been so happy that you put schoolwork before boys. I hope that won't change this year."

"Da-add!" Chelsea gave the word two syllables, her eyes and mouth petulant with dismay. "I don't believe what I'm hearing! All I did was show him how to use the computer in the lunchroom! Is there anything wrong with that?"

"No, honey, there isn't. It's just . . . well . . . ." Tom's gaze flickered to Claire, then dropped. "Forget it."

Claire put in, "He does seem to be a nice boy, Tom. You said so yourself."

"Okay, okay!" He jumped to his feet and headed for the sink to rinse his plate. "Forget it, I said!"

For heaven's sake, Claire thought, *his face is red!*

"There's dessert," she offered, following him with her eyes.

"None for me." He hurried away toward the bathroom, this man who loved desserts, leaving Claire with the distinct impression he was escaping.

He left for his evening meeting at a quarter to seven. Robby went off to the Woodbury Mall to pick up a few school supplies, and Chelsea went to Erin's house to make pom-poms.

Left alone, Claire folded a load of clothes that had been left in the dryer, ironed a couple of wrinkled blouses, and sat down at the kitchen table to read the four-line poems she'd had her honors students compose today about any one hour during their summer.

The first one read:

> *Into a rocket*
> *On a river I stepped*
> *And careened to the bottom*
> *But never got wet.*

She supposed the student had been out at Valleyfair amusement park.

She had read only that one before she found herself thumbing through the papers in search of Kent Arens's, wondering if perhaps she might find in his poem a clue to what had upset Tom so.

> *A thousand lonely miles away*
> *A new house waits. I dread this day.*
> *Eighteen wheels and a big blue van*
> *Changing me from boy to man.*

A lonely boy, leaving his friends and familiarity behind, studying a new house on moving day. It struck a chord of sympathy for Kent but gave no clue to what had rattled Tom so.

She read a dozen more poems, then returned to Kent's and read it three times before rising from the table and roaming around the kitchen listening to the rain, worrying.

Why had Tom gotten so upset?

The house was quiet, the drizzle so steady, collecting on the screens and blurring the view of the twilit yard. The air was damp and oppressive. It seemed to seal the faint cooking smells into the room until they tinged the walls, the curtains, even Claire's clothing.

She had been married to Tom for eighteen years and knew him as well as she knew herself. What had been bothering him in Duluth was still bothering him today, only it was getting worse. Tom Gardner was guilty of something: she knew that as surely as she knew that his favorite part of dinner was dessert.

If it was another woman, what would she do?

At 8:30 she telephoned Ruth. "Ruth, are you busy? Are you alone? May I come over?"

Ruth had lived there since the children were small, had baby-sat Robby and Chelsea when Claire first went back to work, had been there with hugs and help when Claire's mother had died. Ruth had never missed one of Claire's birthdays in sixteen years, bringing cards and thoughtful gifts. Once when Claire was in bed with a terrible flu, Ruth had brought supper over every day for two weeks.

More important, Ruth was the only person who knew that Claire had once been tempted by John Handelman when they were supervising the class play together, and that sometimes when Tom got really busy at school Claire wished he had a different job, and that she worked very hard at squelching her resentment over the evenings he had to spend there. Claire had also confided in Ruth the fact that she had been pregnant when she married Tom and that because of this she harbored a deep-seated insecurity that she hid from the rest of the world.

Ruth Bishop was that person with whom Claire had forged a bond of friendship whose borders were elastic. Whatever the need or the time of day, Ruth Bishop was there.

They sat at opposite ends of a tuxedo sofa in Ruth's den while Chopin played softly on the tape deck and Ruth stitched needlepoint.

"Where's Dean?"

"Working out at the club . . . he says."

"Have the two of you talked yet?"

"No."

"Why not?"

"Because I'm sure now about the other woman. I drove over to the health club and waited in the car till he came out with her. I saw him kiss her goodbye before she got in her car and drove away."

"Oh, Ruth . . ." Claire's voice fell. "I was so hoping this was all in your imagination."

"Well, it's not. It's pretty damned real."

"And you didn't say anything to Dean?"

"No, and I won't either. Let him bring it up, if he's man enough. If he's not, let him live with me and suffer. I hope he does, because I know I am."

"Oh, Ruth, you don't mean that. You can't really go on knowing about a thing like this and not talk about it."

"Oh, yes I can. You just watch me! I don't want to end up like the divorcees I know, going through all that turmoil in the courts, dividing property, losing my home and my husband, and making my kids choose sides. We're less than ten years away from retirement, Dean and I, and where do I end up if I lose him? I'll be a lonely old woman with nobody to travel with, or eat with or sleep with or do anything with, to say nothing about living on a single retirement income. I figure, with a little luck, maybe this thing is just a passing fling with him and it'll blow over soon and the kids will never have to know about it. I don't want them to know, Claire. I don't want them to stop loving him, no matter what he's done. Can you understand that?"

"Of course I can. There's even a part of me that doesn't want to know, that wants everything to be perfect for you and Dean like it used to be.

But it isn't, and I just don't think ignoring the problem will make it go away."

"I don't want to get into it with you, Claire, but you work at that school and everybody there thinks that the only way to face a problem is to confront it. Well, that's not right for all of us. I've had a long time to put all the signs together and decide what to do. I mean, I had hints months ago. Months ago! And I made up my mind that if I ever found out he was chasing around with somebody, he'd have to be the one to tell me, not the other way around."

"What kind of hints?"

"Mostly he was distracted—you know. When you've lived with a man most of your life and he just starts acting different, your woman's intuition clicks on. Sometimes it's not what he does, it's the way he does it. The look on his face, the set of his jaw, the feeling that even when he's with you he's far away, and he'll . . ." Ruth cut herself off to peer more closely at Claire. "Oh, Claire, not you, too. Is it Tom? Has Tom got another woman, too?"

"Tom? Oh, heavens, Ruth, don't be silly."

"You should see the look on your face. What's going on?"

"Going on? What could be going on? We went up to Duluth this weekend for a romantic getaway, remember?"

"Subterfuge."

"Oh, come on, Ruth, you should know that if I thought for one minute Tom had something to hide from me, I'd ask him point-blank what it was."

"So, have you?"

Claire was hit by Ruth's direct gaze, and her bravado crumbled. Doubled forward, elbows to knees, she buried her face in her hands. "It's nothing," she claimed, muffled, hoping it was true. "It's just my imagination, that's all."

"That's what I said when it all started for me."

Claire's head lifted. She gripped one hand with the other. "But he's been so loving! More so than ever! Ruth, I'm not lying to you—the trip to Duluth was just perfect, and lately he's been coming up to me at the most unusual times and kissing me, and he touches me, and acts so affectionate. We've always had this agreement—nothing personal in the school building, but he even came to my room one day and kissed me. And I don't mean just a peck on the mouth. It was an honest-to-God passionate kiss. Now why would he do a thing like that?"

"I told you, subterfuge. Maybe he's trying to throw you off guard. There were a couple of times when I know damned well Dean tried to do that with me. I think I know the first time he actually went to bed with her because he sent me flowers, and it was the middle of the summer when I had all the flowers I needed right in my own garden. Men act that way when they're guilty of something."

Claire jumped up from the sofa, went to a window, and studied the stippled view of the yard through the rain. "Oh, Ruth, that's so cynical."

"You're talking to someone who just saw her husband kissing another woman! I've got a right to be cynical! What else has Tom done?"

"Nothing. Absolutely nothing."

"But that's why you came over here tonight, isn't it? To talk about him, because something is different, isn't it?"

"It's just this gut feeling I have that something is wrong."

"But you haven't asked him? You haven't confronted him with it?" Claire stood silent, her back to Ruth while droplets slid down the window screen and the streetlights oozed on, smearing a blurred gold reflection on Ruth's blacktop driveway. "The way you're telling me I should confront Dean?"

Ruth expected no answer and got none. Claire remained across the room, a forlorn droop to her shoulders while Chopin's sad music played on.

Claire left for home shortly thereafter. She hugged Ruth at the door, extra-long, extra-hard, while Ruth whispered, "Don't ask him. Listen to me. Don't ask him, because once you know, it'll never be the same."

Claire closed her eyes and said, "I have to, don't you see? I'm not like you. I have to know."

A parting squeeze, and Ruth said, "Good luck then."

At home the children had returned and were in their rooms behind closed doors, which she touched with her hand and forehead, drawing comfort from the knowledge of their presence. From Robby's room came the soft reverberations of a rock radio station, while a strip of light showed at the floor beneath Chelsea's door.

She tapped softly and opened it. "Hi, I'm back. I was at Ruth's."

"Hi." Chelsea was doubled over at the waist, brushing her hair upside down. "Wake me at six-fifteen, will you, Mom?"

"Sure."

Whatever worries she carried, Claire realized she could not impose them on her children. She closed Chelsea's door and went into her own bedroom, slipping off her shoes and moving around listlessly. The carpet felt clammy but she resisted putting on the furnace. It was that autumn limbo between the heaven of hot August and the hell of chill October. She turned on one tiny light beside some books on a cedar chest, donned summer pajamas, and found an old, favorite shawl. Wrapped in it, she struck a dramatic pose in the shadows before the dresser mirror. Her reflection looked profoundly sad, the corners of her mouth drawn down like tent corners, her eyes lit only by the furtive light coming from below and behind her. She spoke aloud, quietly, a line from some old movie whose title and star she could not recall. Olivia De Havilland, maybe, in *To Each His Own.* "Tom, Tom, have you forsaken me?" No, the hero in that movie wasn't named Tom, was he? She really couldn't remember.

She left the room and trod with balletic grace to the opposite end of the house to keep the rain company.

When Tom got home she was curled up in a wicker rocking chair on the screened porch off the living room, her updrawn knees wrapped in the brown fringed shawl. A single candle burned in a hurricane lantern on the tabletop. Beyond the screen mist gathered on the brow of the shingles and plopped into the daylilies below. Upstairs Robby's radio still played, but out here the damp, navy-blue night seemed to muffle all sound.

Tom stopped in the doorway from the living room. He'd made no secret of his arrival. She knew he was there. Still, she went on rocking, staring into the shrouded yard beyond the screen, upon which the moisture had created a design like a cross-stitched quilt.

He sighed and stood for a while. Finally he asked, quietly, "Do you want to talk about it?"

She rocked twice, thrice, four times, swiped her lower eyelids with a fist wrapped in the scratchy shawl. "I don't know." The wicker snapped and popped like old bones as she kept it swaying and stared through the screen.

Still dressed in his suit, with his tie loosened, he stood on the track of the sliding door with his hands hanging in his side pockets. She had a penchant for drama, this English teacher, his wife, who directed class plays and was known for a classroom delivery that, in itself, often bordered on the dramatic. He'd long ago stopped blaming her for bringing that overdeveloped sense of drama into their disagreements. He understood it was second nature to her. He understood, too, that the surroundings she'd chosen—the damp, brooding night, the candle, the rocking chair and shawl—were chosen as she might choose a set for one of her school plays.

He sighed once more and let his shoulders sag. "We'd better, don't you think?"

"I suppose."

His loafers rapped out four weary steps on the hollow porch floor as he approached the table, pulled out a wicker side chair, and sat. Her rocker was angled away, giving him a candle-lit view of her left shoulder and the side of her face. He tipped forward with his elbows on his knees and waited.

She sniffled once.

"All right," he said, forcing patience into his voice. "You might as well tell me."

"Something's wrong. I've known it since we were in Duluth."

He sat there, doubled forward, wanting it off his chest but terrified of telling her the truth. For the first time she looked at him over her shoulder, swinging her head as if it were on a film rolling in slow motion.

The candlelight gave depth to her eye sockets and a glimmer to her irises. She wore no makeup, and her hair hung loose.

"Would you tell me, Tom, if you were having an affair?"

"Yes."

"Are you?"

"No."

"What if I said I don't believe you?"

It was easier to dredge up anger with her than to say what he'd come here to say. "Claire, that's ridiculous."

"Is it?"

"What in the name of heaven gave you that idea?"

"Why did you take me to Duluth?"

"Because I love you and I wanted us to get away together!"

"But why now?"

"You know that too—because as soon as school starts my time's not my own anymore. Look, it's started already! Ten o'clock at night and I'm just getting home, but I've been at *school*, not with some other woman!" He was tired. He'd had a grueling day, and he couldn't face the all-night round of tears and recriminations that would probably be set off if he told her about Kent now. Besides, it was so much easier to be the accuser than the accused.

"I've been talking about going to an inn together for at least five years. All of a sudden you go for the idea, then when you get me there you act so distracted that sometimes I had the feeling you forgot I was in the bed with you."

He leaped to his feet. "I am *not* having an affair!"

"Shh! Tom, hold your voice down."

"I don't give a shit if the neighbors at the end of the block hear me! I'm not having an affair! Who the hell would I have one with, and just when do you think I'd find time? I'm at school all day long and five nights to boot. Some affair I could have! I know who put these ideas in your head!" He pointed a finger to the west. "You've been talking to Ruth. That's it, isn't it? What have you two been doing, comparing notes? She thinks Dean is having an affair, so naturally I must be too. For the life of me, I'll never understand how women's minds work!" He picked up his vacated chair, clunked it down exactly where it had been, then stiff-armed it in place, simmering.

"You're the one who said, 'Let's talk about it,' Tom."

"Well, I didn't think I was going to be accused of some bullshit like this! I've got a right to get mad!"

"I asked you to hold your voice down."

"If you wanted me to keep my voice down, you shouldn't have picked the screened porch for Act One! And don't think for a minute that I missed the carefully set stage here." He cut the air with a hand. "The murky lighting and the rain and the hurt wife wrapped up in her shawl with her makeup washed off. Claire, you underestimate me."

From behind him, Chelsea spoke timorously. "Dad?"

He spun around and ordered, "Go to bed, Chelsea."

"But you're fighting."

"Yes, we are. Married people do it all the time. Don't worry, we'll have it all straightened out by morning."

"But . . . you guys never fight."

He went into the living room and put his arms around her. "It's okay, honey." His heart was still jumping with adrenaline as he kissed her hairline. "Kiss Mom and go to bed."

"But I heard what she said, Dad . . . that you're having an affair."

Exasperated, he released her. "I am *not* having an affair!" He tipped his head back, closed his eyes, and tried to collect himself. "Chelsea, will you just do what I say? Kiss Mom and go to bed. We'll both still be here in the morning and we'll all still be at school tomorrow. Nothing has changed!"

Chelsea went into the flickering candlelight and leaned down to kiss Claire's cheek. "Good night, Mom," she whispered.

Claire lifted her face and rubbed her daughter's shoulder. "You weren't meant to hear this, Chelsea. Please don't worry. See you in the morning, darling."

When Chelsea had disappeared into the dark house, Tom went back out to the porch and blew out the candle. "Come on," he said, "let's go to bed."

He went into the bedroom without her and was standing with his back to the door, jerking off his clothing, when she came in and shut the door. She watched him, recognizing anger in every movement. He hung up his trousers, stripped off the shirt, and slammed it into the bathroom hamper, returning to the bedroom without glancing at her.

She got into bed and waited.

He got in, snapped off the lamp, and turned onto his side away from her.

One minute of silence passed, then another and another until finally Claire spoke.

"Tom, you've got to understand."

"Understand what?"

She was trying hard not to cry. "You're right. I did have a talk with Ruth. She's seen Dean with another woman, but she isn't going to confront him with it, because once she does, it'll have to be faced and dealt with. I'm not that way—*we're* not that way, Tom; we deal with confrontations at school all the time. What kind of educators would we be if we taught people that denial is the best way of handling problems? Do you think I wasn't scared tonight, voicing my fear? But what else should I have done? I had my suspicions, so I put them to you. I thought I was doing the right thing."

"All right." He flung himself onto his back, making sure no square inch of his skin touched hers. "You've said your piece, now let me say mine. If I'd been messing around, maybe I wouldn't be so damned mad. But you really caught me off guard. First of all, I love you, and I thought I was doing something great for both of us by taking you to Duluth. Then you turned around and flung it in my face, and that hurts. When I married you I promised to be faithful, and by God, I have been. You want to know the truth, I never even *fantasize* about other women. They say it's healthy, but you couldn't prove it by me. And it really pisses me off, the idea of Ruth Bishop putting these ideas in your head. Ruth Bishop needs a shrink, that's what she needs, so the next time you go over there and she starts gossiping about Dean, *don't* put me on a par with him, because damn it, it hurts!"

Two tears trailed down her cheeks while he went on.

"What hurts even more is that you brought it up where Chelsea could hear."

"You're the one who started shouting, Tom."

"How long do you think it'll stay on her mind? If anything ever goes wrong between us again, do you think it'll come back to her and she'll wonder if I really was having an affair?"

"I'll tell her in the morning that I was wrong."

He flipped onto his side away from her. "Yeah, you do that, Claire."

He knew when she began crying behind him because he could feel the faint trembling through the mattress. He heard her pluck a tissue from the cube on her nightstand, but she was too proud to blow her nose, and lay containing her sobs instead. He had emotions of his own to contain—a real jumble. His daughter had heard him unjustly accused of being unfaithful when he *revered* his wife and had given her no cause to doubt him, ever, not in the last eighteen years! What he'd done with Monica Arens had been done before he spoke his vows, and that was a separate issue from this! But that sin from his past came to rankle and prod him with guilt; after all, he was the one who should be confessing here instead of jumping all over her.

So they lay facing opposite walls, choking on disillusionment and love.

The window on Claire's side of the bed was open a couple of inches. The air felt chilly drifting over Tom's exposed arm, but he lay motionless, damned if he'd move so much as one muscle. He didn't understand this compulsion to lie absolutely still, but it was there. *Don't let her know you're awake. Don't risk moving and touching her. It doesn't matter that she's hurting as badly as you, just let her lie back there miserable for a while, like she's made you miserable.*

She blew her nose, and he thought, *Go ahead and cry! Why should I try to make you feel better when you hurt me this way?* Through several walls he heard the bathroom faucet running and supposed it was Chelsea, troubled and unable to sleep, beleaguered by the unnecessary trauma foisted upon her by this regrettable episode. *All right, I was the one doing the shouting, but damn it, what man wouldn't?*

Behind him Claire shifted her feet so furtively he could tell she, too, suffered from the bizarre compulsion to lie motionless. Inexplicable and stupid, but there you had it—lovers who fought did inexplicable and stupid things.

His body started retaliating in insidious ways. He shifted one arm as furtively as she, sliding the back of his hand slowly along the cool pillow until he could pinch the bridge of his nose, which was stinging, deep inside.

How could she read me so wrong? How could she mistake how much I love her? Can't she tell?

A single hot tear leaked from his left eye onto the pillowcase and made a wet spot that quickly turned from warm to cold.

She twitched once, and he realized she was at last falling asleep. What would he say to her in the morning? Would this constricted feeling be gone from his chest by then? Her eyes would be swollen and she hated that, hated going out in public after she'd been crying.

They'd fought relatively few times in their lives. During those periods of forced abstinence during and after her pregnancies, they'd had the usual spats like most married couples. The worst fight they'd ever had was over a teacher at school, Karen Winstead, who'd flirted with him during the year after her divorce. "I don't want that woman in your office!" Claire had shouted, and he'd said there was no way to keep her out—after all, teachers had to speak to principals about all sorts of things. The whole situation had been exacerbated by his bringing up John Handelman from her department who liked to come to her room and chitchat between classes, and in the end they'd had this drag-out fight spawned by jealousy.

Her eyes had been swollen that time, too.

In the middle of the night he awakened, roused suddenly by the absolute certainty that she was awake behind him. She hadn't moved or spoken, yet he knew her eyes were open, too. After eighteen years of sleeping with her, he knew.

In his sleep he had burrowed under the blankets, and beneath them his heart seemed to be rocking him from side to side with each beat in that magnified midnight way that sometimes happens. He opened only his eyes. Nothing more.

But she knew, too.

They lay back-to-back with their skins tuned to the nearness of each other, their aloneness and aloofness a continuing misery.

After minutes, she finally broke down and moved.

"Tom?" she whispered, and touched him on the back.

He rolled like a cask falling from a wagon, over his own arm to face and clutch her to his empty body, which seemed suddenly to fill from the heart outward.

"Claire . . . oh, Claire," he whispered, clasping her, loving her, sick with sorrow for having been cold and shutting her out, for accusing her when his own guilt was the primary cause of their trouble right now.

"I'm sorry. Oh God, I love you so," she sobbed.

"I love you, too, and I'm sorry, too."

Their limbs, for all the applied pressure, felt inadequate in the face of these emotions. They simply could not hold each other tightly enough.

"I know that . . . I know that . . . please forgive me. I can't"—a sob broke forth and rent her words in half—"can't bear sl . . . sleeping beside you and knowing I hurt you . . . I don't know how to do anyth . . . thing without you."

He kissed her again, cutting off her plea until she had to fight for breath. She tore her mouth free and he heard her soft panting beside his ear as her hands plunged into his waistband to grip him from behind. Moments later she was naked from the waist and he was driving into her, her heels and calves gripping him from behind, forming a heart around his hips. And all that had forged them for eighteen years forged them once again: the vows they had spoken on their wedding day, the disagreements of the past and of earlier tonight, the infrequent jealousy that reminded them of how much they truly loved each other, the love they shared for their children and the wish that their son and daughter could know the very best of life and most certainly that they'd never suffer on their parents' behalf. They had worked hard at their marriage, their careers, their parenting. They had come to respect and love each other for all these reasons and more, and when their union had been threatened they had both known fear.

Fear fled now, chased away by this act that was so much more than sex. It was apology, renewal, and promise.

When it was over and they rested quietly in each other's arms, Claire reached up and touched Tom's cheek.

"Don't ever leave me," she whispered.

"Why would I leave you?"

"I don't know." Some faint pressure of her hand warned him her fear was genuine. "I don't know. Just promise you won't."

"I promise I won't leave you, ever." Sometimes she said these things out of the blue, and he had no idea where her insecurities came from. He rested a hand on her hair and stroked her cheek with a thumb.

"Claire, why do you say those things?"

"I don't know. Maybe because I know you had to marry me. That never seems to go away."

"I married you because I wanted to."

"I know that, really, but deep inside . . . oh, I don't know, Tom." She had never been able to make him understand, the way Ruth understood, the legacy of insecurity left by that premarital pregnancy. Once, years ago, he had told her that it hurt him to know she felt this way, and they'd had a bit of a fight about it. She didn't want that to come between them tonight. "Tom, I'm so tired . . . let's not talk about it anymore."

They didn't. They turned on their left sides and matched their curves like two strips of ribbon. He cupped her breast. They sighed. She looped an elbow back over his hip. And snuggled so, they slept.

Six

At 6:45 Friday night, four days into the school year, the locker room at HHH sounded like a Boy Scout troop when the hot dogs are served. First home game of the season and all seventy members of the football team were geared up and gunnin'. Voices babbled. Doors clanged. Cleats clattered and shoulder pads clacked. The red and white of jerseys put a pinkish cast in the humid, fluorescent-lit air. Boys straddled varnished benches, stretching their quads, taping their hands. Even a sightless person would have recognized the room by its bouquet—sweat, steam, adhesive tape, and concrete permeated by water that never quite dried.

Robby Gardner slipped his hip pads into his pants and stretched them on. He untangled the elastic cords connecting his shoulder pads and began tying them on, while ten feet away Jeff Morehouse said something to Kent Arens, gave him a mock punch on the shoulder, and the two of them laughed. Robby didn't know what it was about the new kid that bugged him so, but he didn't like his best friend getting too chummy with Arens. Pizza Lostetter had begun hanging around with him, too, and more than once Robby had seen his sister Chelsea standing by Kent's locker, talking to him.

Coach Gorman came out of his office carrying a clipboard, dressed in navy trousers, a red-and-white zippered jacket, and a red cap with HHH above the bill. He gave a short bleat on his whistle and bellowed, "Okay, everybody, listen up!" Squat as a garbage can, he stood with his feet widespread and the edge of his clipboard denting his groin. "First home game of the season and we want to set a standard for ourselves tonight. You've all worked hard, but you're going to work a lot harder before this season is over, starting with tonight. Blaine is our toughest opponent and always has been. We're going to need a smart offense and a hair-trigger defense to beat them. You've all been wondering who's going to do the job, who'll play, so I'm not going to keep you in suspense any longer. Here's the starting roster for tonight.

"Gardner, quarterback; Baumgartner, left halfback; Pinowski, left fullback . . ." As he read the names some shoulders sagged and some squared but the room remained quiet. "Arens, running back," he read, and Robby's eyes cut over to Jeff Morehouse, who'd played that position last year on junior varsity and had hoped to be there this year on first string. Robby thought, *Read Jeff's name! Read it!* But when the roster was finished, Jeff's name wasn't on it. It was hard for Robby to imagine handing off to anybody else when he backed away from center for a running play. He'd been handing off to Jeff since the two had played in peewee leagues in third grade.

The coach finished reading the starting lineup and went into his pre-game spiel, reminding everybody of their assignments, based on the coach's scouting report for the opposing team: a repeat of everything they'd been hearing at practice all week long. Robby's eyes skewered Arens, who stood as if at parade rest, scarcely blinking during the four minutes the coach spoke. Even his ability to zero in and fix his attention so totally irritated Robby.

". . . so go out there and show 'em who's the better team!"

Robby came out of his absorption to discover Coach Gorman's speech was finished. He grabbed his helmet and trotted out onto the field with the others, frowning at the back of Kent Arens, who jogged a few paces ahead.

The stands were already filling and the cheerleaders began stirring up applause as the team appeared. The band broke into the school song and the familiar march pulsed across the evening air. Robby caught a glimpse of Chelsea, cheering with the others, half-turning when Arens trotted past behind her. "Hey, Robby! Go, bro!" she yelled when he ran past, breaking out of the school song for a few beats, then falling into routine again.

For as long as he could remember, Robby Gardner had anticipated this time of his life. Senior year, a mild autumn night, soft grass giving beneath his cleats, the tubas making a *pop-pop-pop* against his ears as he ran past them, school colors flashing everywhere, his last high school season ahead with himself as quarterback, and his body resilient and ready for the challenge. Even Chelsea out there cheering. Yeah, that was right, too. But what had just taken place in the locker room took the edge off his total satisfaction. What must Jeff be feeling, benched in his senior year by some Texan who swaggers in, tosses out a couple of *yes sirs*, and makes first string?

Jeff pulled up off Robby's right shoulder and they jogged side by side. Robby said, "Jeez, man, what a bummer."

"Yeah, well, what can I say. The coach calls the shots."

"Yeah, but I think he's wrong this time."

"Better not let him hear you say that or he'll have the team doing twenty-twenties." Twenty-twenties were a grueling punishment no member of the squad wanted to foist upon his teammates.

They reached the fifty-yard line, and as captain of the offensive team, Robby ordered, "Spread out for warm-ups! Let's go!" He marshaled his forces, then led them through a vigorous round of calisthenics and stretches.

"Partner up!" he hollered, and the guys doubled up for leg stretches. "Hey, Arens, over here!"

Kent Arens came over and the air seemed to crackle with Robby's hostility as, without warning, he swung his foot up for a ballerina-style stretch. Kent caught it and held it by the heel while Robby bent forward at the waist until his forehead touched his knee. He took his time, stretching first his right leg, then his left. When he was finished, they reversed roles. Looking down on Arens's head, Robby felt his enmity freshen.

"So what's up between you and my sister?"

Arens straightened and answered, "Nothing."

"I see you in the halls together."

"Yeah, she's a nice kid."

"So what's up then? I mean, you asking her out or something?"

Arens changed feet, swung up the opposite heel. "Any objections if I did?"

"Can't think of any. I mean, it's none of my business . . . long as you treat her decently, right?"

Arens dropped his foot and stood loosely with his hands at his sides. "What's eating you, Gardner?"

"Nothing."

"You sure? So I'm new here, and maybe I bumped one of your friends out of a starting position, but you and I have to play together, and if you've got a problem with that, I think we ought to talk it out."

"No," Robby replied with false aplomb. "No problem at all."

But when he began warming up his arm, he threw the ball at Arens with as much ferocity as he could muster, hitting him in the numbers again and again, unable to make him grunt, retreat, or drop the ball.

Finally Arens threw it back with equal ferocity, catching Robby off guard. As he stepped back to catch his balance, the ball bounced to the grass. "What's with you anyway, Gardner?" Arens yelled. "Why don't you save it for Blaine, man?"

In the last-minute huddle, Coach Gorman said, "Okay, two players to watch. Number thirty-three on offense: Jordahl. Those of you in track know what he can do. He can run the forty in four-seven, so outside linemen, keep him contained. On defense, it's number forty-eight, Wayerson. He's six-foot-five with a reach like King Kong, and he knows how to knock down a pass. Linemen, don't let him get to the ball, y' got that? Those are the two we have to stop to win this game. Don't forget it! Okay, get your hits and play ball!"

They stacked hands, gave a whoop and a holler, and broke huddle.

Three minutes into the first quarter the coach called for a fake veer, curl option play, and Kent curled out, caught the option pass, and ran it into the end zone for six points.

The spectators went wild. The band broke into the school song. The cheerleaders started bouncing. The offensive team rushed Arens and butted his helmet. "Yyyyyesss!" they shouted with fists raised. "Yes, yes, yes!"

Robby Gardner said nothing. He held the football for the point after, then sprinted to the sideline and removed his helmet without a word of congratulations to his running back. He watched seven points go up on the scoreboard and stood beside Jeff Morehouse, feeling a resentment that no good team man ought to be feeling at such a moment.

Arens scored again in the third quarter, on a leaping dive play that carried him into the end zone headfirst over the backs of his linemen.

And in the final quarter he threw the block that opened up a hole for a quarterback sneak, allowing Gardner to score a TD that broke a seventeen-all tie and won the game for the HHH Senators.

On the way off the field, jogging beside Kent, Robby realized his teammates were jogging all around them, and said expressionlessly, "Nice goin', Arens."

"Thanks," Arens said with as little enthusiasm as the compliment offered. Neither of them cast so much as a sideward glance at the other during the exchange.

When the locker room was nearly empty, Coach Gorman approached Robby's locker and said, "Gardner, I want to see you in my office when you're dressed."

Robby glanced over his shoulder. "Sure, Coach." He snapped his letter jacket, stuffed his dirty jerseys into a drawstring bag, and closed his locker door. "Hey, Jeff!" he called. "Be out in a minute. Gotta talk to the coach! Here's my keys." He tossed his car keys. "If you see Brenda, ask her if she wants to go to McDonald's with us, okay?"

The coach was sitting in a battered desk chair, leaning back at a ten o'clock angle while reading his clipboard. "Shut the door," he said, rocking forward and clattering the board onto his desk.

Robby shut the door.

"Sit."

Robby sat.

The coach let silence work its wiles for passing seconds while Robby leaned forward, his elbows spread on the chair arms, his fingers loosely linked. "So . . ." Coach Gorman finally blatted out. "Got something you want to talk about?"

Robby tipped his thumbs toward his chest. His eyebrows rose. "Me?"

"Something was going on out there on that field tonight. Mind telling me what it was?"

Robby's face went blank. His voice was blithe with feigned innocence. "We played a good game, Coach! We won!"

The coach picked up a pencil and let it fall onto the clipboard. "Come on, Gardner, you're not fooling me. You've been nursing some grudge ever since I let Arens on the team. Tonight it was obvious that you were playing with something else on your mind."

"But we won!"

"This isn't about winning, Gardner, and you know it! This is about being part of a team and working as a team and always striving for what's best for that team."

"Yeah?" Gardner's inflection said, *I know that, so why are you preaching?*

"So what's between you and Arens?"

"Nothing."

"Come on, Robby, give me some credit here. I'm your coach. When the unity of my team is threatened, I want to know why. Couldn't be that you resent Arens acing out your good buddy Morehouse, could it?"

Robby sucked his lips against his teeth and stared at a golf ball bookend on the coach's desk.

"That's it, isn't it? That and the fact that the rest of you sweated through hell week and Arens didn't have to."

"Excuse me, Coach, but Jeff worked hard to make first string."

Gorman bellowed, "*I'm* the coach here! *I* decide who'll play and who won't play, and I do it based on who'll make the team perform at optimum. You, on the other hand, seem to have forgotten that when you stop being a team player, it's the team that suffers. Where were the congrats and high-fives when Arens made his first touchdown tonight? And his second?"

Robby dropped his chin and aligned his thumbnails.

The coach took on a confidential tone and doubled forward, crossing his forearms on the desktop. "It's not like you, Gardner. And Arens is good. He's darned good. Everybody's been playing better since he's been here, and tonight when he threw the crucial block that put you into the end zone, I expected you to do some celebrating with him."

Robby mumbled, "Sorry, Coach."

Gorman sat back and threw an ankle over a knee. "If there's personal stuff between you, don't bring it on the field. You're too good a player to forget a rule like that, and too good a quarterback to wind up benched. Don't test me, Robby, because I'll do what's best for the team every time, okay?"

Robby nodded.

Gorman flapped a hand toward the door. "All right then, you're outta here. Have a nice weekend and see you Monday at practice."

Robby had been playing football since he was so young his head barely filled a helmet. Never, in all those years, had he been called on the carpet this way by his coach. Along with his team, yes. But alone? Never.

Leaving the coach's office, he felt more antagonistic than ever toward Arens.

In the girls' locker room after the game, Erin Gallagher stripped off her red sweater and said, "I'd give anything if Kent Arens would ask me out!"

Chelsea said, "Not cool, Erin. What about Rick?"

"Rick isn't on the football team. And besides, he's so bossy!"

"But Erin"—Chelsea lowered her voice—"how can you say that when you and Rick . . ." She stirred the air with one hand and whispered, ". . . you know."

"Rick and I had a fight after school today."

"About what?"

"About Kent. He saw me talking to him in the hall after fifth period. Chelsea, I think Kent's starting to like me. You're his friend. Would you give him the hint that I think he's really studly and that I'd go out with him if he asked me to?"

"Studly? Erin, how can I say a thing like that to him? I'd die of embarrassment."

"Well, you know what I mean. Just drop the hint."

"Erin, I don't know . . ."

"Don't tell me you've got a crush on him yourself!"

"Not exactly."

"You do! Oh cripes, Chels, do you really? I thought you were just showing him around because you had to."

"He's really nice, Erin. I mean, he's got manners and he's not loud like most of the boys. He's not the kind of guy you say 'studly' to."

Erin's spirits deflated. "Well, anyway, I just thought I'd ask. Heck, I didn't know you were scoping him out for yourself."

"I'm not scoping him out, and don't say that so loud. You know how gossip starts."

When the girls had showered and changed, Chelsea said, "I'm going to take my uniform up to my locker, Erin. Meet you by the front door."

"Me too. Three minutes, okay?"

They parted in the hall carrying their red sweaters and skirts on hangers over their shoulders. Around the corner by the first-floor lockers the lights were dim, the classroom doors closed and locked. It seemed so different here at night than during the day. Chelsea could even hear the click on her combination lock as she rotated it with her thumb. Her locker door resounded like a gong as she opened it and hung up her

uniform. She took out a small purse, applied fresh lipstick, then looped
the noodle-thin strap over her shoulder, closed her locker, and headed for
the front door. On the way she passed the five long, narrow banks where
the seniors were assigned lockers. From the shadows between them,
someone said, "Hey, Chelsea, that you?"

She backed up and peered down the middle aisle.

"Kent?" He stood beside his open locker wearing a green windbreaker, jeans, and a baseball cap tipped back on his head.

"Hi," she said softly, in a tone of pleased surprise, moving toward him.
"You played a super game."

"Thanks."

"I can see why you made first string."

"I had good coaches in Texas."

"Mmm . . . no, it's more than that, I think. My dad always says, 'You
can teach plays, but you can't teach ability.'" Dropping one shoulder
against the lockers, she watched him field the compliment with engag-
ing humility. "Hey, it's nothing to be ashamed of."

"I'm not ashamed. Just . . ." He shrugged and they laughed together.
Quiet fell between them.

"Every now and then I'd glance over to the sidelines and see you
cheering, and I'd think, 'Hey, I know her. There's Chelsea.' I liked seeing
you there."

There was silence again while they let their eyes meet and part, meet
and part, both still uneasy with the attraction they were beginning to
feel.

"So, do you ride home with your girlfriends or what?"

"Sometimes. Sometimes I drive, but Robby's got the car tonight. How
about you?"

"My mom came to the game but she didn't want to wait around while
I showered, so she went back home and told me to call her if I wanted a
ride. Pizza said I could catch a ride with him if I want."

"Oh." She took a sudden interest in scratching the dial of a combination lock with her thumbnail.

He closed his locker door and set the lock, but they remained as they were, neither making motions of leaving the dimly lit private spot.

"So how far away do you live?" he asked.

"About two miles."

"That way." He pointed in the direction she'd once pointed for him.

"Yeah, that way."

He moved to stand in front of her, planting his feet wide, with both hands in the pockets of his windbreaker. "I could walk you," he offered.

"It'd be a long walk back home for you."

"I don't care. It's a nice night."

"You sure?"

He shrugged and grinned. "Good for the quads."

Erin came whizzing around the end of the lockers.

"There you are, Chelsea! What's holding you . . . oh!"

"I was just talking to Kent."

"Hi, Kent."

"Hi, Erin."

"Well, are you coming, or what, Chelsea?"

"No, you go on ahead. Kent's going to walk me home."

Erin's expression, dimmed by a sudden tinge of jealousy, lost its vivacity. Her mouth squared. "You don't want to go to McDonald's with us?"

"Next time, okay?"

Erin continued looking sickly over her friend's good fortune. When time began dragging with no one speaking, she said, "Well . . . okay, then, but . . . well, call me tomorrow, okay, Chels?"

"For sure."

"'Kay, then, bye."

"Bye," Chelsea and Kent said in unison.

When her footsteps faded, Chelsea said, "She likes you."

Kent said, "She's okay, but she's not exactly what I'd call my style."

They turned and began walking with the leisurely pace of two on the brink of discoveries with all the time in the world to make them.

"Oh? And what is?"

"I'm not sure yet. When I decide, I'll let you know."

The empty building created an intimacy, surrounding them with its uncustomary quiet and the whispering sounds of their own movement down its corridors. He opened the heavy front door and let her pass before him into the autumn night. Outside some cars were still leaving the parking lot and someone honked at them and waved out an open window. The lights were off above the football field, but those in the front lot created intermittent splotches along the edge of the school grounds. As they crossed the street, the moon, at half-phase, spread creamy light over the world, transforming the sidewalks to pale ribbons and putting thick shadows beneath the trees in the residential areas through which they passed. Somewhere in the distance a dog barked. They moved unhurriedly through the dappled night, a young couple exploring their newfound friendship that hinted of growing into something more.

"Do you miss Texas?" she asked.

"I miss my friends, especially my best friend, Gray Beaudry."

"Gray Beaudry. Southerners have romantic names, don't they?"

"Gray Richard Beaudry. I called him 'Rich,' and it was our own little joke, because he was. His mother's family was named Gray and she came from oil money somehow. You should have seen their house. Swimming pool, guest cabanas . . . the works."

"So do you want to be rich someday?"

"I don't know. It wouldn't be bad. Do you?"

"Not really. I'd rather be happy."

"Well, yeah, who wouldn't? I mean, what good's money if you're miserable?"

They talked about their own parents' relative richness and happiness. Kent said that achieving had always made his mother happy and she'd worked really hard and their new house was a major achievement and source of pride for her. Chelsea said that was probably true at her house, too, and she pretty much got whatever she wanted so she guessed her mom and dad were probably pretty well off. She'd always known they were happy together, too. Kent said he'd always thought it was odd that his mother was perfectly happy even though she'd never been married. Chelsea said wasn't it funny how different people were, 'cause she didn't think her mom and dad would be happy any other way but married.

Abruptly Kent changed the subject. "So what's this I hear about how Pizza got his nickname?"

"He told you?"

"Not him. Somebody else did. He's still scared to admit it."

"But it's true and everybody knows it. On the last day of school two years ago, he called up Domino's Pizza and used my dad's name and had seven large pizzas delivered to our house."

"And your dad paid for them?"

"What else could he do?"

"Man, that's hard to believe." They were both laughing. "Takes a pretty even-tempered guy to do a thing like that. Didn't he even try to find out who did it?"

"Oh, he suspected right away. Roland had been caught driving on people's boulevards and had done detention time at the end of the school year. My dad was pretty sure it was him. So last school year, every time we'd have pizza for school lunch, my dad would go up to his table—you know how he does—and stand behind him and ask, 'How's the pizza today, Roland?' And the weirdest thing happened. Roland started to like my dad so much that this summer he got a summer job working for the school district, mowing lawns and doing maintenance. My dad helped him get it."

They walked in silence for a while before Kent said, "Can I tell you something?"

"What?"

"I envy you your dad. I think I sounded like I had a chip on my shoulder that day you asked me about mine, but since then I've seen how Mr. Gard . . . I mean, how your dad comes up to you in the lunchroom and says hi, and you stop by his office now and then, and he pretty much likes the kids—you can tell. I think he's all right."

"Thanks," she replied, pleased. "I think so, too."

They reached a corner and she said, "This is my street. Fourth house on the left."

Their footsteps slowed. He hooked his thumbs into the back pockets of his jeans so his arm curved behind hers. Sometimes they let their elbows brush. They watched their feet move in slow motion down the edge of the street, beneath tree shadows that appeared blue upon the blacktop.

When they were almost at her driveway he asked, "So, are you going with anybody or anything?"

"No."

He glanced at her secretly, then away, and said, "Good."

"What about you? Any girl back in Texas you're writing to?"

"No," he said. "Nobody."

"Good," she repeated, feeling especially lucky.

They turned and walked up the driveway. The closed garage doors cut off access through the family room, so she led him along the sidewalk to the front door, where she paused at the bottom of two steps leading up to a concrete stoop. Turning, she looked up at Kent. "Thanks for walking me home. Sorry you've got to walk so far back to your house."

"No problem." He stood with his hands in the pockets of his windbreaker and caught the sole of one shoe on the edge of the step behind her, unconsciously hemming her in. "Sorry I didn't have a car to drive you. My mom's going to get one for me, but she hasn't had time since we moved."

"It's okay. I enjoyed walking." She gazed at the sky and gave a protracted shrug. "It's a beautiful night, isn't it?"

He looked up, too. "Yeah, it sure is."

Their gazes returned to earth and to each other. His foot dropped off the step.

"Well . . ." she said with a quirk of the head that said, *I'd better go in.*

They stood transfixed by the idea of a kiss, trapped in that splendid moment of anticipation whereby nights are memorialized in girls' diaries forever.

He shifted, testing the moment, bending toward her in the slight, questioning way of a boy who leaves the choice up to the girl. She waited with her face lifted. He leaned down and kissed her, keeping his hands in his pockets, taking nothing for granted. His lips were soft, innocent, and closed. So were hers.

When he straightened they both smiled, and he said quietly, "See you."

"Yeah . . . see you."

He walked backward several steps before turning to head away.

Seven

It was a rare Saturday morning when Tom stayed home. Community activities kept the school building open to the public, and when it was, he felt his place was there. People put the building to all kinds of uses: senior citizens' pancake breakfasts in the cafeteria, open swimming in the pool, dance-line practice in the gym, and everything from garden clubs to Adult Children of Alcoholics meetings in the classrooms.

The Saturday after the first football game was no exception. Tom got ready to leave the house shortly after 8:30 A.M.

"What are you doing today?" he asked Claire as he rinsed out his coffee cup. They had been treating their relationship as a fragile and precious thing since the night of their disagreement, being especially kind and appreciative to one another.

"Grocery shopping, housecleaning, then class preparation. When you get home, will you take a look at that sprayer on the sink and see if you can get it to work?"

"Sure." He kissed her in passing. "See you later."

She stopped him for a better kiss, and they parted lingeringly, smiling.

"See you," she whispered.

"As soon as I can get home."

There were smiles with ulterior meanings. They exchanged one that promised things sexual later on.

He spent the morning in his office, appreciating the quiet, studying the school's budget and trying to find room in it for a Russian language class, which would be taught by interactive television through a cable network with four other Minnesota school districts.

Shortly before noon Robby came in, dressed in sweats and dirty high-topped tennies.

"Hi, Dad."

"Hi," Tom said, dropping his pencil, flexing backward in his chair. "Been working out in the weight room?"

"Yeah, but now my car won't start. I think the battery's dead."

"Well, I'm ready to go home, too." Tom scraped his papers together and squared them into a pile. "Let's go out and take a look at it."

It was nearly noon, the activities in the building largely over. Tom locked the glass doors to the outer office, detoured through the cafeteria and found it quiet, glanced down the first-floor halls and found them quiet, too. Somewhere in the building the janitors were working; he could hear Cecil's radio playing softly in the west wing. The front doors were propped open again.

Outside, the September day was perfect, the sky a pale blue. The maple trees beside the front sidewalk and the massive elms in the yards of the neighborhood houses were still a deep, rich green. In a driveway across the road a man was washing a red car. The school grounds lay uncustomarily quiet. At times like this Tom felt a peculiar emptiness: this place could feel so forlorn without the hubbub of activity it was made for. He always wanted to hurry home when he found the parking lot empty.

Tom and Robby got into Tom's car at the reserved section near the front door and drove around to the area designated for student parking. The Nova sat all by itself in the huge lot, its oxidized body looking as dull as an old galvanized pail. "Did it do anything when you tried to start it?"

"Naw. Wouldn't even turn over."

"Might as well get out the jumper cables then."

Tom pulled up nose to nose with the Nova, jerked the hood release, and found his jumper cables in the trunk. While he was attaching them to the batteries, Robby came and leaned on the fender beside him.

"I suppose I might as well tell you," Robby said, "'cause you'll find out anyway. The coach reamed me out last night."

"Oh yeah?" Tom kept his face averted.

"It's about Arens. He thinks I've got a burr on my butt about him."

Tom glanced back over his shoulder. "Do you?"

"I don't know." Robby shrugged and looked sullen.

Tom pulled his head from beneath the hood, brushing his hands against one another. "Talk to me. I'm not going to ream you out. Just talk to me."

"Well, hell, Dad, Jeff got sidelined!"

Tom could see Robby was having great trouble puzzling out how to handle the situation; this was not the time to preach.

"So how's Jeff taking it?"

"I don't know. He didn't say much."

Tom paused a beat. "So did you say it for him?"

"Not really. But I've been playing ball with Jeff since we were in third grade!" Robby sounded slightly petulant as he swung around and propped his backside against the fender. Tom studied his shoulders for a minute, wiped his hands on his hanky, then joined him. Side by side, with their arms crossed, they rested against the warm steel fender and fixed their eyes on the man washing his car clear across the parking lot and road. The noon sun warmed their shoulders and the backs of their heads. The wide expanse of gravel-strewn blacktop created the feeling that they were the only two people on an island.

Tom said, "You forget, I was at the game last night. I think I know what the coach was upset about. And by the way, what goes on between you and him in the locker room is strictly private. I don't ask, nor does he tell me, how he chooses to coach you."

Robby glanced over, but made no reply.

Far off at the fire station a noon whistle blew. Above the distant trees north of the parking lot a flock of blackbirds lifted, made black confetti against the sky, then disappeared once more into the foliage.

"Life changes," Tom said ruminatively. "You get it all lined up just the way you like it and then something beyond your control comes along and bumps you off center. How nice it would be if you could get everything just the way you want it and say, 'Okay, now, stay.' But nothing stays the same. You grow up, make friends, lose friends, go to college, lose track of people, meet new ones, and sometimes you ask yourself why. But all I can tell you is that every single experience you go through like this changes you in some way. Every new person who comes into your life changes you. Every moral dilemma or emotional experience you come up against changes you. It's your job to decide *how*. That's how character is developed."

Robby kicked at some gravel with the toe of his tennis shoe, then looked off across the street. "So you're saying the team comes first, before Jeff."

"I'm saying you've got to decide for yourself."

Robby stared at the blackbirds, who flew up again, chattering, and made a shifting pattern of motion against the sky. Tom curled a hand over his son's shoulder and boosted himself off the fender. "Come on. Let's try to get this junk heap started."

A short while later they arrived home in two cars. Tom parked in the garage and Robby at the end of the driveway. When he tried to restart the Nova, nothing happened. Tom stood listening to the sound of the starter grinding fruitlessly and mentally calculated the price of a new battery.

Robby slammed the Nova door and said, "Deader than a doornail."

"I've been expecting it. At least it happened before winter."

They entered the house together. The vacuum cleaner sprawled on the family room floor and the kitchen was a mess, as if putting away groceries was in interrupted progress.

Claire called from the porch, "We're out here eating soup! Bring a couple of bowls and spoons!"

Tom opened a cupboard door, Robby the silverware drawer, and they went through the family room toward the sunny side of the house.

On the screen porch Claire and Chelsea sat at the round patio table, where a stainless-steel kettle and a tube of crackers shared space with the day's mail. Chelsea was painting her toenails, wearing an oversized white T-shirt sporting a chartreuse parrot. She finished one nail, ate a spoonful of soup, and began painting another. Claire, dressed in jeans, a chambray shirt, and a baseball cap, clinked her spoon into her bowl and said, "Help yourselves."

Tom's hand drifted over her shoulder as he passed behind her chair. "What's new?"

"Mmm . . . not much. Your dad called. Nothing important, just said hi. What's new with you two?"

"The Nova probably needs a new battery. We had to jump-start it at school; now it won't start again."

Robby lifted a cover off the soup kettle and peered inside. "What kind?"

"Broccoli-and-ham chowder."

"With cheese?" he asked, his eyebrows rising.

"Of course."

"All *right*, Mom! I'm starved."

"So what else is new," she remarked, as the guys filled their soup bowls and sat down. "Here, have some crackers." Claire pushed a tube across the table.

Robby began breaking some into his soup and pushing them beneath the surface, keeping one eye on his sister. "What are you painting your toenails for? That's the dumbest thing I ever heard of."

"Yeah, well, what would you know, Big Neck?"

"Hey, you know how many hours of weight lifting it took to get my neck this big? And who sees your toenails anyway?"

She gave him a *look* that said, *Your stupidity is showing.*

"Does Kent Arens like painted toenails or what?"

"If he did, it's none of your business."

"I hear he walked you home from the game last night."

A spoonful of soup stalled halfway to Tom's mouth. A warning crimped his insides.

"That's none of your business either," Chelsea shot back.

"Can't he drive a car yet, or what?"

"My goodness, that makes you sooo manly when you belittle others you're jealous of." She blew down the length of her shin, trying to dry her toenails.

"That'll be the day I'm jealous of Kent Arens. Talks like a Confederate, and you can't understand half of what he says."

"Well, I happen to like it, and yes, he walked me home last night. Anything else you want to know?"

"All right, you two, enough," Tom said, forcing down the flutters in his stomach and the hot shot of fear whizzing through him. "I swear to God, the way you talk to each other, a person would think you were mortal enemies. And Robby, don't forget what we talked about at school."

Chelsea said, "What did you talk about at school?"—her bearing suddenly alert with typical sibling nosiness.

Tom chided, "Chelsea."

"Oh, all right." They had rules about privacy, this family who bumped against each other twenty-four hours a day; Tom and Claire had laid them down early on. "But tell him he'd better not say anything to scare Kent Arens off. He's really nice and I like him a lot."

Chelsea's words struck Tom full force.

His throat closed.

The chowder seemed to curdle in his stomach.

Good God, what had he done? Coward that he was, he'd withheld the truth, and now Chelsea probably had a crush on her own brother.

He had to get away, be alone, sort this through. He rose to carry his soup bowl into the kitchen.

Claire watched him go. "Tom, you hardly ate anything."

"Sorry, honey, I'm not too hungry."

In the kitchen he rinsed his bowl. He should have admitted his wrongdoing a week and a half ago, the day he'd first laid eyes on Kent Arens. All these lives—six lives—affected by this father-son relationship, and he'd stalled long enough from doing the honorable thing. Above the sound of the running water he called, "Listen, honey, I'm going to run up to Target and buy a battery for the Nova. I'll try to get to the kitchen faucet later, okay?"

"But shouldn't you take a look at the faucet first in case you need to pick up any parts?"

He went out to her, gave her a kiss on the hairline, worried sick about the mess he'd caused.

"The car's more important. Be back soon, okay?"

He drove to the Target Greatland store at the Woodbury Mall and called Monica Arens from a pay phone in the customer service area. She answered on the third ring.

"Hello, Monica. This is Tom Gardner."

A surprised pause, then "Oh," as if she'd looked up warily at someone else in the room. Probably Kent, Tom thought.

"I need to talk to you."

She said nothing.

"Immediately."

"I can't."

"It's important."

"I'm in the middle of something here and—"

"Monica, I don't give a damn what you're in the middle of! This can't be put off! Kent walked my daughter Chelsea home from the game last night!"

Again came a pause, then, "I see." He sensed her fumbling for code words before she asked a question, pretending she was speaking to someone at work. "Is the front door to the reception area open on Saturdays?"

"He's there in the room with you, is that it?"

"Yes."

"Will he believe you've been called to work?"

"Yes."

"I'm at the Woodbury Mall. Can you come here?"

"Yes, I guess so, but I can't work very long. I'm still getting settled and there's so much in the house to do."

"Do you know where it is?"

"Yes."

"How soon can you meet me there?"

"All right. I'll be there in fifteen minutes."

"There's a restaurant called Ciatti's that stands all by itself. I'm driving a red Taurus. I'll park on the northwest side of the building. Fifteen minutes."

"Yes, okay, goodbye."

He didn't remember buying the battery at Target, going through the checkout line, or writing a check. He was conscious primarily of a sharp ache across his shoulders, a bulky lump in his throat, and a headache across the base of his skull. It was Saturday. The shopping center was busy. He could run into any of his students anywhere. Had he done the right thing telling Monica to meet him in a parking lot? He checked the time: 1:35, so hopefully the lunch business would be tapering off and the restaurant parking lot wouldn't be too busy by the time she got there.

He drove to the meeting spot, parked, turned off the engine, and sat with the sun beating through the windshield, turning the car into an oven. The lot was about half full, but even as he arrived two cars left. He rolled the windows down, rested one elbow on the window ledge, pinched his lower lip, and stared at the brick wall of the restaurant, his mind working.

The blue Lexus pulled up on his right and he felt suddenly guilty of much more than a premarital peccadillo eighteen years ago. Two cars, side by side, a woman getting out of one and getting into the other—it had the appearance of a clandestine tête-à-tête. He jumped out of his car as she got out of hers—an effort to allay his sense of wrongdoing—and waited to see what she'd do.

She moved toward the tail end of the cars and he did the same.

Neither of them said hello. They stood near their rear bumpers searching for comfortable places to fix their eyes, casting about for grace in the midst of this unsettling debacle.

"Thank you for coming," he thought to say.

"I didn't know what else to do. Kent was right there in the room with me when the phone rang."

"I didn't know what else to do either except call you."

She was wearing sunglasses and a purse over her shoulder with her thumb caught beneath the strap. Her dress was another one of those sacky shapeless things that made him happy he'd married a woman with a perkier style. He braved a glance at Monica but her body language and the slant of her sunglasses suggested she'd be damned if she'd glance back.

The autumn sun drummed down on the blacktop and reflected off the paint of their cars, into their eyes.

"Should we sit in my car and talk?"

Her sunglasses flashed his way. Her lips remained a thin, colorless ribbon. Without replying, she walked toward the passenger door of the Taurus and got in.

When he'd slid behind the wheel they sat in weighty silence. Each was embarrassed to be there. Had they any sort of sentimentality about their past, it might have eased them, but they had only regret and very little recollection of the brief intimacy that had caused this meeting today.

Finally he cleared his throat and said, "Look, I was running on adrenaline when I called you. I didn't really think through how or where we'd meet. I just picked up the phone and dialed. If you want to go someplace where we can have a soft drink and—"

"This is fine. You said Kent walked your daughter home from the game last night."

"Yes. I just found out about an hour ago."

"So I assume you want to tell your family who he really is."

"I've got to. I've known the truth for only ten days and it's been a living hell for me ever since. I'm no good at keeping secrets from my wife, no good at all."

She lowered her forehead to the butt of one hand. Her arms were crossed on the purse in her lap, its leather strap gone slack and floating free of her shoulder.

Tom said, "The only reason I didn't tell them this noon was because I thought you and I should discuss it first. You should tell Kent sometime over the weekend, too, so that they all find out at the same time. I don't want one of my kids to be the one to tell him at school."

"No, that wouldn't be good."

Time passed, great chunks of silence, while they envisioned telling their families.

"I got pretty panicky when I heard he'd walked her home."

"Yes," she said, rather detachedly, Tom thought. She seemed a very unemotional woman, tightly reined, giving away little in her facial expressions or the inflection of her voice.

"Has he mentioned Chelsea at all?"

"Once."

"What did he say?"

"Not much."

"Nothing about her personally?"

"No."

He thought about how secretive teenagers could be. "It's uncanny how they took to each other. I've been watching them all week long meeting by their lockers before school, sitting next to each other in the lunchroom. I just kept hoping it was because she was showing him his way around school, but . . . well . . . no such luck."

Someone came out of the restaurant, got into a car sitting a couple of parking slots to their left, and drove away, leaving space all around their two cars.

"Listen," Monica said, shifting in her seat as if uncomfortable not with it but with herself, "I didn't tell you the truth just now. Kent did say something more about Chelsea."

"What?"

She shot him a glance, as brief as a blink before facing front. "That he envied her for having a father."

Tom took the news like a kidney punch. For a minute it was hard to breathe normally.

Monica went on. "We fought about it, and that's rare for us. It made me realize how important it is for him to know about you. It's . . . it's time I told him."

"So you'll do that? Before school on Monday?"

"What else can I do?"

"You know," Tom said, "my son Robby hasn't been exactly congenial to Kent on the football field. If you want to know the truth, I think he's jealous. I don't know what this will do to them."

"Be honest, Tom. We don't know what it'll do to any of us with the possible exception of me. My life will probably go on just as it was. It's all the rest of you who'll have to work through a tangle of emotions over this."

Tom thought about it and sighed. He slumped lower in his seat and let his head fall back against the headrest.

"It's peculiar. I had this talk with Robby today about how every person you meet changes you, how every moral dilemma you face shapes your character. Maybe I was saying it for my own benefit and didn't realize it till now."

A car pulled in on their left. Its windows were down and the radio on. Tom glanced over just as the driver reached down to shut off the radio. The woman saw him, smiled, and waggled her fingers.

"Hi, Tom," she called through their two open windows.

He straightened in his seat. Heat shot up his body. "Hi, Ruth."

She got out of her car and headed his way.

"Oh, shit," he mumbled.

"Who's that?"

"My next-door neighbor."

Ruth reached his open window and leaned down. "Hi, Cl . . . oh . . . sorry, I thought it was Claire with you."

"Monica Arens, this is my neighbor, Ruth Bishop."

Ruth gave a quick smile, her eyes bright with interest. "Just came over to pick up some of their bread sticks for supper. They're Dean's favorites, and for once he's going to be home for a meal." She strained forward and studied Monica with unveiled curiosity even while speaking to Tom. "Is Claire at home?"

"Yes. She's housecleaning today."

"Oh." Ruth seemed to be waiting for more, an explanation perhaps, but with none forthcoming she let her hand slip off the window ledge and chattered, "Well, I'd better get going, get my bread sticks. Nice to see you, Tom. Say hi to Claire."

"I will."

Watching her retreat toward the restaurant Tom said, "Well, that clinches it. If I don't get home and tell Claire first, Ruth will do it for me."

"And I've got to go home and tell Kent, too." Monica put her purse strap up over her shoulder but stayed where she was. "I never know what to say to you at moments like this. I just always feel so awkward."

"Me too."

"Good luck telling your family, I guess."

"Good luck to you, too."

Still they remained where they were.

"Should we talk again?" she asked.

"Let's wait and see."

"Yes . . . yes, I suppose you're right."

"I think it'll be unavoidable."

After considering awhile Monica asked, "This is the right thing to do, isn't it, Tom?"

"Absolutely."

"Yes . . . absolutely," she repeated, as if trying to convince herself. "Then why am I so hesitant to go home and do it?"

"Fear," he said.

"Yes, I suppose."

"It's not much fun, is it?"

"No. It's awful."

"I've been living with it ever since you walked into my office, and to tell the truth, it'll be a relief to get it out in the open and face it, whatever needs facing. My mind's been . . . oh, scattered, I suppose you'd say."

"Yes . . . well . . ."

"Here she comes again." Ruth Bishop came toward them carrying a white paper bag. Tom watched her all the way.

"Do you have a strong marriage, Tom?" Monica asked, her eyes, too, following the woman.

"Yes, very."

Ruth Bishop went to her car, hefted the bag up so it could be seen above the roof, and called, "I got a whole dozen of 'em! Dean better make sure he comes home now!"

Tom sent her a perfunctory smile and an empty wave of acknowledgment.

Monica said, "Good, because you're going to need it." When Ruth had driven away, she added, "Now I guess I'd really better go. I'm anxious to have this day over with."

"Good luck," he said again. "And thanks for coming."

"Sure."

There was a certain sadness to their parting, the sadness of two people whose past has caught up with them and who—in spite of feeling no physical attraction toward one another—feel drawn together by their similar fates. She would go to her family and he to his. They would both face a baring of conscience that would forever alter their lives. Leaving the parking lot, driving in opposite directions, they felt once more a melancholy regret, for they had not even one warm memory of each other to carry as consolation for the upheaval their lives were about to undergo.

Kent was on the portable phone when his mother returned home. She came through the living room, where he was sprawled on the wide-armed sofa with one heel on the coffee table, his foot waggling back and forth like a windshield washer. His chin rested on his chest and he was grinning.

Passing through the room, Monica said, "Get your foot off the furniture."

He crossed it over his knee, imperturbable, and continued with his conversation. "No, I told you, hardly ever. So are you going to teach me, or what? . . . No, where? . . . No, we never had school dances. A couple of times they had these big parties out at Beaudry's house with live bands and everything, and Rich asked me over, but we just sort of watched the old people dance because we were the youngest ones there. . . . Homecoming? . . . Who says you have to dance just because it's Homecoming? . . ."

His mother came out of the kitchen, drying her hands on a linen towel. "Kent, I have to talk to you. Could you cut your call short, please?"

He covered the mouthpiece and said, "I'm talking to a girl, Mom."

"Cut it short, please," she repeated, and disappeared.

He removed his hand from the mouthpiece and said, "Sorry, Chelsea, I have to go. Mom needs me for something. Listen, you gonna be home later? . . . Maybe I'll call you then. . . . Yeah, sure. You too . . . Bye."

He rocked up out of the sofa and sprang to his feet, taking the phone along. "Hey, Mom," he said, rounding the corner into the kitchen, tossing the phone from hand to hand. "What's so important I can't finish my conversation first?"

She was unnecessarily rearranging fruit in a white glass latticework bowl, shifting peaches, bananas, and apples.

"Who was the girl?" she asked.

"Chelsea Gardner."

She leveled her eyes on him, one hand resting on the bowl while holding a green apple, all of her gone so still and sober he wondered if she'd lost her job or something.

He stopped playing hot potato with the phone and said, "Mom, what's wrong?"

Unconsciously, she took the apple along and said, "Let's go in the living room, Kent."

He sat on the sofa where he'd been. She sat at a right angle, in a deep tapestry chair, leaning forward with both elbows on her tight-pressed knees, working the apple on an axis in her fingertips. "Kent," she said, "I'm going to tell you about your father."

He got very still, everything inside him seizing up like during those last few seconds before he dove off the high board the first time.

"My father?" he repeated, as if the subject were new.

"Yes," she said. "You're right. It's time."

He swallowed and fixed his gaze on her, gripping the telephone as if it were the handlebar on a roller coaster. "All right."

"Kent, your father is Tom Gardner."

His lips fell open. He couldn't seem to close them. "Tom Gardner? You mean . . . Mr. Gardner, my principal?"

"Yes," she said quietly, and waited. She had stopped rotating the apple. It hung suspended in her fingertips above the carpet.

"Mr. Gardner?" he whispered croakily.

"Yes."

"But he's . . . he's Chelsea's father."

"Yes," she said quietly, "he is."

Kent fell back against the sofa, his eyes closed, the phone still gripped in his right hand, his thumb crooked sharply against it with the nail bent over.

Mr. Gardner, one of the nicest men he'd ever met, who'd been smiling and saying hi every day this week in the halls and who sometimes put a hand on his shoulder, a man he'd liked from the minute he met him, partly because of how he treated his kids, partly because of how he treated other kids. A man he would see on Monday and every school day for the rest of the year. The man who would hand him his high school diploma.

Chelsea's father.

And good God, he'd kissed Chelsea last night.

Reactions came tumbling too fast to sort. Shock turned him quivery. He opened his eyes and saw the corner of the ceiling looking blurry through his tears.

"I walked Chelsea home from the game last night."

"Yes, I know. I just left Tom fifteen minutes ago. He told me."

Kent sat up. "You met Mr. Gardner? Are you . . . I mean, is he—"

"No, he's nothing to me beyond the fact that he's your father. We only met to talk about this, about us telling our families how you two are related. That's all."

"So he does know about me. You said he didn't."

"I know, and I'm sorry, Kent. I don't make a habit of lying to you, but you can see why I didn't think you should know. Not until this thing with Chelsea came up."

"Yeah, well, nothing happened between us, okay?" he declared somewhat belligerently.

"Of course not," she said, her eyes falling to the green apple.

He could see she was relieved to hear it, though he'd never given her reason to believe he'd been promiscuous with girls. He hadn't.

"So how long has he known about me?" Kent asked.

"Since the day I registered you at school. I had no idea he was the principal there till he walked out of his office."

"So he never knew I existed?"

"No."

Kent doubled forward, dropping his head to his hands, the telephone pushing his hair against his skull above one ear. The room grew terribly silent. Monica set the apple on the coffee table as if both pieces were made of spun glass. She sat almost primly, hands crossed and both wrists turned upward while she gazed at a rectangle of sunlight falling across the living room carpeting. There were tears in her eyes, too.

After more than a minute of misery Kent raised his head.

"So what made you tell him?"

"He recognized you and asked."

"*Recognized* me?"

"You look a lot like him."

"Oh, do I?" The idea took hold and rattled Kent.

She nodded at the carpet.

The surfeit of emotion erupted in a sudden watershed of anger that Kent did not understand. "I spend my whole life being told nothing, now all at once you not only tell me who he is, you tell me he's this man I like, and that I even look like him!" He paused a beat, then shouted, "Well, talk to me, Mom! Tell me how it happened! Don't make me ask sixty-four thousand questions!"

"You aren't going to like it."

"Do you think I care by now? I want to know!"

She took some time to collect herself before beginning. "He was a boy I used to see around the college campus sometimes. We had one class together—I don't even remember which one anymore. I always thought he was handsome, but we never dated. I didn't really even know him. In my senior year I worked as a delivery girl for Mama Fiori's Pizza, and one June night we got a call for a half dozen pizzas to be delivered to a bachelor party. I delivered them, and he was the one who answered the door. He . . ." She inverted her linked fingers and shrugged. "I don't know . . . he grabbed my wrist and pulled me into the apartment. There was a lot of noise, and they'd been drinking, of course. There were beer kegs, and some rather scantily clad girls there. He remembered me and rounded up a big tip from all the guys and said why didn't I come back after I got off work and have a beer. I'd never . . . well, I'd never done anything like that before. I was what you'd probably call a tight-ass. A scholar. Very straight and disciplined. Very goal-oriented. I can't say why I did it, but I went back after work and had a couple of beers, and one thing led to another and I ended up in bed with him. Two months later I discovered I was pregnant."

Kent let it sink in a minute, staring at her balefully. "A bachelor party," he said in a rusty voice. "I was conceived at a bachelor party."

"Yes," she whispered. "But that's not the worst of it."

He only waited.

"It was his bachelor party." She had colored some.

"His?"

"He was getting married the next week."

It took only a split second for everything to add up. "Oh, don't tell me . . ." Their eyes met, his distraught, hers embarrassed. "Aw, come on . . . to Mrs. Gardner, my *English teacher*?"

Monica nodded and dropped her gaze, rubbing the cuticle of one thumb with the pad of the other. Kent tossed the telephone onto the sofa, where it bounced once while he fell back against the cushions with a forearm flung over his eyes.

"A one-night stand," he said.

His mother watched his Adam's apple bob and replied, "Yes," offering no self-defense.

"Does she know?"

"None of them know. He's telling them now."

He went on hiding behind his arm while his mother's eyes took in his long body, dressed in blue jeans; the mouth that was held firm as if to keep from crying, the chin and jaws with the patchy beard that now needed shaving every day, the throat that pulsed each time he swallowed his tears.

She reached over and rubbed the coarse blue denim covering his knee. "Kent, I'm sorry," she whispered.

His mouth moved. "Yes, ma'am, I know."

She kept rubbing his knee; she didn't know what else to do.

He jolted to his feet as if to escape her touch, sniffing, running the back of a hand under his nose. "Listen, Mom." He pelted toward the door. "I just gotta get out of here for a while. I gotta . . . I don't know . . . my mind's a mess. I gotta go, okay? Don't worry. I just gotta go."

"Kent!" She rushed to the railing overlooking the entry, but he'd descended the steps in three giant strides and the door was already closing behind him. "Kent!" She ran down the stairs and jerked the door open. "Kent, wait! Please, honey, don't take the car! We can talk some more . . . we can—"

"Go on back in, Mom!"

"But, Kent—"

"You took eighteen years getting used to the idea! At least give me a few hours!"

The car door slammed, the engine revved, and he backed down the driveway too fast, bumping and turning off the curb, leaving a pair of rubber marks on the pavement as he squealed away.

Eight

For Tom, the ride home from Ciatti's parking lot was a journey through purgatory. How would he tell Claire? How would she react? How would he tell the kids? Would they think him an immoral weakling? A phony? A liar who had wronged their mother on the eve of their marriage and hid it all these years?

He would tell Claire first—she deserved that much—before he broke the news to the kids and the four of them got into the heavy scene that was sure to follow. Claire deserved to be told in private, to hit him, blame him, shout, cry, call him names, whatever she felt like doing, without her children watching or listening.

When he got home she had them busy cleaning their rooms, the vacuum cleaner wheezing upstairs. He found Claire on her hands and knees in the living room, dusting the lower shelf of an end table. How unsuspecting she was, how vulnerable, working away, thinking they'd straightened things out the other night by forgiving each other and making love. Little did she know.

He squatted down on one heel behind her, regretting how he had to hurt her.

"Claire?"

She reared up and bumped her head.

"Ooo, damn," she said, rubbing it through her baseball cap, wincing as she turned and let her weight sink against the carpet.

"Sorry, I thought you heard me come in."

"No-o-o, I didn't. Jeez, that smarts."

She looked twenty-five years old in her HHH cap, jeans, and wrinkled shirt. He felt his heart swell with incontrovertible love, and suffered a fresh stab of guilt.

He squeezed her arm. "You okay?"

"I'll live."

"Claire, something's come up that I need to talk to you about . . . away from the kids. Would you take a ride with me?"

Her hand dropped slowly from her head. "What is it, Tom? You look terrible." She rolled to her knees, facing him. "What's wrong?"

He took her hands and drew her to her feet. "Let's take a ride. C'mon."

He called the children. "Robby? Chelsea? Come here a minute." When they came, he said, "Mom and I will be gone for an hour or so. When we get back I want you to be here, okay?"

"Sure, Dad. Where you going?" Chelsea asked.

"I'll tell you all about it when we get back. Get your rooms finished and make sure you're here, understand? It's important."

"Sure, Dad . . ."

"Sure, Dad . . ."

Their voices reflected puzzled obedience.

In the car, Claire said, "Tom, you're scaring me to death. Will you tell me what's wrong?"

"I will in a minute. Let's drive over to Valley Elementary first. The schoolyard should be empty. We can talk there."

She sat as if wearing armor whose only movable part was the head-piece, studying his profile while he drove to the nearby building and pulled around the back, where the blacktop abutted the playground. Here their kids had gone to elementary school, had drawn hopscotches, hung on jungle gyms, and competed on Field Day. The sight of the building and playground swathed in late afternoon sunlight brought a wave of nostalgia.

Tom turned off the engine and said, "Come on, let's take a walk."

She followed reluctantly, sensing calamity ahead. Tom took her hand. They trod across a stretch of grass and a corner of a softball diamond, their footsteps raising blossoms of dust on the infield. Beyond the ball field, a sturdy gathering of playground equipment created a geometric pattern against a violet sky, while at their backs, the sunset hour approached. They went to the equipment and sat side by side on swings shaped like horseshoes. The seats were low to the ground, the earth beneath them covered with wood chips through which paths had been worn down to hard-scraped earth.

Claire's hands clung to the cold steel chains; Tom tipped forward like a basketball player on the bench.

Neither of them swung. They sat for a while, smelling the forest-musty smell of the wood chips, feeling the swings cinch their hips and the earth anchor their feet.

Finally, Tom cleared his throat. "Claire, I love you. That's the first thing I want to say, and the easiest. The rest is a lot harder."

"Whatever it is, just say it, Tom, because, damn it, this is horrible!"

"All right, I will, straight out." He drew a deep breath first. "Six days before school started a woman walked into my office and registered a boy who, it turns out, is my son. I never knew he existed till that day. She never told me, so I had no reason to suspect. His name is Kent Arens."

Their eyes were locked as he finished. He supposed he would never forget the shock in hers, the drained look, the disbelief. Not one muscle moved while her wide-eyed gaze remained fixed on him and her hands clung to the chains.

"Kent Arens . . ." she whispered, ". . . is your son?"

"Yes, Claire, he is." He said it as gently as possible.

"But . . . but that would mean . . ." She struggled with dates.

"I'll make it easy for you. He's seventeen years old, the same age as Robby. He was conceived in June of 1975."

This time she didn't have to struggle. "The month we got married?"

"The week we got married."

The tiniest, pained word came out of her. "Oh . . ." and again while her eyes widened and got glossy, "Oh . . ."

"I'm going to tell you exactly what happened, because she never meant anything to me, nothing. Above all, you've got to believe that."

"Oh, Tom," she managed, covering her lips with three fingers.

He hardened his resolve and continued, determined to tell this straightaway, for only in absolute truth could he see a modicum of dignity. "The weeks before our wedding are pretty hard to remember now, the actual events that were going on at that time. But one thing stands out crystal clear in my mind: I wasn't ready to get married yet, and I felt—I'm sorry to have to say this, Claire—but I felt trapped. Maybe even a little desperate. Sometimes it was almost like . . . like I was being railroaded. I'd just spent four years in college and I had plans for the next couple of years. I wanted to take the summer off, and get a teaching job in the fall, live with the guys, be free for a while after all the years of keeping schedules and studying. I wanted to buy a new car and some nice clothes, and vacation in Mexico and maybe do a weekend in Las Vegas now and then.

"Instead, you got pregnant and I ended up at pre-marriage courses, picking out rings and china patterns and renting tuxedos. Everything just seemed to . . . well, it escalated so fast! The truth is, for a while I got just plain scared. Then after the first shock wore off, I got angry.

"That's probably the mood I was in the night of my bachelor party, when this girl I hardly knew at all delivered a bunch of pizzas. I talked her into bed with me, and it was simple rebellion, nothing more. She went off to live her life, and I went off to live mine, and we never met again . . . until she walked into my office with her son last week."

Claire's brimming, disillusioned eyes rested on him, then veered away while the shock waves rattled through her. She began to rise from the swing.

"No, stay." Tom held her arm. "I'm not done. That's the trouble with telling something like this. I don't want to leave anything out, but I have to work through all the bad stuff to get to the most important thing, and that's the fact that I changed. After I married you, I changed." Softly, he added, "I came to love you very, very much, Claire."

"Don't!" She pulled her arm free and twisted the swing till she faced west, her back to him, her front to the brightening orange sky. "Don't offer me platitudes. After what you've just told me, don't you *dare* offer me platitudes!"

"They're not platitudes. I started realizing what I had in you the day Robby was born, and ev—"

"And that's supposed to make me feel good?"

"You didn't let me finish. And every year got better. I found out I love being a father, I love being a husband, I love you."

He could tell from the quivering of her shoulders, she was crying.

"You did that . . . with another woman . . . the same week that we got married?"

He'd known that fact would weigh heavier than any other and that he'd have to be patient with her while she dealt with it.

"Claire . . . Claire, I'm so sorry."

"How could you do that?" Her voice had grown pinched and high from contained emotion. "How could you do that and walk down an aisle with me a week later?"

He dropped his elbows to his knees and let his head hang low, feet spraddled while he stared at the dirt and wood chips between them. Since learning about Kent he had held his own emotions in check, but tears stung as he realized how he'd hurt Claire. He let them gather, pinching them away only to find his eyes refilling immediately. He was a man without excuses, so he offered none as the afternoon aged and they sat on their separate swings, facing separate directions, she west and he north.

She was still crying when she said, "I never knew that before . . . how you . . . how you r . . . resented marrying me."

"Past tense, Claire, honest, it's all past tense. I told you I came to realize how lucky I was."

She hurt too badly to be soothed. "Wouldn't you think a woman would sense a thing like that on her wedding day? I guess I was just so glad to have the f . . . father of my baby marrying me that I . . . that I . . ." She began crying audibly, muffling the sound with her hand.

He reached out and squeezed her shoulder from behind. Her body shook with her weeping; it tore at his heart. "Claire, don't," he pleaded, aching as much as she. "Jesus, Claire, I didn't want to hurt you this way."

She shrugged his hand away. "Well, you did. I hurt and it's b . . . because of you and I hate you at this m . . . moment for doing this to us." She was using the sides of her hands to wipe her nose. He passed his handkerchief over her shoulder.

She used it, then said, "You've been acting so strange lately. I knew something was wrong, but I couldn't figure out what."

"I tried to tell you in Duluth, but I just . . ." His words trailed away and he ended softly, "Aw, hell."

Silence pressed down, thick, oppressive, stilling all but their burrowing thoughts. Sorrow sealed them to their swing seats and held them prisoners of each other and this cruel foible sprung upon them at mid-life, when they'd been so serene and smug. The autumn evening progressed, the edge of the world closing the sun's lower eyelid, turning the sky the hues of fruit. A faint chill drifted across the playground.

After many minutes Claire finally asked, "Does he know?"

"She's telling him today."

He could tell she was adding things up and drawing the wrong conclusion. All this time she'd been turned away from him with the swing chain crossed above her head. She let it uncross and throw her into line with him so she could see his face. Though her expression seemed dulled by sorrow, her gaze seemed to penetrate clear to his viscera.

"You saw her, didn't you? That's where you were when you said you were going to buy the battery."

"Yes, but Claire—"

"Have you seen her other times?"

"Listen to me. He's grown up not knowing who his father was. I couldn't tell you about him without her permission, and that's what we talked about today, the decision to tell the truth to everyone at the same time so nobody would find out from anyone else."

"You didn't answer my question. *Have you seen her other times?*"

Some muscles tensed, altering his jawline, reflecting movement at his temple. "Yes. Once. The day I found out he was my son."

"Where?"

"At her house. But all we did was talk, Claire, honest."

Claire said nothing for the longest time, staring at him with puffy, red, mistrusting eyes. Finally she dropped her gaze to her knees. "She must live around here someplace."

"In Haviland Hills Addition. She moved here from Texas just before school started. When she walked in to register Kent, she had no idea I was the principal. Claire, I'm answering all these questions because I have nothing more to hide. That one night back in 1975, that was it. I swear to God, there has never been anyone but you since the day I took my vows."

She let her shoulders slump and dropped her hands between her legs, where they hung loosely. Her eyes closed and her head lolled backward, pointing the bill of her baseball cap at the sky. She sighed once—a great, noisy shudder of a sigh, then sat, motionless, the picture of one who simply wishes to escape. She gave herself a tiny jog and set the swing in motion—a few degrees only—as if somewhere in the depths of her mind she pretended she was beyond all this. Her chambray shirttail hung behind her, and her crossed shins laid the outsides of her tennis shoes against the dirt.

He waited, sick at heart for having caused her despair.

"Well," she said finally, pulling her head up as if marshaling fortitude, "we've got some children to consider, don't we?" The swing continued in waggling figure S's. Then abruptly it stopped as she clapped a hand to her mouth and turned away while the tears built once again. "Oh, God, what a mess." Her voice had gone squeaky.

What should he say? Do? Give? Offer? His misery was as complete as hers.

"I never meant to hurt any of you, not you or the children, not in any way, Claire. It happened so long ago. It was just an incident out of my past that I'd forgotten about."

"It was long ago for you, but it's now for us. We've got to deal with it *now*, and it's so unfair to foist this on the children."

"Don't you think I've been thinking about that?"

"I don't know. Have you?"

"Of course I have. Claire, you act as if I've suddenly gotten heartless because of this thing. Can't you see that I hurt, too? That I'm sorry, and I wish I could undo it? But I can't. All I can do is be honest about everything and hope that's the way to cause the least amount of pain to everyone involved. As for the children, I intend to tell them today. I can do that by myself or you can be with me, whatever you want."

"Chelsea's going to be so . . . so . . . ." Claire motioned vacantly. "Who knows what went on between them? I know she's got a crush on him."

"Nothing went on between them, I'd stake my life on it."

"Oh, I know that!" Claire shot back angrily, glaring. "On a first date that wasn't even a date? Give us credit for raising a daughter with a few more scruples than that! I'm talking about kisses. If he *kissed* her, and certainly kids that age are going to kiss!"

"Well, we'll never find out, because I'm surely not going to ask her."

"No, of course not. But she'll be chagrined just the same. And what about Robby? He's already antagonistic toward Kent . . . they have to play football together, and *I* have to face him in a classroom Monday."

"I have to face him, too."

"Oh, well, pardon me if I can't feel too sorry for you over what you've got to face!"

She left her swing and moved to one of the diagonal struts, propping a shoulder against it. With her hands slipped into her front hip pockets she looked sunward. He actually felt sick to his stomach studying the back of her. Always now, the back of her. Fear had congealed into a sickening lump within him. Need skulked there too, the need to touch her, hold her, have her in his arms and feel reassured that they could work this through.

He left his swing and moved up behind her, hesitant to touch her, afraid not to, awkward with his insecurity. He stared at the messy ponytail she'd drawn through the back opening of her cap, at the sun-speckled tips of her hair, the sleeves of her washed-out old shirt whose wrinkles appeared dusted by the low sun. Her youthful clothing and untidiness gave her a childlike defenselessness.

"Claire . . ." He put his hands on the soft chambray below her collar.

"Don't." She shimmied free and settled against the pole again, defiant. "I don't want to be touched by you right now. You should know that."

He dropped his hands and waited.

And waited.

Facing the same direction as Claire while their shadows grew longer and the dull tarnish of distress settled over their marriage.

"It's the betrayal that hurts worst of all," she said, finally. "Thinking you know someone, then finding out you don't know him at all."

"That's not true, Claire. I'm the same man I was."

"Not in my eyes. Not anymore."

"I still love you."

"You don't do this to someone you love. You don't go to another woman's house. Especially not a woman who had your baby."

"Oh, come on, Claire, I told you, that thing with her happened in 1975. She's a damned stranger to me!"

Claire snorted quietly and stood despondent, looking down at her feet. Finally she turned around and the expression in her eyes chilled him.

"I never thought I could feel this way about you. Never. I thought that what we had built together was inviolable, that we had the kind of marriage that nothing could damage, because we'd worked so hard at it. But at this moment, Tom Gardner, I hate you. I want to strike out at you and hurt you because you're doing this to us and to our family."

"If it'll make you feel any better, do it. God knows I deserve it."

She swung with her right and slapped him so hard that it knocked him off balance. Immediately she stepped back and gasped, realizing what she'd done. His cheek flared with her handprint. His eyes widened in surprise. Never in eighteen years of marriage had either of them struck the other.

He stepped back, putting space between them, each of them somewhat embarrassed, uncertain of their footing. Slowly the flush of anger came to join that from the handprint on his face.

"What do you want me to do, Claire? It's done. It's history. What do you want me to do?"

"Tell your children. Tell them their father isn't the kind of man they thought he was. Try to explain to Robby why you had sex with another woman while I was carrying him. Try to explain to Chelsea why she mustn't do things like that with boys, although it was all right for you to do it because you really didn't want to marry her mother!" Claire pointed a finger toward home. "You drive back there and tell them, Tom Gardner, and break their hearts, because this is more than just the announcement that they have a half brother! This is a betrayal, and don't think they'll see it as anything less!"

She had, of course, capsulized the gist of his guilt toward the children. He hated hearing it.

"You sound as if you plan to ask them to choose sides. Don't do that, Claire."

"Oh, don't be so damned self-righteous!" She made two fists and strained to keep them against her hips. There seemed to be more rebuffs scrabbling to be shouted, but, as if she didn't trust herself, she turned and stalked toward the car.

She slammed the passenger door vehemently and lashed her arms around her midriff as if to keep her very skin from falling off. She fixed her eyes on the pebbles at the edge of the tar where the grass was worn thin. That line where the black met the green suddenly snaked into motion, skewed by fresh tears as self-pity took a turn on her.

On our wedding week . . .

He never really wanted to marry me . . .

Home Song

He said I railroaded him . . .

He was out there on the playground, standing under the swing set with his head hanging, probably playing for her sympathy and understanding. Well, she had none to spare, not for him. Not today, not tomorrow, or anytime soon. No husband could dump a load like this on his wife and expect her to rebound like the infatuated girl she'd once been.

She was the wronged one here. *She*, not he!

All her married life she had worked toward an ideal, not only in her relationship with him, but in their family relationship as a whole. To discover it was predicated upon a marriage he'd never wanted, a first child he felt he'd been saddled with, made a mockery of all the hard work and emotion she had invested in these eighteen years.

Eighteen years . . . condensing into this.

She felt like a fool never to have suspected, and blamed him for bringing these feelings upon her at a time in her life when all she wanted was blissful harmony. But if she had not suspected then, she did now. The woman who had offered a reprieve from his obligations was back in the area, still single, the father of his son. And he admittedly had seen her more than once.

What intelligent man with a home and family at risk would not deny anything illicit?

The thought terrified Claire even while exacerbating her anger.

I don't want to be a woman sorting through suspicions! Not one of those pitiable creatures who are whispered about in the teachers' lounge. I want to be the woman I was one hour ago!

Anger and self-pity were still roiling her thoughts when she heard his footsteps on the cinders.

He got in and slammed the door. Put the key in the ignition. But emotional inertia held him motionless. He let the hand drop and his eyes rest unfocused on the hood. "Claire, I don't know how I'm going to tell them."

"Neither do I," she said to the blacktop, not a wisp of sympathy in her voice.

"I suppose I should just say it straight out like I did to you."

"I suppose so."

"Do you want to be there?"

"To tell the truth, I want to be in Puerto Rico right now. Calcutta, Saudi Arabia . . . anywhere but here, going through this!"

The stretches of silence were growing longer and more oppressive.

Eventually he started the car and drove them home while she never once looked at him or spoke. He parked in the garage and followed her into the house, taut with dread of telling his children and losing honor in their eyes.

He hung his car keys in the kitchen on a hooked board that Robby had made in elementary school. He went to the kitchen sink for a drink and found there a red mug that said DAD, given to him by Chelsea last Father's Day. All around him, evidence of their love and respect for him. He filled the mug and drank slowly, postponing his final fall from grace.

He shut off the water and turned to find Chelsea had entered the kitchen and stood on its far side, all her housework completed, present as ordered for whatever it was that would happen. Robby stood with her, both of them silent and wondering. Claire had disappeared.

"Let's sit down," he said. "I've got something to tell you."

They sat at the kitchen table, glancing from him to each other in confusion and wariness.

"Some things have happened in the last week and a half that . . . well, they're going to change our lives to some degree. Not"—he motioned as if stirring the air above a crystal ball—"not our family life, as such, but in a way each member of our family, because it concerns all of us.

"Now, before I say anything more, I want you to know that Mom and I have talked about it. We're working it out between us, okay? So there's nothing to be scared of."

He cleared his throat. "This concerns Kent Arens."

"Kent?" Chelsea repeated, surprised.

Claire appeared silently behind the kids and leaned against the kitchen doorway where only Tom could see her. He linked his fingers on the tabletop, fitting the pads of his thumbs together.

"Kent Arens is my son."

No one moved or spoke. But the blood rose in Chelsea's face and Robby's lips parted. He sat back against the kitchen chair, his long arms hanging, his oversized hands curled around the edges of the chair seat. Chelsea merely stared at her father, stunned.

"I knew his mother when I was in college, but I never knew she'd had him, not until the Wednesday before school started, when she brought him in to register."

The silence roared on for a long time.

Robby spoke first. "Are you sure?"

Tom nodded silently.

"But . . . but how old is he?"

"The same age as you."

He whispered, "Oh, jeez." And after a beat, "Does Mom know that?"

"Yes, she does."

Robby whispered, "Wow."

"There are some things about all this that I believe should remain private between your mother and myself, but some things I think we all have to know and understand. Kent was never told who his father was, but he's being told today, too, so there'll be no mistaking our relationship the next time any of us meet him. Nobody at school knows about this, so it's up to you—up to us—to . . ." *To tell the truth or conceal it?* ". . . to . . . well, set the tone for our future relationship with him. I don't know what it will be any more than you do, but I'm asking you to understand that there'll be difficulties for all of us. For us, for him. I'm not telling you how to react to this news. I'm not saying, 'He's your brother, you have to love him, or even like him.' Chelsea, I know you've already become his friend and I . . . well, I'm sorry if this is an embarrassment for you. Robby, I know your feelings, too. This isn't going to be easy, and I'm sorry I have to put you through it. But, please . . . if you've got feelings to work out, talk to Mom and me about it. Will you do that?"

One of them mumbled something, but both refused to lift their eyes from the tabletop.

"I want you both to know that what I've done was very wrong. I've always valued your respect for me as a father and been proud of it. Telling you the truth about this has been . . . has been—" Tom swallowed visibly—"well, it's been the worst couple weeks of my life. I knew you had to be told but I was afraid your opinion of me would change. What I did was wrong, and I accept responsibility for that. I ask your forgiveness, because in wronging your mother, I've wronged you. I have no excuses. There are no excuses for dishonorable behavior, but I love you both very much, and the last thing in the world I'd ever do is hurt you or your mom. Because I love you all . . . very much." He lifted his eyes to Claire. She stayed against the doorway, her expressionless face as immobile as if baked in ceramic. Neither of the children had lifted their eyes.

He spoke to them again. "There's something more I need to say about this. It has to do with morals." He realized he had clasped his joined hands hard against his belly. Inside, it was trembling fiercely. "Please don't . . . don't follow my example. You've been good, honest kids. Stay that way . . . please." His last word came out a little hoarsely.

Silence followed, another one of those stretches of misery that were becoming standard fare on this soulful day.

"Is there anything you want to say . . . or ask?" Tom said.

Chelsea, solemn and red, her eyes downcast, whispered, "What'll we tell our friends?"

"The truth, when you must. I would never ask you to lie for me. He's my son, and it seems absurd to believe that in the environment where all four of us—five of us—spend five days a week, the truth won't be known. Kent will have some things to work out, too, remember. I'd imagine he'll rely on his counselor to help him sort out his feelings. The same might even be true for you."

Chelsea made an L of her arms and dropped her face into one hand. "It'll be so embarrassing. Our dad . . . the principal."

"I know and I'm sorry, Chelsea."

Tom wanted to reach across the corner of the table and squeeze her arm, but felt he'd somehow lost the right. Robby's embarrassment seemed to have ebbed and been replaced by a half scowl. "So what are we supposed to do? I mean, is he gonna be hanging around here, or what?"

"Hanging around here? No, I don't think so. I mean . . . Robby, that's hard to answer. He's finding out today that he not only has a father living right across town, he's got a half brother and half sister, and even aunts and uncles and a grandfather he didn't know he had. I would imagine the time will come when he'll be curious about all of us."

Robby set the edges of his teeth together. His expression was hard. He too had linked his hands on his stomach, but the set of his shoulders looked uncompromising.

"So, what's going on between you and Mom? Did you just tell her today, or what?"

"Yes, I just told her. Mom's pretty upset. She's been crying." From the corner of his eye, he saw Claire fade away from her place in the doorway and slip around the corner. Robby swung around just as her shirttails disappeared. It was obvious he hadn't known she was standing there, and that he was scared to death as he went on quizzing his father.

"So what's between you and this woman? I mean, is there something going on, or what?"

"There's nothing going on. She's a total stranger to me now, and absolutely nothing is going on. Let's say it straight out; you're both old enough—no affair, nothing sexual, okay? On the occasions I've seen her and spoken to her, it was only to clear things up about Kent and how to handle it."

Chelsea said, "Then why did Mom ask you if you were having an affair that night?"

Robby's head snapped around. "When? You never told me that!"

"Dad?" She kept her attention riveted on Tom. "Why?"

"I don't know why. Because I was tense and distracted, I guess. I found out about Kent and knew it was only a matter of time before I'd have to tell you, and I was afraid. Mom misread me, that's all. If I'd been honest with her and told the truth as soon as I found out, this would be a week behind us by now and you'd never have heard that conversation."

Their exchange was suddenly interrupted when a car came tearing into their driveway just beside the kitchen window. A car door slammed, footsteps pounded up the front walk, and the doorbell rang.

As Robby pushed his chair back it rang again and again, was still ringing when he reached the door and came to a surprised halt, gaping out through the screen.

Kent Arens stood there, glaring in at him. His voice carried clearly into the kitchen. "I want to see your father." Without being invited, he opened the screen door and stepped inside just as Tom and Claire converged on the entry from two different parts of the house. Chelsea hovered at a distance, watching, and Robby stepped back out of Kent's way.

Father and son faced off in the crackling silence, replicas in spite of their age difference. Kent stared, confronting the image he would look like in twenty-odd years. The dark skin, brown eyes, arched brows, full mouth, straight nose.

The cowlick.

His defiant eyes catalogued it all while he stood with outrage in his pose. No smile, no movement softened his bearing.

He said, "I just had to see for myself," and stormed out as full of bluster as when he'd arrived.

"Kent!" Tom shouted, heading after him, hitting the door with both palms. "Wait!" When he sailed off the front stoop onto the sidewalk, Kent was standing on the far side of the Lexus with the driver's door open, wearing a hard-bitten expression.

"You never even tried to find her! You never even asked!" he yelled. "You just screwed her and left! Well, I might be a bastard, but even a bastard has more scruples than that!"

The car door slammed and the Lexus roared down the driveway, barreling away at breakneck speed.

Tom watched it go, sighing, feeling laden by the weight of emotional weariness. This day, when would it end? It had been one scalding encounter after another until he actually felt like crying again. Instead, responsibility prodded and he squared his shoulders to go into the house and face it.

The kids were standing where he'd left them.

"Where's your mother?"

"Upstairs."

"Claire?" he called from the mouth of the stairs. "Claire, come here!"

He went halfway up the stairs until his eyes were level with the upper hall floor. She came out of their bedroom and stood at the far end of the hall, her arms crossed as if she were tied to a stake. It seemed as if she'd had her arms crossed that way for the last two hours.

"What?"

He shouted so the kids could hear, too. "He's very upset. I've got to call his mother, and just so there'll be no question about what I'm doing, I'm telling you first, all of you! I've worked with kids too long to mistake the emotional state he's in." He headed for the kitchen phone, passing Chelsea and Robby on the way. "You can all stand right here and listen if you want to, but I *am* going to call her."

He dialed and Monica answered after a single ring.

"Monica, this is Tom."

"Oh, Tom, thank heavens. Kent took off with my car and—"

"I know. He was just here. He barged in and confronted me, then stormed away driving like a maniac. It might be the best thing if you'd call the police, have them pull him over for his own safety. He's really worked up."

"I was afraid of this." She took only a moment to think. "All right, I will. Was he crying, Tom?"

"No, I don't think so. He was angry."

"Yes, that's how he was when he left here. How did your family take it?"

"Not well."

After a pause, she said, "Well, I'd better go . . . make that call. Thank you, Tom."

"It's okay. Would you call me when he comes back and let me know he's okay?"

"Sure."

When he'd hung up, the house returned to its funereal somberness, everybody occupying their little square of space, keeping carefully separate, not speaking, hiding within themselves. The children crept off to their rooms. Claire stayed in her and Tom's bedroom while he was left in the kitchen staring at a red mug that said DAD.

It was done. The secret unveiled. The guilt confessed. But now came this hopeless transition period when it felt as if his family's unity would never be restored. The house remained quiet—no TV, no music, no footsteps, doors opening or closing, water running. Only silence. What were they doing, these three people he loved? Coiling on their beds hating him?

Chelsea sat on her bed pillow, her spine curled against the headboard, knees drawn up, stocking feet overlapped, a red cheerleading pom-pom in her lap. Long-faced, she repeatedly straightened the crepe paper squiggles, scraping them flat with the edge of her middle fingernail as if unsnagging hair. The pad of her thumb was stained red. A few strands of crepe paper had accidentally snapped off. They collected at her hip in a trembling pile as she drew on the pom-pom again . . . and again . . . and again . . . staring . . . remembering . . . mortified . . .

She had kissed her own brother.

What would she say to him the next time she saw him? How could she ever face him again? And would she be forced to, maybe even in her home sometimes, now that he knew they had the same father? It would be bad enough seeing him at school without thinking about him coming back here again. She pictured herself walking into school on Monday morning and passing his bank of lockers, meeting his eyes above the crowd and trying to act normal. What was normal in a situation like this? How could she even tell her friends? Her dad was their principal. Their principal! The person they were supposed to look up to and respect. Whether she confided in them or not, the word would get out. It was bound to, the way Kent was acting, charging into their house, staring at her dad, yelling accusations at him. Then all her friends would find out that her dad had a kid he'd never accepted responsibility for. It didn't matter what the circumstances were, he had two sons in the same grade, and only one was legitimate.

Chelsea doubled her arms across her knees and dropped her forehead to them. Her breath stirred the pom-pom in her lap. It rustled like wind through autumn leaves and brought as little comfort.

What would happen to her family? If she was upset by the news about Kent, her mother must be dying.

She knew her mom and dad's wedding anniversary. They'd been married in June, and Robby was born in December. What month was Kent born? It hardly mattered what month. If it was the same year—and it seemed to be—her dad had some explaining to do. Chelsea tried to imagine being her mother and hearing the news, but the idea of her father's unfaithfulness was too immense to ponder. Other kids' parents had affairs. Not hers.

Please, she thought, please let Mom and Dad get over this. Let it not cause great big trouble because we've never had trouble in our family before, and I don't know what I'd do if anything went wrong between my parents. Tell me what to do to make it easier on Mom and I'll do it. Anything at all and I'll do it.

But Mom was holed up in her room across the hall, and Dad was wandering around someplace in the rest of the house. And even though he'd said not to worry, it would take an idiot not to see how bad Mom felt, and how this had already caused tears and hurt and distance between them. Heck, between the whole family.

Robby sat on a hard maple chair in his room, rotating a football in his hands. Ceiling-to-floor shelving surrounded his desk, where a computer thrust its blackened screen into the silent room. The bed was freshly made, the blue carpeting vacuumed, the collected junk stacked on the bookshelves and chest and piled in the corners. His letter jacket hung on a pegboard behind the door. Though dusk had fallen, his lights remained unlit.

He sat now much as his father had sat earlier on the swing, doubled forward, elbows to knees while the football flipped over and over in his outsized teenage hands.

A brother. No, a half brother. Same age. Conceived when? Under what circumstances? Living clear across the country most of his life and never knowing his father. Finding him now, to do what? Make people whisper, tease, ask all kinds of questions Robby didn't have the answers for? Horn in on the family and start hanging around here, making everybody uncomfortable? Be better than Robby on the football field? Look at him sideways as if to accuse him of having a dad all to himself all these years while Kent had none? Well, heck, it wasn't his fault, was it?

But Dad—jeez, how could it happen? What was going on between Mom and Dad back then? Sometimes the two of them talked about old boyfriends and girlfriends, but Robby had never heard the name Monica before.

He remembered his dad saying, just this afternoon, "Every person you meet changes you." Well, Kent Arens had already changed this family! And who knew how many more changes he'd make, and how serious they'd be? All that stuff Dad had said about facing moral dilemmas and that's how character is developed—so what kind of character did that give his dad? Robby had figured out long ago that his mother was pregnant when she and Dad got married. Well, maybe he'd been pretty naive, but he'd always guessed that his mom and dad had never done it with any others, only with each other. Seemed like his own generation was the only one that had to sit through health classes about AIDS, and sermons about using condoms, and lectures from parents about being *good*. So what was *good*? He'd always thought his parents' generation was naturally more good than his own, just because that was so long ago, when being good came easier. He ought to know. He and Brenda had come so close to doing it so many times that he was a wreck. Actually, under pressure, he'd told his friends he *had* done it, just because if you didn't, you were a nerd. The truth was, he was scared as hell to go all the way, and so was Brenda, so they just sort of, well . . . messed around *a lot*.

But his dad had gotten two girls pregnant at the same time. Bum-mer.

And anybody with gonads could scope out a calendar and figure out that if Robby and Kent were born the same year to two different women, their dad had been pretty busy.

Robby flipped the football into a metal wastebasket and threw himself onto his back on the bed.

Kent Arens. His illegitimate brother. And he had to hand off the football to this kid for the rest of the season while Mom watched from the stands.

Poor Mom. Gosh, what was it going to be like for her if word got around the school? What was it like for her right now, closed up in her room across the hall, thinking about what had happened today?

Claire sat on the edge of her bed, a wide dresser drawer on the bedspread beside her. She pulled out a handful of tangled socks and sorted them into pairs, folded them neatly, and made organized piles. She dried her eyes with a thick pair of white ones, went on doggedly putting stockings, nylons, and underwear in precise order as if the new order in her dresser drawer would transmute into the same in her life.

Match a pair of anklets, fold them, stack them; check the pantyhose for runs, halve them, quarter them, roll them neat; double the bras upon themselves, lean them in a corner in a growing pile; fold the wrinkled nylon pants, press them with your hand, try to keep the stack from leaning, sliding out of order as her life suddenly had.

Abruptly she doubled forward, covering her face with a lump of white cotton.

I can't . . . I can't . . .

Can't what? No answer came, only aftershocks and the picture of that boy faced off against Tom in the front hall, looking so much like the younger Tom that she'd felt agonized merely looking at him.

How could she have missed the similarity before? How could she deal with all this now? How could she walk into the kitchen and resume her duties as a wife and mother and maintain an air of normality when suddenly her faith in her husband had been shattered? How could she do the same at school on Monday?

I can't . . . I can't . . .

She had no idea why it seemed so important to restore order to that dresser drawer, but she dragged her body upright and continued straightening its contents while her tears flowed faster and she began to sob. Her head hung and her hands fussed, fussed, fussed over a silly drawer that had been a mess for at least two years and could go on being messy for another two, and who cared?

Finally she gave up the needless task and toppled over on her side, her body bent around the wooden drawer, her forehead at its back panel while a high-pitched keening squeezed from her throat.

Ohh . . . ohhh . . . he didn't want to marry me . . . he didn't love meee . . .

She wanted him to come in and find her lying there in her misery, to witness what he'd reduced her to, because it was genuine and shattering, this state of weeping lethargy.

On the other hand, she didn't want to face him yet because she didn't know what she would say to him, how she would even be able to look at him.

He stayed away, and she lay for an hour while dark fell and the streetlights came on. The air coming in the cracked window grew chilly and tapped the tieback against the window frame. Occasionally a car droned by, and once a motorcycle.

After a long time she heard the phone ring and picked it up at the same moment Tom did on another extension. She held her breath and listened.

"Tom, it's Monica."

"Is he back?"

"Yes."

An unburdening sigh. "Thank God. And he's okay?"

"Yes."

"Did you talk to him?"

"I tried, but he wouldn't say much. He's still too hurt and angry."

"I guess he's got a right to be, but I just wasn't expecting it. When he came charging in here he really threw me."

"What did he say?"

"He called me an unscrupulous bastard who just screwed you and left without bothering to find out afterwards if you were pregnant."

"Oh, Tom, I'm sorry."

"But he's right. I should have at least given you a call."

"Or I should have given you a call."

"Oh, Monica, hell . . ." Another exhausted sigh. "Who knows what we should have done."

During the following silence Claire imagined the two of them clinging to their separate receivers. She wondered what Monica Arens looked like, what her house looked like, and what part of it he had seen.

"I imagine this is pure hell on your family." Her voice held great empathy.

"It's killing them. It's . . . oh, shit." He sounded too emotional to go on.

"Tom, I'm sorry. So much of the blame is mine." She sounded as if she cared very deeply about him. "Is it going to work out, do you think?"

"I don't know, Monica. Right now I really don't know."

"How did your wife take it?"

"She cried. She got angry. She hit me. Now nobody in the place is talking."

"Oh, Tom."

Claire listened to the two of them breathe for a while, then Tom cleared his throat and spoke hoarsely.

"I guess Claire said it best. She said, 'Oh, God, what a mess.'"

"I don't know what I can do at this point, but if there's anything . . ."

"Just try to get Kent to talk, and if you see any danger signs, call me. You know what to look for—depression, withdrawal, if he starts to smoke or drink, break curfew. I'll watch him from this end and keep an eye on his grades."

"All right. And Tom?"

"Yes?"

"You can call me too, you know. Anytime."

"Thanks."

"Well, I guess I'd better go."

"Sure. Me too."

"Well, goodbye then. Good luck."

"Yeah, you too."

When they'd hung up, so did Claire, to lie on her bed with her heartbeat jarring her entire body. I should not have listened, she thought, because now she's real. Now I've heard the care in her voice for Tom. I've heard them speak with pauses as poignant as dialogue. I've been silent witness to the fact that Kent truly is their son, and I can never deny it: there will always be that tie between them.

And now I know this is not the last conversation they'll have.

She waited for him to come to her and tell her about the call. When he didn't, she grew certain there were feelings between him and Monica. How could there not be, she reasoned, when they were going though all this together?

A long time later another car went by, forcing her from her lethargy. She propped herself up and sat there feeling shaky, her hip against the dresser drawer, her cap fallen off, reading the aqua blue digits on the bedside clock. Not even nine. Too early for bed yet, but she would not impose herself into his half of the house, risk encountering him some-place out there and having to make decisions about how to act.

She put the drawer back into the dresser by the clock light, took off her shoes and jeans but left her anklets and shirt on. Lacking all energy to find and change into proper sleepwear, she crawled under the covers and curled into a ball, tucking her hands between her knees, facing away from Tom's side of the bed.

A while later she heard him rap quietly on the kids' doors—first one, then the other—going in to talk to each of them, his voice only a distant murmur before he opened their own bedroom door and came inside.

He, too, undressed in the dark, then stretched out on his back without touching her, as if slipping into a pew beside someone who is deep in prayer.

Once again came the absolute stillness, the inexplicable necessity to lie motionless and pretend the other wasn't there, even when bone and muscle seemed to begin humming with the need to move.

All the crying had given Claire a headache, but she stared at the clock, watching numbers change until finally her eyelids grew heavy.

Sometime in the night she awakened to the feeling of his hand on her arm, imploring, trying to turn her over. But she knocked it off and withdrew tighter onto her side of the bed.

"Don't," she said.

Nothing more.

Nine

Claire awakened in the post-dawn haze of an eight o'clock Sunday morning. Outside, fog was shredding and lifting, leaving behind leaves polished by moisture. The sun was up, bathing the yard in coppery light. Behind her, Tom got out of bed and moved quietly across the carpet to the bathroom, closing the door.

She listened to water run, to life resuming, deadened by the events of the previous day. She replayed the dialogues of yesterday, and midway through the rehashing, felt anger seeping in to replace her lassitude. Each drip coming through the bathroom door spurred that anger as she pictured Tom moving about at his morning ablutions. He was carrying forth as if nothing had changed.

It had.

Within the wife who had been wholly committed to her marriage in every healthy way possible, a stranger reared her ugly head, a stubborn, hurt, vindictive woman where a kind, forgiving one had been before. She wanted to hurt him as deeply as he'd hurt her.

He came out of the bathroom and moved to the closet, where the soft rustle of cotton was punctuated by the ting of metal hangers as he selected a shirt and put it on. She followed his routine as he moved around the room, lying with her eyes open and her cheek to the pillow while his figure glanced across her peripheral vision.

He came to the bedside trouserless, knotting his tie. "Better get up. It's eight twenty-five already. We'll be late for church."

"I'm not going."

"Come on, Claire, don't start that. The kids need to see a united front here."

"I'm not going, I said!" She threw back the covers and stormed out of bed. "My face looks like hell and I'm not in the mood. You take them and go without me."

A conflagration of anger burst out of nowhere, surprising even him. "Look, I said I was sorry." He grabbed her arm as she flew past toward the bathroom. "Now, I think it's important that we keep up appearances until we settle this thing."

"I said, don't touch me!" She jerked free violently. The expression in her eyes shocked him as greatly as the slap she'd delivered yesterday. It warned him not to make a molehill out of this mountain. He stood faced off with her, his heart clamoring as he witnessed a stubborn and aggressive side of her nature that had lain dormant till now.

"Claire," he pleaded to her back, experiencing a small stab of fear. The bathroom door slammed. Through it, he said, "What should I tell them?"

"You don't have to tell them anything. I'll do my own talking."

She came out a minute later, belting a robe, and left their bedroom, still in her fat, white stockings, which by now were bulged like gourds. Whatever she said to the children he didn't hear. When they got in the car he could tell their night had been as troubled as his own, and that they were thrown into a state of fearful confusion by their mother's unlikely balking at a time when she had always been with them before.

"Why didn't Mom come with us?" Chelsea asked.

"I don't know. What did she tell you?"

"That she wasn't emotionally prepared to go out this morning, and that I shouldn't worry. What does that mean, 'not emotionally pre-pared'? Did you two have a fight last night?"

"We talked at the park. The rest you heard. After that, nothing more happened."

"She looked awful."

"She always looks awful after she cries."

"But, Dad, she always goes to church. Is she going to stop doing things with us just because she's mad at you?"

"I don't know, Chelsea. I hope not. She's very hurt right now. I think we have to give her time."

A knot seemed to be gathering around Tom's heart as he saw how, overnight, his children had been affected by his past indiscretion. Chelsea was the one asking the questions, but Robby wore a distressed look, riding in uneasy silence.

Chelsea asked, "You still love her, don't you, Dad?"

She had no idea how her question wrenched his heart. He reached over to squeeze her hand reassuringly. "Of course I do, honey. And we'll get this thing worked through, don't worry. I'm not going to let anything happen to Mom and me."

After church Claire had breakfast waiting. She was showered, dressed, and made up, moving around the kitchen using snappy efficiency as both shield and weapon. She forced some smiles for the children's benefit. "Hungry? Sit down." But their eyes lingered on her to watch what would happen between her and their father. Like an insect around repellent, he kept his distance, buzzing only so close to her before pulling back, conscious of how she pointedly ignored him while pouring juice and coffee, taking warm muffins from the oven. She found a bowl and a spatula for the scrambled eggs. He went to take them out of her hands, his heart racing as he neared her. "Here, I'll do that." She flinched away, avoiding contact with any part of him as he commandeered the utensils. Her aversion to him was so obvious it threw a pall over the entire meal. She spoke to the children, asking questions—how was church, what were they going to do today, did they have any homework to finish? They answered dutifully, wanting only that she look at their father, speak to him, smile at him as she had before yesterday.

It did not happen.

Her aloofness pervaded the thirty minutes they spent at the table. And when she said to the children, "I thought I'd go to a movie this afternoon. Either of you want to go with me?" they glanced up from their plates with gaunt expressions and made excuses, then slinked off to their bedrooms the minute the breakfast dishes were cleaned up.

It was amazing to Tom how facilely she could avoid all contact with him. She spoke to him when the need arose, answered his questions when he asked them, but he understood as he never had before how simple it was for this woman to slip into a role and stay in character. She was playing the part of the wounded woman, extending civilities only for her children's sake, and she was playing it with Academy Award–winning prowess.

Around one in the afternoon he found her in the living room with student papers stacked on the sofa around her and Streisand singing softly on the stereo. She was wearing a pair of half-glasses on the tip of her nose, reading a composition and making occasional comments in the margin. The autumn sun filtered through the sheer curtains and threw an obelisk of cinnamon across the carpet near her feet. She wore a French terry jogging suit and thin white canvas shoes. Her knees were crossed, one toe pointing at the floor. He'd always admired the line of her foot when she sat that way, how the forefoot angled down more sharply than other women's and gave the arch a pronounced curve.

He paused in the doorway, rebuffed by her so many times this morning that he hadn't the fortitude to place himself anywhere near her and risk being cold-shouldered again. With his hands in his pockets he watched her.

"Could we talk?" he asked.

She finished reading a paragraph, circled a word, and said, "I don't think so," without flicking an eyelash his way.

"When?"

"I don't know."

He sighed and tried to keep from getting angry. This woman seemed a stranger to him, and it was terrifying that he suddenly didn't like her very much.

"I thought you were going to a movie."

"At three."

"May I go along?"

There might have been a quarter beat when her eyes stopped roving over the paper, just before her eyebrows rose haughtily, her gaze still trimmed on the sheet in her hand. "No, Tom, I don't think so."

He tried even harder to keep from getting angry. "So how long are you going to treat me as if I'm not in the room?"

"I've spoken to you, haven't I?"

He snorted derisively and twisted his head as if water were in his ear. "Is that what you call it?"

She flapped a pair of stapled sheets into order, laid them aside, and picked up another set.

"The kids are scared," he said, "can't you see that? They need to know that you and I are at least *trying* to work this out."

Her eyes stopped scanning the composition, but she deigned not to lift them to him.

"They're not the only ones," she said.

He risked it, pulling forward from his position in the doorway to go to her, sitting down on the edge of the sofa, separated from her by a stack of student papers.

"Then let's talk about it," he urged. "I'm scared too, so that makes all four of us, but if you won't meet me halfway I can't do it all by myself."

With the red pen crooked in her finger she picked up a batch of papers and tamped them on her knee. Over her glasses she leveled him with a gaze of faint disdain.

"I need some time. Can you understand that?"

"Time to do what? Perfect your acting technique? You're at it again, you know, but you'd better be careful, Claire, because this is real life and there's a whole family hurting."

"How dare you!" she snapped. "*You* betrayed *me*, and then accuse me of pretending to be hurt when—"

"I didn't mean it that way—"

"—I'm the one who had to hear that my husband didn't want to marry me—"

"—I never meant that I didn't want to marry you—"

"—and that you were screwing another woman. *You* try getting a slap in the face like that and see how you react!"

"Claire, keep your voice down."

"Don't tell me what to do! I'll shout if I want to, and I'll hurt if I want to, and I'll go to the movie by myself, because right now I cannot bear to be in the same room with you, so get out and let me lick my wounds the way I please!"

The children were still in their rooms and he didn't want them to hear any more, so he left, stung afresh by Claire's tirade. He had made things worse. All he'd meant to do was warn her that they needed to talk things out, not accuse her of having no grounds for hurt. She had grounds, all right, but her stubbornness was wearing thin, and no matter what she said, she *was* indulging in some role-playing. Always before, whenever they disagreed, they'd discussed it sensibly, right away. Disagreeing with respect was what had made their relationship endure. What had gotten into her? Slapping him, shunning him, refusing to communicate, then bursting into a rage and throwing him out.

Claire?

He still found himself stunned by this reaction he had not expected from a woman he thought he knew, so stunned that he had to talk to somebody about it.

His dad's log cabin looked like something straight out of the Smoky Mountains. The walls were the color of sorghum, the chimney stone and the front porch unscreened.

Wesley's voice came around the corner as Tom opened his car door.

"Who's comin'?" he yelled.

"It's me, Dad."

"I'm on the front porch! Come on around here!"

Wesley had never put in a driveway. Just the two tire ruts leading up to the back door and beyond to an old shack near the water, where he stored his boat and motor in the winter. Neither did he bother to mow his lot very often. Two or three times a year if he felt like it. Clover and dandelions thrived in the sunny stretch out front, between lofty white pines whose carpet of needles was so thick the earth beneath them rolled like sand dunes. They gave off a dry pungency that Tom associated with his youth, those days when his dad had first put a cane pole in his hands and said, "This one's for you, Tommy. All your own. When it starts looking bleached out, you give it a couple coats of spar varnish, and it'll catch you fish for years."

It was one of Wesley Gardner's peculiarities that he could live an entire life surrounded by a weedy lawn, a muddy driveway, and clothing that could have used changing a lot more regularly, but he kept his fishing equipment in mint condition, lavishing hours of care on it and on his boat and motor.

Tom found him at it when he came around the end of the porch, where Wesley sat working on a rod and reel with an open tackle box at his feet.

"Well, look who's here."

"Hi, Dad." Tom climbed the wide front steps.

"Pull up a chair."

Tom settled into an ancient Adirondack chair to which paint was only a memory. It creaked, taking his weight.

Wesley sat in a matching one, a fiberglass rod between his knees, transferring monofilament line from one reel to another, applying line-cleaning fluid with a dab of cotton, and checking the line for kinks and irregularities. He held the cotton with his left thumb and worked the take-up reel with his right hand. It hissed quietly while the oily smell of the fluid mixed with the fishy one from his clothing. The legs of his plumber-green pants were wide enough to hold three men's legs, short enough to show most of his socks. On his head lolled the ever-present soiled blue fishing cap.

"Whatever brings you out here, it ain't no good," Wesley said, eyeing his son askance. "I can tell that already."

"Nope. No good at all."

"Well, I never knew a problem didn't get a little less serious out here on this porch with that lake out there smiling at a person."

Tom looked at it, silver-blue and twinkling: this might be one time his dad was wrong.

Wesley refolded his cotton ball and tipped more cleaner onto it. The reel sang once again.

"Dad," Tom said, "could I ask you something?"

"Asking don't hurt."

"You ever step out on Mom?"

"Nope." Wesley didn't miss a beat, cranking the reel. "Didn't need to. She gave me all and plenty of what a man needs. Did it with a smile, too."

That was the thing Tom liked about his dad: Tom could sit here dropping lead-ins all afternoon and Wesley wouldn't ask. He was a person so comfortable in his own skin that he didn't need to be scratching that of others to see what was below the surface.

"Never, huh?"

"Nope."

"Me either. But we've got a situation at home that stems from way back when I was engaged to Claire. Mind if I talk to you about it?"

"I got all day."

"Well, this is how it is: I did step out on her then, one time, and it seems—you'd better prepare yourself, Dad, because this one's a shocker—seems like you've got a grandson you never knew about before. He's seventeen years old and he's going to my school."

Wesley stopped cranking the reel. He whipped a look over at Tom, then let his weight sink back against the chair. After half a minute or so, he set down the reel and said, "You know, son, I think we need a beer here."

He pushed out of the deep, slatted chair and went inside, curled forward a little like a fishing line in the middle of a long cast. The warped wooden screen door banged behind him. He came back out with four cans of Schlitz, gave two to Tom, and sat down, bearing his weight on the creaking arms of the chair before lowering himself into it.

They popped open their first cans.

Heard the twin hisses.

Tipped back their heads.

Wesley wiped his mouth with knuckles like old walnuts.

"Well now . . . that's something," he said.

"I just found out the week before school started. I told Claire last night. She's pretty broken up about it."

"I don't doubt it. This old heart of mine might've taken a couple of good licks itself when you told me."

"She's hurtin', man, I mean, really hurtin'." Tom squinted out at the lake. "She won't let me touch her. Hell, she won't even look at me."

"Well, you've got to give her a little time, son. This is some backlash you've thrown."

Tom took two swallows of beer and rested the can on the flat arm of his chair. "I'm scared, Dad. I've never seen her like this before. She slapped me yesterday, and an hour ago she asked me to leave, said she couldn't stand to be in the same room with me. I mean, for God's sake, Dad, we don't treat each other that way! We never have!"

"I don't suppose you deserved it."

"Well, I did. I know I did. I said some things that really hurt her, but I had to be truthful, didn't I? And you know how it is between Claire and me. We've worked so damned hard to have the kind of marriage where we respect each other. Through thick and thin, respect is our byword. Now she won't even sit down and talk."

Wesley took a beat to compose his opinion. "Women are fragile creatures. Changeable."

"Whoa! . . . You can say that again. Only I'm just learning it!"

"Well, son, you've put her in a ticklish position. Two boys born the same year . . ."

"The other woman was nothing to me, ever. When she showed up at school registering Kent she didn't even ring a bell at first. I wouldn't have given her a second glance if it weren't for the boy. Only Claire doesn't believe that, I don't think."

"Would you?" Wesley finished off the first beer and set the can down on the porch floor. "I mean, just for the sake of getting into her mind, would you?"

Tom rubbed the bottom of the beer can on his knee. He was still dressed in the gray trousers he'd worn to church, though his tie hung loose under his white collar. "No, I suppose not."

"Well, then, that tells you you've got to take it slow with her. She'll need a little wooing." Wesley opened his second beer. "'Course, that part could be fun."

Tom glanced sideways at his dad and found Wesley doing the same at him. Momentarily the mischief faded from the older man's eyes.

"So his name is Kent, is it?"

Tom nodded several times. "Kent Arens."

"Kent Arens . . ." Wesley sampled it. Quietly, he asked, "What's he like?"

Tom wagged his head slowly, in wonder. "Aw, God, Dad, he's incredible. He was raised in the South and he's got impeccable manners, calls his teachers 'ma'am' and 'sir.' Exemplary grades, impressive school records, goals, the works. And he looks so much like me it'll knock your socks off. Nearly knocked mine off when I put it all together."

"Can't wait to meet him."

Tom went on as if Wesley hadn't spoken. "Even the pictures of him down through elementary school. They were all there in his file, and when I looked through it . . . well . . ." Tom watched his thumbnail working against the paint on his beer can. "It was one of the most emotional moments of my life. I sat there at my desk, all alone, looking at this kid . . . this boy who's mine. I've never seen him before, and all of a sudden there before me are pictures not just of him, but of *me*. It felt as if I was looking at myself at those ages, you know, Dad? And I realized I was responsible for giving him life, yet I'd been robbed of sharing that life with him, and he'd been robbed of knowing me. And I felt guilty, and deprived, and sad. So damned sad I wanted to cry. Matter of fact, I did a little bit. I've had tears in my eyes more in the last couple weeks than in the last ten years, over this."

"Does Claire know that?"

Tom glanced at his father and shrugged. Then he finished off his beer and put his can on the floor. They sat for a while, smelling the dusty pine duff from beneath the monstrous trees and the musty dog-days smell of aging cattails and lake shore, tipping their heads to watch a couple of mallards fly over the shoreline. The birds yelled, *braack, braack,* fading off in the distance as the porch roof cut them off from view. The sun warmed the men's pants legs. The roof shaded their heads. Wesley reached into his tackle box for a whetstone and a fishhook and sat back passing time sharpening it.

Finally, Tom said, "Kent was conceived one week before I married Claire."

Wesley finished the first hook and started on another.

"And Chelsea was beginning to get a crush on him, and Robby resents him on the football field because he bumped Robby's best friend off the starting lineup. Also because he's probably a better player than Robby is. Tomorrow at school we all have to face one another. It might possibly be the hardest for Claire, because she's Kent's English teacher."

Wesley started on another fishhook. It rasped pleasantly against the stone, like some insect chirping in the garden. He took his time, studying his work myopically, checking the shiny tip again and again before finding it to his liking. He finished it and set it aside before he spoke again.

"Well, I'll tell you what . . ." He leaned back in his chair with his knees spread wide, resting his hands on them with the knuckles curled under. "A man sets a code for himself at some point in his life, and he lives by it. If he's a family man, he gives his children something to live up to. If he's a husband, he gives his wife something to rely on. If he's a leader, he gives those under him standards to guide them. A man lives a life like that, he's got nothing to be ashamed of. There isn't a one of us didn't do things in our younger days that we wouldn't do now, if we could go back and change it. Only, we can't. Living with mistakes, now that's a tricky business. Tells a lot about a man, how he handles that. I think it's always okay to feel a little guilty about some things—keeps a man in line, actually—as long as you don't give guilt undue sway. Yessir, it's a hard taskmaster, that guilt. I say, feel it, and wriggle a little bit if you have to, but then put it away. Get on with what you can change.

"Now you, Tom, you can't change the first part of Kent's life, but you can change the rest of it, and judging from what I've heard today, you have every intention of getting to know this son of yours. Be patient with Claire. Just keep loving her the way you always have. She'll get over the shock, and once she does she'll realize that this boy is going to bring something into your lives, not take something away. *That's* the point when all this fuss will have been worth it for all of you.

"Meanwhile, you've just got to struggle along like the rest of us, and tell yourself that one big mistake doesn't a bastard make, and I'm speaking of you, not your new son. Bring him around here sometime. I'd love to meet him, maybe show him how to pop for bass at the edge of the reeds or catch those sunnies out there off the point. Cook up a mess of 'em in beer batter, maybe tell him what kind of little boy his dad was. Be good for him, don't you think?"

By the time Wesley was done, Tom's heart had eased some. He sat relaxed with his head resting against the back of the chair; the situation at home seemed a little less dire.

"You know what?" he said.

Wesley chuckled. "That's a dangerous question to ask an old windbag like me."

Tom grinned and rolled his face toward his dad. "Every time I come out here, I go away realizing why I'm such a good principal."

Wesley's eyes held a glint of appreciation, but all he said was, "Want your other beer?"

"No. Go ahead." Tom sat on, a little healed, watching his father.

Wesley rested his old eyes on the lake, a soft smile on his lips, and thought of how cool and tangy a beer tasted on a gorgeous fall afternoon like this, and how nice it was to have a son like this stop by and confide in him, cull a few bits of wisdom out of such a soft old brain as his, treat an old duffer like him as if he still had something to offer. Yup, it sure was fine, sitting here on the porch chairs with the sun on your legs and your fishing gear all in order and your boy at your elbow and Anne waiting on the other side. *Yessiree, Anne,* he thought, lifting his eyes to the blue-washed sky above the lake she had loved as much as he, *we did a good job with Tom here. He's turned into one damned fine man.*

The Monday morning routine never changed. Tom left home at quarter to seven, Claire a half hour later. They saw each other again in the teachers' lunchroom at a 7:30 staff meeting, over which Tom presided.

Nothing had changed at home. Claire had slept hugging her edge of the mattress. She had dressed behind the closed bathroom door. The kids had been remote and quiet. Nobody ate breakfast at the table, but took juice to their rooms instead. When Tom had gone to find Claire and say, as usual, "I'm leaving. See you later," she hadn't said a word.

The place had felt like a torture chamber. And now he faced another.

As he walked toward the teachers' lunchroom for the staff meeting, he thought of what a relief it would have been to work anywhere else today, to be able to immerse himself in concerns unrelated to his family life. Instead he already felt drained, preparing to face Claire in front of all their co-workers with the weight of their domestic estrangement between them.

Before the door closed behind him he was scanning the teachers' lunchroom for his wife. She was sitting at the farthest table among others from her department, drinking coffee, taking no part in the conversation and occasional laughter. The moment he entered, her eyes met his above the cup and she hastily looked away. He turned to the stainless-steel percolator, filled a cup for himself, returned some 'good mornings,' and attempted to gather his emotional equilibrium.

They'd had disagreements before, but he'd never faced Claire as her principal with hostility of this magnitude between them. It was uncomfortable being her superior at a time when his guilt weighed heavily.

The cooks had left a tray of warm caramel rolls. He helped himself to one and took his mug of hot coffee to his usual spot at the near end of the center table. Coach Gorman came in, dressed in sweats and a baseball cap, garnering congratulations on Friday night's game. When he carried his coffee past Tom's chair, Tom, too, said, "Nice game, Coach."

Ed Clifton from the science department said to Gorman, "Looks like you've got a new star on your hands, Bob. That running back, Arens, might just be all-state material."

It was no different from any other Monday morning after a game. HHH excelled in sports; remarks like this always drifted across the staff meetings. But when the talk centered on Kent Arens, Tom felt Claire's eyes click into him and dig. The boy was making impressions—that was obvious already. He was the kind who'd be very noticed by both students and staff, so that when and if Kent's relationship to Tom became fodder for school gossip, Claire would be exposed to plenty of speculative glances, maybe even outright questions from the curious.

Tom stood and called the meeting to order with his usual informality. "Well, let's get this thing going. Cecil," he said to the head janitor, "we'll start with you, as usual."

Cecil read off a list of the week's events that would need special attention. Following that, someone brought up the issue of students without parking permits taking up teachers' parking spots, an annual complaint that always took a few weeks to straighten out.

The head of the social studies department invited Tom to a citizenship meeting and asked the teaching staff to encourage all students to become involved in visiting senior citizens' homes, becoming big brothers and big sisters, and other civic-minded pursuits.

One by one, Tom called on the head of each department until he came to Claire.

"English department?" he said.

"We're still missing textbooks," she replied. "What's the status on them?"

He said, "They're on their way. We'll take that up in the English department meeting tomorrow. Anything else?"

"Yes. Senior-class play. I'll be supervising it again this year, so if anyone has time to help, I'd appreciate it. You don't have to be in the English department to help, you know. We don't turn anyone away. I won't start auditioning the cast until late this month, and the performances will be just before Thanksgiving, but it's never too early to put out an appeal."

Tom added, "For those of you who are new to our staff, Claire puts on some impressive productions. Last year she did *The Wizard of Oz*. This year it'll be . . ."

He deferred to Claire, who pointedly refused to glance his way.

"*Steel Magnolias*," she supplied.

The tenured staff, who had known them for years, could feel the chill as if a window had been flung open on a sub-zero day. For the remainder of the meeting their antennae were up, gauging the unusual tension between their principal and his wife, especially the antagonism emanating from Claire.

When the meeting ended, Tom turned his back to speak to someone else while Claire left the room behind him, taking the long way around the tables to avoid going near him.

Several minutes later, still keyed up from the staff meeting, Tom was at his post, monitoring the front hall just inside the entry doors as the school buses began arriving. Through the ceiling-to-floor glass wall he watched the students leap off the bus steps onto the sidewalk, talking and laughing as they funneled toward the building.

He saw Kent the moment he stepped from the bus. Watching him approach, Tom felt his heart start clubbing. It required no lifetime of father-son intimacy to recognize that the boy was troubled, stern-faced, speaking to no one. He walked with a portfolio riding his right thigh, shoulders back and head straight: an athlete's stride. His hair caught the morning sun, dark, gelled into a popular style that showed the coarse furrows of some stout styling tool. He wore jeans and a nylon windbreaker over a paisley shirt with an open collar. As usual, his clothing was clean and crisply ironed. His appearance spoke volumes about the quality of care provided by his mother. Among the students issuing from the bus he stood out not only for his neatness, but for his dark good looks and superior physique as well. It caught Tom like a barbed-wire fence across the gut, the swift clutch of pride tinged with awe that this impressive young man could be his son.

Anxiety gripped him, born of the complexity of their relationship, their past that needed discussing, and their future that remained a question mark. Tom's last encounter with Kent came back in vivid detail as he watched his son stalk toward the door. *You just screwed her and left,* the boy had shouted.

A student came by and said, "Hi, Mr. G."

Tom swung around and said, "Hi, Cindy." When he faced the door again Kent was coming through it and heading his way. Their eyes met and Kent's forward motion flagged. Tom could feel his pulse pound high in his throat, bulging veins as if he'd knotted his tie too tightly. The encounter was inevitable; Tom stood at the intersection of two halls, and Kent had to take one of them. He sped ahead as if to move past without speaking.

Tom wouldn't let him. "Good morning, Kent," he said.

"Good morning, sir," Kent replied obediently, without pausing.

Tom's voice stopped him. "I'd like to talk to you today if you have a few minutes."

Kent fixed his gaze on the backs of the students flowing past him. "I have a heavy schedule, sir, and after school I have football practice."

Tom felt embarrassment creep up his face. He, the principal, was being rebuffed by one of his own students.

"Of course. Well, someday soon then." Stepping back, he allowed the boy to pass, sending from behind a silent message of apology and appeal.

Robby had gone to school early to work out in the weight room, so Chelsea rode the bus, speaking to no one, staring out the window for minutes at a time, registering nothing but sad memories of home while the seat jiggled and bounced beneath her. When the bus stopped, she filed off and headed for the building, buffeted along by a surge of students, seeking out her father even through the plate-glass wall. She swam through the wide front doorway and there he stood, same as always, at the junction of the two halls. For a moment she was reassured by his presence in the place where she was accustomed to finding him every morning. But over the weekend everything had changed. A pall hung over every simple movement that used to make her happy. Terror lodged in her chest.

"Hi, Dad," she said quietly, stopping before him, hugging a yellow portfolio.

"Hi, honey." The words were familiar, but his smile was forced. She felt like a stranger in a foreign land where customs were different than those she knew. Already she hated picking her way so carefully through the tangled family tensions for which no protocol was available to guide her. She, who had always been so blithe in the exchange of conversation and affection with her parents, no longer knew how to approach them, what to say or do.

"Dad, what's . . . I mean . . ." Tears spurted into her eyes. "When are you and Mom going to make up?"

Tom put his arm around her and drew her away from traffic. He turned them to face a wall and bent his head to her.

"Chelsea, honey, I'm really sorry you have to be caught in the middle of this. I know it's asking a lot, but could you please just go on as you were? Just concentrate on school the way you always have, and enjoy it without spending your worries on us. We'll work it out, I swear we will, but I don't know when. In the meantime, if Mom doesn't act the same, please forgive her. If I don't act the same, forgive me, too."

"But, Daddy, it's so hard. I didn't even want to come to school today."

"I know, honey, but the danger of something like this is that it draws all the vigor out of us as a family, but I want us to be the way we were just as badly as you do."

She put her head down, trying to keep her tears from spilling and ruining her makeup. "But we've never had anything like this happen before. Our family was always so perfect."

"I know, Chelsea, and we will be again. Not perfect. No family is perfect. I guess we're finding that out. But happy, like we used to be. I'll try really hard, okay?"

She nodded and her tears fell onto the yellow portfolio. They still faced the wall, Tom with his arm around her shoulders, both of them aware that curious students were passing behind them, probably gawking.

Chelsea tried to scrape her tears away unobtrusively. "Dad, can I use the mirror in your office?"

"Sure. I'll come with you."

"No, it's okay. You don't have to."

"Honey, I want to. You're the first one who's talked to me in two days, and it feels good."

They went into his office and Chelsea took a sharp right, opened his cupboard door, and hid behind it where the secretaries couldn't see. She looked in the mirror and tried rubbing away her smeared mascara while Tom went on to his desk and picked up some telephone messages. After flipping through half of them, he dropped them and came to stand behind her.

She gave up trying to fix her makeup as their eyes met in the mirror. Two sadder reflections she had never seen in her life. "Dad, what should I do about Kent? I don't know what to say to him."

He turned her around gently by the shoulders. "Be his friend. He'll need one."

"I don't know if I can be." She had worried herself sick about facing him again after that kiss.

"Give it time, then. He probably doesn't know how to treat you either."

"I don't even know what I'll say to Erin. She's going to be able to tell that something is wrong. I said I couldn't talk to her on the phone when she called yesterday."

"Honey, I don't know either. Maybe we'd all better give it a day or

two. A lot of feelings are involved here, not the least of which are Kent's.
Whether or not he'll want the general population of this school to know
he's my son is his call."

They stood awhile, Tom with his hands on her arms, she staring at a
design on his tie. How could lives change so drastically, so fast? they both
wondered. Last week they'd been part of a happy family of four, and look
at them now. She sighed and turned away, got eyeliner and mascara out
of her purse, and began putting them to use while he walked back to his
desk, picked up the phone messages but gave up reading them and went
back to her.

"So what do you think of this whole deal?" he asked quietly.

She looked at him in the mirror with the mascara wand poised near
her eyelashes. She shrugged. "I don't know."

"Are you shocked?"

She looked down. "A little."

"Yeah, me too."

They stood close, wondering what to say next. Tom said, "I guess
you'd be pretty bummed out if everybody found out who he is." He
deliberately chose the slang he heard so often in the halls. It seemed very
appropriate today, and put them on equal footing.

With her chin on her chest she mumbled, "Yeah . . . I guess."

Again he turned her around. "You angry at me?"

When she refused to lift her head he dipped his knees and got his face
where she couldn't avoid it. "Just a little, maybe?"

"Maybe," she admitted unwillingly.

"It's okay, Chelsea. I guess I'd be mad too if I were you."

She closed the closet door and turned around. "Does Grandpa know
yet?"

"Yes. I went out and told him yesterday afternoon."

"What did he say?"

"Oh, you know Grandpa. He doesn't place blame on people for much
of anything. He says that in time your mom will come to realize—that all
of us will come to realize—that Kent will probably bring something into
our lives instead of taking something away from us."

Home Song

She studied her dad's face, drawn with sleeplessness and worry. The bell rang, warning that classes would start in four minutes. She wanted to say, "But he's already taken something from us, hasn't he? He's taken our family happiness." But speaking it aloud would make it too real and scary. Maybe if she didn't say it, it wouldn't be true.

Tom put a hand between her shoulder blades and started her toward the door. "You'd better go now, honey, so you aren't late for class."

Suddenly she loved him very much, and some of her anger with him slipped away. She reached up and pressed her cheek to his, just because he looked so forlorn and tired. From the doorway she gave him a wistful parting smile, then went away carrying the memory of his hurt and worried face.

Ten

Chelsea and Kent managed to avoid each other until classes passed between third and fourth periods. Until then he'd kept clear of his locker, where they used to meet, and she took alternative routes. But before fourth period he needed a notebook he'd forgotten and she—short of time—picked the quickest route to her social studies class, leading her past the spot where they used to rendezvous, exchange smiles, and feel their pulses quicken.

The memory stung them with embarrassment now.

Sure enough, she was barreling along behind a flock of kids when Kent came out of his locker aisle and they came face-to-face. They halted, pivoted, and veered apart as fast as humanly possible. They both blushed, and he hurried to get away in one direction while she did the same in the other.

They both felt stupid.

And embarrassed.

And guilty of something obscure.

Home Song

. . .

Honors English, fifth period, was a fact of life. Mrs. Gardner, teacher, had been dreading it as much as Kent Arens, student. But the clock moved, the bell rang, and during the 12:13 shuffle he approached the door of room 232, where she stood as her class filed in.

She knew she should greet him, but couldn't.

He knew he should say something, but couldn't.

They encountered each other with the bristling stares of a cat and dog meeting in a doorway, each knowing it can hurt—or be hurt by—the other.

She saw in him the spit and image of her husband.

He saw in her the woman who'd married his mother's seducer.

Each viewpoint had its deserved antagonisms, but a profound respect for authority had been drilled into Kent from the time he could grasp it, and he nodded stiffly as he passed Mrs. Gardner.

She tipped up the corners of her lips but no smile domed her cheeks or touched her eyes. When she closed the door to begin class, he was seated along with everybody else. Avoiding eye contact with him became a concentrated study throughout that hour while she faced him and spoke of Greek plays and mythology, passed out copies of the *Odyssey*, and gave historical background about the classic. She explained why they were taking the chronological approach to literature, listed the segments of study, recommended available videos and paperback books that would bring Greek classics alive for them, and passed out a paper listing suggestions for extra-credit work for this unit.

Throughout her lecture Kent kept his frosty gaze fixed on her shoes. Peripherally, she was aware of this, and of the fact that he sat with his spine curved slightly to the right, an elbow on the desktop and a finger covering his upper lip, scarcely moving through the entire fifty-two minutes. Once she forgot herself and looked him square in the face, startled by how much he resembled Tom. That glance touched off a peculiar sense of déjà vu, as if she were teaching the seventeen-year-old Tom Gardner, whom she'd never actually known.

The bell rang, her students began filing out, and Claire stood behind her desk, making herself appear busy, keeping her eyes downcast, giving herself and Kent a graceful means of separating without contact. But he lagged till the others had left, and stood before her desk like some sinewy Greek warrior, afraid of nothing.

"Mrs. Gardner?"

Her head shot up. A force field of negative ions seemed to dance between them, repelling them from one another.

"I'm sorry I barged into your house that way. I had no right to do that."

Abruptly he spun, leaving only the squeak of his rubber-soled shoes and no chance for her reply as she watched his dark head and straight back disappear out the door.

In the empty room she plopped onto her chair as if he'd placed ten fingers on her chest and pushed. There she sat, an emotional tourbillion, her heart bumping around inside her body like two cats in a gunnysack. What was it she felt for that boy? More than resentment. He was Tom's son, and divorcing herself from that fact was impossible. Did she feel pity? No, not yet. It was too soon for pity, but she had to admire his forthrightness and courage. Warm shame rose to flood her face for having shunned him when she—as an adult and a teacher—should have been the one to set the example. Instead, he, a mere boy of seventeen, had done the dirty work of speaking to her first. What else had she expected? He was, after all, Tom's boy, and it's exactly what Tom would have done.

The thought of Tom reopened her wound. She sat on at her desk, gathering her grievances about her like weapons, sharpening them against the whetstones of her own faithfulness and honesty during all the years she'd known him.

During the last period of the day Kent had weight training with Mr. Arturo. He was straddling a blue padded bench doing slow arm curls with a fifteen-pound dumbbell when a student aide from the main office walked in and handed Mr. Arturo a note. The teacher glanced at the name on the front, then approached Kent and extended it, folded and unread, between two fingers.

"Something from the office," he said, and walked away.

Kent uncurled his right arm and left the dumbbell on the bench. Inside was a pre-printed "Message from the Principal." One of the student aides in the office had filled in the blanks with the time and the words *See Mr. Gardner in his office now.*

Kent felt as if he'd dropped the dumbbell across his neck. He wasn't altogether sure he could swallow his own spit. On the other hand, his adrenaline was spurting so hard he figured he could have changed a tire without a jack.

No fair, he thought. *Just because he's the authority around here doesn't mean he can force me to do something that's got nothing to do with my being a student and his being a principal. I'm not ready to face him. I don't know what to say.*

He put the note in an inside pocket of his shorts, picked up his dumbbell, and continued doing arm curls. He followed them with a series of bench presses, incline presses, butterflies, and bent-arm flies, and eventually a full workout on his legs, bringing him to the end of the hour.

He went straight into the locker room for football practice and was lacing on his gear when Robby Gardner came in. Robby's locker was twelve feet from Kent's on the opposite side of a long varnished bench. He moved straight to it, opened the door with one hand and his jacket snaps with the other while between him and Kent four other boys dressed and rattled metal doors.

Tension buzzed across the twelve feet separating the half brothers.

Robby hung up his jacket.

Kent laced on his shoulder pads.

Robby pulled his shirt out of his jeans.

Kent reached for his jersey.

They both looked straight into their lockers. Their posture was exemplary. Their profiles were stern.

Okay, okay, so he's there. So what!

But each of them was burningly aware of the other. Each fought an urge to turn and search for physical similarities.

Robby's head turned first.

Then Kent's.

Their eyes locked, fascinated, against their wills, drawn by blood and a shared secret.

Half brothers. Born the same year. If our fates had been reversed, we might have lived in each other's shoes.

Rosy color climbed their necks while they searched for likenesses, linked by events that had happened to their parents in an era that seemed too long ago to make this present revelation seem valid.

It lasted only seconds.

Simultaneously they returned their attention to dressing, letting today's antipathy take its place between them again with all its painful and convoluted relationships. Relationships aside, one thing dominated their thoughts: each of them stood to face a gossip mill if the word ever got out, and both were busy working out the full ramifications of that possibility.

They might be brothers genealogically, but on the football field they remained rivals.

By tacit agreement their animus was established during those first five minutes in the locker room: play together, but never let your gazes lock; present a unified appearance for the team, but remain aloof in principle; give the coach the impression of harmony, but never let your hands touch, not even when you're getting your hits in the huddle.

They headed outside for practice. The weather had turned gray and clouds roiled, ragged and raw with promised rain. The grass felt cold beneath their knuckles. Their mouthguards tasted like mildew. Across the ear holes of their helmets the wind played like a flute in low register. Dirt smeared on their bare calves and never seemed to dry. By four-forty, when the drizzle started, they were anxious to hit the showers and go home to warm kitchens and supper.

Practice wasn't over yet, however. As usual, the coach broke them up

Home Song

into four groups and yelled, "Ten good plays!" signaling at least another half hour of work before he blew the three short blasts on his whistle that dismissed them.

They were lining up for their second play when Robby and Kent both saw him at once: their principal, their father, standing on the bleachers with his back to the wind, hands driven deeply into the pockets of a gray trench coat that whacked at his calves. His dark hair flapped against his forehead, and his trouser legs rippled, but he stood motionless, his attention riveted on the playing field like that of a felon before a magistrate. Alone he stood, the sole figure on that long stretch of aluminum, while rain darkened his shoulders. Forlornness telegraphed itself from the set of those shoulders and the stillness of his stance. They caught him watching them and felt his regret reaching across the bleak autumn afternoon toward them both. Powerless against a force greater than any miserable, stubborn fixing of wills, the half brothers turned, meeting each other's eyes across the churned stretch of turf separating them. And for one brief moment, contrary to all that called out for divisiveness, they felt themselves unified by a stab of pity for the man who'd fathered them both.

Chelsea made supper that night. Her eagerness to please nearly broke Tom's heart as she presented her conciliatory offering—Spanish rice and green Jell-O with pears—then waited with hopeful eyes darting back and forth between her mother and father to see if her ploy would work.

They sat. They ate. They spoke.

But when their eyes met, his were seeking and hers unforgiving.

After supper Tom went back to school because the French Club was having its first meeting to discuss a trip to France next summer, and they had invited him to sit in. Also, adult education pottery classes were starting in the art department, and the city policemen and their wives were beginning their mixed volleyball league in the gym, so he stayed until the building was empty.

At home, Claire finished her classroom prep and prowled around like a caged cat, trying to make herself do one more load of laundry but needing a vent for her frustrations instead.

She called Ruth Bishop and Ruth said, "Come on over."

Dean was gone again, working out at the club, and Ruth was writing a letter to her parents. She pushed her stationery aside and poured two glasses of wine.

"All right," she said across the kitchen table. "Let it all hang out."

"It seems my husband has a son nobody bothered to tell me about till now."

Claire spilled it all, crying some, cursing some, wailing out her hurt and disillusionment, drinking two glasses of wine while venting her anguish on Ruth. She told of her initial shock followed by anger, then her chagrin while facing the boy at school. But she returned to the moment that stung worst.

"I wish I'd never picked up the phone when she called back, but I just couldn't help myself. And now I've heard him talking to her and it makes it all so real. Oh, God, Ruth, do you know what it's like to hear your husband talking to a woman he's been in bed with? Especially after he's told you he didn't want to marry you? Do you know how that hurts?"

"I know," Ruth said.

"It was as much their silences as what they said. Sometimes I could hear them breathing. Just . . . just breathing, like . . . like lovers who are dying to see each other; and then he said she could call him anytime, and she told him the same thing. For God's sake, Ruth, he's my husband! And he's saying that to her?"

"I'm sorry you have to go through this. I know exactly how you feel because I've been there myself. I told you, I've heard Dean hang up a dozen times when I walked into the room. Then he'd lie when I'd ask who he'd been talking to. Take it from me, Claire, all men are liars."

"He claims there's nothing between them anymore, but how can I believe him?"

A look of disgust put an edge on Ruth's features. She refilled her wineglass with a poke of the bottle. "Take my word, you're a damned fool if you do."

Her acerbic glance lifted and seemed to leave some things unsaid.

"Ruth, what is it? Do you know something about this? Has he talked to you . . . or Dean?"

Ruth considered before replying.

"Has he?" Claire persisted.

"Not because he wanted to."

"What does that mean?"

"I saw them together last Saturday, at least I think it was her. Monica Arens?"

"Oh God . . ." Claire whispered, covering her lips. "Where?"

"In front of Ciatti's in Woodbury."

"Are you sure?"

"I walked right up to his car window and leaned down and talked to him. At first I thought it was you with him, but then I saw her, and to tell the truth, I felt like a fool. I didn't know what to say once I realized it wasn't you."

"What did he say?"

"Nothing. Just introduced her."

"What did she look like?"

"Nondescript. Blondish hair parted on the side, hardly any makeup. Kind of a long nose."

"What were they doing?"

"If you're asking did he kiss her or anything like that, the answer is no. But I have to be honest with you, Claire. What do you think a man and woman are doing when they meet in a car in the middle of a parking lot? If you ask him, I'm sure he'll deny it, but it looks to me like you're getting the shaft just like I am."

"Oh, God, Ruth, I just didn't want to believe it."

"Neither did I when I first suspected Dean, but evidence piled up."

Claire whispered, "It hurts so much."

"Of course it does." Ruth covered Claire's free hand. "Believe me, I know."

"He's gone right now, supposedly at school. He's gone so much. But how will I ever know if he's telling the truth from now on? He could be anywhere." Ruth gave no reply, and Claire felt her despair increasing along with a faint muzziness from the wine. "So this is the moment of truth that you warned me about," she realized.

"It's not fun, is it, deciding what to do about it?"

"No, it's not." Suddenly Claire felt a fragment of her spunk return, and she pushed away her wineglass, still full. "But I won't be a two-timed wife! He'll tell me the truth because I'll make him!" She shot to her feet. "I'll be damned if I'll sit here getting drunk over it either!"

The billow of anger felt much better and she rode it home, where she plunged herself into the job of putting blond highlighter in her hair. He returned around ten o'clock and she heard him come up the stairs to their room. He shuffled to a stop in the bathroom doorway and stood tugging tiredly at his tie. She continued kneading her damp locks into question marks around her face, refusing to glance his way.

"Hi," he said.

"Hi." She replied colorlessly, ignoring the plea in his voice.

He pulled his shirttail from his pants and let it hang. Stood there a long time before finally sighing and coming out with what was on his mind. "Look, I've been lugging around this question ever since supper, and I can't lug it anymore. I've got to ask. How did it go today with Kent?"

She went on jabbing at her scalp with her fingers, lifting her hair and spreading the sweet-and-sour chemical smell in the room.

"It's difficult. Neither one of us knew how to handle it."

"Do you want me to pull him from your class?"

She shot him a glance. "Mine's the only honors English for seniors."

"Still, it might be better if he had another teacher."

"Not very fair to him though, would it be?"

Softly, guiltily, he replied, "No."

She let him suffer awhile before snapping, "Leave him."

Tom turned away into the shadows to finish undressing and put on pajama pants. She came into the bedroom and opened a dresser drawer in search of a nightgown. He went into the bathroom to brush his teeth. When he came out she was in bed. He snapped out the bathroom light and picked his way through the dark to his spot beside her. Covered to the armpits they lay as separate as two railroad ties.

Minutes went by while each remained fully aware of the other's wakefulness.

Finally, Tom said, "I called him into my office today, but he refused to come."

"Can you blame him? He's just as mixed up as the rest of us."

"I'm not sure what to do."

"Well, don't ask me." Claire put a bite in her words. "What does she say?"

"Who?"

"The boy's *mother*."

"How should I know?"

"Well, don't you consult her on *everything*?"

"Oh, for God's sake, Claire."

"How did you know her phone number, Tom?"

"Don't be ridiculous."

"Well, *how*? You went storming into the kitchen and jerked the phone off the hook and dialed in a split second. How did you know it?"

"It's in my records at school. You know how good my memory is for numbers."

"Sure," she said sarcastically, and tossed onto her side facing the dresser.

"Claire, she's nothing more than—"

"Just *don't*!" Claire reared up and glared over her shoulder, one hand slicing the dark above the covers. "Don't defend yourself because I don't know what to believe anymore, and I'm having a hard enough time as it is. I talked to Ruth tonight and she said she saw you in a car with that woman in front of Ciatti's last Saturday."

"I told you I'd seen her that day."

"In a *car*, for God's sake! You met her in a car like some . . . some sneaking, low-life philanderer! In a *car* in some *parking lot*?"

"Where else was I supposed to meet her? Would you feel better if I said I went to her house?"

"Hell, you've done that too, haven't you? And where were you yesterday?"

"Out at Dad's."

"I'll bet."

"Call him."

"Maybe I'll do that, Tom. Maybe I'll just do that."

"We sat on the porch and drank a couple of beers and I told him about Kent."

"And what did he say?"

"I thought you were going to call him and ask him yourself. After all, you wouldn't believe it, coming from me. You just said so."

He plunked over and presented his spine, too.

Back to back, they simmered, devising retorts that would have been sharper and more cutting than those already delivered, wishing they had twin beds.

It seemed hours before they dropped off into fitful sleep, during which any movement from the other half of the bed roused them, the slightest touch made them draw back sharply across the line of demarcation down the center of the mattress. In the deep of night, though each woke at various times, there was no dissolving of anguish, no melting together with whispered words of apology. Only two people who, even in sleep, knew that tomorrow would likely be no better than today.

The following morning before school, Tom faced Claire at the English departmental meeting. Once again he felt uncomfortable as her superior. Once again he felt speculative glances cast their way by their fellow workers, who could easily sense the strain between them. Monitoring the hall as the students arrived, Tom watched and waited for Kent, but the boy must have decided to enter through another door and avoid him. At noon, he noticed that Chelsea and Erin were sitting alone and Kent was clear across the cafeteria at a table with Pizza Lostetter and a bunch of other football players. Though Robby usually sat with them, today he sat apart. Tom followed his customary pattern of cruising the lunchroom, pausing here and there to smile and talk with students, but he avoided Kent's table. He watched him leave, dropping his milk cartons in the garbage can. Following Kent's progress from the immense, noisy room, Tom felt the same longing within, a reaching that drew upon him and made heartache a real human condition. His son. His dark-haired, stubborn, hurt, and haunted son, who had defied his order yesterday and left Tom sitting with his heart in his throat until the end of seventh period before finally admitting Kent wasn't going to come.

Later that afternoon, shortly after two o'clock, Tom was putting his desk in order, preparing to leave for the district office, where the superintendent had called the monthly cabinet meeting of all sixteen principals and assistant principals in the district. He closed the budget books on which he'd been working, made a stack of correspondence that needed filing, and was trying to decide how to handle a student report from a probation officer when Dora Mae came to his door.

"Tom?" she said.

"Hm?" He looked up, distracted, with the paper in his hand.

"That new student, Kent Arens, is out here and wants to see you."

Had Dora Mae said, "The President of the United States is out here and wants to see you," she could not have rattled Tom any more. The inner chaos he suffered was both divine and daunting. It shone plainly in the leap of color to his face, his gawky expression, and the uncharacteristic, useless flutter of a hand to his tie.

"Oh, well . . . then . . ." Tom realized too late he was giving himself away. He cleared his throat and added, "Send him in."

Dora Mae went out and did as ordered, then whispered to her fellow secretary, Arlene Stendahl, "What in the world is wrong with Tom lately?"

Arlene whispered back, "I don't know, but everybody's talking about him. And Claire, too! She's been treating him like some leper."

Kent appeared in his doorway, grave but with a faint giveaway of color in his own cheeks. He stood foursquare to his principal, dressed in the jeans and windbreaker Tom already knew. The boy could hold himself so motionless that Tom became thrown into even greater disquiet.

"You wanted to see me, sir," Kent said from the doorway.

Tom rose, his right hand still near the middle of his tie, his heart doing a mad dance in his breast. "Come in . . . please. Close the door."

Kent did so, keeping ten feet between himself and Tom's desk while Tom waited breathlessly.

"Sit down," Tom managed. The boy came forward and sat.

"I'm sorry I didn't come yesterday," he said.

"Oh, that's okay. I probably handled it badly, summoning you that way."

"I didn't know what I'd say to you."

"I wasn't sure what I'd say to you either."

An awkward beat passed.

"I still don't."

"Me either."

Had their situation been less grave, they might have chuckled, but too much remained electric between them. Casting about for courage to go one step further, Kent let his eyes graze impersonal objects in the office until at last they settled on Tom. The father and son sat taking each other in under the first unhostile conditions since their relationship had been made known to both of them. What they saw rocked them both. Tom watched the boy's eyes move up to his hairline, across his cheeks, nose, mouth, throat before returning to his eyes. The room was bright with afternoon light coupled with overhead fluorescence. No detail was lost during that intense exchange.

"On Saturday when Mom told me . . ." The thought went unfinished as Kent swallowed and looked down.

"I know," Tom said, low in his throat. "It was the same for me the day you registered and I found out about you."

Kent fought for control and succeeded. "Did your wife tell you I apologized for barging into your house that way?"

"No . . . no, she didn't."

"Well, I am sorry, and that's the truth. I was just really bummed out."

"I understand. So was I."

A lull fell, filled only with the murmur of voices from beyond the door and the electronic nibbling of office machinery.

Finally Kent said, "I saw you watching me on the football field yesterday. I guess that's when I decided I should come and see you."

"I'm glad you did."

"Saturday was bad though."

"For me, too. My family didn't handle the shock too well."

"I could tell."

"If they've been acting differently toward you—" When Tom's words faltered, Kent made no reply, leaving Tom to scavenge around for pertinent dialogue. "If you want to change English classes, I can see to it."

"Does she want me out of there?"

"No."

"I bet she does."

"She says no. We talked about it."

Kent considered this news. "Maybe I should anyway."

"It's up to you."

"I know I'm going to be a big embarrassment to her."

"Kent, listen . . ." Tom leaned forward. His arm fell onto his oversized desk calendar. "I don't even know where to begin. There's so much we have to work through. Mrs. Gardner and I . . . we need to know what you want. If it'll be too uncomfortable for you to have the other students know, they don't have to. But if you want to be claimed in any public fashion, I'm ready to do that. Our situation here at school forces some issues that could otherwise have been left alone. Robby and Chelsea, for example . . ."

He watched Kent color at the mention of Chelsea, and felt sorry for him.

"We're all struggling, Kent, but I think our relationship—yours and mine—has to be worked out first, and while we're doing that the others will have to honor our wishes."

"But I don't know, Mr. Gardner . . ." When he raised his eyes again, Tom saw not a young man exceedingly mature for his age, but a troubled teenager like any other. The formal mode of address hung awkwardly between them until Kent admitted, "Heck, I don't even know what to call you anymore."

"I think you should go on calling me 'Mr. Gardner' if you're comfortable with that."

"Okay . . . Mr. Gardner . . ." He said it as if testing it before continuing. "I lived my whole life long not even knowing I had a dad, and now it's not just you, it's a half sister and half brother, too. I don't think you understand what it's like when you don't know where you came from. You think for sure that your father had to be some kind of bum, some . . . some homeless guy on welfare, since he never married your mother. You think only a real immoral creep would leave your mother pregnant, right? So I go through seventeen years thinking whoever you are, you're some jerk who I'd spit on if I ever got the chance. Only when I met you you weren't that kind. It takes some time to get used to that, and a half brother and half sister to boot."

Tom's reactions were rioting. There was so much more to be said while time ticked away and nudged at him to remember his meeting at the district office. Uppermost in his thoughts, however, was the fact that this boy had been seventeen years late meeting him, and Tom could not summon the wherewithal to draw their talk to a precipitous close.

"Just a minute," he said, and picked up the phone. With his eyes on Kent, he said, "Dora Mae, would you let Noreen know that I won't be going to the meeting at the district office? Tell her she'll be going without me so she can drive her own car."

"Not going? But it's the superintendent's cabinet meeting. You have to go."

"I know, but I just can't today. Ask Noreen to take notes for me, will you please?"

After a surprised pause, Dora Mae said, "Okay."

Speculation might run rampant among the office ranks and from there throughout the entire faculty, but Tom was a decision maker, and his decision was made within minutes after this boy walked through the door. He would not have dreamed of walking out and leaving this conversation unfinished.

He hung up and sat back in his chair. The interruption had cut some of the tension and given them a fresh starting point.

Kent took advantage of it. "Could we talk about you and my mom?" he asked.

"Of course."

"Why did you do that—meet her at some party and just . . . well, you know."

"What did she tell you?"

"That I was the product of a one-night stand. That she had one class with you and she'd always sort of liked you."

Tom swiveled his chair slightly to the right and picked up a glass paperweight shaped like an apple. It was transparent, imbedded with a pattern of air bubbles, topped off with two pointed brass leaves. He pressed one into the pad of his thumb as he spoke. "Nothing I say now will make it right. Nothing excuses an impetuous act like that, especially since I didn't use any birth control."

"I still want to know."

Tom considered the wisdom of telling one of Claire's students the intimate history of their relationship. Before he could reply, Kent asked, "Is it true that you were getting married the next week to Mrs. Gardner?"

The brass leaf riveted Tom's thumb. He set the apple down.

"Yes, it is."

"And Robby's the same age as me?"

"Yes, he is."

"When's his birthday?"

"December fifteenth."

Tom could see the math wizard compute the fact in a millisecond, along with the ramifications of Tom's guilt.

"You're right," Tom admitted. "I was rebelling, plain and simple. I wasn't ready to get married yet. But the rebellion ended then and there.

Mrs. Gardner and I have had a very happy marriage. I want you to know that, and I think I deserve to say that much in my own defense."

Kent absorbed the information, ran his hands back across his jaws, and clasped them momentarily behind his head, then let them slide down to his lap. "Wow," he breathed. "That's some can of worms I opened. No wonder they hate me."

"They don't hate you, Kent."

"Robby does."

"Robby . . . well, it's hard to characterize what Robby's feeling. If you want to know the truth, I think when you first came here he was jealous of you. Now I don't think he knows how to treat you. He's been laying pretty low over the weekend."

"And Mrs. Gardner won't talk to me."

"Give her time. She will."

"I'm not sure I want her to. What I mean is, I don't know where I belong in the middle of all this. Before—when I didn't know any of you—at least I knew where I belonged. With my mother. Just the two of us . . . we've always gotten along. Maybe I didn't know who my father was, but Mom and I did okay. Heck, I don't even know how to say this. It's just that since Saturday afternoon when I found out about you, everything changed. Only it didn't. I'm still with my mom, and you're still with your family, so what do we do now? Do I keep staring at Mrs. Gardner's shoes in English class? And trying to keep ten yards between me and Robby at football practice? And Chelsea . . . well, I'm so mixed up about her I just want to run the other way when I see her in the hall."

"I take it from things she said at home that the two of you had formed rather an attraction for each other?"

Kent stared at his knees. "Sort of," he admitted sheepishly.

"That's a tough one."

Kent nodded.

"She's not talking much around home yet, but I think she feels pretty much like you do. Like she was duped by me. And I'm at fault for not bringing this thing out in the open the day I first met you. But time is going to make a big difference between you two, and between you and

Robby, too. I think, as you grow older, you're going to realize that having a brother and a sister can be a blessing. At least, that's how I hope it turns out. My dad said as much when I talked to him yesterday."

Kent's head shot up.

"Your dad?"

Tom nodded solemnly. "Yes . . . a grandfather, too."

Kent swallowed and his lips parted. He stared in stupefaction.

"I told him about you because I needed his advice. He's a good man, full of old-fashioned morality and common sense." Tom thought to ask, "Would you like to see his picture?"

Kent replied, quietly, "Yes, sir."

Tom cocked his hips and drew a billfold from his rear pocket. He flipped it open to his parents' twenty-fifth wedding anniversary photo and passed it across the desk. "You'll probably never see him dressed in a suit and tie again. He wears his fishing clothes every place he goes. He lives in a cabin out on Eagle Lake next to his brother, Clyde. The two of them spend most of their time fishing and arguing and telling lies about who caught the biggest fish last year. And that's my mom. She was the salt of the earth. She died about five years ago."

Kent stared. On his palm the billfold lay warm with the body heat of the man across the desk. Staring up at him was the picture of a woman he wished he could have known. "I think I got her mouth," he said.

"She was a very pretty woman. My dad worshiped her. And though I heard her tell him off a time or two, I never heard him raise his voice to her. He called her names like 'my little petunia,' and 'my little dove,' and he loved to tease her. 'Course, she wasn't above teasing him back. As soon as you meet him, he'll probably tell you about the time she put the smelt in his boot."

"Smelt?" Kent lifted his eyes from the picture.

"It's a little fish, not even as big as a herring, indigenous to Minnesota. They run in the spring, and people flock to the streams up north to haul them out by the tubfuls. Mom and Dad went together every single year."

Mesmerized by the story, Kent handed the wallet back across the desk.

Tom folded it and put it away. "Dad would love to meet you. He said so right away."

Kent met Tom's eyes, his throat working. Tom could see that the idea of meeting a grandparent had him struggling with emotions.

"Somehow I don't think your children would like the idea of sharing their grandfather with me."

"Perhaps the choice isn't theirs to make. He's your grandfather as well as theirs, and a lot of people's wishes need to be considered here."

Kent thought awhile and asked, "What's his name?"

"Wesley," Tom answered.

"Wesley."

"After his mother's brother, who died as an infant. I have a brother, too. He'd be your uncle Ryan."

"Uncle Ryan," Kent repeated. And after a thoughtful moment, "Do I have any cousins?"

"Three of them: Brent, Allison, and Erica. And your aunt Connie. They live in St. Cloud."

"Do you see them often?"

"Not as often as I'd like."

"Are there any other relatives?"

"My uncle Clyde, the one who lives next to Dad at the lake. He's the only one."

Kent considered awhile and said, "I had a grandfather when I was little. But I don't remember him much. Now there's an aunt and uncle, cousins, even a grandfather." With a note of amazement, Kent said, "Gosh."

Tom dared a very small smile. "A whole family in a day."

"It's a lot to discover."

A bell rang, signaling the end of the school day. Kent looked up at the clock.

"Stay where you are," Tom said.

"But don't you have to be in the hall?"

"I'm the principal here. I make the rules, and this is more important than any hall duty. There are a couple of things I'd like to tell you."

Kent settled back in his chair, showing signs of surprise that he was allowed to command so much of his principal's time. Suddenly he remembered, "I have football practice though."

"Let me take care of that." Tom picked up the phone and dialed. "Bob, this is Tom. Will you excuse Kent Arens if he's a little late for practice today? I've got him in my office." He listened for a reply, said, "Thanks," and hung up. Letting his weight back in his chair he said, "Where were we?"

"You had something you wanted to tell me."

"Oh, yes. Your permanent record." Tom shook his head as if with a fond recollection. "That was something. The day after I found out about you, your records arrived, and I sat here at my desk, going back over every word that was written about you, and looking at your class pictures."

"My class pictures?"

"Most of them were in there, way back to kindergarten."

"I didn't know that. I mean, that teachers put things like that in there."

"They put a lot more than pictures in there. Samples of your first handwriting, an Easter poem you wrote one time, teachers' personal observations, as well as your very impressive report cards. I suppose what I felt that day was a lot like what you felt just now learning that you have a grandpa and an aunt and uncles. A little heartsick because I'd missed it all."

"You felt that way, too?"

"Of course I did."

"I thought it was just me."

"No, not just you at all. If I had known about you, I would have insisted on seeing you. I don't know how *much* we'd have seen each other, but I know we would have, because regardless of the circumstances between me and your mother, you're my son, and I don't take that responsibility lightly. I've already told your mom that I want to pay for your college education. I can do that much, at least."

"You'd do *that*?"

"I knew I'd do that within an hour after learning I was your father.

That feeling we were talking about"—Tom thumped his heart with one clenched fist—"in here. When I was looking at your school pictures, it felt like I was being crushed, and I knew—I just knew—that I had to try to make up for what we'd lost. But that's a lot of years, and I don't know if they can ever be overcome. I hope so though. I really hope so."

It was as close to making a prediction about their future as either of them had come. Kent was left uncomfortable by it, Tom could tell, so he went on.

"There's something else I want to say about going through that file. While I was reading it I came to respect your mother tremendously for the job she did raising you. Everything I saw told me how *there* she was for you, how vitally interested she was in your academic and personal life, how she stood up for you, taught you values and a respect for both education *and* educators. I have to tell you, there aren't a lot of parents like that anymore. I know. I deal with parents every day, and yours is the kind we could use more of."

Kent's face took on an even greater expression of amazement. Undoubtedly, he'd expected antagonism rather than praise for his mother, given the present situation. Hearing her lauded raised his respect for Tom another notch.

"Well, listen . . ." Tom pushed his chair back and stretched his arms against the edge of the desk. "I've kept you from your practice long enough, and if I hurry I can still get in on the end of the meeting at the district office." Tom stood, pushed his suit jacket back, and tugged up his belt. Kent got to his feet and went around behind his chair to keep farewells on an impersonal basis.

"We can talk anytime," Tom offered.

"Thank you, sir."

"You know where to find me."

"You know where to find me, too."

With a desk and a chair between them they felt buffered from the unwanted urge to touch each other some way.

"May I tell my mother about our talk?"

"Certainly."

"Will you be telling your family, too?"

"Do you want me to?"

"I don't know."

"I'd like to, with your permission."

"Robby, too?"

"Only if you say so."

"I don't know. It's been pretty hard on the football field, and now that I understand about our birthdays . . . well, I don't want to antagonize him any more."

"How about if I play it by ear? If I sense that he's still jealous or that he feels threatened in any way, I'll hold off."

Kent let his fingertips slip off the back of the chair as if to give approval by preparing to leave.

"I'm glad you came," Tom said.

"Yes, sir."

"Well"—Tom raised a hand—"have a good practice."

"Thank you, sir."

"And I'll be keeping my eye on you during the game Friday night."

"Yes, sir."

Kent took one step backward toward the door. Their hearts and wills strained toward one another, their connection reaching clear back to ancestors neither one of them had ever known or seen, bringing with it the compulsion to hug.

But touching in any way would have been absurd; they were, after all, still strangers.

"Well, goodbye," Kent said finally, opening the door.

"Goodbye."

He stood with his hand on the knob, looking back at his father—one last impulsive study—as if reconfirming how much they looked alike before heading for football practice.

Eleven

Homecoming was scheduled for the last Friday in September. Every year Tom dreaded Homecoming week. It meant disrupted and skipped classes, a lot of ornery teachers, an upsurge in student drinking, and general wildness, including necking in the halls. It brought complaints from homeowners in the vicinity of the school whose yards were TP'd, torn up by tires, or, on occasion, even urinated on. It meant, for Tom, a lot of after hours at school, where floats were being constructed, the gym decorated, and signs painted.

Homecoming had its upside though. During that week groups of students came together in a marvelous camaraderie that would, for many, bond them for the remainder of the school year. A similar fellowship blossomed between teachers and students who worked together on the various projects. The faculty had the opportunity to see a new and different side of the kids, who became enthusiastic and inventive as they threw themselves into undertakings in which they were vitally interested. The students often surprised the teachers by showing dependability and resourcefulness they'd hidden until now, and in some cases, remarkable leadership qualities as well. During those days of planning floats, dances, pep fests, and painting signs, they used their ingenuity to solve problems, delegate work, and meet schedules.

But Homecoming week brought something more to Humphrey High, a vitality it lacked at other times of the year, an upbeat tempo that caught and motivated the entire school population. For many, the excitement would culminate not at the football game on Friday night, but at the crowning of the king and queen candidates on Friday afternoon.

First, though, came the announcement of the candidates.

Stationing himself just inside the main door of the gym for the Monday afternoon pep fest, Tom felt the tension everywhere—in the office secretaries who had counted the votes of the senior class; in Nancy Halliday, the speech teacher and the only member of the faculty who knew the results; in ten of her speech students, who had been sworn to secrecy and had prepared introductions that they would deliver in the next thirty minutes; in the faces of the class leaders, the popular ones who stood a chance of being singled out by one of Nancy's students and escorted to the stage.

The excitement was infectious and the student body rambunctious as they crowded into the gymnasium. The pep band was blaring. Drum-beats reverberated off the ceiling. The sun streamed through the sky-lights and lit the hardwood floor, turning the room gold. Red, red everywhere: on the bleachers and the folding chairs set up on half the gym floor where the senior class would sit—red sweaters, red pom-poms, red baseball caps, and red letter jackets with white H's sewn proudly in place.

While they filed past Tom, he waited only for a glimpse of Claire.

Nothing had changed at home. For two weeks the deep freeze had continued, until bedtime had become an exercise in stoicism. She had begun play practice in the evenings, so most days the two of them hardly saw each other until they claimed their distinct halves of the mattress to lie stiff and tense, pretending the other wasn't there.

When she finally entered the gym Tom's heart actually jumped. He smiled, but she glanced aside, her expression disdainful, and moved on with the crowd.

The festivities began. The band played the school song. The cheerleaders cheered. The co-captains of the football team spoke. Coach Gorman was roasted. Six of the less inhibited members of the football team came on the floor in line-dance formation, with bare midriffs, stuffed bathing suit tops, and miniskirts, kicking their hairy legs in an oafish parody of the cancan.

One of the dancers was Robby.

Tom stood near the wall off one end of the bleachers, laughing. The boys swung around, presented their butts and wiggled them, faced the bleachers, joined arms, and went for a high kick, as graceful as a herd of buffalo. They put their hands on their knees, jumped in, jumped back, shimmied until their fake breasts flopped, and raised an uproar of laughter that nearly drowned out the music.

It had been weeks since Tom had lost himself in a hearty bout of laughter. He turned to look up at the bleachers and find Claire. She too was belly-laughing at their son, rearing back with her mouth open and her cheeks curved like red apples. Her merriment wrenched Tom's heart. He wanted back what they'd had, this ability to enjoy all of life again, to be restored by its amusements. They should be sitting together in the midst of this celebration, sharing their uninhibited son, turning from him to the mirth in each other's eyes. But Claire was alone up there, sitting in the crowd with some other English teachers, and he was alone down here. *Look at me, Claire,* he thought, *you know where I am. I'm down here wanting an end to this cold war between us. Please, look down, now while Robby is showing us all we have to fight for.*

But she refused.

The parody ended and the senior class president quieted the crowd with a brief explanation of how the king and queen candidates had been chosen. Tension erased the buzz of voices from the student body. It brought a deeper slouch to the burnouts and a squaring of posture to the leaders. Nancy Halliday's speech students were brought forward to the middle of the gym floor to introduce the royalty-elect.

Home Song

Sabra Booker, a pretty and poised girl, with a rich contralto voice, read a brief bio of the first candidate: honor student, student council member, lettered athlete in various sports, member of the yearbook staff, member of the Math Club—the credits could have belonged to dozens of seniors, both boys and girls. As she left the mike stand, the band struck up a tinny rendition of "Beauty and the Beast." She strolled the center aisle of the main floor, stopping to scan various rows of seats, reversing directions, drawing out the suspense until finally reaching toward the third seat from the aisle and summoning a stocky blond boy named Dooley Leonard. As he got to his feet, surprised and pleased, his face flushed, the entire school population burst into applause and started thrusting their fists in the air, chanting, *"Duke, Duke, Duke!"* while he walked up to the stage on Sabra Booker's arm.

A queen candidate was named next, another achiever named Madelaine Crowe, who was escorted to the stage by a tall senior boy named Jamie Beldower.

After that, Terri McDermott, who had dated Robby last year, went out to pick another king candidate. She, like the others, extended the anticipation by walking back and forth, up and down, pausing to consider sections of students before finally marching toward a row of boys with a step that said, *This is it.*

She pointed straight at Robby Gardner.

Pride shot through Tom while he watched Robby unfold and tug at his clothes with the typical self-consciousness and shy pride of a normal teenage boy. As Robby made his way past six sets of knees, Tom flashed a glance at Claire. She was on her feet, beaming and applauding like a rabid rock fan. Her gaze veered to Tom, the pull too strong, the habit too established to resist—and he felt her first real warmth in weeks. It redoubled the swell of emotion in his breast as they stood lauding their son, separated by rows of noisy people, still surprised by the realization that the boy who'd been introduced, among other credits, as "someone who's lettered in every sport imaginable" was actually Robby.

Chelsea was on her feet jumping and clapping with the other cheerleaders. Some teachers beside Tom offered congratulations, and Claire, too, was enfolded in felicity as she sat down and diverted her attention to those seated nearby.

Tom watched Robby walk to the stage with Terri McDermott, a girl he'd always liked, the two of them talking and smiling from their disparate heights while the student body chanted, "Rob, Rob, Rob!"

After that, "Beauty and the Beast" swelled and faded, and the candidates seemed to wane in importance as their principal watched them plucked from among their peers and singled out for this honor that would keep them in the limelight for the rest of this school year and in the memories of their classmates for the rest of their lives.

Claire had been a homecoming queen candidate in high school, but he hadn't known her then. He'd seen pictures of her though, in her yearbook, her long ironed hair parted down the middle.

The last candidate was being introduced, and the list of credits sounded like so many others that Tom paid little attention—student council, Math Club, DECA Club, honor student, a whole range of sports. Then something caught his ear, some organization HHH didn't have, some club with a Spanish name, and he perked up as a stately speech student named Saundra Gibbons executed the tension-mounting search for the right candidate.

Some gut instinct told Tom, even before Saundra paused in the aisle beside him, that she would single out Kent Arens.

When she did, the auditorium broke into riotous applause. "K.A.! K.A.! K.A.!" they shouted. The football team did high-fives, and the student population cheered their newest gridiron hero. Over the PA system a voice overrode the band. "Oh yeah, we forgot to tell you . . . most of his life he lived in Austin, Texas. He's only been here for three weeks. What a way to welcome him to HHH and Minnesota!"

Kent acted too stunned to rise. While Saundra was still reaching out a hand, Tom fired a glance at Claire. She was drop-dead shocked and clapping as lamely as if under the influence of a sedative. He found Chelsea, standing totem-straight with both hands over her mouth. Up on the stage, Robby was clapping dutifully, unable to do otherwise, showcased as he was before the entire school population. By the time Tom's eyes found Claire again she was bending at the hip to resume her seat. For a moment she was cut off from view, then those around her sat and he caught her laser stare shooting at him like a thin red line capable of cutting the retinas out of his eyes.

She looked away first. Whatever smile she'd given earlier had left no more mark than the band director's baton. "Beauty and the Beast" droned on and on as Kent moved up the steps to the stage and shook hands with the other candidates. He reached Robby, and from thirty feet away Tom felt their reluctance to touch. They did what protocol demanded, perfunctorily, then Kent took his place beside one of the queen candidates, who gave him a kiss on the cheek.

Tom was their principal. His congratulations were expected, even prized. He moved toward them with emotions warring within him, the irony of this day creating a pain between his shoulders as if a hatchet were buried there.

Robby's was the third hand he shook. As he smiled into his son's eyes he saw the questions that others didn't see. He saw this moment of glory addled by the muddle of relationships represented in this gymnasium. And though he was a principal who wasn't supposed to play favorites, he was a father, too, and he caught Rob's neck in the crook of one arm and gave him a hug.

"I'm so darned proud of you," he said at Rob's ear.

"Thanks, Dad."

He moved on down the line—girl, boy, girl, boy—until he came to Kent and shook his hand, the first touch they had shared since discovering their relationship. Tom covered their joined hands with his free one and felt his own gripped so strongly his wedding ring gouged his other fingers. He was quite unprepared for the vehemence of his own reaction, the urge to hug Kent, to hide his stinging eyes in a paternal embrace. But behind him Claire glared and Chelsea watched, mystified and confused, so he could only hide his feelings and hope Kent read them in his eyes.

"Congratulations, Kent. We're so proud to have you at our school."

"Thank you, sir," Kent answered. "I'm proud to be here, but I'm not sure I deserve this."

"Your classmates say you do. Enjoy it, son."

The word quavered both their souls while this first crushing grip continued. Tom saw surprise darken Kent's eyes before he finally pulled free and turned to address the student body.

It was difficult to marshal his thoughts with both of his sons standing behind him, his daughter and wife before him, but he suppressed his personal involvement to do his job.

"I look forward to this day every year, the day when you seniors cast your vote of approval for ten of your classmates who exemplify all the best that a student, a friend, a member of the school community can represent. In the past it might have been true that the election of a homecoming king and queen was nothing more than a beauty contest. But the ten students standing before you today are leaders, each and every one of them. They're kids who spend far more than thirty hours of classroom time in this building every week. They represent friendship, generosity, respect, academic and athletic leadership, and more."

Tom let his eyes scan the bleachers while he went on speaking. Frequently they stalled on Claire, who sat for the first minute with one forearm over her crossed knees, studying the underside of her watchband. The next time he looked she was staring at Robby and gave the impression of adamantly refusing to lock eyes with her husband.

His speech ended. The coach said one parting sentence and thanked the students and teachers who'd planned the program. The cheerleaders led the assembly in the school song, and the pep fest concluded.

The stage became a mob of people, Claire among them. She hugged Robby but managed to sidestep Tom. His heart sank while he wished she'd come to him, slip her arm around his waist, and say, "Can you believe it? Great son we've got, huh?"

But their estrangement had only been exacerbated by this ceremony today, and he was left to bump around the crowd accepting congratulations from everyone but the one who mattered most.

Then he turned, and there was Chelsea, looking up at him with wounded eyes. She had heat spots in her cheeks and he read very clearly how it hurt her to see Claire giving him the cold shoulder here at this auspicious moment. Her confusion over Kent showed clearly in her eyes, and in her hesitation to hug her father. Before she could, someone spoke at Tom's side and he turned his attention elsewhere.

As Chelsea sought out her brother she felt as if she were on an emotional bronco ride, one minute airborne, the next jarred to earth by underlying realities.

"Robby!" she said, reaching him, hugging him, feigning glee for his benefit. "I'm so proud! Mr. King Candidate!"

"How about that?" he said, bending down to reach her. She heard the subdued note in his voice, and knew he shared the same confusion of feelings as she, with their mother ignoring their dad, and Kent Arens sharing this stage.

When he released her they became an island of suppressed emotion in the middle of the celebration. What was happening to their family? And when would everybody in the whole school know about it?

"Listen," she said, "you deserve it. I know you're going to win."

He gave her a weak smile and she was turned loose to face the daunting prospect of coming eye to eye with the half brother she had kissed. She glanced his way and caught him quickly looking away from her. She had seen scenes like this in movies, two people in a crowd, pretending indifference while the maze of others hemmed them both in and out of each other's reach. He swung his head and their eyes met while voices and motion swirled between them, but the kiss was too grievous a mistake to bury, and their embarrassment too profound to be breached.

She turned away without congratulating him.

The Gardner family reconvened over supper that night and put on a mighty fine show for one another. But Chelsea was not convinced. The divisiveness pervaded even the celebration for Robby's benefit.

Its threat was evident in the careful distance Tom and Claire always kept between them, even when scurrying around the kitchen like busboys. It was evident in the quick flicking departure of her eyes from his whenever their glances met, and in the fact that Kent's name was never mentioned though all the other candidates were discussed and dissected as potential kings or queens.

Toward the end of the meal Robby said to Tom and Claire with a look of abject love in his eyes, "Listen, you guys, I know the custom is for every candidate to be escorted into the coronation ceremonies by his parents, and I just want to make sure you'll both be there."

"Of course we will!" they said in unison.

"One on either side of me."

"Absolutely."

"Yes."

"And you'll come to the dance afterwards, together?"

"Absolutely," Tom answered.

And after a pause, "Sure," Claire said, glancing safely down at her plate.

Always now, there was this stutter step whenever Robby or Chelsea made a move to get the two of them to reconcile. Tom would have made every effort, and Claire pretended she would, but it was a false front.

Neither of her children knew how to make her forgive their father.

That night in her bedroom, Chelsea sat on her bed staring at the wall. On the chair in the corner her homework waited. She had no ambition to open a book or lift a pencil. The house was too quiet, her mother gone to play practice as usual, and her dad sitting in the living room with some financial reports on his lap. Robby had gone to Brenda's house as soon as he could to escape the tension around this place, but Chelsea couldn't even call Erin to talk about it, because if she did everyone in school would find out and their family would be the subject of gossip from one end of the district to the other.

Erin had been asking questions lately and watching Chelsea curiously, especially whenever Kent's name was mentioned. She knew something major was up.

Home Song

Something major, for sure, Chelsea thought. Her family was falling apart, and she was trying to get her mother and father to talk to each other, and crying secretly in her room at night, and trying to avoid Kent, and wishing she could tell Erin everything. But she just *couldn't!* Because underneath she was mortified by what her dad had done, and by what she had done with Kent. And she didn't know whether her mom was right to shun her dad or not, and if she herself was right to shun Kent, and how she should treat him now that she knew they were related. If only she could talk to Erin about it. Talk to somebody! But even her counselors at school were bound to gossip. Heck, their offices were right next to Daddy's, and if they knew, it would be just awful for him.

She curled on her side in her oversized letter sweater and lay in the dark with the sleeves pulled over her hands.

Meanwhile, at play practice, a forty-year-old single English teacher named John Handelman supervised the building of the flats and watched Claire closely, offering only a smile of invitation to talk about whatever was bothering her that neither one of them had spoken about.

On the day after the naming of the Homecoming royalty, Tom found a note in his mailbox at school.

Dear Mr. Gardner,

Mrs. Halliday told all of us candidates that the custom is to have our parents escort us into the coronation ceremonies. I just wanted you to know that if it were possible, I'd have you walk in beside me, and that I'd be proud to have you there. Don't worry, I won't ask you because I'd never want to make any trouble for you. But I just wanted you to know.

Kent

Tom's eyes welled up and he had to go into the boys' washroom and hide in a stall while the emotion leveled itself out.

That night when Claire got home from play practice, Tom was freshly showered and sitting up in bed wearing pajama bottoms and smelling of after-shave. When she slipped between the sheets and shut the light out, he put his hand on her in the dark and tried to kiss her, but she pushed him away and said, "Don't Tom. I just can't."

The coronation ceremony was held in the school auditorium at two o'clock Friday afternoon. All the parents gathered in a room at the rear, preparatory to escorting their children into the festivities.

For the first time, Claire saw Monica Arens.

She wasn't pretty, but she had a boardroom chic that stemmed from expensive clothing and understated jewelry. Her chosen hairstyle did little to flatter her face, but open any classy magazine and it could be found on a dozen pages. What she lacked in pulchritude she made up for in bearing. Everything about her said, Don't mess with me.

Claire turned her back on Monica and her son, pretending they were not in the room. She was aware, however, that Tom, as principal, was forced to divide his loyalties and congratulate the parents of *all* the candidates. When he spoke to his long-ago lover and shook her hand, Claire could not control a perverse urge to watch. Jealousy and hurt robbed her of all pleasure in this day, and she blamed Tom for robbing her of the joy she should be experiencing on this once-in-a-lifetime event.

Little warmth radiated from Claire on her walk up the aisle with Robby. She flanked him on the left while Tom did so on the right. At the stage steps they kissed him, then sat side by side in the front row. Throughout the ceremonies she spared no word or touch for her husband, focusing on Robby and no one else.

Beside her, Tom read brittle animosity in her every movement and pose. She held her hands too high while applauding, and lifted her chin too sharply while watching. Sometimes she actually tossed her head. When Duke Leonard was pronounced king, Tom sensed Claire bristling and knew she'd wanted Robby to win for many of the wrong reasons.

With a sinking feeling he admitted again that he didn't like her this way at all. The many virtues for which he'd fallen in love with her were gone, and he was the one who had chased them away.

They danced together at the Homecoming dance and he discovered that a man could dislike a woman's hard side and still love her. And he did still love his wife. When his hand touched the small of her back he felt sick with longing and tried to pull her closer. She arched away and said, "I guess this is as good a time to talk to you as any, Tom. I've made a decision, but I held off telling you until Homecoming was over so I wouldn't spoil it for the kids. Well, now it's over, and I can't live like this any longer. I want a separation."

His feet stopped. Fear gripped him.

"No, Claire, come on, we can—"

"I thought I could get over it, but I can't. I'm miserable. I hurt. I feel like crying all the time. I can't keep on facing you in bed every night."

"Claire, you can't mean this. You don't throw away eighteen years without trying."

"I've been trying."

"Like hell you have! You've been . . ." He realized he'd shouted and two students dancing nearby turned to gape. "Come on!" he ordered, and hauled her by the hand out of the gym, down the hall past the swimming pool to the core of the building, where he unlocked the glass doors to the office. "Let me go!" she ordered halfway there. "Tom, for heaven's sake, you've already made a spectacle out of us by storming out of the dance that way!"

Once inside his office he slammed the door. "We're not separating!" he shouted.

"You're not the only one making this decision!"

"Before we even try counseling or anything?"

"Counseling for what? *I* didn't do anything!"

"Including forgiving me! Can't you even *try* to forgive me, Claire?"

"Not while you're having an affair with her."

"I'm not having an affair with her! Claire, I love you!"

"I don't believe you."

"Oh, you don't believe me. And you think you don't need counseling?"

"Don't you criticize me, mister!" She poked him in the chest. "Don't you *dare* criticize me! I'm not the one who was unfaithful! I'm not the one who fathered a son that our children have to cringe about! I'm not the one who kept it a secret for eighteen years. I watched your eyes when the king candidates were announced. I saw the expression in them. You need to acknowledge him, Tom, can't you see that? You're dying to let the world know he's yours. Well, let them know! But don't expect me to be living with you while you do it. It's embarrassing enough to be working in this building with you, to take orders from you day after day! Have you even considered what an object of pity I'm going to be when this gets out?"

"Then why let it out? Work with me. We'll go to counseling together. This is worth saving, Claire."

She took a step back, spread two hands in the air, and took a long, slow blink. "I need to be away from you, Tom."

His panic spread.

"Claire, please . . ."

"No . . ." She retreated another step. "I do. I feel betrayed and angry and like . . . like lashing out at you all the time! The stress is so god-awful I wake up in the morning and don't know how I'll be able to function at school all day long. I take orders from you in teachers' meetings when all I want to do is curse at you. I see you in the hall and I'd walk two miles the long way around to avoid you if I could. And I just can't fake it at the dinner table in front of the kids anymore."

"Listen to yourself! Claire, what's happening to you? You used to fight fair. What about that respect we always promised to one another when we disagreed?"

"It's gone." She spoke more calmly. "That's the scariest thing for me, Tom. My respect for you is gone. And when I felt it go, I realized that all these years I've been spouting platitudes. Respect, sure, it's easy enough to preach about when your marriage has never been tested. Now that mine has, I find myself reacting a little differently."

"And I hate it!"

"It or me?"

"Oh, come on, Claire, when have I ever acted as if I hated you? It's the brittleness I hate, the calculated coldness you can turn on like a tap when you want to. You seem to be taking joy in punishing me. You treat me as if my sin was unpardonable."

"To me right now, it is, especially when I have to be reminded of it every day when your son walks into my classroom."

"If you want him transferred, I'll transfer him. I told you that."

"Transferring him won't cancel his existence. He *is*. And he's *yours*. And his mother is here in this school district, and you've been seeing her again, and I can't live with that, so I want out."

He declared through bared teeth: "*I am not having an affair with Monica Arens!* Why won't you believe me?"

"I wish I could, Tom . . . I wish I could. Why didn't you tell me about talking to her in your car that day?"

"I . . ." He raised his arms to shoulder level and let them drop. "I don't know. I should have, but I didn't. I'm sorry. I was scared."

"Well, I'm scared too. Can't you see that?"

"Then why are you running away from me?"

"Because I need time, Tom." She put a hand on her heart. Her voice had softened. "I can't forgive you. I can't face you. I can't sleep with you. I don't know what to say to the children. I need time."

"How much time?"

"I don't know."

With the dimming of her anger his fear escalated.

"Claire, please, don't do this."

"I have to."

"No, you don't." He took her arm, but she turned away.

"Don't. I've made up my mind," she said calmly.

"We could—"

"Don't make it any harder, Tom, please."

Terrified, he turned away and stood at the window near the gallery of family pictures. Against the blackness outside, his reflection showed as a silhouette with no face. The fluorescent lights behind him put a halo around his form. He could see Claire's reflection, too. She was standing in front of his desk, studying his back with her chin high and resolution clear in the set of her shoulders.

He sighed and asked sadly, "What about the kids?"

"They should stay with whoever remains in the house."

"You're not willing to try counseling, not even for their sake?"

"Not right now."

"It'll kill them. Especially Chelsea."

"I know. That's the hard part."

He felt as if a catheter had shot dye into his veins, a swift burning all along them, straight from the heart. He turned, pleading, "Then try, Claire, for their sake."

Had her animosity not fled he might have believed there was hope in arguing further, but she spoke as calmly as if she were putting a child to bed. "I can't, Tom. For mine."

"Claire," he appealed, reaching out, taking two steps toward her, but she warned him with the faintest retreat not to touch her. "Jesus," he whispered, and moved defeatedly around his desk. He dropped heavily into his chair and sat with an elbow on his calendar and a hand to his face.

A minute ticked by. Two. Claire stood as before, waiting, while the idea of separating brought its dreads to be reckoned with. Finally he let his hand drop and looked up at her. "Claire, I love you," he said as earnestly as ever in his life. "Please, please, don't do this."

"I can't help it, Tom. I know you won't believe it, but you're not the only one who's scared. I'm scaring myself." She pressed her heart. "I was always one of those women who loved so intensely, always worrying in the back of my mind how I could possibly live without you. I always thought, 'Gosh, he had to marry me,' and that was my insecurity, eating away at me, always making me think I loved you more than you loved me. And then I found out what you'd done and this . . . this very, very frightening person took over inside of me, this woman I didn't know was there before, and she stood up and demanded to be heard, and I thought, 'Where did she come from? This can't be me speaking and acting this way, can it?' But it is, and right now I have to be this way. I have to distance myself from you because I hurt so badly. Can you understand that, Tom?"

He tried answering once, but his throat wouldn't cooperate. "N . . . no," he finally managed in a broken voice.

She remained dry-eyed and calm. "How can you understand it when I don't understand it myself?"

She walked over to study the pictures on his windowsill—their family, so happy and carefree in years gone by. She touched one of the frames as she might have touched the fine hair of their children when they were infants.

"I'm sorry, Claire. How many ways can I say it?"

"I know you are."

"Then why won't you relent a little and give us another chance?"

"I don't know, Tom. I have no other answer for you."

They remained a long time in silence broken only by the distant sound of music from the gym, where their children were dancing. Once he sighed and wiped tears from his eyes. Once she picked up a picture of the four of them and studied it awhile before replacing it on the sill, very carefully, the way an intruder would if she knew someone were dozing in the next room.

Finally she turned and said, "I'm perfectly willing to be the one to go. You may stay in the house if you want."

He wondered if a man could actually die of a broken heart. "I couldn't do that. I couldn't ask you to leave."

"I'm the one forcing the issue. I should be the one to go."

"This'll be bad enough for the children without losing you, too."

"Then you want me to stay and you to go?"

"I want us both to stay, Claire, can't you understand that?" He felt himself on the verge of full-scale weeping.

She walked toward the door and said quietly, "I'll go."

He was up like a shot, around the desk, holding her by one arm. "Claire . . ." He'd never been so scared in his life. "Jesus . . ." She didn't even pull away. She didn't need to, for she'd done it days ago. "Where would you go?"

She shrugged, staring forlornly at the carpet.

After a while she looked up and asked, "Where would you?"

"To my dad's, I suppose."

She dropped her chin. "Well, maybe . . ."

Thus it was decided: two simple words and a wife dropping her chin, and his course of action was set.

They left the dance together, left their children celebrating youth and victory in a loud gymnasium abounding with life. Now that it was decided, Claire remained amenable to walking at his side into a blue-lit parking lot, sitting beside him in his car while they rode the couple of miles home, waiting while he opened the door and let her into the house before him.

They stopped in the dark, surrounded by familiar, looming shapes of possessions they had accumulated over the years—furniture, lamps, pictures on the walls—things they had chosen together in times when their future seemed unshakable.

"When will you go?" she asked.

"Tomorrow."

"Then I'll sleep on the sofa tonight."

"No, Claire . . ." He caught her hand. "No, please."

"Don't, Tom." She gently pulled away, and he heard her moving toward the hall. He lifted his face, as if shouting at God, and pulled in some huge drafts of air to keep himself from bawling. Faster, deeper, faster, deeper, until he'd bested the urge. Then he went toward the distant bedroom light and stood in the doorway looking in. She was already in her bedclothes, crossing the room, but stopped warily when he appeared, as if expecting him to come in and make advances.

Instead, he said, "You can stay in here. I'll sleep on the sofa."

Chelsea found him when she came in near one o'clock, out on the screened porch in the chilly night air, sitting on a rocker without rocking, staring at the night without seeing.

"Dad, you okay?" Chelsea asked, rolling the door back a few inches.

It took a bit before he responded. "I'm okay, honey."

"How come you're sitting out here? It's cold."

"I couldn't sleep."

"You sure you're okay?"

"I'm sure. Go on to bed, honey."

She paused uncertainly. "It was a nice dance, Dad, wasn't it?"

In the dark she could make out his form. He didn't even turn his head her way. "Yes, it was a nice dance."

"And I'm proud of Robby even though he didn't win."

"So am I."

She waited uncertainly for an explanation that didn't come.

"Well . . . okay then, 'night, Dad."

"'Night."

Chelsea was waiting in Robby's room when he came in fifteen minutes later.

"Shh," she whispered. "It's me."

"Chels?"

"Something's wrong."

"What do you mean?"

"Did you go through the family room?"

"No."

"Dad's still sitting up on the screen porch."

"He and Mom left the dance early."

"I know."

They worried awhile together, then Chelsea said, "He never sits up late. He always says there aren't enough hours in the day."

They worried some more, to no avail.

"Well, heck . . ." Robby said. "I don't know . . . Did you talk to him?"

"Just for a minute."

"What'd he say?"

"Not much."

"Yeah, that's the trouble around here lately, he and Mom never say much."

In the morning Chelsea awakened shortly after nine and got up to go to the bathroom. Passing the open doorway of her parents' bedroom, she saw her dad moving around inside. He was dressed in old clothes and there were cardboard boxes and two open suitcases on the bed. She stood in the doorway barefoot, an oversized dinosaur T-shirt brushing the tops of her knees.

"Dad, what're you doing?"

He straightened with a stack of underwear in his hands, then stuffed them into a suitcase and reached out a hand toward her. "Come here," he said quietly.

She advanced cautiously, put her hand in his, and they sat on the edge of the rumpled bed between the boxes. He took her in his arms and rested his cheek on her hair. "Honey, your mom wants me to leave for a while."

"No!" she said, gripping his sweatshirt in a fist. "I knew that's what it was! Please don't do it, Daddy!" She hadn't called him Daddy since the end of elementary school.

"I'm going to move out to Grandpa's cabin for a while."

"No!" She tore herself out of his arms, screaming. "Where is she? She can't make you do this!" Her rampage carried her out the door and down the hall with Tom at her heels. She shouted all the way down the stairs to the main level. "You can't make him do this! Mother, where are you? What is going *on* around here? You're married! You can't just pretend you're not anymore and send him to Grandpa's house!" Claire intercepted her at the foot of the stairs. "You're his wife, Mother! What are you doing?"

Robby came flying out of his bedroom, awakened by the shouting, stumbling downstairs, too. "What's goin' on?" He was tousled, puffy-eyed, disoriented.

"Dad's moving out of the house, Robby. Tell him he can't! Tell Mom she can't make him go!" Chelsea was weeping wildly.

"Chelsea, we're not getting a divorce." Claire tried to calm her.

"Not yet, you aren't, but you will if he goes! Mom, don't let him! Daddy, please . . ." She spun from one parent to the other. The family seemed misplaced in the front entry hall among all the tears and shouting so early in the morning.

Tom tried for calm. "Your mother and I talked it over last night."

"But why are you doing it? You never tell us anything! You pretend nothing's wrong, but the two of you don't even look at each other anymore! Are you having an affair, Daddy, is that it?"

"No, I'm not, Chelsea, but your mother won't believe me."

"Why won't you believe him, Mother?" She swung on Claire.

"It's more than that, Chelsea."

"But if he says he isn't, why won't you believe him? Why won't you talk to us? Robby and I are part of this family, too, and we should have a say. We don't want him to go, do we, Robby?"

Robby was hanging back, still reeling from the violent wake-up call. He stood near the coat-closet door, looking tentative and confused in a stretched-out black T-shirt and gray sweatpants.

"Mom, why are you asking him to go?" His more controlled bearing slowed the emotional gait of the entire scene.

Claire said, "I need some time away from him, that's all. The situation is smothering me and I don't know what else to do."

"But if he goes, Chelsea is right. How can you work it out again?"

She looked down at the carpet.

Robby looked at Tom. "Dad?"

"I'll still be here whenever you need me, or when she needs me, for that matter."

"No you won't. You'll be at Grandpa's."

"You can call anytime and I'll come over, and I'll see you at school every day."

Robby sank against the door frame and whispered to the floor, "Shit."

Nobody rebuked him as they would have before. The silence was oppressive, laden with fear, confusion, grief. They were all thinking about school, where they'd bump into one another and everyone they knew would be asking questions. They imagined the future, when they'd be split apart, living in two houses.

Tom finally spoke. "Hey, listen, you two . . ." He collected them each in an arm and curled their inert forms against him. "I still love you. Your mom still loves you. That's never going to change."

Chelsea said, "If you loved us you'd stay together."

Tom met Claire's eyes beyond the children's heads but there would be no dissuading her, he could see. She hurt for the children, and for herself, but not for their relationship. She wanted the separation and nothing would sway her. She had developed a body language as readable as an English textbook. It said, "Keep away. I'm taking care of me and that's the way it is." While he hugged his children, he saw through her needs to her selfishness and detested it. She stood near the kitchen doorway with her damned arms crossed again while he was left to offer the children what little consolation he could muster. He glared at her and she finally budged to come over and rub the children's shoulders.

"Come on . . . I'll make you some breakfast."

But it wasn't breakfast they wanted.

Leaving was so damned painful Tom felt as if his heart were being eviscerated. He slammed the trunk and stood beside it. A Saturday in autumn, sharp-edged, resplendent, with the trees turning to gilt and a leaf falling there and here. Sounds carried from neighbors' yards, each crystalline in clarity, even the smallest metallic click from a combination window being lifted. The time of year in itself held a sadness, with its final days of warmth and welcome to the outdoors, its fading flowers at doorsides even as the verdant grass put on a late show.

He heaved a sigh and forced his legs to carry him back to the house to say goodbye.

Chelsea's bedroom door was closed. He tapped. "Chelsea?" No answer, so he intruded. She was sitting on her pillow hugging a pink teddy bear, staring at her window curtain with her mouth pulled small and defensive. He went and sat beside her.

"Gotta go," he said in a croaking whisper, tucking a single strand of hair behind her left ear.

She refused to acknowledge him. Tears trembled on her lower eyelids.

"You know Grandpa's number if you want me for anything, okay, sweetheart?"

Her chin and lips were set like a plaster cast of themselves. A fat tear spilled over and left a shiny streak on her cheek.

"I love you, honey. And who knows, maybe your mother is right. Maybe some time apart will get her mind straight."

Chelsea refused to blink though her eyes must have been burning. He rose and turned away.

"Daddy, wait!" She catapulted off the bed into his arms. Her voice came to him muffled against his sweatshirt as she clung to his neck. "Why?"

He had no answer so he kissed her hair, set her from him, and left.

In the kitchen Claire was standing beside the table, making sure a chair stood between him and her. Did she have to guard herself that way? As if he were a wife-beater, he thought. He still loved her, didn't she really understand that? Didn't she know he was dying here, walking away from all that was dear?

"They shouldn't be left alone so much now. What about play practice? You want me to come over in the evenings when I don't have meetings?"

"Since when don't you have evening meetings?"

"Look. I'm not going to stand here and argue anymore. You want me out, I'm going. Just pay attention to them. They're going to be vulnerable to a hundred new problems, and I don't want them hurt any more than they've already been."

"You talk as if I don't love them anymore."

"You know, Claire, I'm beginning to wonder."

He left her with that stinging rebuke and went out through the family room and garage. Robby was leaning against the front fender of Tom's car, his arms crossed, scuffing at the surface of the blacktop driveway with the rubber toe of his sneaker.

Tom got his keys out and studied them on his palm awhile, then studied his son's downcast head. "You help your mom now whenever you can. This is hard for her too, you know."

Robby nodded, still scuffing.

Autumn, uncaring, shimmered around them. The late morning sun reflected off the windshield. The shadows from the trees grew thinner every day. It wasn't too long ago he and Robby had leaned against a car and talked like this about moral dilemmas that formed a man's character. The irony of that day stung them both as they remembered.

"Listen, son." Tom shifted his stance and placed himself squarely before Robby with both hands on Robby's shoulders. "I'm going to be worried about you and your sister. If you see any fallout from this threatening her in any way, you'll tell me, won't you? I mean, if she should start smoking, or drinking, or running around with different friends, or staying out late—anything, okay?"

Robby nodded.

"And I'm going to ask her the same thing about you."

Robby gave up scuffing and let his mournfulness show. Big jiggly tears blurred the outline of his Nikes. His nostrils worked like bellows and he simply could not lift his head and face his dad.

Tom grabbed him and hugged him hard.

"And don't ever think it's not okay to cry. I've cried plenty myself lately. Sometimes it makes you feel better." He stepped back. "I gotta go. Call me at Grandpa's if you need me."

Only when he'd slammed himself into the car and was rolling down his window did Robby pull away from the fender and look at him.

Where will he go? Tom wondered. Who will he talk to? What will it be like in this house after I'm gone? Don't let him fall prey to depression and retaliation like the hundreds of kids who've come through my office over the years, destroyed by their parents' divorce. Don't let this ruin him or Chelsea.

"Hey, heads up," Tom said, summoning some false cheer. "I'm not done with her yet."

But he received no smile from his son as he started the engine and backed away.

Twelve

At the lake autumn was even more resplendent, adding torment to this already tormented day. The water, at rest, reflected the shoreline like glass. The sound of a distant motor carried from a full mile away, while a small fishing boat marred the perfection of the surface, curling it back like blue rose petals. The summer birds had left the yard in the keeping of a flock of cedar waxwings who were dining on cotoneaster berries around the edge of the porch.

Tom climbed the two wide wooden steps and opened the screen door. It had an old-fashioned spring, the kind you can pinch your fingers in if you're a boy with nothing better to do than open and close, open and close it until your mother comes to see what in the world you're doing. The *twin-n-ng* of that spring brought a nostalgic ache to a heart already sore.

Tom stepped into the cool, woody dimness of his dad's front room.

"Dad?" he called, stopping, listening. Bird chitter, a falling pinecone clattering on the roof, and nothing more. The room hadn't changed much in thirty years: an old sagging sofa covered with an Indian rug and some square green-and-orange pillows for his dad's afternoon naps; a couple of stuffed large-mouth bass hanging on the log walls that had aged to the color of maple syrup; overstuffed rockers with overstuffed magazine racks beside them; a round hassock of taffy-colored Naugahyde with a removable lid, filled with his mother's old piano music; the piano itself, an ancient and venerable upright giant with a crazed black finish and a hundred water rings to the right of the music rack where his mother used to set her lemonade glass; at one side of the great room, a deplorable yellowed gas range that always seemed to give off fumes, the same stove his mother had fried fish on and baked bread in and made all of her boys' favorite dishes on.

Tom paused to take in the room while at his back the east door opened to the shaded porch light that forever kept the room dim.

"Dad?" he called again, getting no answer.

Behind him he heard the soft chuckle of the boat motor nearing and went out, leaving the spring serenading after the screen door clacked, across the snake-length grass through which a path had been trampled toward the lake. The cabin sat on high ground; he saw the V in the water before catching sight of the dock below, where his dad was tying up.

Wesley heard footsteps on the bleached wooden steps and straightened, pushing back his fishing cap.

"Fish aren't bitin' worth a damn. Alls I got is three little pan fish, but it's enough for two. You come to help me eat 'em up?"

"Sure, why not," Tom replied, though food hadn't the dimmest appeal.

He walked out on the dock that shuddered with every footfall, and shuffled to a stop, looking down on his dad's dirty blue cap and wrinkled neck. The old man carefully removed a hook from his rod and reel, wiped it on his pants, and stored it in his tackle box.

"How come Uncle Clyde isn't fishing with you today?"

"He had to go into town and get his prescription renewed for his blood pressure pills. He told me he was going to visit the whorehouse, but I says to him, 'Clyde, what the Sam Hill you gonna do there? Your blood pressure's high everywhere 'cept where you want it to be.'

Anyway, I know he was going to the drugstore." Wesley chuckled to himself and rose to his feet, holding a stringer of three large sunfish. "Come on, I'll clean these."

Tom followed him to the north side of the tipsy boathouse, where Wesley handed him a blue plastic bucket. "Here, dip me some lake water, will you, son?"

While Wesley scaled and gutted fish on a chunky table made of weather-beaten wood, Tom stood by watching.

"Well, you might as well spit it out," his dad said. "Standin' there with your hands in your pockets like when you were little and all the kids went out catching frogs and forgot to ask you along."

Tom's eyes suddenly began stinging. He spun to face the lake. The fish scales stopped flying, and Wesley lifted his head to study his son's broad shoulders, slumped as they so seldom were, his hands buried in his trouser pockets.

"Claire and I are separating."

Wesley's old heart did a flop like the fish waiting on the tabletop.

"Oh, son . . ." He abandoned his work and dipped his hands in the bucket, keeping an eye on Tom. He dried his hands on his trousers, then put one on Tom's shoulder. "That's a shame. That's just a gol-dang shame. This just happen?"

Tom nodded. "Just this morning. We told the kids about an hour ago, and I packed up the car and left."

Wesley gripped the sturdy shoulder and hung on as much for himself as to offer support. Boy-oh-boy, how he loved Claire. She'd been the best wife and mother Tom could've had.

"I suppose this is about that other woman and your boy Kent."

Tom nodded—barely—still staring at the lake. "She just can't forgive me."

"That's a shame. How are the kids taking it?"

"Not good. Chelsea was crying. Robby was trying not to."

"Well, that's understandable. This all happened mighty fast."

"You're telling me. One month ago I'd never even heard of Kent Arens, and I had absolutely forgotten his mother."

Wesley heaved a great big sigh. "Well, hell . . ." He stood there hurting for his son, for all of them, and after a while, added, "It's a damned sad thing, breaking up a family."

Tom said nothing.

"I suppose you'll be needing a place to stay. Might as well get you settled into your old room."

"You don't mind?"

"Mind? Why, what's a dad for? For the good times only? Come on, I'll have to see if I can scout up some sheets for the bed in there."

"But what about your fish?"

"I'll get to 'em later."

"Why make the trip up the steps twice? Come on, I'll help you finish."

Wesley finished cleaning the fish while Tom rinsed them in the bucket, then buried the entrails. They walked up to the cabin together, Tom with the bucket, Wesley with his rod and reel and tackle box. The situation seemed to call for reverent quiet, so Tom spoke softly as they trudged along.

"I was hoping you'd let me stay. Actually, I brought sheets and pillowcases from home."

When the car was unloaded and the bed made, they sat down to a lunch of beer-battered fish, sliced tomatoes sprinkled with sugar, and thick, tart slabs of vinegar-soaked cucumbers and onion rings, which they piled onto slices of rye bread spread with butter. Though Tom had imagined himself too overwrought to eat, he did so with surprising relish. Perhaps it was the simplicity of the food, or eating it with his dad, who had no pretensions. Perhaps it was the need to draw himself back to a safer time when he was a boy here in this cabin and the cares of life had not yet affected him. The simple foods like his mother used to serve seemed to do just that.

In the middle of the meal his uncle Clyde came in. He was eighty if he was a day.

Without glancing at the door, Wesley asked, "So how was things at the whorehouse?"

"Whores ain't what they used to be." Clyde sat down at the table without being asked.

"Not hardly. They used to be twenty years old and pretty as the dickens. Nowadays the only ones who'll look at old geezers like us are sixty and look like the underside of mushrooms. You sure you was at the whorehouse?"

"You accusing me of lying?"

"Never said you was lying. I said I agree with you, whores ain't what they used to be."

"And how would you know? You was never in a whorehouse in your life."

"Was never in a doctor's office either, except for that once when that bullhead stung me and I got an infection in my finger. You ever been in a doctor's office, Clyde?"

"I *have not!*"

"Then how do you know your blood pressure's high, and how'd you get that prescription for those blood pressure pills you went in town to get more of?"

"I didn't say my blood pressure was high. You did."

"Oh, so your blood pressure's low?"

"Ain't low, ain't high. It's just right. Everything about me's just right, and that little whore in the whorehouse said so no more'n an hour ago."

"Was that before or after she quit laughin'?"

"Wesley, my boy, let me tell you somethin'"—Clyde pointed at his brother with his fork tines, smiling slyly— "that wasn't laughin', that was grinnin', and I'll tell you what put that grin on her face. A man of experience, that's what."

Wesley never lifted his eyes. "You ever hear so much bullshit in your life?" he asked his plate while he mopped up tomato juice with a last crust of bread, then pushed it in his mouth. "Comes in here and sits down and eats my fish and the last of the tomatoes and cukes from my garden and tries to tell me his sap still runs."

"It don't just run, it spurts!" the old geezer boasted. "That's what's got those little gals grinnin'."

And so it went, on and on for Tom's benefit. They never changed, Wesley and Clyde. They'd been carrying on this trumped-up pettifoggery for as long as Tom could remember, though where they got the material, he couldn't guess.

Finally Tom said, "It's okay, Dad, you can tell Uncle Clyde."

Everyone hushed. The silence felt harsh in the echo of the brothers' outlandish palaver.

"I guess you're right. I might as well tell him." Wesley sat back in his chair, looking somber. "Tom left Claire," he said. "He's moving in with me for a while."

Clyde looked poleaxed. "No."

"Not by choice," Tom put in. He told the two old men everything, and before he finished he was trying to ward off some sharp stabs of pain that knifed through his stomach.

He spent the day doing little, going to the bathroom more often than natural, otherwise trapped by an overwhelming lassitude such as he'd never suffered before. He lay on his bed, sleepless though exhausted, hands beneath his head, staring at the ceiling, memorizing the pattern of the dead flies in the light fixture. He sat on a lawn chair on the dock with his outstretched ankles crossed, fingers knit across his belly, staring at the water for so long that Wesley came out to see if he was all right. When his father asked if he wanted to eat supper, Tom replied no. When Wesley asked if he wanted to watch TV, play a little cribbage, start a jigsaw puzzle, the reply was always the same. Energy was something Tom had taken for granted. Feeling it prized away by depression brought him to wonder how he would be able to face a workday and function normally.

His father's cabin proved additionally depressing. When Tom had first come in, nostalgia had beckoned, but upon settling into the room with its sunken mattress and scarred furniture and the faint smell of bat shit funneling through the cracks from the attic above, he couldn't help comparing it to the house he'd just left, and he felt the full measure of what he would lose if he and Claire parted permanently: all they had built, bought, and banked—halved, sold, or both; their comfortable home with all its conveniences, favorite chairs, the screened porch they'd added on five years ago, the yard he'd mowed so many times, his garage with all his tools hanging on the wall; the sound system, records, tapes, and CDs representing a lifetime of favorites they'd bought together.

If they parted they would have to divide it all—not just the property and bank accounts but maybe even their children's loyalties. His eyelids sank closed at the repulsive thought. It shouldn't happen, ever, not to anyone who'd worked at a marriage as hard as he and Claire had. Oh God, he didn't want to be single, adrift, alone. He wanted commitment to both his wife and his family.

At 9:15 he called home. Robby answered.

"How's everything there?" Tom asked.

"It sucks."

Tom was unprepared for the answer. Somehow he'd expected Robby to remain the blithe one who downplayed the gloomy aspects and cracked jokes.

"I know," Tom replied throatily. And after a while, "How's Chelsea?"

"Incommunicado."

"How's Mom?"

"She's crazy, as far as I'm concerned. What did she do this for?"

"Could I talk to her?"

"She's over at Ruth's."

"At Ruth's." Probably heaping aspersions on her husband and getting applause for dumping him. Tom sighed. "Well, tell her I called, will you? Just to check and see if everything's okay."

"Yeah, I'll tell her."

"You going out tonight?"

"Naw."

"On a Saturday night?"

"I just don't feel like it, Dad."

Tom understood fully. "Yeah, I know. Well, you get some sleep. You didn't get much last night."

"Yeah, I will."

"All right then, see you tomorrow at church."

"Yeah, right."

"And tell Chelsea I love her. And I love you too."

"I will. Love you too, Dad."

"Well, good night then."

"'Ni—'" Robby's voice cracked into a falsetto. He cleared his throat and tried again. "'Night, Dad."

After he'd hung up, Tom stared at the phone. How pathetic, wishing his kids good night by telephone. A barrage of anger hit him, refreshing after the dead calm that had held him prisoner much of the day. What the hell was Claire thinking, doing this to them? Damn her anyway!

As the evening wore on, his emotions swung from high to low, low to high, lassitude and anger, then pain and guilt followed by frustration and helplessness. Sometimes he'd rise to his feet as if Claire were in the room, and in his imagination he'd fire a salvo of blame on her while reassuring himself that he'd done nothing wrong since he'd spoken his vows— nothing!—and she should have been willing to forgive him for his one grave sin before that.

Damn you, Claire, you can't do this!

Unfortunately, she could. She had.

He slept poorly and awoke to the grim prospect of showering in his dad's tin shower stall with its soap-coated plastic curtain and gooey walls. He'd always excused his dad's lack of cleanliness since his mother died, but maybe he'd have to talk to the old man about it if he was to live here indefinitely.

His trousers had gotten wrinkled jamming them into the tiny closet beside the chimney stack, and so had his suit jacket. When he asked where the iron was, he got a relic whose steam holes were packed solid with tartar. The condition of the ironing board cover made him set his jaw with grim determination.

But he was too excited about seeing Claire and the kids at church to complain.

To his dismay and anger, they weren't there.

He called home afterward and said, "Claire, what are you trying to pull? Why weren't you in church?"

"The kids were tired, so I let them sleep till a later service."

They had an argument that led to nothing but more frustration, setting the tone for the rest of the day.

On Monday morning he pulled out more wrinkled clothes and had as little success with the corroded steam iron. Checking his reflection in the mirror before leaving for school, he tried unsuccessfully to get a wave out of the hem of his suit coat by pressing it against his thigh with his hand.

Finally he muttered, "Aw, shit," and clattered out of the cabin cursing his father for living in semi-squalor. Without a garage his car windows had gathered moisture and the rear window needed to be squeegeed before he could set out, irritating him further when he couldn't find a squeegee in his car and his dad didn't have any paper towels. The search for rags made Tom late. When he was finally under way he kept thinking about frost coming soon and how he'd have to scrape his window every morning. He understood now why people said that it never worked when adult kids moved back in with their parents after being out on their own.

At school he was faced with the regular Monday morning faculty meeting, where he arrived five minutes late and confronted Claire without the reassurance of perfect grooming. When he looked at her with desperate longing and a need to be recognized, she gave him nothing.

They made it to the end of the meeting without exchanging any personal words, but his stomach immediately began its nervous dance. He ran into the nurse's office and begged for some Kaopectate, which he gulped in haste because the school busses had already begun arriving, and the worst disaster in the world that morning would have been to miss Chelsea when she walked through the door. Robby always came in early and worked out in the weight room, so he was already somewhere in the building.

Rushing toward the front hall he actually felt panic at the idea that he might have already missed Chelsea. But he hadn't, and when he saw her approaching the building with Robby at her side as well, he felt as if his heart had exploded inside him. They came through the door and headed straight for him as if they, too, needed the contact. Their eyes were sad and their faces long. He touched them both and felt heartsick and afraid the way so many of his students had told him they felt when their families were breaking up because of a divorce. Such a parade of sad stories he'd heard in his years as an educator, never believing he'd be the one experiencing them.

He and Chelsea shared a hug, there in the hall with students streaming past while the two of them—helpless victims of Claire's decision—felt their eyes sting.

He broke free and gripped Robby's arm. "Come on, you two, let's go into my office for a minute."

"I can't, Dad," Chelsea said, blinking hard to control her tears. "I didn't do my homework over the weekend and I need to write something quick for health class."

Tom turned to Robby. "What about you? Did you do yours?"

"I didn't have any."

"What about weight lifting? Don't you usually go in before school for that?"

Robby averted his gaze. "I didn't feel like it this morning."

Tom hated chiding them first thing, but he and Claire hadn't been apart for forty-eight hours and already the kids were showing signs of typical divorce fallout.

"Listen, you aren't going to start this now, are you? No matter what happens at home, you can't slough off on your schoolwork and extracurricular activities, okay? You just keep on doing everything the way you were . . . promise?"

Robby nodded sheepishly.

"Okay, Chelsea?"

She nodded too, but refused to meet his eyes.

"All right then, I'd better let you go," he said, even though he felt as if he would buckle into a heap and die the minute they walked out of his sight.

Chelsea seemed reluctant to head away.

"What is it?" he asked.

"I don't know. It's just . . . well, it's hard to act normal when nothing's normal at all anymore."

"What else can we do?"

She shrugged and looked glum. "Can we tell our friends, Dad?"

"If you must."

Robby said, "I don't want to tell mine."

Chelsea finally decided she couldn't handle getting into this at the beginning of the day. Her eyes were blinking hard and fast, and in a minute her tears would win. "I've got to go, Dad."

She went off without further remarks.

"I'd better go too, Dad." Robby sounded absolutely defeated.

"Okay. See you later." Tom touched Robby's back and watched him drift into the traffic. Left behind, Tom realized that neither of the children had inquired about his emotional state, about how it was staying out at Grandpa's, if he was getting along okay. They were all so busy coming to grips with their own emotional upheaval that they couldn't handle anyone else's. His trained mind realized this was typical, but he couldn't help feeling hurt that no one seemed concerned about *his* needs.

Heading back toward his office he made a silent vow that he would never get so wrapped up in his own grief that he grew immune to the children's.

It was inevitable that some situation would force the truth to be told around the school building. It simply happened faster than Tom expected.

He was passing the teachers' mailboxes when the band director, Vince Conti, stopped him. "Oh, Tom . . . I was wondering if I could come over and get that canoe one night this week. Duck hunting season opens next Saturday."

Weeks ago he and Tom had talked about Vince borrowing the canoe because his teenage boys wanted to take up the sport, which he had enjoyed years ago but had given up after he was married.

Nonplussed, Tom stammered, "Oh . . . oh, sure, Vince."

"Your schedule is busier than mine, so you name the night."

"Ahh . . . well, any night is fine, actually. I'll ahh . . ." Tom cleared his throat and felt a spear of panic at the idea of divulging that his marriage was in trouble. He'd never guessed it would be this hard, or that he'd feel like such a loser when he made the admission. "The truth is, Vince, I'll have to tell Claire where the paddles are and you can make arrangements with her to come and get it. I'm not living there anymore."

"You're not?"

"Claire and I are separating for a while."

He watched Vince battle shock and search for the proper response. "Gee, Tom . . . I'm sorry. I didn't know."

"It's all right, Vince, nobody knows. You're the first one I've told. It just happened over the weekend."

Vince looked grossly uncomfortable. "Tom, I really *am* sorry. You'd offered to let me borrow your canoe and—well, hell, I mean, I don't have to—"

"No need to change your plans, Vince. You can still borrow it. I'll make sure Claire knows you're coming and that she has the paddles out for you. If you need some help loading it on your car I can make sure Robby is home to help you, or I can meet you over at the house."

"No, no, I can take one of my boys."

"Fine. Well . . . you know where it is, then. Out behind the garage."

"Sure."

"Claire can show you."

It was obvious from the look on Vince's face that he was curious, but to his credit he asked no questions. When he walked away it was clear to Tom that in spite of the commonness of divorce, people still found it awful, and got uncomfortable when they were told about it. Perhaps Vince didn't want to intrude. Perhaps he didn't know what to say. The fact remained that the instant he was told, he put up a barrier that had never been there before.

Vince wasn't the only one who had to be told that day. A school the size of HHH functioned much like a small community with many interdependent parts. As its head, Tom had to be accessible at all times, in case of emergencies, or simply to answer questions, necessitating his having to give his dad's phone number to his assistant principal, his secretary, the liaison law enforcement officer, the chief of police, the head of the school board, the school counselors, and Cecil, the head janitor, who often called at night when his crew did the bulk of their cleaning. With all those people apprised of the situation, it took no time at all before the word seeped out to the general population of the building. Once it did, it spread faster than an Elizabethan plague.

Erin Gallagher came hustling to find Chelsea between classes. "Is it true, Chelsea?" Erin looked owl-eyed and dopey. "Everybody's saying your mom and dad are getting a divorce!"

"They are *not* getting a divorce!"

"But Susie Randolph told me that Jeff Morehouse told her that your dad moved out." Chelsea's battle to control her tears confirmed the rumor. Erin immediately became sympathetic. "Oh, Chels, you poor thing. Oh, gol, how awful. Where did he go?"

"To my grandpa's."

"Why?"

Chelsea's face began to corrugate. "Oh Erin, I've just got to tell somebody. I can't keep it to myself anymore." Her tears began running even before the words were out. The girls went and sat in Chelsea's car, and Chelsea told her friend everything, then swore her to secrecy.

"Oh my gosh," Erin whispered in wonder, "Kent Arens is your brother . . . wow . . ." Then she added, "I bet you're bummed."

The girls hugged, and Chelsea cried, and Erin asked if Chelsea thought her dad would ever move back home, which made Chelsea cry even harder. They skipped all of sixth period and part of seventh, and by the time they were ready to go back inside, Chelsea looked so puffy and red that she said, looking into the rearview mirror, "I wouldn't be caught dead looking like this."

Erin said, "Maybe you better skip cheerleading practice tonight, and by tomorrow you'll be feeling better. You'll look better, too."

"What are we going to say to our sixth- and seventh-period teachers?"

Erin, usually the follower where she and Chelsea were concerned, suddenly became the leader. "Come on," she ordered, opening the car door and heading straight for Tom's office.

"No, Erin, I'm not going in there! I'm not going to talk to my dad!"

"Why not? He'll give us excuses."

"No! He'll kill me if he finds out I skipped classes!"

"How are you going to keep him from finding out? Come on, Chels, you're not making much sense."

"But he and Mom don't let us skip for anything, you know that! If there's one thing at our house that's inexcusable, that's it." Chelsea balked in the hall outside the main-office doors.

"Well, I don't care if you're not going in. I am." She left Chelsea in the hall and went into the front office. Dora Mae let her go right into Tom's office.

"Hi, Mr. Gardner," she said from the doorway. "Chelsea and I have been sitting out in her car talking. She told me what's going on at home, and she's been crying a lot, but she wouldn't come in here and tell you we skipped two classes. Would you give us excused absences?"

"Where is she?"

"Out in the hall. She said you'd kill her if you found out, but I didn't think so since you know what we were talking about."

Tom was up and heading for the hall, with Erin at his heels.

Chelsea stood around the corner where she could not be seen through the glass wall. When she saw him coming toward her, her eyes began to fill. When he hugged her, she clung. "Oh, Daddy, I'm sorry I told, but I just had to talk to somebody. I'm sorry . . . I'm sor—"

"Shh, it's okay, honey."

Erin felt out of her element, watching her principal and her best friend hugging while he choked back tears and she bawled on his shoulder.

"I understand," he murmured, rubbing Chelsea's hair. "It's a hard day for all of us."

A student came out of the main office and gaped as she walked past.

"Come on," Tom said. "Let's go into my office. You too, Erin."

"I can't go in there looking like this," Chelsea cried. "All the secretaries will see me."

"You're not the first student to come in crying." He handed her a handkerchief from his hip pocket. "Just dry your eyes. I want to talk to you."

He ushered them inside and closed his office door. "Sit down, girls."

They sat facing his desk and he perched on the edge of it, close to them. "Now listen. I'll give you excused absences because I understand that you couldn't cope with everything today, but honey, you can't skip any more classes. I know that's a tall order, but I want you to try really hard for me."

Chelsea nodded, eyes downcast and brimming, while she stretched Tom's handkerchief over her thumbs.

"Because no good will be served if you start letting your grades slide on top of everything else."

Chelsea kept nodding.

"Erin, you did the right thing coming to me today, but in the future, if you skip classes I won't be able to excuse you."

"Okay, Mr. Gardner."

"Now I want you both to do something for me. I want you to see Mrs. Roxbury and get appointments to talk to her." Mrs. Roxbury was the counselor for the junior class. "Chelsea, the sooner the better for you. Erin, I think it might help if you talk to her too, because you're going to be one of Chelsea's support people, and it's important that you understand what she's going through right now."

Erin murmured, "Okay . . . sure."

"Is it okay with both of you if I go and get Mrs. Roxbury and have her come in here now?"

The girls both nodded.

"Okay, I'll be right back."

When Tom went out, Erin whispered, "Gol, Chelsea, your dad is so nice, I don't see how your mom could ever kick him out."

Chelsea said sadly, "I know. She's just spoiling everything."

Mrs. Roxbury, a fortyish woman with rimless glasses and a shag haircut, came in and took the girls to her office. As they left, Chelsea looked back at Tom and said softly, with a wan smile, "Thanks, Dad."

He smiled for her benefit and she went out.

Three minutes later Lynn Roxbury returned to find Tom sitting glumly at his desk, staring at the pictures on his window ledge.

"Tom?" she said quietly.

He swung his gaze to the door. "Thanks, Lynn. I appreciate your fitting them in."

"No problem. I've got appointments with them tomorrow." She crossed her arms and leaned against the door frame. "Listen, I've got time for you too, if you find you need to talk. There have been a lot of rumors flying around here today, so I have a pretty good idea why Chelsea's eyes were red and you look like you've just lost your best friend. I believe you have."

He sighed and ground eight fingertips into his eyes, tipping his desk chair back at a sharp angle. "Ohh, Lynn . . . shit. To quote my son."

She discreetly closed the door. "I hear that a lot in my business."

"It's been a hell of a month around our house."

"I don't think I need to say it, but anything you choose to unload will be held in strictest confidence. I imagine this is particularly hard for you and Claire, being you both work in the same building."

"It's just plain hell."

She waited, and he said, "Sit."

"I only have a few minutes right now." She took the chair Erin had vacated.

He rocked forward, his forearms on his desk, his shoulders rounded. "I'll give it to you short and straight. Claire and I have separated at her request. I'm living with my dad out at his cabin on the lake, and the kids are living with Claire in the house. The reason goes way back into my past and it's kind of a shocker. It has to do with the new senior here, Kent

Arens. I've just discovered that he's my son." Lynn sat with a finger against her lips but said nothing. Tom went on. "I didn't know about him until he walked into the office to register for school. I never kept in touch with his mother, so I never knew, but as it turns out, he was born the same year as Robby. My indiscretion was a one-night stand the night of my bachelor party. Claire believes I've revived an affair with Kent's mother, which I haven't. Nevertheless, she left me."

It said a lot about the walloping punch packed by this revelation that Lynn gave away a hint of astonishment upon hearing it.

"Oh, Tom, no! You were the last two I ever thought this would happen to!"

He spread his hands and let them fall. "Me too." Neither of them spoke for a while. Finally, he said, "I love her so damned much. I don't want this separation at all."

"Do you think she'll relent?"

"I don't know. It's brought out a side of her I've never seen before. She acts almost fearless, almost . . . I don't know what to call it but aggressive, and absolutely convinced that she has to get away from me for a while."

"The key words here are *for a while.*"

"I hope so. God, Lynn, I hope so."

Lynn Roxbury continued to look stunned by the news. "Tom, I'm sorry I can't talk any longer, but I've got another appointment. We can talk more after school though. I'm free around four-thirty today."

Tom rose to his feet. "I've got meetings at the district office right after school, so I'll be busy, but thanks for listening now. It helped."

He went around his desk and she squeezed his sleeve. "You going to be okay?"

He gave her a weak smile. "Sure."

But it had been a difficult day for Tom. His attention span was short. His mind wandered—most often, to Claire.

He looked up once and saw her through his open doorway, in the outer office, speaking to Dora Mae. His response was as swift and consuming as passion, a desperate yearning for her to turn and look his way, to offer him that much. She knew his door was open, that he was probably sitting at his desk.

But she moved on without offering him a crumb, and her rebuff hurt worse than anything he could remember.

At lunchtime he saw her again, walking through the cafeteria on her way to the teachers' lunchroom. She was with Nancy Halliday, listening to Nancy talk, and she glanced over at Tom, who stood in the center of the room beneath the round skylight watching over the kids.

His heart damn near knocked him off his feet. But she glanced away indifferently and continued through a door that closed on a pneumatic hinge, whisking her out of sight.

He forced himself to stay away from her until the break between the last two periods of the day. Then he went to her room, waiting in the hall while the sixth-period kids spilled out, unconsciously checking the knot in his tie before stepping into the room. She was seated at her desk, which faced the door, searching for something in a lower drawer. Catching sight of her, he felt his skin go hot—his neck, cheeks, forehead—felt the whole chain reaction begin again, combined with a rush that was unquestionably sexual. He grew angry with her for putting him through this. He didn't want this separation, damn it!

"Claire?" he said, and she looked up, leaving a hand between the file folders.

"Hello, Tom."

"I ah . . ." He cleared his throat. "I told Vince Conti he could come over and pick up our canoe some night this week. He wants to use it for duck hunting. Do you know where the paddles are?"

"Yes."

"Would you give them to Vince when he comes?"

"Sure."

"He'll probably talk to you about when."

"All right."

"It was a few weeks ago I told him he could borrow it. I didn't think he'd have to be bothering you to . . . well . . . you know. You've got play practice most nights."

"It's okay, Tom. We'll work it out."

When he remained where he was, pink-faced and humble, she said, "Is there anything else, Tom?"

It suddenly angered him, being treated like some vassal at the foot of a feudal princess. "Yes, there's plenty more!" He strode toward her, piqued. "Claire, how can you be so damned cold? I don't deserve to be treated this way!"

Once again she bent to the files in the drawer. "Nothing personal in the schoolroom, Tom. Have you forgotten?"

He reached her desk and braced his hands on it, thrusting his head toward her. "Claire, I don't want this separation!"

She withdrew a file and slammed the metal drawer. Two students came in, talking and laughing, as she rolled her desk chair backward.

"Not here, Tom," she admonished quietly. "Not now."

He straightened slowly, colored by anger, realizing he should not have come in here. No man needed this in the middle of his workday. In the middle of his life!

"I want to come back home." He kept his voice quiet so the students could not hear.

"I'll make sure Vince gets the canoe paddles," she said, dismissing him as surely as if she'd picked up a bell and rung it, like the teachers of old.

He had no choice but to turn and push his way through the incoming students.

Thirteen

The word spread through the locker room at football practice that day: Mr. Gardner is getting a divorce.

Kent Arens heard it from a kid named Bruce Abernathy, who—as far as Kent knew—wasn't even a friend of Robby's, so how would he know? Kent went to Jeff Morehouse and asked if he knew anything about it.

"Yeah, Robby's dad moved out."

"Are they getting a divorce?"

"Robby doesn't know. He says his mom threw his dad out because he had an affair with somebody."

No! Kent wanted to shout. No, not them! Not the family who had it all!

When he had time to recover from the first bolt of news, another bomb exploded in his mind. Suppose it was true, and the other woman was his mother. The thought made him sick.

In that muddled moment he realized he had come to hold up the Gardner family as an ideal: somewhere in this world of half families and screwed-up values, there was one unit of four who'd survived all the treacheries of modern times to hang together and love each other. They had seemed inviolable, and even though he, Kent, had envied Chelsea her father, he had never wanted to take him from her. And if his mother was a party to it, how could he respect her anymore?

He dropped to a bench, half dressed and shaken, gripping his knees and struggling with a whole new crop of emotions. The locker room thrummed with conversation, and when it suddenly ceased, he looked up to find that Robby Gardner had walked in. Nobody said a word. Nobody moved. The silence was awesome and filled with the echoes of gossip that had been whispered and wondered about all day.

Gardner looked at Arens. Arens looked back, steadily.

Then Gardner continued toward his locker.

But something had changed in his stride. Its brazenness was gone, its spunk. As he passed among his silent teammates, their knowing eyes followed him. Some held pity, some questions. Some were embarrassed for him as he opened his locker door, hung up his letter jacket, and began dressing without the usual joshing.

Kent suppressed the urge to rise and go to him, put a hand on his shoulder, and say, "I'm sorry." Somehow this was his fault, Kent's, though reason told him perfectly well that his conception was the act of two others, nothing he had willed or wanted or wrought. Still, he'd been born, hadn't he? And it appeared his mother and Mr. Gardner had started up again, and all this had driven a wedge between Robby and Chelsea's parents.

Surely there was some guilt inherent in these facts.

The team went on poking their heads through their jerseys and slamming locker doors until finally they started filing out to the field, the clatter of their cleats fading. Robby, who usually led them, remained behind.

Kent turned to look at him down the length of the varnished benches. Robby faced his open locker, his head hanging as he worked his jersey over his pads.

Kent moved toward him . . . stopped behind him, his helmet hanging from one hand.

"Hey, Gardner?" Kent said.

At last Robby turned around. They stood grounded in place, dressed in their red-and-white uniforms and stocking feet, holding their cleats and helmets, wondering how the hell to get around the morass of emotions that had been forced upon them in so short a time.

The coach came out of his office, opened his mouth to order them to get a move on, changed his mind, and left them alone. He went away, his cleats *tack-tacketing* on the concrete floor, leaving the two boys in silence broken only by the drip from some shower head on the other side of a tiled wall.

They stood separated by the low bench and the difference in their birthrights. Kent had expected Robby's face to hold scorn. Instead, it held only sadness.

"I heard about your mom and dad," Kent said. "I'm sorry."

"Yeah." Robby dropped his chin and kept his eyes lowered in case any telltale tears should appear. None did, but their threat was as clear to Kent as if his own eyes had stung.

He reached across the bench and for the first time ever, touched his half brother on the shoulder . . . one singular, uncertain touch.

"I mean it. I really am," he offered kindly.

Robby only stared at the bench, unable to lift his head.

Then Kent dropped his hand and turned to the door to give his half brother time alone.

Kent went home from practice that night angrier than he ever remembered being with his mother. When he stormed into the house, she was coming up the basement stairs with a stack of folded towels.

"I want to talk to you, Mom!" he bellowed.

"Well, that's a fine hello."

"What's going on between you and Mr. Gardner?"

She froze in mid-step, then continued past on her way to the linen closet with him dogging her. "Are you having an affair with him?"

"I most certainly am not!"

"Then why is everybody at school saying you are? And why has Mr. Gardner left his wife?"

She spun with the towels forgotten in her hand. "He has?"

"Yes, he has! And everybody in school is gossiping about it! Some kid in the locker room said his wife threw him out because he was having an affair."

"Well, if he is, it's not with me."

Kent peered at her more closely. She was telling the truth. He sighed and gave her some space. "Jeez, Mom, is *that* a relief."

"Well, I'm glad you believe me. Now maybe you can stop yelling at me."

"Sorry."

She stuffed the towels into the closet. "So you think it's true? Tom's left his wife?"

"It looks that way. I asked Jeff, and Jeff said it was, and he ought to know. He's been Robby's best friend forever."

She hooked Kent by an elbow and led him back toward the front of the house. "You seem upset about it."

"Well . . . yeah . . . yeah, I guess I am."

"Even though I'm not a part of it?"

He shot her a reproving glance.

"Presently a part of it," she amended.

"I am upset, Mom. You just have to look at Robby Gardner to see that he's really bummed out. I suppose Chelsea's the same way. She really loves her dad, Mom. The way she talked about him was . . . well, it was different, you know? The way kids hardly ever talk about their parents. And I took one look at Robby in the locker room today and . . ." They had reached the kitchen and Kent dropped onto a stool at the counter. "I don't know. The look on his face was pretty awful. I didn't know what to say to him."

"What did you say?"

"I said I was sorry."

She had opened the refrigerator to get out some hamburger and half an onion in a plastic bag. She set them on the counter and went to Kent.

"I'm sorry too," she said.

They commiserated together, he perched on the edge of the high stool, she standing beside it, affected by the news of one family's breakup, touched by obscure guilt over it. But they could not change the past. Monica got out a frying pan and started preparing supper.

"Hey, Mom?" Kent said, still sitting glum and gleeless.

She looked over. "What?"

"What would you think if I sort of . . . well, like . . . I don't know . . . tried to become his friend or something."

Monica had to think about that for a while. She went to the sink and pulled out the breadboard beside it, opened the package of hamburger, and started forming patties. "I guess there's no way I can stop you." The *pat slap pat* of her hands on the meat filled the room.

"So you don't approve?"

"I didn't say that."

But something in the way she slapped that hamburger told him his question threatened her somehow.

"He's my half brother. Today when I was looking at him I really thought about that. My half brother. You've got to admit, that's pretty awesome, Mom."

She turned her back and switched on a stove burner, opened a lower cabinet door and found a bottle of oil, squirted some in the pan, and made no reply.

"I thought maybe I could help some way. I don't know how, but it's because of me they're breaking up. If it's not because you're having an affair with him, then it's because of me."

Monica swung around, faintly exasperated. "It's not your responsibility, and you certainly aren't guilty of anything, so if you've got that idea in your head you can just get it out!"

"Well, then whose responsibility is it?"

"It's his! Tom's!"

"So I should just stand by and watch their family break up and not do anything about it?"

"You said it earlier—what can you do?"

"I can be Robby's friend."

"Are you sure he wants that?"

Meekly, Kent answered, "No."

"Then, be careful."

"Of what?"

"Getting hurt yourself."

"Mom, I'm already hurt—you don't seem to understand that. This whole mess hurts me a lot! I want to get to know my father, but if I have to circle wide around his kids every time I want to see him—well, wouldn't it be much easier just to try to make friends with them?"

She dropped a patty in the pan, sending up sizzle and smoke. It was exceedingly hard for her to give her blessing to his making friends in Tom Gardner's camp.

"You afraid I'll change loyalties or something, Mom?" He came over and draped his arm over her shoulder cajolingly. "You should know me better than that. You're my mom and that's not going to change if I get to know them. But I've got to do this, don't you see?"

"I do." She spun and hugged him so hard he couldn't see the heavy sheen in her eyes. "I do see. It's why Tom insisted that I tell you he was your father. But I'm scared of losing you."

"To them? Come on, Mom, that doesn't make any sense. Why would you lose me?"

She sniffed and chuckled at her own foolishness. "I don't know. It's such a mix-up, you and them, you and me, me and him, and him and you." She turned out of his arms to tend the hamburgers, leaving him standing with one wrist still crooked over her shoulder. They watched as she flipped the patties, then sliced wedges of onion against her thumb, dropping them into the pan beside the meat. The aroma intensified and he drew her harder against his side.

"Boy, it's really hell growing up, isn't it, Mom?"

She chuckled, poked at the onions with the knife tip, and said, "You know it."

"Tell you what . . ." He took the knife and poked at the onions, too. "Just so you won't feel threatened, I'll come back and report everything to you. I'll tell you when I see them and what we talk about. And I'll tell you how we're all getting along. That way you won't think I'm being lured away from you; how's that?"

"I would have expected you to do that anyway."

"Well, yeah, but this way you'll know for sure."

"Okay, it's a deal. Now how about buttering some buns?"

"Right."

"And getting out a couple of plates."

"Right."

"And the jar of pickles."

"Yeah, yeah, yeah." As he turned around to help her, she turned around to watch him, and while the hamburgers sizzled and the onions cooked and he buttered buns with his back to her, she realized that she had been silly to feel threatened by his wish to get closer to Tom's children.

She had raised too good a boy to lose him over this. She had done such a good job that *he* was teaching *her* that love need not be competitive.

At play practice that night Claire checked her watch, clapped her hands, and shouted above the jabbering onstage. "Okay, everybody, it's ten o'clock, time to wrap it up. Make sure all the props are locked up! Work on those lines and I'll see you tomorrow night!"

Beside her John Handelman shouted, "Hey, Sam, you're going to make a copy of the lighting script and give it to Doug, right?"

"Yo!" the boy called back.

"Good. Paint crew, wear old clothes tomorrow night. The art department's got the flats sketched and we'll be filling in the background!"

A syncopated chorus of good nights drifted back to the pair left onstage. The kids' voices drifted off, leaving the auditorium quiet.

"I'll get the lights," John said, heading toward the wings.

A moment later the spots disappeared from between the overhead travelers, leaving Claire in shadows. She made her way to rear stage, where only one dim light threw murky gray bands down between the drops. Some folding chairs stood higgledy-piggledy beside a rough wooden crate, her jacket thrown across the seat of one. She leaned over tiredly to stuff her script and notes into a cloth bag along with some fabric samples and a book on costuming. Straightening with a sigh, she picked up her jacket and drew it on.

"Tired?"

She turned. John stood behind her, putting on his jacket, too.

"Beat."

"We did lots of work tonight though."

"Yes, we accomplished a lot." She reached for her bag and he put a hand on her arm.

"Claire," he said, "could we talk a minute?"

She left the bag on the chair seat. "Sure."

"Lots of rumors flying around the school today. Rather than wonder if they're true, I decided to ask. Are they?"

"Maybe you'd better tell me what you heard, John."

"That you left Tom."

"It's true."

"For good?"

"I don't know yet."

"The gossips are saying he had an affair."

"He did once. He says it's over."

"So what's your take on that?"

"I'm hurt. I'm mixed up. I'm angry. I don't know whether to believe him or not."

He studied her awhile. Their faces looked like masks of Tragedy, eyes mere sockets in the meager light from some distance away.

"You threw the faculty into a major shock, you know."

"Yes, I suppose we did."

"Everybody's saying they never thought it could happen to you and Tom."

"I never thought so either, but it did."

"You need a shoulder to cry on?"

She picked up her bag and started walking. He fell into step beside her. "You offering one?"

"Yes, ma'am. I certainly am."

She had known for years that he was attracted to her, but was nonetheless surprised by how fast he made his move. She had been married for too long to find this situation comfortable.

"John, it just happened day before yesterday. I don't even know yet if I should scream or cry."

"Well, hell, you can scream on my shoulder, too, if that's what you want."

"Thanks. I'll remember that."

At the stage door he snapped off the last remaining light and let her go out first. It was a clear autumn night, complete with stars and the smell of dry leaves. Walking across the parking lot, she put plenty of distance between them.

"Listen," he said, "you're going to need a friend. I'm just offering my services, nothing more, okay?"

"Okay," she agreed, relieved. He walked her to her car and waited while she unlocked the door and got in.

"Good night, and thanks."

"See you tomorrow," he said, and slammed the door with a two-handed push.

She left him standing there watching as she drove away. Her heart was thumping with a response resembling fear. John Handelman wouldn't hurt her. Why was she reacting this way? Because she hadn't expected that the announcement of her separation would make her into immediate date bait. She didn't want to date, for heaven's sake! She wanted to heal! How dare John move in on her that way?

At home Robby's and Chelsea's rooms were empty and dark. She clunked around her bedroom, angry that they hadn't even left a note. They came in together at 10:30.

"All right, you two, where have you been?"

"At Erin's," she answered.

"At Jeff's."

"Your curfew is ten o'clock! Or have you forgotten?"

"So it's ten-thirty. Big deal," Chelsea said, walking away.

"You get back here, young lady!"

She returned with an air of long-suffering. "What?"

"Nothing is changed because your dad isn't here anymore. You're in the house by ten and in bed by eleven on school nights, is that clear?"

"Why should we be here when nobody else is?"

"Because we have rules in this house, that's why."

"I hate it here without Dad."

"It's no different than when he lived here and stayed at school for meetings."

"Yes, it is. It's morbid. And you're gone to play practice every night, so I'm going to go to Erin's."

"You blame me for all of it, don't you?"

"Well, you're the one who threw him out."

Robby had stood by saying nothing.

"Robby?" Claire invited.

He shuffled his feet and looked uncomfortable. "I don't see why you couldn't have let him stay here while you two worked it out. I mean, heck, he's pretty miserable. You could tell just by looking at him today."

She subdued the urge to yell out her impatience, and made a sudden decision. "Come here, you two." She took them into her bedroom and made them sit on the edge of her bed while she perched on a cedar chest beneath the window. "Robby, you said you don't see why I couldn't just let him stay here. Well, I'll tell you, and I'll tell you as honestly as I can, because I think you're old enough to hear it. Your dad and I are still very sexual beings, and it was a part of our marriage that I—we—enjoyed very much. When I found out that he'd had sex with another woman a week before I married him, I felt betrayed. I still feel betrayed by that. Then some other things came to light that led me to believe there's still something between him and this other woman. I'm not going to elaborate because I don't want to pit you against your dad. But for me there's still some doubt about his faithfulness, and as long as I feel that, I can't live with him. You may think that's old-fashioned by today's standards, but I don't care. A vow is a vow and I cannot and will not live as an alternate wife.

"Then there's the very real living proof of his betrayal. Kent Arens. I see him every day in class, and what do you think it does to me when he walks in? Do you think it doesn't hurt all over again? Do you think I can just simply forgive your dad for putting you two in the embarrassing position of having to attend school in the same building with your illegitimate half brother? If it weren't so tragic it would almost be ludicrous, the five of us all in that school building, bumping into each other, pretending we're just one big happy family.

"Your father is Kent's father, and that fact—pardon me—is a little hard for me to swallow. And I'm sure you found out that everybody in the school building thought it was some pretty juicy news. It spread through the place like wildfire today. I hate that you two have to be subjected to it. That all *three* of us have to be subjected to it.

"Now I know you miss your dad. You may not believe it, but I do too. You don't stay married to a man for eighteen years without missing him when he's gone. But I hurt." Claire put a hand over her heart and leaned toward them earnestly. "I hurt very badly, and if I need some time to get over that hurt I expect you to understand me, not blame me for being the one to cause our breakup."

She sat back on the cedar chest and took a deep breath. The children sat on the edge of the bed looking chastised. The room held a sadness so profound it seemed to press them in place. Claire saw she was the only one who could dispel it. "Now come here . . ." She opened her arms wide. "Come and give me a hug. I need one really badly right now. We all do."

They came. They hugged. They lingered in their parting, smitten with the realization that there were two sides to this argument, and that their mother deserved her share of understanding.

"I love you," Claire said with her cheeks sandwiched between theirs. They both said, "I love you too."

"And your dad loves you. Don't ever forget that. No matter what, he loves you, and he never meant to hurt you."

"We know," Robby said.

"Okay then . . ." She gave them a gentle nudge away. "It's been an awful day and we're all tired. I think it's time we got some sleep."

Fifteen minutes later, with her face scrubbed and her nightgown on, Claire lay beneath the covers of her and Tom's bed with tears leaking from the corners of her eyes. She missed him. Oh God, she missed him so horribly. And she damned him for making her into this stubborn, defensive woman who had to show him she could live without him and would! He said there was nothing between him and Monica Arens anymore, but then why had Ruth seen them together? Why had his voice been so emotional when he talked to her on the phone? It hurt so badly being unable to believe him after all the years of implicit trust. And it hurt even worse imagining sexual images of him with another woman.

But the images came and would not be dispelled. They appeared every night when Claire lay down in this bed where she and Tom had been intimate, where the smell of him still lingered in the sheets, and the wrinkles on his pillowcase could still be faintly seen. If she lived alone until she was a hundred she'd never get used to his warm, breathing presence being absent from the other half of the bed.

Sometimes a contrary thought came, though she didn't mean to be thinking in terms of getting even.

All right, so maybe you've got a mistress, Tom Gardner, but just don't think you're the only one who's still got some sex appeal left, because all I'd have to do is snap my fingers and John Handelman would be right in this bed beside me!

Afterward she'd feel guilty, as if she were actually considering committing adultery, even though it had been only a hollow threat.

One of them had to honor their vows for the children's sake, and if Tom hadn't, she would. After all, children needed role models, and part of her greatest disappointment in Tom was his falling from grace in their eyes.

Her eyes would be bloodshot again in the morning . . . damn him, too, for causing that . . . and for making her live without him, which she hated . . . and for making her the subject of school gossip . . . and the target of John Handelman's flirting . . .

She was still missing him when she finally lurched off to sleep.

. . .

The following day, she knew the moment Kent Arens walked into her classroom that he'd heard about her and Tom's breakup. He'd always been distant and watchful. Today he seemed to be studying her with a somber intensity she could feel even when her back was turned.

She should have let Tom transfer him out when he'd suggested doing so. It was difficult to remain objective—let alone friendly—with your husband's illegitimate child. Her disfavor showed. She never called on him, let her eyes linger on him, or said hello when he walked past her door. When their gazes tangled, neither of them smiled. She felt terrible treating him that way, but his work remained exemplary, his average a perfect 4.0, so she excused herself and submerged her guilt.

That Tuesday when fifth period ended and the students filed out, Kent remained behind in his seat. Claire pretended not to see him while she tamped papers and checked her lesson plan book, but his presence was hard to miss. He unfolded his leggy body and came to stand smack in front of her.

"I heard about you and Mr. Gardner," he said.

She leveled a loveless gaze on him and said, "Did you?"

He stood at ease, wearing jeans and a pale yellow V-necked sweater, looking so damned much like Tom.

"I suppose it's my fault," he said.

Her heart melted as he faced her foursquare, owning up to guilt that wasn't his.

"No, of course not."

"Then why do you treat me as if I'm not here?"

She blushed. "I'm sorry, Kent. I didn't realize I was doing that."

"I think you do it on purpose, to punish me for being in this school."

Hit squarely in her conscience, she took to her chair as if a blow truly had been delivered. It left her short-breathed and quivering inside.

"You're very much like him," she whispered.

"Am I? I wouldn't know."

"He'd stand up to me the same way if he were in this situation. I admire you for it."

"Then why did you leave him?"

"Really, Kent, I don't think that's any of your business."

"If it isn't mine, whose is it? This wouldn't have happened if I hadn't moved into this school district. Am I wrong?"

They locked eyes for several seconds before she admitted, softly, "No, you're not."

"So if you're not punishing me, who are you punishing? Him? Because if that's what you're doing, you should know that your kids are suffering too. I just don't see any sense in that. I grew up without a dad, so I know what it feels like. Your kids have one and you're taking him away from them. I'm sorry, Mrs. Gardner, but I don't think that's the right thing to do. Chelsea told me once how much she loves him, and yesterday in the locker room everybody could see that Robby was acting different already. He didn't even lead the team outside for practice."

"I had a talk with my children last night. I think they understand my reasons for leaving Tom."

"Do you think he's having an affair with my mother, or what? Because I asked her, and she said they're not. Why don't you just ask him?"

Claire was so stunned she couldn't respond. What was she doing discussing the intimate details of her marriage with one of her students?

"I think you're out of line, Kent."

He iced over and backed up a step, a model of overstrained politeness.

"All right, then I apologize, and I'll go." He turned on his heel and made for the door with a military correctness, more in control than any seventeen-year-old she'd ever met. Good Lord, had he no fear of retribution? The average high school senior wouldn't have had the temerity to speak up to a teacher that way. The remarkable thing was he'd done it with the utmost respect, the same kind of respect she and Tom had always maintained while disagreeing with each other. When she saw Kent's back going around the doorway she was left with a grudging respect herself.

By the end of that week more details had leaked out and everyone at HHH knew that Kent Arens was the illegitimate son of their principal.

Kent was being stared at.

Robby and Chelsea were being questioned.

Claire often detected sudden hushes when she walked into a room.

Tom had done some talking with Lynn Roxbury, who'd told him to forget about what people thought; he needed to reconcile his relationship with Kent in some concrete way before he could go on with his life.

He sent a note to Kent's first-hour class, and this time Kent showed up at his office door in five minutes. When they were alone the two of them stood gazing at each other, still acclimating to the idea that they were father and son. It was a more precious moment than before, devoid of some of the complications and secrecy that had permeated their previous meetings. They could study each other wholly, searching eyes, shapes, musculature, and coloring without recoiling in shock at their similarity.

"We do look a lot alike, don't we?" Tom said.

Kent nodded, barely perceptibly. He was still staring at his father, who had come around his desk and stood a mere four feet away. Between them hummed a ripe fascination.

"Everybody in school knows about it now," Kent said.

"Does that bother you?"

"At first it did. Now though, I don't know. I'm . . . well, I'm sort of proud of it."

Tom's heart gave a little kick of surprise.

"I would like sometime for you to see the pictures of me when I was your age."

Kent said, "I'd like that too."

Silence hovered again while they thought of possibilities, considered making up for lost time, and wondered if they could create some future as father and son.

Tom said, "My father would like to meet you."

"I'd . . ." Kent swallowed hard. "I'd like to meet him too."

"I'm living with him now, you know."

"Yes, I know. I'm sorry I caused that."

"You didn't, I did. But it's my problem and I'll handle it. Anyway, Dad and I were wondering if you could come out to the cabin this weekend, maybe on Saturday."

Kent's face flushed. "Sure. I'd . . . well, heck, I mean that'd be great!"

"You could meet Uncle Clyde too, if you want."

"Sure." Kent was smiling outright.

"Uncle Clyde and Dad like to rib one another a lot, and you never know what it'll be about, so I warn you, you'll have to take it with a grain of salt."

Kent looked awestruck, perhaps a little giddy. "I just can't believe it, that I'm really going to meet my grandfather."

"He's a great old guy. You're going to love him. I surely do."

Kent just smiled and smiled.

"Well, listen," Tom said, "I shouldn't keep you away from class anymore. Do you need a ride on Saturday? Because I could come and get you."

"No, I think Mom will let me use the car."

"All right then . . . two o'clock maybe?"

"Two would be fine."

"Here, just a minute . . ." Tom returned to his desk. "I'll draw you a map."

While he slashed lines with a pencil, he was conscious that Kent had come right around the desk to stand beside him. "Watch for a line of pine trees along here, and then when you turn in, bear right at the Y, and Dad's place is only about a hundred yards in. It's a little log cabin, and you'll see my red Taurus parked by the back door beside his pickup."

Tom straightened and handed the paper to Kent.

"Thanks. Two o'clock . . . I'll be there." He folded the paper and creased it with his thumbnail. Once. Twice. Thrice, unnecessarily. There was nothing more that needed saying at the moment. They stood near, held in thrall by the possibility of touching, realizing that if they did they would cross a threshold that would forever alter their relationship. Their eyes gave away what they felt, how they yearned . . . and feared . . . and faced the moment with fast-tripping hearts.

And then Tom took him, and he came, and they pressed together heart to heart. They stood motionless, holding fast to one another in a flood of emotion. To have found each other became a miracle, a gift they had not expected life to give. At that moment they felt rich with it, blessed.

When they parted and looked into each other's eyes, they saw well-springs near flowing.

Tom touched his son's face, a mere resting of a palm on a cheek, while Kent's arms slid free of his father's sides. He tried to speak but failed. No smile intruded on the moment, no word marred its perfection. They stepped back, Tom's hand fell, and Kent left the office in the kind of silence reserved most times for temples.

Fourteen

On Saturday morning Tom said, "Dad, come on, let's clean up the place."

"What for?" Wesley took in the exploding magazine rack, the tilting pile of newspapers, the skewed slipcovers, and the disastrous kitchen sink. Junk everywhere, and none of it clean.

"I don't know how you can live in this pigpen."

"Doesn't bother me none."

"I know, but Dad, please, could we just make it look presentable for once?"

"Oh, all right." Wesley budged himself off his kitchen chair. "What do you want me to do?"

"Just one thing. Throw away every single thing that you haven't touched in six months, and after that, take a shower and put on clean clothes. I'll do all the rest."

Wesley looked down at his baggy trousers and khaki shirt. He looked up at Tom. *What's the matter with these?* was written all over his face. He looked down again, flicked a scale of dried egg yolk off his shirtfront, and gave a sniff that could have meant anything. Then he started sorting newspapers.

Clyde came over at quarter to two, looking spiffy. He, unlike his brother, took great pride in dressing the part of a dandy. He took one look at Wesley and said, "Great balls of fire, would you look at him! Tom, give me a jackknife so I can carve this date on the wall."

"Just shut your trap, Clyde, before I shut it for you!"

Clyde chortled in his throat. "What'd you have to do, Tom, handcuff him to the shower wall? By God, you clean up real purty, Wesley. You play your cards right, I'll take you to the whorehouse later on."

Kent arrived promptly at two. He pulled up in the Lexus and got out to be greeted by all three of the men waiting on the back stoop.

Tom went forward. Here was that awkward moment again, like back before the two of them had hugged, filled with uncertainty on both their parts.

"Hello, Kent."

"Hello, sir."

"Well . . . you're right on time."

"Yes, sir."

After a clumsy pause, Tom said, "Well, come on . . . meet Dad." He ushered the boy forward to the base of the step, shot through by indecision about how to introduce them. In the end he decided to forgo any mention of their blood relationship and let time take care of that.

"Kent, this is my dad, Wesley Gardner, and my uncle, Clyde Gardner. Dad, Uncle Clyde, this is my son Kent Arens." *My son Kent Arens.* The effect of that first declaration was far more powerful than Tom had expected. My son, my son, my son . . . Happiness flooded him as he watched the encounter between his dad and the boy.

Wesley reached out as if to shake Kent's hand, but held it at length, smiling at his face, looking from it to Tom's and back again.

"Yessir," he proclaimed, "you're Tom's boy all right. And darned if you haven't got a little bit of your grandma in you too. I can see it in the mouth, can't you, Clyde? Hasn't he got Anne's mouth?"

Kent smiled self-consciously. Then he let himself chuckle, and by the time he shook hands with Clyde, the worst moments were over.

"Well, come on inside, I'll show you where I live." Wesley led the way. "Your dad had me gussying the place up this morning, getting rid of the fish smell. I don't know about you, but I don't think there's anything wrong with a little fish smell. Makes the place feel homey. You like to fish, son?"

"I've never done it."

"Never done it! Why, we'll fix that, won't we, Clyde? Too late this year, but next summer when the season opens, you just wait! I put a cane pole in your dad's hands when he wasn't even as high as my hemorrhoids, and I want to tell you, that boy knew how to fish! We're startin' a little late with you, but maybe you ain't spoiled yet. You ever seen a Fenwick rod, Kent?"

"No sir, I haven't."

"Best rod in the—" Wesley stopped himself and spun, directing a fake scowl at the boy. "Sir? What's this 'sir' business? I don't know about you, but I'm feeling pretty lucky today. Just found myself a new grandson, and if it's all the same to you, I'd like to be called Grandpa, like all the rest of my grandchildren do. You want to try it out one time?"

Kent couldn't help grinning. It was hard not to around a lovable old windbag like Wesley. "Grandpa," he said.

"That's better. Now come on over here. I'll show you my Fenwick Goldwing. Just put a new Daiwa reel on it. It's a whisker series, you know."

Clyde piped up. "You listen to him and your mind'll get tainted right off the bat. He thinks he's got the best rod and reel in the world, but mine's better. I got a G. Loomis with a Shimano Stradic two thousand, and you can ask him whose rod and reel caught the biggest walleye this summer. Go ahead, ask him!"

"Whose rod and reel caught the biggest walleye, Grandpa?" Kent asked, falling right in with their shenanigans.

Wesley scowled at his brother. "Well, damn it, Clyde, you hung your fish on that damned old rusty scale that was prob'ly used to weigh the whale that swallowed Jonah!"

"Old, but accurate." Clyde grinned.

"Then tell him whose rod and reel caught the biggest northern!"

"Hey, wait!" Kent interrupted. "Wait, wait, wait! What's a northern? What's a walleye?"

Both men gaped at him in rank stupefaction. *"What's a walleye!"* they blurted out simultaneously. They looked at him . . . at each other . . . back at him. Their expressions seemed to say, *poor slighted child.* Then Wesley shook his head. "Boy-o-boy, do we have our work cut out for us!" he said, reaching up to remove a fishing cap that wasn't there, intending to scratch his head beneath it. "Boy-o-boy-o-boy."

They had a fabulous day. Kent learned much more about his grandfather and great-uncle than he did about his father. He sat on a slip-covered sofa and listened to the two of them tell about when they were boys in Alexandria, Minnesota, and their folks had run a resort. He learned that in the summers they'd slept in an unfinished loft over a shed, and at nighttime they peed in a fruit jar they kept under the bed until their mother found it while cleaning one time, and made them each lay a turd in the jar and leave it uncapped for two weeks before they could throw it away. It was a hot summer. The loft was ninety-five degrees by midafternoon, and well before the two weeks were up Wesley and Clyde had vowed to their mother they'd never again leave a pee jar under their bed, but would make the long walk down the path in the back even in the deep mosquitoey night.

Back then they'd had a friend they called Sweaty, who wasn't the brightest light on the Ferris wheel, but he was so much older than the rest of the boys they claimed he'd had his driver's license in sixth grade. Old Sweaty was mighty popular with the pre-driving crowd in their early teens. A bunch of them used to run around in Sweaty's car, stealing watermelons and putting Limburger cheese on manifolds, leaving snakes in people's mailboxes, gluing dimes onto sidewalks, and putting sugar in saltshakers at the local hangouts. They laughed and laughed about the Halloweens when they'd filled paper bags with dog shit, lit them on fire on people's doorsteps, then rung the bell and run. And once

they stole a huge bra and underpants from the clothesline of their
English teacher, Mrs. Fabrini, and hoisted it up the flagpole at school.

"Hoo-ey! Remember how big she was?"

Clyde held out his hands as if holding two overstuffed grocery bags.
"Like a couple of yearling pigs in a gunnysack."

"And back here, too!" Wesley swatted his rump.

"Why, when the wind blew them underpants the science teachers
took their classes outside 'cause they thought we were having an eclipse
of the sun!"

"And remember her mustache?"

"Sure do. She shaved more regular than the boys in the junior class.
Matter of fact, I think a lot of them envied her. Not me though. I
'member, I had a pretty thick beard already by that time." Clyde rubbed
his jaw, squinting one eye. "Girls were eyeing me up pretty good
already."

"Oh, sure. I suppose you were goin' to whorehouses already, too."

Clyde only chuckled, self-satisfied. "You jealous, Wesley?"

"Shee-it." Wesley pressed back on his kitchen chair, expanded his
chest, and scratched it with two hands. "At'll be the day I'm jealous of a
pack of lies from a man with blood pressure that's four times higher than
his IQ."

Tom let them carry on, watching Kent's face, catching his eye occasionally and exchanging secret smiles of amusement. At the mention of
the whorehouse, the boy looked a bit startled, but he was bright enough
to figure out this was an ongoing refrain between the two old men. After
they were done showing off, Wesley got out some photo albums and
showed Kent pictures of Tom as a boy.

"This here's your dad right after we brought him home from the
hospital. I 'member how colicky he was and how your grandma had to
walk the floor with him, nights. Here he is with the little neighbor girl,
Sherry Johnson. They used to play together in the backyards, and I used
to take them to swimming lessons together. Seemed like your dad was
born swimming though. Did he tell you he went all the way up through

Senior Lifesaving? Now this here"—Wesley's hard fingertip tapped the page—"this I remember." The photo review went on through Tom's high school football pictures to college graduation and his wedding day.

The albums were still strewn on the kitchen table when a car horn sounded and everyone looked at the back door. It had a window with a limp red-and-white-checked curtain through which four people could be seen getting out of a red Ford Bronco.

"Danged if it isn't Ryan and the kids," Wesley said, rising and going to the door. "Doesn't look like Connie's with 'em though."

He opened the door and called, "Well, look who's here!"

An assortment of voices called, "Hi, Grandpa!" and "Hi, Dad."

Tom rose, too, feeling a faint grip in his stomach. He hadn't been expecting this—his older brother and kids, who knew nothing about Kent. They lived an hour and a half north, in St. Cloud, so Tom didn't see them very often unless their get-togethers were planned.

Things happened all at once. The four new arrivals crowded into the cabin, Kent rose to his feet in slow motion, casting a questioning glance at Tom; Clyde got up to do some hand shaking and back whapping, and Ryan spotted his younger brother.

"Well, I'll be damned. Thought I'd have to go over to your house to find you."

They shook hands and gripped arms affectionately. "It's your lucky day, big bro. Where's Connie?"

"At some big antique show with her sister. I rounded up the kids and said, 'Come on, let's go visit Grandpa.'" He cast a curious glance at Kent while inquiring of Tom, "Where's Claire?"

"At home."

"Kids too?"

"Yeah."

"They okay?"

"Yeah. Everybody's fine."

"And who's this?" Ryan turned his attention fully on Kent. He was a big, bluff replica of Tom, gray above the ears, full-chested, wearing glasses.

"This . . ." Tom moved near Kent. "This takes a little explaining." Certainly fate had handed him this opportunity for a perfectly good reason. He curled a hand over Kent's shoulder. "Which I'll be happy to do if it's all right with you, Kent."

Kent looked directly into his father's eyes as he answered, "Yes, sir." But the boy's fascination could not be held from this unexpected gold mine of relatives: a real uncle . . . and cousins—three of them!— close enough to his age to maybe become his friends, if things went right.

Tom squeezed his shoulder and in a strong, resonant voice devoid of apology, announced, "This is my son, Kent Arens."

The room grew so silent you could have heard moss growing on the family tree. Nobody moved. Nobody breathed. Then Ryan, suppressing his bewilderment, reached out with a mitt like a boxing glove and shook Kent's hand while Tom spoke.

"Kent, this is your uncle Ryan."

"How do you do, sir."

"And your cousins Brent, Allison, and Erica."

Everybody stared at everybody else. Quite a few faces blushed. The two old men watched carefully, gauging reactions.

Wesley finally said, "Well, isn't anybody going to say anything?"

The girls murmured, "H'lo," and the boys shook hands perfunctorily. Erica, age fifteen, still gaping at Kent, breathed, "Well, gee . . . I mean, gosh, where have you been all these years?"

A few chuckles eased the strain, one from Kent before he answered, "Living with my mother in Austin, Texas."

Everyone looked embarrassed again, so Tom said, "Sit down, everybody, and Kent and I will tell you all about it. There are no secrets anymore. Everybody at school knows, and everyone in the family—with the exception of Connie, of course, and you can tell her when you get home. It's not every day you find an extra relative, so we might as well start this relationship out right—with the truth. Dad, maybe you better make an extra pot of coffee."

They all sat down and Tom told them the unvarnished truth, omitting nothing. Sometimes Kent filled in details, exchanging gazes with Tom, or running his eyes past the others, awed yet by this plethora of relatives after a lifetime of having nearly none. They drank coffee and root beer and ate some store-bought cupcakes, and Kent found personal trivia to exchange with Brent, who was in his last year of college at the University of Minnesota, Duluth, studying to be a speech therapist. Allison was nineteen and working at a bank. Erica seemed unable to get over her stunned amazement at Kent's existence, and every time she spoke to him she got rattled and red.

Ryan and Tom found time to be alone later in the afternoon when dusk was gathering and it was nearly time for Ryan and the kids to head home.

"Come on outside for a minute," Ryan said, and the two brothers put on jackets and went out into the frosty gloom of October. Side by side, they leaned against the cold fender of Ryan's truck, looking up at the lowering clouds that were stacked like corrugated steel in the opening between the pine trees. A pair of mallards wheeled past. The wind swirled in the clearing around the cabin, plucking at their hair and twisting the long dried grass beside the untended driveway. Sometimes they thought they felt flakes of snow on their faces, but could not see it against the metallic sky.

"Why didn't you call?" Ryan asked.

"I didn't know what to say."

"Hell, I'm your brother. You don't have to dream up what to say, you know that."

"Yeah, I know." Chin tucked, Tom stared at the toes of his shoes.

"You left Claire," the older brother said empathetically.

"No, she left me. It's just a technicality that I'm the one who moved out."

"I can't believe it." Ryan sounded as if he was still in shock.

"Neither can I."

"I always thought you two had it so together that *nothing* could bust you up! Hell, Connie and I fight more than you do."

They spent some time feeling as gloomy as the day, each sensing the sadness in the other. Finally Ryan dropped an arm across Tom's shoulders.

"So how you doin'? You doin' all right?"

Tom shrugged and crossed his arms and ankles. "Living with Dad is for shit."

"Yeah, I can imagine."

"I'm going to have to get an apartment. The dirt is driving me nuts."

"You got furniture?"

"No."

"Then what are you going to do, live with somebody?"

"No, nothing like that."

"So there's nothing between you and this woman?"

"No, not a thing."

"Well, that's good. At least you haven't got that complication. You going to try to get back together with Claire, or what?"

"If she'll try. So far she's sticking to her guns. She doesn't want me around at all. She says she needs space, needs to figure things out, needs to get over the hurt."

"How long do you think it'll take?"

Tom sighed and tilted his face to the sky, closing his eyes. "Hell, I don't know. I can't figure her out."

Ryan tightened his arm around Tom. "Yeah, who can figure out women?" After a while, he offered, "What do you want me to do? Anything, you name it."

"Nothing you can do."

"I got some old furniture, a recliner that wouldn't fit in Brent's dorm room, and a couple of old Formica-topped tables."

"Naw, thanks anyway, but I'll probably go and rent some. Nothing too permanent, you know?" Permanent or not, it still sounded pretty dismal to them both. "I've just been putting it off because it's going to be pretty lonely living alone, especially with the holidays coming. Dad's not the cleanest, but at least he's company. And Uncle Clyde comes over every day and they throw bullshit at each other, you know how they do."

"Yeah." Ryan chuckled. "I know how they do."

A couple more ducks flew over. During happier times one of the brothers would have said, "Teal," or "Bluebills," or "Mallards." Today they watched the colorful pair whisk past and said nothing. When the whistle of wings had faded away, Ryan said, "I know how much you love her. This must be hell for you."

"Pure, living, unmitigated hell."

Ryan gripped Tom and jostled him in a side-by-side hug, then rubbed his jacket sleeve a bunch of times. "The boy is mighty impressive."

"Yeah, isn't he something? I have to admit, his mother did a fine job of raising him."

"Listen, you want me to talk to Claire or anything?"

"I'm not sure what good it would do."

"Well, I can try."

"Yeah, I suppose you can try."

"I'll give her a call one day next week. Anything else I can do, just say it."

"Well, I might need someplace to go on Thanksgiving."

"You got it."

They both got quiet. Ryan looked at the rectangle of light coming through the window of the cabin door. "Well, I suppose we should be going. Connie will be home by now, and we've got a ninety-minute drive."

"Yeah, I suppose. . . ."

Tom boosted off the car. Ryan boosted off the car. They could easily count the number of times they had forthrightly hugged. They did so now, with the sadness of a broken marriage bringing them close, and the knowledge that more sadness lay ahead for Tom.

"Hey, listen, little brother, you call if you need me, okay?"

"Yuh." Tom backed away, blinking hard, turning toward the cabin. They walked to it together, and on the step Tom turned, his hand on the doorknob. "Hey, listen, in case you try to call Claire, she's got play practice every night, so call late, okay?"

"Sure thing."

"And call me afterwards, okay? Tell me what she said."

"I will."

Ryan again dropped a hand on his brother's shoulder. It slid off as Tom turned to go inside, his usual vigor sadly absent.

Ten minutes later Tom stood on the stoop watching the two vehicles back up and turn around. He raised a hand as they rolled away. Full dark had fallen, and he thought of Ryan going home to Connie, with the kids all gathered around, talking excitedly over the supper table. He pictured his own home without him: Claire, Robby, and Chelsea, subdued now, with nothing much to say. He imagined Kent going home to his mother and telling her about the cousins, grandfather, uncle, and great-uncle he'd spent the afternoon with. Behind him the two old men had shut the door and were probably going to get out the playing cards and settle down for a long night of squabbling over canasta or cribbage. There had been many sad moments since the day he'd told Claire about Kent, but none seemed as forlorn as today, when everyone moved off into a world that operated mostly in pairs. Even the ducks that flew overhead did so in pairs. And here he stood, mateless and lonely while the autumn gathered force for the coming winter.

He went inside and found he was right. The cribbage board was on the table and his dad was coming out of the bathroom. Uncle Clyde was getting out a couple of beers.

"I'm going to go out for a while," Tom said.

"Where to?" his dad asked.

"To the drugstore for some cough drops." Wesley's expression said he wasn't born yesterday. "All right," Tom relented, exasperated at having to explain himself to these two. "I don't suppose you'd believe me if I said I was going to the whorehouse."

"Nope. I wouldn't."

"Okay, I'm going to talk to Claire."

"Now, that I believe. Good luck."

He wasn't at all sure what he felt as he drove toward home. Fear, yes, and hope. A lot of self-pity and a tremendous mantle of insecurity, to which he was unaccustomed. He kept thinking, *What if I make it worse? What if she's got somebody there? Would she ask John Handelman over? Would she do that? What if I upset the kids again? What if she cries, yells, tells me to get out?*

Sometimes a quick flash of anger would strike and it would feel good; after all, he'd done the best he could to ask her forgiveness for his past mistakes, and she was putting too much emphasis on one single misguided night of his life, and not enough on the years since.

It was the damnedest thing, walking up to his own house and wondering if he must knock before going inside. He'd paid for this house, damn it! He'd painted this very door and replaced the doorknob when the tumblers got fouled up. The key for it was right in his pocket! Yet he should knock?

No damned way.

He walked right in. The kitchen was empty, the light on over the table. Somewhere upstairs a radio was playing.

He walked to the bottom of the steps and saw a bedroom light faintly illuminating the ceiling at the far end of the upstairs hall.

"Claire?" he called.

After a pause, "I'm in the bedroom!"

He climbed the stairs slowly, passed the open doors of the kids' empty, dark rooms, and stopped in the last door on the right.

Claire was standing at the dresser mirror inserting an earring, wearing high heels, a midnight-blue skirt, and a pale floral blouse he'd never seen before. The room smelled of the Estée Lauder perfume she'd worn for years.

"Hi," he said, and waited.

"Hi," she returned, picking up the second earring and tipping her head sideways while putting it on.

"Where are the kids?"

"Robby's out on a date. Chelsea's at Merilee's."

"Merilee Sand's?" Merilee was a girl neither of them particularly liked. "She's been spending a lot of time over there lately, hasn't she?"

"I make sure she's home when she should be."

"What happened to Erin?"

"Chelsea hasn't been seeing much of her lately."

He stayed in the doorway, feet planted wide. Watching Claire lean close to the mirror and twist both earrings in her earlobes, he felt the first stirrings of arousal and wondered what to do about it.

"And where are you going?"

"I'm going to a play at the Guthrie with Nancy Halliday."

"You're sure about that?"

She went to her nightstand and opened a drawer, selecting a long gold chain he had given to her for their fifteenth anniversary. "And just what is that supposed to mean?" She returned to the mirror to put the chain over her head.

"You put on perfume and high heels to go out with Nancy?"

"No, I put on perfume and high heels to go to a theater where a lot of classy people hang out." Facing the mirror, she arranged the chain flat against her blouse.

"Who are you trying to kid? I've been to the Guthrie. Half the people who go there look like leftover flower children from the sixties. The women wear black tights and stretched-out sweaters, and the men wear corduroys worse than anything my dad ever put on!"

"Don't be ridiculous, Tom." She headed for the bathroom to switch off the radio and light.

"Look, Claire!" He advanced two steps into the room and pointed at the floor at her feet. "We're separated, not divorced! That doesn't give you the right to go out on dates!"

"I'm not going out on dates! I'm going to the Guthrie with Nancy Halliday."

"And where's her husband?"

"At home. He doesn't like the theater."

"And where's John Handelman?"

Glaring up at him, Claire blushed. Realizing her mistake, she spun toward the closet to yank her suit jacket off a hanger.

"Yeah, I hit the nail on the head there, didn't I, Mrs. Gardner?" He stalked her and grabbed her arm, swinging her to face him while her half-donned jacket hung from one arm. "Well, you listen to me!" he shouted, trembling with anger. "I've watched that man eye you up for ten years, sidling around your door between classes and waiting like a damned vulture for his chance. Now that the word is out that we're separated and he's got access to you every night at play practice, I suppose he thinks he's got free rein, doesn't he? *Over my dead body, Claire!* You're still my wife, and if John Handelman so much as lays a hand on you, I'll have the sonofabitch castrated!"

She jerked free of his grip, massaging her arm. "Don't you dare yell at me, Tom Gardner! Not when you're standing there accusing me of what *you* did just so you can feel vindicated! I am not doing *anything* with John Handelman but directing a play!"

"Are you denying that he's been drooling at your classroom door since the day he laid eyes on you?"

"No!"

"Because it's true!"

"I've never encouraged him! Never!"

"Oh, come on, Claire," he said disdainfully, "how stupid do you think I am? I come up with an illegitimate son and your ego is hurt, and John Handelman is hovering in the wings every night after play practice, slobbering all over you, and you expect me to believe you're not encouraging him?"

She jammed her other arm into her suit coat and slammed the closet door. "I don't care what you believe. And the next time you come into this house, you knock!"

"Like hell I will!" He snagged her before she reached the doorway and hauled her toward the bed. Three stumbling steps and she was on her back beneath him.

"Damn you, Tom, get off me!" She fought a losing battle against his superior strength, and in a trice he had her pinned by the wrists.

"Claire . . . Claire . . ." His anger softened to supplication. "Why are you doing this? I love you. I didn't come over here to fight with you." He tried to kiss her but she swung her face aside.

"You're giving a damned fine imitation then!"

"Claire, please"—with one hand he forced her chin around—"look at me."

She wouldn't. There were tears at the corners of her closed eyes.

"I came over here to ask you to let me move back home. Please, Claire. I can't live at my dad's anymore. It just isn't working out there, and I realize that I'm going to have to get an apartment, and the first of the month is coming up fast, but before I make a move . . ." He paused, hoping she'd take pity on him, but she still refused to open her eyes. "Please, Claire . . . I don't want to live alone in some godforsaken one-bedroom apartment. I want to live with you and the kids right here in this house, where I belong."

She covered her face with her free hand and let out one enormous sob. "Damn you, Tom . . ." She tried to roll to one side and he let her, sliding from her body in the opposite direction, leaning above her while she coiled away from him. "You don't have any idea how you hurt me, do you?"

"No, Claire, I suppose I don't. It was so long ago, I don't see how it can bother you this much."

She swung her head to glare up at him. "You went from me to her to me in three days! Did you know that? I read my diary and I used to keep track of when we made love. From me to her to me—bang! bang! bang!—did you realize that, Tom?"

He hadn't. His memory was very vague about that time.

"I was your fiancée," Claire went on, her hurt pouring forth in each heart-torn word. "I was carrying your baby, and I thought . . . I thought my body was this sacred vessel to you. Giving it to you was like . . . like taking part in a sacrament. I loved you so incredibly much. I had from almost the very first time we went out together. You were, plainly and simply, a god to me. I realize my mistake now. Holding you up as an idol became my undoing, because when you fell off your pedestal, you shattered in my eyes.

"And now I'm facing your illegitimate son every day, and not only him but the gossips, and the curiosity seekers, and—yes, I'll admit it—the come-ons of John Handelman, which are quite embarrassing for me, because I don't know quite how to handle them. Do you think this is what I want, Tom? *Do you?*"

He had been looking down into her face. The longer she spoke, the more he realized his problems wouldn't be solved by storming into their house and tossing her on a bed. He fell to his back with an arm over his eyes.

She said quietly, "I want things to be like they were. Only they'll never be again. There are moments when I hate you for doing that to us."

He swallowed hard. His desire had faded, in its place a hollow yearning, a fear that he had trivialized what she was going through and would pay for it with the loss of her and his children.

She dragged herself to the edge of the bed and sat with her back to him, making no move to go further. He lay on the rumpled bedspread, hiding beneath his upflung arm because he was afraid of what he might read in her face when he asked the question he had so feared asking. "Do you want a divorce, Claire? Is that what you want?"

She sighed and sat silent for so long that he finally let his arm fall.

"I don't know," she said softly, so softly he realized the depth of the danger into which their marriage had been thrust. He lay studying her with love and hurt and fear forming a knot in his throat. He had messed her hair. It had been fluffed and soft when he came in, but now it was flattened against her skull like a used pillow.

He sat up, braced on one hand with his shoulder close behind hers so she couldn't see his face. He touched her hair, tried to restore its shape, but failed.

"Claire, I'm sorry."

Though she made no reply, he knew she believed him. The pitiful part was that she could not forgive him.

"We have to work this out somehow," he said. "Don't you see that?"

"Yes."

"Will you go to counseling with me?"

She sat forlornly, staring at her knees, her feet not quite touching the floor. She nodded dispassionately as if she'd given up, and he closed his eyes, restraining a sigh of relief, letting his chin sink to his chest.

"But I think you'd better take that apartment, Tom."

He opened his eyes in surprise. "Now? Before the holidays? Please, Claire . . ."

"Take it, Tom." She got off the bed and went to the bathroom to repair her hair and makeup. He let himself fall back and lay staring at the texturized ceiling where the lamplight slanted and put oversized shadows behind each tiny lump. She ran the water, turned it off. Her cosmetics made small sounds—a compact opening, closing; a mascara wand dropping into a drawer; the drawer closing. A sniff from her, then a tissue being extracted from a box. Though he still stared at the ceiling, he knew when she came to the bathroom doorway and stood looking at him.

"I have to go," she said calmly.

His insides twisted in fear. He'd thought she wouldn't be able to face going out after the emotional wringer he'd just put them through. But she was stalwart in her attempt to move on without him, for a while anyway.

He remained where he was. "I'll just stay here awhile, if that's all right with you."

"As long as you're gone by the time I come home."

"Don't worry, I will be."

"All right then. Do you want me to leave the light on?"

"No, you can turn it off."

She snapped off the bathroom light and went out, switching on the hall light, her belated consideration wounding him in a way she would never know. She went downstairs without a further word, and when she reached the bottom turned off the upstairs light, leaving him in darkness.

Fifteen

❧✠❧

Parent-teacher conferences were going to shorten the school week, so Claire had extended play practice for an additional hour on Monday, Tuesday, and Wednesday. They had all worked hard and the kids were uncomplaining about spending the extra time at school. However, they were overjoyed at the prospect of having four days off without practice. The backdrops had been finished with the cooperation of the art department, and the set promised to look extraordinarily convincing. Some mothers had done volunteer sewing, and the costumes were coming together beautifully. Tickets had been printed up, and the local newspaper had sent a photographer, who got some good photos for a rousing article about the entire project. It had appeared in this morning's paper and given the entire cast and crew stuff to crow about. The mood was upbeat when the gang broke up at eleven o'clock that Wednesday night.

It had become habit for Claire and John to walk out to their cars together. The parking lot was deserted at this hour of the night. Scudding white clouds drifted past a half-moon, blotting its reflection off the roofs of the two cars parked near each other.

"Good night, John," Claire said, passing his car without slowing.

"Good night."

She was unlocking her car door when he said at her shoulder, "You in a hurry to get home, Claire?"

She spun with a hand on her heart.

"Lord, John, you scared me half to death."

"Sorry. I didn't mean to. Could I buy you a cup of coffee?"

"At this time of night?"

"Well, how about a glass of Coke?" When she remained hesitant, he added cajolingly, "Glass of milk? . . . Water?"

"I don't think so, John. It's after eleven and tomorrow's going to be a long day. You know how conferences are. By this time tomorrow night I'll be hoarse and grouchy."

"Then it's better that we have that drink now, isn't it?" When she still hesitated, he said, "I'm just all keyed up tonight. Everything went so well, and the kids are being such good sports. I'm enjoying the class play very much and I want it to last. What do you say—just half an hour?"

"No, John, I'm sorry."

"Are you still scared I'll make a move on you?"

"When did I say I was scared?"

"You don't have to say it. It shows."

"Oh, I . . . I didn't realize that."

"You practically jumped out of your skin when I came up behind you."

Yes, she had.

"Claire, I know you're very much aware of me. A man senses these things."

"Please, John, I have to go." She bent as if to unlock her car, but with a gentle grip on her arm he turned her to face him.

"Would you just tell me, Claire, what's the status between you and Tom?"

She sighed and let her weight settle back against the car door. "We're apart. He's living with his father but he's going to be getting an apartment soon. I've agreed to start joint counseling with him."

"Do you still love him?"

Nobody had asked her that since she'd left Tom. It felt quite good to think about it and come up with the right answer.

"Yes, John, I do."

John leaned forward, resting the heels of his hands on the car roof on either side of her shoulders, stapling her loosely into place.

"Well, I'm going to take a chance and tell you something that I hope will change your mind about me. When I first came here to teach, I was coming off a relationship that had absolutely annihilated me. I'd been engaged to a woman who had an affair with somebody else and gave me back my ring. I caught them in bed together in the apartment Sally and I shared. My self-esteem was about as low as it could go when I met you. But you encouraged me to talk, and you said that what she'd done was reprehensible and that I must not let it defeat me. Remember how you used to tell me that she wasn't the only fish in the sea, and just because one woman had treated me like crap, that didn't mean they all would? We used to stand there between our classroom doors, and I swear to God, I almost went crazy, waiting for that bell to ring at the end of every hour so I could beat it out there and see you. All I could think about was getting to you, talking to you, because everything you said about relationships and commitment was the way I wanted it to be, and you were teaching me so many important lessons."

His voice softened. "I fell in love with you, Claire, so many years ago—what is it now? Ten? Eleven? I fell in love with you, and I watched you and Tom smile at each other when you'd meet in the halls, and I'd ache because I couldn't tell you how I felt.

"I did the honorable thing, Claire. I never once spoke my feelings. I wouldn't have dishonored you that way—because to me it would have been a dishonor to imply that you were susceptible to my advances.

"But now things have changed. All right, you say you still love him, but you're living apart, and I've been waiting to meet some woman who measures up to you, but nobody comes close. So here I am, taking the only chance I might have in my lifetime to lay it on the line and tell you how I feel.

"I love you, Claire. I've loved you for a very long time, and if there's any chance in the world for me, this old heart of mine feels like you'd be saving its life if you'd say so right now."

"Oh, John." She had not imagined the depth of his feelings. "I didn't know."

"I told you, Claire, I didn't want you to know. I'm not that kind of man who'd try to seduce a happily married woman."

"But don't you see, John? Happily or not, I'm still married."

"But there are mitigating circumstances, aren't there?"

"Not really. Not where vows are concerned."

He studied her at point-blank range by moonlight, their faces so close the shadow of his head darkened her chin. "What if I kissed you?"

"It would complicate our work relationship."

"So what? It's been complicated for me for over ten years. Would you be angry if I did?"

"I have to go, John." She made a motion as if to pull away from the car door but he remained as before, hemming her in.

"Would you be angry? Because if you will be, I'm not going to risk it."

She released one nervous huff of laughter. "John Handelman, you know exactly what you're doing, don't you? I'm not made of wood. I am, after all, susceptible to compliments and flattery, especially when they're accompanied by an honest declaration of feelings. If you think I'm not reacting here, guess again. But I can't say yes. I'm married."

"You're separated."

"Not legally."

"Only emotionally." He gave her time to respond. When she failed, he added, "Is that it, Claire?"

She thought for a moment, confused and tempted by him. "Maybe . . . yes. I don't know. Good night, John, I've got to go."

"Good night, Claire. You can blame me for this," he said as his head cut off the moon and he kissed her. She put her hands on his shoulders to push him away, but they rested there without resisting him. She arched away from him, taking little part in the contact of their mouths, but feeling his body curve against hers from the waist down. He was wearing jeans and a short jacket, she a full-length coat, unbuttoned. His mouth was warm and persuasive, open slightly, and the shock of feeling another man's tongue caused her to recoil, for much to her amazement, she liked it. He was a clean, good, attractive man whom she'd always liked, whom she'd worked well with over the years. Nothing he had ever said or done had repulsed or even aggravated her. He'd declared his love for her and had stolen one single kiss, which she'd verbally denied.

She drew back and forced him to end the kiss, but he lowered his face to her jaw and whispered thickly, "Just one, come on, Claire, one with you taking part in it a little bit. One, because I know it'll be the only one I ever get. Come on, Claire, give me that much . . . Claire . . . one single kiss . . . Claire, lovely Claire . . . you've been my dream for so long . . ."

He slipped his arms inside her coat and fit himself against her in every place that counted, sliding one hand clear up between her shoulder blades until he gripped the back of her neck and urged her to turn her head. She gave in and their mouths aligned. He had soft, full lips, not at all off-putting, and he knew how to use them. He, like Claire herself, enjoyed drama and had an instinct for putting it to good use when the time was right.

The time was right, there in that late moonlit autumn night in the surrounding emptiness of the dark parking lot.

She succumbed to the loveliness of the kiss, to its deep delights and deeper perils, adding her own motion at the beck and call of his. John Handelman, for his part, decided that if it was to be the one and only kiss he ever shared with her, he'd make it count, and he followed nature's way, flexing his knees and striking her in upsweeps like bent grass releasing when the wind wanes, again and again until she arched in reply and made a soft sound in her throat.

What constitutes betrayal, Claire wondered, even while enjoying the kiss. She knew this was wrong midway through the buildup, but she had been lonely, and had missed kisses so very much. Maybe Tom had done this with Kent Arens's mother in the last few weeks, and if so, didn't she, Claire, deserve recompense? It could happen this easily, she knew now, starting out in unadulterated innocence, ending in innocent adultery.

But she would not be a party to it. Nor would she drop her head in shame for having wrongly indulged.

"Stop, John." She drew away and pushed at the bend of his elbows. "That's enough." Much to her dismay, they were both breathing stridently, and all within her had welled up, proving that chastity had its price. His breath beat at a swath of her hair, battering it against her temple in the white night light. He rested his lips against her forehead.

She said, "We'll never do this again. That's a promise. I want you to promise, too."

"Not on your life."

"Tom said he'd castrate you if you did this to me."

He pulled back and lifted her chin with a finger. "So you talked about me. You knew."

"No." She withdrew from his touch. "I didn't. Tom suspected, that's all."

"What did he say?"

She fended off further questions with two widespread hands. "No. Don't. I'm not going to discuss him with you or divulge any more of his feelings. I've done enough already. Please forgive me."

"*Forgive* you?"

"Yes. I shouldn't have let this happen. It means nothing. I want to save my marriage, not ruin it. I'm sorry, John, really I am. Listen, I've got to go. Please, let's both try to forget this tomorrow." When she moved to open her car door he did it for her. A part of her expected him to detain her, maybe even try to further this ill-advised tryst the two of them had perpetrated. He was as good as his word, however, and, having claimed his one kiss, stood back and waited while she got behind the wheel and put her key in the ignition. As she started the engine he slammed her car door, then stepped back and raised a hand in farewell as she pulled away.

She drove home in a state of arousal and guilt, and climbed into her cold, empty bed alone. She was so angry with Tom she cried and stretched herself diagonally across his half of the bed with her breasts on his pillow, missing him so damned much she wanted to drive out there to

Wesley's house and whap the living piss out of him for getting them into this impasse in the first place!

After tossing and crying sporadically, she called him at one-thirty in the morning from the kitchen phone, a house length away from the sleeping children, trusting that the old man would be a sounder sleeper and farther away from the phone than Tom.

It took five rings before he picked up, and then a full two seconds before his first utterance. He cleared his throat and answered groggily, "Hullo?"

"Tom?"

A long pause, then, "Claire?"—hopefully, but with a voice still off duty.

"I couldn't sleep. I've been thinking."

He waited.

"We've got to make that appointment with the counselor right away."

"All right. Which one?"

"Not any of them from school. I don't want them to hear all of the sordid details of our troubles."

"I've got a list of clinics at school."

"Then pick one. Any one."

"Do you think we should go together the first time, or separately?"

"I don't know."

"Together," he decided.

"I don't know. Maybe the counselor will recommend what's best."

"Or I've got a better idea. Why don't I come over there right now and crawl into bed with you, and in the morning we won't need any counselors."

"Oh, Tom, can't you see that's not going to solve this?"

"Then why did you call me in the middle of the night?"

"Because I miss you, damn it!"

"Claire, are you crying?"

"Yes, I'm crying!"

His pulse raced at her admission. "Please let me come over there, please, Claire."

"Tom, I'm so scared. I don't . . . I don't know the me I've become."

He hunkered on the Naugahyde footstool on top of his mother's piano music, gripping an old-fashioned black telephone receiver in one hand and his forehead in the other.

"Claire, do you love me?"

"Yes!" Exasperated.

"And I love you. So why are we going through this?"

"Because I haven't forgiven you and I'm not sure I ever can, and don't you see that I'll hold it against you until I *do* forgive you? Oh, God, I don't know . . ." She sounded beyond exhaustion. "I did something tonight that . . ."

He bristled and his elbows came off his knees.

"What did you do?"

"See? You're mad at me already and I haven't even told you what it is."

"You were with Handelman, weren't you?"

"Just get the counselor lined up, the sooner the better."

"What did you do with him!"

"Tom, I don't want to get into it now. It's almost two o'clock and I've got ten hours of conferences to get through tomorrow."

"Damn it, Claire! You call me up at two in the morning and tell me you were with another man and then *you* say you don't want to get into it now!"

Wesley came shambling out of his bedroom in the dark and mumbled, "What's all the shouting about?"

"Go back to bed, Dad!"

"You talking to Claire?"

"Yes, now go back to bed!"

Wesley did. And closed his door.

Claire said, "Oh, hell, now we woke up your dad."

"This is really playing dirty, you know that, Claire? All right, so I had a fling eighteen years ago, but you're just twisting the knife, and you know it." His anger grew ripe, his yelling unbridled. "You want to go to a counselor, you make your own goddamned appointment! And look for John Handelman's balls on your lunch tray tomorrow!"

He slammed down the receiver and rocketed to his feet, stood like a samurai staring down at the dark lake, stood for all of thirty-seven seconds before marching into his bedroom and scrabbling through his briefcase for the phone number of John Handelman. He left the bedroom light on and marched back to the phone, growing additionally pissed off because his dad still had a rotary albatross that seemed to take fifteen minutes to dial! *Why the hell couldn't the old fart keep up with the times and get himself a Touch-Tone phone?*

Handelman answered on the seventh ring.

"Handelman? This is Tom Gardner! You keep your slimy hands off my wife or I'll have you out of this school district so goddamned fast that you'll need a nose cone to reenter. You got that?"

Handelman took a moment to wake up to what was happening. "Well," he finally replied, unruffled, "that didn't take long."

"You hear me, Handelman?"

"I hear you."

"And you keep away from her door between classes, you got that too?"

"I got that too. Anything else?"

"Yeah. Stick to play practice instead of practicing plays on my wife! If you're hard up for a woman, go get one of your own!"

Tom slammed the receiver down so hard it jumped off and clattered to the tabletop. He slammed it down even harder. Then he sat a long time on the plastic ottoman, gripping his head while the ridge around the legs of his briefs began to dig into his buns, and his thighs stuck to the plastic. He pulled himself up in slow motion, peeling his skin free with a sound like rattling paper.

Goddamn it, he thought, shuffling off to bed like an old man. Goddamn it all to hell. When was she going to come to her senses?

He slept terribly after that and awakened in the morning with a headache. To top it off, he turned on the shower to discover that his father's creaky old water system had a burned-out heater. He showered in the river of ice water and arrived at school still shivering, and in a vile temper prompted by the Claire/Handelman incident, wondering about its particulars.

The teachers had a one-hour prep time before conferences started, so he poured himself a mug of steaming coffee and took it to her room.

When he entered, she was standing at a worktable with her back to him, stuffing manila folders into a marbleized cardboard box. Only when he closed the door did she glance over her shoulder.

"Open the door."

"You said you didn't want the whole school to know the sordid details of our fights."

"Not in the school building, Tom! Now, open that door!"

"I want to know what you did with him."

"Tom . . . *not now!*"

"You call me in the middle of the night and—"

She spun and faced him angrily. "Look! I have three days of solid meetings with parents ahead of me, and so help me, if you make me start crying and ruin my makeup, I'll do something with John Handelman's balls that you won't be too happy about when I find them on my lunch tray! Now get out of here!"

"Claire, you're still my wife!"

She pointed the way with one trembling finger. Her voice turned menacing. *"Get . . . out . . . of . . . here!"*

She was right. Their workplace was totally inappropriate for carrying on their row. He spun in place, yanked open the door, and stormed out.

The way conferences were handled at HHH, all the teachers were stationed at tables set up around the perimeter of the gym, and parents ranged freely, seeking the shortest lines, until they'd spoken to all the teachers they needed to see. There were lulls, short stretches when some teachers had no lines at all, but for the most part the center of the gym remained an arena of motion with parents crossing, searching the name placards taped to the gym walls, stopping to visit with other parents before moving on and forming lines that snaked into the crowd four and five deep.

It was shortly before noon of the first day when Claire hit a lull, pushed back, and stretched. The stretch abruptly ended when she saw Tom standing just inside the gym doors talking to Monica Arens.

The blood seemed to push at Claire's neck and face. Try as she might, she could not tear her eyes away. Monica had changed her hairstyle to something much more flattering. She was dressed in an attractive sienna-brown suit with a gold pin on the lapel that matched her earrings. Someone had once told Claire that when people start having an affair they suddenly start taking pride in their appearance.

Claire couldn't stop staring.

Tom started out in his *principal's stance*, arms crossed, feet flat, knees locked, leaning back from the waist. Monica said something and he chuckled, pushed back his unbuttoned suit jacket, caught his hands on his hips, dropped his chin, and relaxed his knees. He looked back up into Monica's face and said something. They both laughed.

Laughed!

Then they sobered as one and exchanged a gaze that Claire couldn't see on Tom's face, only on Monica's. If she wasn't a woman in love, Claire would eat everything on her next lunch tray!

Suddenly Monica's eyes swung Claire's way, and Claire bent to appear busy, digging through the materials in the box on the floor.

She came up with Kent's folder, opened it on her lap, and studied its contents, aware that Monica Arens was moving toward her through the crowd.

Her presence overwhelmed Claire with threat, this woman who had carnal knowledge of her husband, who had lain with him one week before his wedding, whose body had accepted his seed while Claire was already pregnant with his baby, and who only a moment ago had stood across this gym laughing with him.

"Hello," a voice said, and Claire feared looking up. When finally she did, she found the woman standing before her poised and seemingly undaunted by this meeting. "I'm Monica Arens, Kent's mother." She extended her hand, looking more attractive than Claire remembered. She had applied makeup that added a curve to her mouth and size to her eyes. Her hair lifted at the crown and wisped forward in a deceptively simple shag that cupped her face without ever quite touching it, like a fading blossom of Queen Anne's lace. Her suit was expensive and draped exquisitely upon her frame, her jewelry tastefully simple.

"Hello," Claire replied, keeping her hand intentionally limp while touching her nemesis. Monica sat and said nothing further.

Claire cleared her throat and placed Kent's folder on the table. "Well . . ." She had been a speech teacher at one time, a drama teacher another, and she included a unit on extemporaneous speaking every year in her senior honors class. How many times had she instructed her students never to open any dialogue with the word *well?* Yet here she sat doing it, like a stagestruck idiot. She cleared her throat and repeated her mistake. "Well . . . Kent is certainly a good student . . . um . . ."

They proceeded along this bumpy road, one of them rambling on nervously, the other listening attentively, asking occasional intuitive, bright questions.

Nobody ever said, My son is going through emotional hell since he found out who his father is.

Or, Your son tried to lecture me about saving my marriage.

Or, My son met his grandfather and cousins last weekend.

Or, My family is falling apart because of you.

They merely conferred—a teacher, a parent at conferences, like two supportive fakes.

But at the end of their discussion, they didn't shake hands. And when Monica rose and paused beside her metal folding chair, tension skewered her there for a moment. She drew breath as if to speak, and Claire waited expectantly. The silence grew uncomfortable, and finally Claire said, "Well . . ." yet again, thinking to herself, *Oh, you silver-tongued devil, you.*

The spell had broken and Monica retreated one step, caught her purse beneath an arm, and said, "Goodbye. Thank you."

"Yes . . . goodbye."

Two other parents were waiting for Claire, but even as they seated themselves, she watched Monica moving away through the crowd, then swung her gaze to Tom, still standing by the entrance to the gym. He'd been watching them intently.

When their gazes caught, he started moving toward Claire, but whatever denial he had planned could be waylaid: She turned her attention to greeting the new set of parents who had taken Monica's place.

Tom came forward anyway, taking the liberty of walking around behind the table where his wife was seated. "Excuse me," he said, and placing one hand on the tabletop, the other on the back of Claire's chair, he leaned down right in front of her, his shoulder forming a barrier between her and the parents.

"Friday next week, five o'clock at Family Networking. The counselor's name is Mr. Gaintner."

"I thought you said I could line up the counselor myself." She kept her expression deliberately flat. His face was nearer than it had been in weeks. She wanted to spread a hand on it and push him onto his trim little ass on the floor.

"I changed my mind. You're busy today. I thought I might as well do it."

"Couldn't you get an appointment sooner than that?"

He shrugged. "What can I say? The world's a screwed-up place. Lots of people doing lots of things to mess up their lives."

His flippancy burned her. "Does he want to see both of us?"

Tom nodded, dragged himself upright like James Dean, and went away.

He had consulted a man! Damn his manipulative hide—a man! He knew perfectly well she preferred women counselors after all the discussions they'd had on the subject! Women were better counselors than men any day. Men couldn't let themselves get teary-eyed. They held their distance instead of hugging, though even Claire had to admit that men had just cause to worry about accusations of sexual misconduct, given today's litigious climate. Every male educator she knew was terrified of touching girl students, even on the shoulder. Nevertheless, Tom knew Claire liked women counselors.

But he'd consulted a man.

She was angry and distracted for the rest of the afternoon and evening, while she watched the clock creep toward nine P.M. and sucked throat lozenges and felt her voice growing hoarser from all the talk, talk, talk. Their esteemed principal had warned them that no teacher was to leave her assigned table until the tick of nine, and far be it from Claire Gardner to seek his royal highness's retribution!

At nine she slammed the cover on her storage box, scooped it beneath her arm, and ran to find Joan Berlatsky before Joan left the building. She caught her in her office as Joan was slipping on her coat.

"Joan, can you spare one minute, please?"

Joan glanced at the clock and restrained a sigh. "Sure." She dropped into her chair with a sigh.

"I don't mean to take advantage of you, but I need some advice."

"Do you want to shut the door?" They both knew Tom could very well walk past at any moment on his way to his own office.

Claire closed the door and perched on the edge of a visitors' chair. "I assume you know that Tom and I are apart and why."

"Yes, I do, Claire. I'm really sorry about it."

"You know that Kent Arens is his son?"

Joan nodded.

"I have a confession to make. First of all, let me say in my own defense that I'm a good teacher. I care very much about my students and their welfare, but I did something tonight that I've never done before. I avoided talking about something that should have been discussed with a parent. You see, I had a conference with Kent's mother."

Joan had sat back in her chair and joined her hands. Her steepled fingers rested against her lips while she studied Claire with a faint frown.

"Tom suggested weeks ago that he put Kent in someone else's English class, but I had the only honors class, so I stubbornly insisted he stay with me. Now . . . well, now things have grown so complex and the relationships have changed between all of us. I can't help thinking it's affecting that boy much worse than he lets on. I should have talked about it honestly with his mother, but I just couldn't. Kent's grade has been a perfect four point oh, and I rationalized with myself that since his grades haven't suffered, I didn't need to bring up anything personal during the conference. I know it was cowardly of me, and I know I'm using you as a confessor here, but . . . well . . . you see, I think . . . that is, *sometimes* I think Tom is having an affair with her. There. God, I've said it. I've got it off my chest at last."

Joan sat as before, thinking, frowning, tapping her fingertips against her mouth. Finally she asked a few pertinent questions, and the answers filled in the necessary past history.

" . . . and now he's made an appointment with a male counselor. Joan, I know he did it to get a man on his side, and I wanted a woman!"

"Did you tell him that?"

"No, but he knows it!"

Joan did nothing more than change the position of her arms. It had been a long, grueling day for her too. She had been talking to stupid parents and recalcitrant teenagers since nine o'clock that morning. She had a headache from the buzz of the gym lights, and a heartache from some of the genuinely pitiful situations she'd handled today. She wanted to go home, flop into bed, and sleep into the next century. Along comes this normally well-balanced, kind, caring woman who was throwing away her marriage and wrecking her family because she couldn't see through her own red haze of jealousy. Claire Gardner was a well-educated woman who'd had her share of psych classes, but a college education didn't necessarily guarantee common sense, and sometimes Joan grew downright fed up with these teachers who ought to have more of it. Joan Berlatsky—bless her weary counselor's heart— had had it!

"Claire, listen to yourself. How many times have you read and heard that the basis of most relationship problems is lack of communication? If you wanted a female counselor, you should have said so. You're blaming Tom because you're upset with him about something else entirely. Ask any divorce lawyer—this is how the big-time fights get up a head of steam. Do you want to save your marriage?"

Claire's recoil said very clearly she hadn't expected rebuttal of this sort.

"Yes," she replied meekly. "At least I think I do."

"Well, you're surely not acting like it. I've known Tom for twelve years, and in that time I've never heard him do anything but praise you. I'm at meetings and on committees with him that you aren't in. What he says behind your back would probably make you blush with joy. That man loves you, and he loves his children, and what you're putting them all through gets no sympathy from me, because I don't think you've got just cause. He made a mistake in judgment eighteen years ago, and he's apologized and asked your forgiveness for it, and whatever you're accusing him of now is all based on circumstantial evidence. I don't think he's having an affair because I know how he loves you. You're embarrassed by having to face his son day after day while the whole school population knows who Kent is, but—hey, so what? So we know. Big deal. We accept it. The boy is our student, and we haven't ostracized him, or Tom, for that matter. You're the only one doing that. And in the process, you're alienating your own family. I'm probably not sounding much like a counselor right now because I'm not. I'm turning down your request to talk to me about this any more because, quite frankly, this is one case where I've taken sides, and I'm not on yours. I'm squarely on Tom's, because what I see ahead for you is a broken home and four unhappy people if you continue the way you have been. He's miserable. Your children are miserable. Truthfully, I think you probably are too. Now I'm tired, I've been talking all day, and I want to go home to bed."

Joan stood up, bringing the discussion to a close. She moved to the door, opened it, and snapped the light switch off—quite rudely, actually—as Claire attempted to gather her wits and realize she was being roundly reprimanded and turned out.

Joan bent and locked her door behind them, then led the way toward the plate-glass door. There she turned and looked down past the secretaries' desks to where Tom's office light fell through his open doorway across the blue carpet.

"Tom, are you still there?" she called.

Momentarily, he appeared in his doorway.

"Yes, Joan, you can leave it unlocked."

"Will do. Good night then."

"Good night."

He said nothing to Claire, and she said nothing to him. But their gazes met across the deserted stretch of office, and pride held them aloof.

She thought, *Oh, Tom, I know I should do exactly what Joan said.*

And he thought, *You know what you can do, Claire? You can just haul yourself off to John Handelman if you've gone to bed with him, because I sure as hell don't want you back.*

Sixteen

At 8:30 that night, Chelsea left a note on the kitchen table. "Dear Mom," it read, "Drake Emerson called and invited me to go to Mississippi Live with a bunch of his friends. I said yes because it's not a school night so I can sleep late tomorrow. I know I should have asked you first, but I couldn't get ahold of you since you were having conferences. See you in the morning. Love, Chels."

Chelsea made one last check in the bathroom mirror, added a layer of lip gloss, pouted at her reflection, and shut off the light. She went to the doorway of Robby's room.

"I'll be out of here in a minute. What're you doing tonight?"

His eyes swung to the door and scanned her length, down, then up. She was wearing black leggings and a fishnet top over a little tight black thing that showed her belly, sort of like what the aerobics dancers wore on TV. Her hair was bushed out in wild corkscrews, and she had too much makeup on her eyes, plus her lipstick was red and shiny instead of coral and soft the way she used to wear it. Her earrings were big and dangly and noisy; he'd never seen them before.

"I'm going to the second show with Brenda. She had to work till nine. Are you going out dressed in *that?*"

She flicked a glance downward, then gave a toss of her head. "Sure. This is how all the girls dress up there."

"You should have asked Mom about going there."

"I couldn't. She's in the gym, and there are no phones in the gym, or have you forgotten?"

"You should have gone over there then. And you should have asked her about going with Drake Emerson."

"What's wrong with Drake?"

"You know what's wrong with Drake. He hasn't got a very good reputation."

"Listen, he called me like a gentleman, and he talked very politely on the phone. And besides, maybe if kids like that get a chance to prove they're okay, they will be. Mom and Dad have never said anything about him getting called into the office or anything."

"Are any of your other friends going along?"

"My other friends are so *boring.* We do the same old things all the time, and I figure this is a good chance to make some new ones."

"Mom wouldn't like it. Neither would Dad."

Chelsea's face hardened. "Well, maybe I don't care. Did they ask us if we liked what *they* did? And besides, they're not here, so how can I ask permission?"

"Chelsea, I don't think you should wear that."

Chelsea rolled her eyes and pivoted on one foot. Her parting remark could be heard coming back down the hall. "Oh, brr-other, I really don't need this."

She made sure she had her jacket on and was ready to slip out the door the moment the bell rang, so Drake didn't have to come into the house. She wouldn't put it past Robby to subject him to some grand inquisition, like he was her father or something.

As it turned out, Drake was late and Robby had already gone by the time the car pulled into the driveway to collect Chelsea. She ran out to meet him on the sidewalk leading up to the house.

"Hey, so how'z it goin', babe?" he greeted her.

"Just fine. Can't wait to see this place."

"If you want to do some illin', this is the place."

She disqualified the tiny shiver of misgiving and told herself she was a good girl. Tonight would be nothing but innocent fun.

The car waiting in the driveway was such a wreck she wasn't sure it would make it all the way to downtown Minneapolis. Someone named Church was driving, and beside him were Merilee, and Esmond, whom she had never met; he was twenty-three, Merilee had told her. In the dark, Chelsea barely caught a glimpse of them. Throughout the ride they remained three bodyless heads framed by the green lights from the dash. She sat in the back between Drake and a girl from Robby's senior class named Sue Strong. Sue was a burnout who—it was rumored—had a tattoo of a serpent on her butt and had once been caught bare-breasted in a janitor's room with a boy who'd flunked out of school the year before. Chelsea had heard Sue's name around the kitchen table on more than one occasion, and it hadn't been good.

"Hi, Sue," Chelsea said when introduced.

Sue blew smoke at the roof and said, "You the principal's daughter?"

"Yes, I am."

"This's cool, Drake," Sue said. "Her old man busted my ass more'n once for shit that wasn't none of his business. This's gonna be a real drag, man, havin' her along."

Chelsea felt her stomach clench, but Drake slung an arm up and rocked her over against him, grinning into her eyes.

"Hey, Sue, watch your mouth. She's not used to talk like that, are you, sugar?"

Chelsea smiled tensely and caught the smell of leather from Drake's jacket. The faraway dash lights picked out his dark eyes and lopsided smile. He reminded Chelsea of the carny who'd run the bullets at the state fair last summer. He said all the right things, but in his grin salaciousness lingered, as if every word he spoke had a second meaning. Drake whispered, putting his mouth nearly against Chelsea's ear so Sue couldn't hear, "Never mind her. She and Esmond are jugglin' insults tonight, that's all. But we're going to have a good time, you and me. This place'll really rock your world. You're going to like it."

He was right. Mississippi Live really rocked her world. Located in Riverplace, in a historic district of downtown Minneapolis on the banks of the Mississippi River, it was a multiplex dance hall, a music lover's dream, a rocker's delight, an assault on the senses even before one stepped inside. Crossing the courtyard out front, Chelsea heard the music pounding through the glass wall. She could see motion and lights even before they went through the door. Inside, the beat magnified and drove itself into her stomach. The crowd of upbeat dancers and cruisers was dominated by young people in their twenties. Just inside the front door a young man was strapped into the human gyro machine with his limbs outspread like a Michelangelo sketch while he whirled like a beach ball going over a waterfall. The gyro was centered between a pair of curving steel staircases leading up to an open balcony. Both the balcony and stairs were packed with humanity, every pair of eyes captivated by the whirling human form. Many of the spectators held bottles of beer or glasses of mixed drinks.

Chelsea followed Drake up the stairway. On the second floor the beat from downstairs segued into that from the karaoke show, where a high-energy master of ceremonies clapped and stirred things up while a young man sang "Soul Survivor" and the words flashed across multiple TV screens mounted on the ceiling. A different press of people surrounded the karaoke stage, the clientele constantly shifting, moving on its feet, turning sideways when moving through the crowd to the next attraction. Drake and Chelsea turned left into a black cavern where a DJ sat in a glass booth and rap music blasted out of speakers while strobe lights spattered a collection of dancers into disjointed fragments of motion on the dance floor. One girl wore a crop top, a coarse calf-length burlap skirt, and cossack boots. One man wore black-and-red leather pants with a design like foot-long sharks' teeth taking gouges out of his legs. One dancer wore suspenders, Spike Lee–style glasses low on his nose, and a silver-sequined bowler on his head. As he whirled, his hat seemed to levitate off his head five times a second in the strobe lights.

Home Song

The music hurt Chelsea's ears. It made the center of her chest feel as if it would implode.

Drake put his lips to her ear. "Want something to drink?"

She yelled back, "A Coke!"

He grinned at her while turning away. She watched him from behind as he moved toward the bar. His pants were so tight she figured something on him must be hurting. He had thick boots on his feet like those of a mountain climber. His tapered, waist-length leather jacket had zippers on the arms and chest.

At the bar he must have been carded because he pulled a billfold out of his pocket and flashed what had to be a fake ID before the bartender began mixing a drink.

In a minute he returned with two plastic glasses and handed her one. She yelled thank you and sipped cautiously, finding, thankfully, that it was plain Coca-Cola. She turned, fascinated, back to the dance floor. Nobody in the place seemed to be using the chairs, except occasionally to hook a foot on. Across the way a couple danced beside their table, apparently practicing some moves. Nobody paid them the least attention. After a few minutes Drake confiscated Chelsea's glass and set it down, then led her onto the floor. She danced until sweat dampened her bra and her hair stuck to her hot neck, never once touching Drake, though she felt as if she'd been touched by him in most of the erogenous zones of her body. He had a sinewy body that moved like smoke, and a way of keeping his gaze riveted on her that made her feel daring.

Soon they moved on to another dance floor, another bar, followed by another and another until they had sampled five. They danced in most of them, bought drinks in most of them. In the last, country music played and people were line-dancing. A sequined cowboy boot turned slowly above the dance floor, casting diamond spangles across the dancers below. The song changed to a slow one and Drake said, "Come on, babe, one more time." He wound his arm around her waist, plastered his pelvis against her, and dropped his hand down low over her spine, where he massaged her with his fingertips in time to the music. She reached back and pulled it up.

"What's the matter?" He grinned down at her, thrusting his hips more firmly against her. "Never danced this way before?"

"Not where anybody could see me."

"How about where people couldn't see you?"

"Mmm . . ." She smiled suggestively and tossed her head.

"Feels good if you let it." He commandeered her arms and urged them up over his shoulders, holding them in place until she doubled them across his neck. Then he rubbed his hands down to her hips, gripping and steering them to his liking. Below, she could feel bones and flesh impress themselves upon her like fossils in clay as he kept on moving, moving, always moving against her, cradling her, keeping his knees spread and eventually working his right thigh between hers. His right hand stole up beneath her fishnet top onto the bare flesh above her waistband. He spread his fingers wide until his thumb intruded under the back elastic of her bra.

She thought of secrets Erin had divulged about having sex with Rick. She thought of her parents. *Hey, Mom and Dad, what do you think of this, huh? Your perfect little girl's not so perfect anymore, is she?*

Above her, the sequined boot threw light chips across the dancers. A spell of vertigo struck her, and she closed her eyes. "Did you put something in my drink, Drake?"

"Don't you trust me?"

"Did you?"

"Just a little rum. You couldn't even taste it, could you?"

"I said I wanted plain Coke."

"Okay, no more rum. Just plain Coke from now on."

"But I think maybe I'm drunk already. I don't know. I've never felt like this before."

"You aren't getting sick, are you?"

"No, just dizzy."

"Just keep your eyes open, you'll be okay."

"Drake, you shouldn't have done that. I'm not allowed to drink."

"Sorry. I just thought you might like to have a good time like the rest of us. A little drink sort of loosens you up, takes away all the inhibitions, makes dancing this way more fun." This time he slid both hands down her buttocks. But the way Drake kept swaying, the way his knees were spread, it felt good to wallow up close and use him for balance as her world grew more tipsy. Her body conformed with surprising ease, and no matter where he moved, her flesh seemed to follow. Over his shoulder she saw a bunch of other couples dancing the same way—so she figured it was how it was done in a place like this.

"Drake, I'm really getting dizzy. I think maybe I have to go."

"Hey, it's early yet."

"What time is it?" Over his shoulder she tried to read her wristwatch, but the numbers refused to focus.

His hands left her rump as he checked his watch. "Midnight. A little after."

"I have to be home by one. I really have to go." It was her first time at overt rebellion, and reverting to form came spontaneously.

"All right, whatever you say. Let's go find those guys."

It took some time to round up the other four. By the time they headed for their car it was a quarter to one and Chelsea knew she'd never make her one o'clock curfew.

Outside, the brisk air felt bracing, but when they got in the backseat and began moving, her world started spinning. She tipped her head back against the seat and felt as if she'd been packed into a shipping carton and sent down a conveyor belt. There were four people in the backseat, and she was sitting between Drake and the door. He kissed her at the same moment he slipped a hand inside her coat and under her fishnet top. It was nothing at all like the kiss she'd shared with Kent. Nothing that innocent. In a rush it struck her that the guilt she'd carried for that one kiss with her half brother had been misguided. Here was something she could really feel guilty for, and would—tomorrow. Drake kissed her deep and wet, with a hand up under her bra, then down behind, where he'd been touching her on the dance floor, and pretty soon between her legs.

"Stop it, Drake," she whispered, mortified because something worse seemed to be going on on the far side of the backseat. Obviously, Sue and Esmond had made up.

"Hey, come on, nothing's going to happen."

"No, stop."

"You ever felt a guy?" He carried her hand between his legs and cupped it hard against himself. "Bet you haven't. Go ahead, little girl, explore. This is how a guy feels. See? Hot . . . hard . . . no, no . . ." He turned her head back his way when she tried to peer past him at their seatmates. "Don't worry about them. They can't see us. They're busy."

"Drake, don't."

"Bet you've been a good little girl, haven't you? Always done what your mommy and daddy told you to do. So tonight you decided to try what the bad girls do, and I bet you like it, don't you? You ever had anybody kiss you here before?" He moved so fast she couldn't combat him—up with her stretch top and down with his head, and his mouth fastened on her nipple.

She was starting to cry, trying to force his head up, and afraid she'd get sick because her stomach was starting to heave, and if she vomited on the car floor she'd just die!

He lifted his head himself and put his thumb where his tongue had been and made circles on her wet flesh.

"Bet you're gettin' hot, aren't you? Nothin' wrong with that; hell, everybody does it."

"Drake, I think I'm going to be sick. Tell Church to stop the car."

"Aw, Jesus," he said in disgust. "Hey, Church, pull over. Chelsea's got to hurl."

She hurled, all right. She would never as long as she lived forget how she retched into the frosty weeds beside some highway while the cars whooshed past and the couple in the backseat went right on humping as if this were the Garden of Eden and they were the only two in the universe.

When her mortification was complete, Chelsea climbed back in the car, where Drake at last kept his hands and legs and pelvis off her. In lieu of fornicating, he rolled and lit up a foul-smelling cigarette.

"Want a hit, little girl?" he asked when the car stank completely.

"No thank you."

"Never tried that either, huh?"

She hugged herself harder and gazed out the dark window through tears that transformed the freeway lights into many-pointed stars. She thought about her real friends and tried to understand why she'd been seeing less of them, and why she'd hit on Drake Emerson, for it was true—she'd singled him out and done some flirting. It hadn't taken much before he'd asked her out. But he was such a major sleaze, and she missed Erin so much. All of a sudden all she wanted was to be in Erin's room eating popcorn and talking, sitting cross-legged on the bed or trying out new hairdos.

At home a kitchen light glowed, and Drake let her walk to the house alone. As she reached the door, he called, "Yo, goody-girl! You got to learn to loosen up some. Anytime you want to try again, just give me the high sign."

The door opened and her mother stood above her.

"Get in here, young lady!"

In the harsh kitchen light, Chelsea could not escape Claire's scrutiny.

"Where in the world have you been? Do you know it's one-thirty in the morning?"

"So?"

"We have curfews in this house! And rules about where you go and with whom! Robby says you were with Drake Emerson. Were you?"

Chelsea refused to look at Claire. She stood with her jacket hanging open, mouth drawn into a tight, defiant bundle. Claire took Chelsea's chin and forced it up with a snap. "Dressed like that? And smelling like that? Chelsea, have you been drinking?"

"It's none of your business!" Chelsea pulled free and hit for her bedroom.

Claire stood in the empty kitchen with fear constricting her throat, the fetid smell of her daughter's breath lingering in the air around her. Dear God, not Chelsea. Not her sweet daughter who'd never given her a moment's worry, who'd picked nurturing friends and kept early hours and taken part in wholesome activities that had always made her a parents' dream. It didn't even seem like the same girl who had just come through the kitchen. This one was dressed like a whore, and had been in the company of a boy whose truancy, drug use, and pathetic scholastic record made him a subject of disdain whenever his name came up in faculty circles. Judging from Chelsea's attire, Claire guessed that there was at least the possibility that she had done something sexual with Drake Emerson. *AIDS, pregnancy*—the fears flashed past along with sordid stories about other girls from school, so many that she'd almost become accustomed to them. But when the subject was your own daughter and the fault was your own, it was another matter.

Claire had one instinctive thought as she stood in the kitchen with a hand over her mouth and tears in her eyes: *Tom, I need you.*

But Tom wasn't there. She had thrown him out because she could not forgive his deceptions of the past. Now those deceptions seemed to weigh less in light of Chelsea's defiance and the very real danger she seemed to have put herself in tonight. Oh, to have Tom here now, to be able to slip her hand into his and feel the quick pressure of his fingers. To turn and whisper, "Tom, what should we do?" After all, these things happened to other people's children, not their own! But it was twenty-five to two in the morning, and Tom had had as long a day as Claire. By the time she called him and he drove in from his dad's cabin, it would be after two, and both of them simply had to be at school tomorrow for the last day of conferences, had to be there early, as a matter of fact, to attend conferences for their own children.

So Claire had to handle this alone.

She snapped out the kitchen light and headed upstairs. Robby was asleep behind his closed bedroom door and Chelsea was in the bathroom. Claire knocked softly and waited, listening to the sink faucet running and being shut off, the squeal of the plastic soap dish on the marble vanity top. She knocked again—"Chelsea?"—and opened the door, letting it swing back on its own while remaining where she was with her arms crossed and her weight against the door frame. Chelsea was scrubbing her face, bent over the sink.

"Chelsea?" Claire said quietly, terrified because she didn't know what to say, ask, do: no parenting manuals had prepared her for a moment like this. "Why?"

Chelsea pushed the plunger, releasing the water, and buried her face in a towel. Claire waited until Chelsea's eyes reappeared, staring straight into the mirror as if she were alone in the room.

"Is it because of Dad and me?"

Chelsea's hands dropped, still holding the towel. She stood lifelessly for some time before whispering, "I don't know." The water dripped from the faucet, which would have been fixed days ago if Tom had been living at home. Otherwise the room was silent.

Tom, Tom, I don't know what to say.

"Were you drinking tonight?"

Chelsea's mouth and chin quivered. Her head hung. She nodded, her eyes filling.

"Did you take any drugs?"

Chelsea wagged her head no.

"Did you do anything sexual with him?"

"No, Mom, I didn't." Chelsea's pleading eyes swung to Claire. Her face was back to girlish, though framed by a wiry, streetwalker's hairdo. "Honest, Mom."

"I believe you."

"Are you going to tell Dad?"

"Yes, I am, Chelsea. I have to. I don't know how to deal with this alone. You're not allowed at places like that. You broke curfew and you used alcohol. He has to know."

"Will he come back home then?"

If there was a moment when Claire's heart broke completely, this was it. As she stood in the bathroom watching tears spring from the eyes of her sad, pitiful, misguided daughter, Claire felt her own eyes sting. "Is that why you did it?" she asked gently. "So Daddy would come back home?"

A sob broke forth from Chelsea as she whirled and flung herself into her mother's arms, clinging frantically, pleading in broken phrases.

"I don't know, Mom, maybe I d . . . did, but it's so awful here w . . . without him. Won't you please tell him he can come b . . . back and live with us? Please, Mom? Nothing's the s . . . same without him, and I hate it in this house, and you're not the s . . . same anymore, and I just don't know why you're doing this to us!"

Guilt, fear, and love. All exerted an awesome force on Claire. She hurt in ways she had never experienced hurt before. Holding Chelsea, realizing what desperate measures her daughter was willing to risk to bring about her family's reconciliation, Claire realized they were on the brink of so much more than the dissolution of a marriage. She petted Chelsea's hair in hard, desperate strokes while reassuring her.

"Dad and I have agreed to go to a marriage counselor. We're going to start working on it."

"R . . . really?" Chelsea drew back, sniffing.

"Yes, the first appointment is already set up for next week."

"Then does that mean Dad will move back home now?"

"No, darling, not right now."

"But . . . but why?" Chelsea sniffed again. "If you want to get back together with him, why are you putting it off?"

Claire reached for some tissues and handed them to Chelsea, who began mopping her face and blowing her nose. "Because there are things we have to work out first."

"What things?"

"Kent Arens, for one."

"And Mr. Handelman?"

"Mr. Handelman?"

"Some of the kids are saying that you and Mr. Handelman are dating."

"Oh, that's ridiculous! We are *not* dating!"

"But you spend a lot of time with him at play practice, and he's got a crush on you, hasn't he?"

Claire grew flustered and felt herself blushing.

Chelsea wailed, "Oh, Mom, don't tell me it's true! There *is* something going on between you two, isn't there? Gol, Mom, how could you?"

"I told you, there's nothing! And how did this conversation get turned around and centered on me? We were talking about you, and the flagrant breaking of rules tonight. There's got to be some punishment, you know that, Chelsea, don't you?"

"Yes, I know."

"But I . . ." Claire put a hand to her forehead and rubbed it with four fingertips. "I'm just . . . I'm not prepared to handle this alone. I'll have to talk to your father about it. Meanwhile, you're not to leave the house tomorrow, and the car is off limits. I want you to give me your keys."

Chelsea answered docilely, "All right, Mother," and went to her room to get them. Left behind, Claire dried her eyes and felt her love for Chelsea welling up and closing her aching throat even as her disappointment brought panic edging closer. She felt lonely and forsaken, uncertain of tens of things that seemed to be directing her life right now: Tom, the children, Kent, Monica, the class play and her mis-moves with John Handelman, Chelsea's accusations and disappointment in her mother.

A great parental guilt pressed down heavily as Claire cowered in the hall wishing for Tom, regretting the past two months. Finally she dashed the tears from her eyes and went to Chelsea's bedroom door to collect the keys. As Chelsea put them in her hand, the girl's sudden tractability seemed the saddest of postscripts to this disastrous day, and Claire recognized there was one vitally important thing left to say, one thing that she needed to hear as badly as Chelsea did.

"Chelsea, you know that I love you, don't you?"

"I guess I do." Chelsea could not look at her mother. "But sometimes lately I've been wondering."

"I do . . . very much. But parents aren't infallible. Sometimes we do the wrong thing, even though we think what we're doing is right. Sometimes it's the same with kids, isn't it?"

Chelsea nodded glumly, refusing to lift her head. She and Claire stood in the doorway, dusted by ocher light from one small bedside lamp, surrounded by the girlish belongings from Chelsea's childhood days, which in the past two years mingled with the trappings of a young woman: roller-skate pom-poms and lip gloss on the same dresser top, dolls and nylon stockings on the same rocking chair, an elf-shaped jewelry box below a poster of Rod Stewart. Standing in the wee-hour shadows, they both felt the sadness that growing up sometimes exerts upon a mother and daughter.

It was late; they were both exhausted. Claire drew her wandering gaze back to Chelsea and sighed, as if punctuating both their thoughts.

"Well . . . could I have a hug?"

Chelsea bestowed one gingerly.

"I love you," Claire said.

"I love you too."

"Clean your room and catch up on your ironing tomorrow, and I'll see you when I get home around six-fifteen. We'll talk about everything then."

Chelsea nodded without looking up.

The following morning a block of conference time had been set aside for those teachers whose children attended HHH. Tom and Claire were scheduled to see Robby's and Chelsea's teachers between 8:00 and 8:30.

Claire went in with fifteen minutes to spare. Tom's office lights were on though the reception area was empty and unlit. He was working at his desk when she stopped in the doorway. Unaware of her presence, he worked on, dressed in a slate-blue suit she'd always loved and an attractive tie she had bought him at Dayton's for Father's Day last summer. He had a trim body made for well-tailored clothes. Observing him across the room, neatly dressed and groomed, still had the power to stir her. Yesterday when she had watched him across the gym with Monica Arens she had been blindsided by a powerful shot of jealousy.

What had they laughed about? How many other times had they talked and laughed? Had they gotten together with Kent sometimes so Tom could get to know the boy? In the midst of those meetings, had he gotten to know Monica as well? The picture of the three of them together brought Claire a sharp visceral ache and the realization that she had never stopped loving him.

"Tom?" she said, and he looked up. Absent were the smile and look of yearning she'd come to expect since asking him to move out.

"You're fifteen minutes early."

"Yes, I know. May I come in anyway?"

"I'm working on some budgeting stuff that's on a deadline."

"It's important."

He dropped his pencil in annoyance and said, "All right."

She closed the door and took a guest chair. "Why do I feel like one of your students who's been sent in here with a pink slip?"

"Maybe because you're guilty of something, Claire."

"I'm not, but we'll have to put that on hold. I have to talk to you about Chelsea."

"What about her?"

She told the whole story, watching his face grow more and more drawn with concern, watching his back come away from his chair.

"Oh, God," he said when she finished. They sat awhile in silence, sharing a common guilt. Then he closed his eyes, fell back, and whispered, "Drake Emerson." He gulped once so loudly she could hear it from where she sat. "Do you think she's telling the truth when she says she didn't do anything sexual with him?"

"I don't know."

"Oh God, Claire, what if she did? Who knows what she could be carrying?"

They both thought about the range of possibilities.

Claire said, "I guess all we can do is believe her."

"And the drinking . . ."

"I know . . ." she said softly, followed by silence. He looked very sad and his eyes got glisteny.

"I remember when she was born," Tom said, "how we'd lie on the bed with her between us and kiss the bottom of her feet."

They sat separated by a desk, longing to go to each other, needing to hold and be held, drawn by mutual love for their children and the call of their consciences to put things right. But each had been hurt by the other. Each was afraid, so they remained where they were. Claire got teary-eyed too, and left her chair to go stand at the window staring out above the family pictures. It was nearly November. The sky looked as though it held snow, and the grass on the football field had gone brown.

With her back to Tom, she dried her eyes and turned to face him once more. "I didn't know what to do exactly, so I told her she's grounded for today until you and I could talk, and I made her give me her car keys."

"Do you think that's the right thing to do—punish her?"

"I don't know. She did break the rules."

"Maybe we're the ones who broke the rules, Claire."

Distanced by the room, their eyes met and held. Their need for each other had amplified tenfold since they'd been in this office together.

"Did you," she asked, "with Monica?"

"No. Not in the last eighteen years. Did you with Handelman?"

"No."

"Why can't I believe you? It's all over school that the two of you are flirting with each other every night at play practice, and that your two cars are the last ones left in the parking lot."

"Why can't I believe you? I saw you with her yesterday when she walked into the gym, and you were laughing together like old friends, and it's obvious that something's put a sparkle in her life. She looks like a new woman."

"What can I say?" He raised both palms and let them fall, then rolled back his chair and pushed to his feet. The defenses were back up between them, firmly in place. "I guess we'll just have to sort it out at counseling. We have to go now or we'll be late."

"What about Chelsea?"

"I'll have a talk with her."

"Without me?"

"Whatever you prefer." His politeness wounded her as they left his office. She missed the touch of his hand on the small of her back as it would have been in the old days. She missed looking forward to encountering him in the halls and exchanging intimate jokes in voices too quiet for others to hear. She missed his kisses and lovemaking, his reassuring weight on the other side of the bed at night, and listening for his car to pull into the garage. She missed the sound of their children's laughter in the house, and the four of them around the table at supper time talking about what had happened at school that day.

She missed the happiness.

While they were walking to their first conference he said, "I want you to know that Kent has been out to Dad's house. He's met everybody, even Ryan and the kids. I thought he should have the chance to know them all."

Oh, what have I done, Claire thought, stunned by a wave of remorse. Ryan had tried to reach her by phone this week, but she hadn't called him back.

"Also, I've found an apartment I'll be moving into. As soon as I have a phone number I'll let you know."

Claire's shock redoubled as she realized the tables had suddenly turned: she had thrown Tom out to express her hurt; had withheld her forgiveness, refusing to work toward healing the relationship and denying him any outward display of affection.

So he had turned to others for it, to his newfound son and probably to that son's mother, who appeared to be responding to the attention in a most impressive fashion. Now he was getting an apartment.

If not for privacy, why else?

Claire sat down across from the first teacher with her emotions in such turmoil she was having difficulty keeping dry-eyed. As if the first half hour in the school building hadn't brought enough distressing news, the conferences with Chelsea's teachers brought more. Most of them reported that Chelsea had let her schoolwork slide, had failed to turn in assignments, and had done poorly on those she had completed. For the first time ever, two teachers reported that she had skipped some classes.

Tom and Claire stood in the hall afterward, feeling shell-shocked.

"All this . . . because we separated?" Claire said.

Their eyes met—fearful eyes admitting they had done everything to bring this on themselves.

"You didn't know she was letting her homework slide?" he asked.

"No. I've . . . I guess I've been busy with the class play and everything, and . . . well, I . . ." Her admission trailed away.

"And I haven't been coming over as often as I should."

They wanted, needed to hug, touch, something more than stand there with their guilt and longing laying their emotions bare. But they had stopped in the cross fire of traffic as parents came in and out of the gym. Office staff stood nearby, welcoming the parents who were just arriving. Furthermore, Tom and Claire Gardner had this rule about intimacy in the school building.

But if there was one thing they were united on, it was the fact that they loved their children and would do whatever it took to raise them right.

"I'm coming home with you when conferences are over," Tom said, with sudden decisiveness.

"Yes," she agreed, feeling her heart lurch to life. "I guess you'd better."

But neither one of them ventured a guess about whether he meant *home to stay.*

Seventeen

That Saturday morning, the last day of conferences, Robby got up late and washed his football jersey—Claire had taught him years ago how to do that himself—because it had to be turned in. The Senators had lost their last game, killing their chances of going to the state tournaments.

End of the season, end of his high school football career.

The thought made Robby scuff around the house disconsolately.

Finally, at midafternoon, he decided to run his jersey over to school and work out in the weight room a little while. It was depressing at home. Chelsea was grounded and had barely poked her head out of her room all day. Mom wouldn't get home from conferences until around six, and Dad was ostracized from the house. Heck, he'd only been back a few times since he'd moved out to Grandpa's, and both times Mom had been so bitchy and cold to him that he hadn't hung around long.

It was hell looking at his dad's haunted face every time he drove away. Even in school he wasn't the same. He just wasn't cheerful like he used to be. Sometimes Robby got so mad at his mom that he wanted to yell at her, ask her what the heck did it matter anymore if Dad had been unfaithful to her before they were married! After all, it *was* before. So what was the big deal now? Heck, Robby admitted to himself that he'd even gotten used to the fact that Kent Arens was his half brother. The kids at school had stopped being so bummed out about it and no longer pried him with questions.

The truth was, Arens had turned out to be an okay guy. He'd even been pretty respectful about the fact that they shared the same father. He had a way of standing back and not pushing, just minding what they were supposed to be minding about their game, doing what Coach Gorman said, and not letting their personal differences interfere. Besides that, the coach was right: he was a good athlete.

It was hard for Robby to keep from noticing similarities between himself and Arens in terms of their athletic ability. No question, they'd inherited it from their dad, and sometimes when Robby handed off or threw a short pass to Kent, it was almost like watching his dad catch the ball and run with it. Those moments brought the most peculiar catch to Robby's throat, almost like love.

Sometimes, especially when he couldn't sleep at night, Robby would wonder about Kent's life, and how it had affected him, not knowing his father. He'd replay his childhood memories and imagine telling Kent what it was like growing up with Tom Gardner as your dad. If he did that he thought it might make up in some small way for Kent's not being there to live it firsthand.

Sometimes he'd fantasize about the two of them going off to the same college, playing ball together there, hanging out at the same pizza joints, driving home together on weekends. When they got older, got married, and had kids—wow, that'd be something, wouldn't it? Their kids would be first cousins!

The realization never failed to put a lump in Robby's throat.

He'd been thinking about all of this that Saturday afternoon on his way to school to turn in his uniform. It was still on his mind as he jogged down the locker room stairs, yanked open the door, and heard it hiss shut behind him. For once the coach's office was dark, the door locked. The long varnished benches were bare. Somebody had left a single overhead light on. It shed a few dismal rays from inside its metal cage, but the whole place held a postseason gloom, with its ever-pervasive dank smells conjuring up reminders of the sweat and camaraderie exchanged here. In the corner beside the office, three large blue plastic barrels were labeled in the coach's slanty scrawl: *Uniforms, Shin Pads, Shoulder Pads*. Robby's rubber soles squeaked as he crossed the concrete floor and tossed his uniform and gear into the proper containers.

He turned around . . . and halted in his tracks.

There stood Kent Arens at the opposite end of the bench. As surprised as Robby. And as cautious.

Both of them scrabbled around in their minds for something to say. Robby spoke first. "Hi."

"Hi."

"I didn't know you were here."

Kent thumbed over his left shoulder. "I was in the lav."

Again a void while they searched for more to say.

"Turning in your uniform?" Robby asked.

"Yeah. You?"

"Same."

"Hate to see the season end."

"Yeah, me too."

They both drew blanks and wondered where to rest their eyes.

"Well . . ." They were forced to pass each other to get to their respective lockers, and did so making sure they stayed on separate sides of the bench. They poked around inside their lockers, took things out, stuffed them into their duffel bags, never glancing at each other, even once. A loud clatter told Robby that Kent had tossed some pads into a plastic barrel, and he leaned back an inch to peer past his locker door and watch him return. Their eyes met and he immersed himself in the depths of his cubicle again.

Then Kent left his locker and stood behind Robby. "Could I talk to you about something?"

Blood seemed to pound frantically up Robby's neck, very much like when he'd first kissed a girl, the same scary, exhilarated, fearful, hopeful, awful need to face this thing; scared to break down, scared not to, needing to have it behind him at last so that he could get on with the next step of his life.

"Sure," he said, trying to sound natural, pulling his head out of the locker but leaving one hand curled over the open door because he wasn't sure how steady his knees were.

Kent swung a leg over the bench and straddled it. "Why don't you sit down?" he asked.

But sitting down face-to-face was still a problem for Robby. "No, I'm . . . I'm okay here. What's on your mind?"

Looking up, Kent told him, "I met our grandfather."

The immense relief of alluding to their common parentage, in even so circumspect a fashion, finally took the starch out of Robby's legs. He straddled the bench too, a good six feet from Kent, meeting his half brother's gaze head-on.

"How?" he asked quietly.

"Your dad took me out there and introduced us."

"When?"

"A couple of weeks ago. I met our uncle Ryan, too, and all three of his kids."

They took a while to adjust to the idea of sharing those relatives, nudging closer to the idea of forming some relationship of their own.

But both of them were afraid to initiate it.

Finally Robby asked, "What'd you think?"

Kent waggled his head in wonder. "It was pretty awesome."

They sat awhile, picturing it, both of them.

Robby admitted, "It's funny, I was thinking about that on my way over here, about my cousins, and that you never got to know them, you never got to spend time out at Grandpa and Grandma's with them the way I did, and how it was too bad you had to miss out on that."

"You were thinking that? Really?"

Robby shrugged. "That was a pretty great part of being a kid. I guess I didn't realize it until I thought about you never having it."

"I don't have any other grandparents. I used to when I was small, but I don't remember them very well. I've got one aunt here, and she's got two kids, but they're practically strangers to me. I never expected to be meeting a grandpa when we moved here. He's really great."

"Yeah, he is, isn't he? He stays with us sometimes when my mom and dad go away alone together. At least . . . they used to. They're not . . . well, you know . . . I mean, not living together anymore." Robby's voice faded and his gaze had dropped to the varnished wood.

"I guess that's because of me and my mom moving back here."

Robby shrugged. With the pad of one index finger he rubbed and rubbed one brighter strip of gold hardwood, up and down, up and down, until the oil from his finger had dulled an area the size of a Popsicle stick. "I don't know. My mom, she just sort of went crazy, you know? She threw him out, and he moved in with Grandpa, and Chelsea got all screwed up and started running around with wild kids, and . . . I don't know, our family's just really messed up right now."

"I'm sorry."

"Yeah . . . well . . . it's not really your fault."

"I feel like it is."

"Naw . . . it's just . . ." Robby found himself unable to express his feelings. He quit rubbing the bench and sat motionless, staring at the dull spot. Finally he looked up at his half brother. "Hey, could I ask you something?"

"Sure."

"You won't get mad?"

"It takes a lot to get me mad."

"Oh yeah?" Robby let a hint of teasing play around his eyes. "Like that day you came storming into our house?"

"Oh that. Sorry about that. I kind of lost it."

"Yeah, we noticed."

"I knew I shouldn't have done it, but *you* try finding out who your father is and see how *you* react."

"Yeah, I suppose. Sort of like getting shot with a stun gun, isn't it?"

For the first time ever their gazes held the hint of a grin, and the silence between them became a little more comfortable. This one grew lengthy before Kent brought himself back to the gist of their conversation.

"So . . . what were you going to ask?"

"Oh . . . well, it's kind of a hard thing to say."

"This is all hard to say. Say it anyway."

Robby drew a deep breath for courage. "Okay, I will then. Do you think my dad and your mother are having an affair?"

Much to Robby's surprise, Kent took no offense. He answered forthrightly, "I don't think so. I'd know if she was."

"My mother thinks so. That's why she asked him to move out."

"Honest, I really don't think they are."

"Does he . . . like, hang around your house or anything?"

"No. He was there only once that I know of, and that was when he first suspected who I was and came to ask my mother about me."

"So you don't think they go out on dates, or . . . or meet secretly or anything?"

"No. The truth is, my mom doesn't date much. All she lives for is work. And me, of course. She's one of those high achievers who really gets off on it."

"Then my mom's all jealous and bent out of shape for nothing?"

"Well, there's still me. She's not too happy about me showing up in this school, I can tell you that."

"I wasn't at first either, but I got over it. Why can't she?"

"You got over it?"

Again, the shrug. "I guess I did. You never rubbed my nose in it or anything, and by the end of the season we were getting along pretty well on the football field, and I don't know . . . I guess I just sort of grew up a little and started putting myself in your place. I guess if I were you, I'd want to get to know my dad and my grandfather, too. I mean, who wouldn't?"

They sat on, absorbing the newness of being frank with each other, even beginning to project into a future in which they might actually become good friends, more than good friends.

Kent took a stab at what was on both of their minds. "You think we could ever, I don't know, like maybe do things together? Not really like brothers but . . ."

"You think you'd want to?"

"Maybe." And after a pause, "Yeah, I guess I would. Sure. But your mom probably wouldn't like it."

"Mom might have to get used to it."

"Your sister wouldn't like it, for sure."

"Hey, listen, she liked you a lot when she first met you. I don't know what happened, but she thought you were the greatest."

"I'll tell you what happened. I kissed her one night. That's what happened."

"You kissed her!"

Kent threw his hands wide. "Well, heck, I didn't know we were related! How could I have known a thing like that! I liked her. She was pretty and bright and really friendly and we got along really well together, and one night after a football game I walked her home and I kissed her. Right after that we found out we were related, and ever since then, whenever we run into each other in the hall, we can't even *look* at each other, much less stop and talk. It's like we both run the other way. Heck, I don't know . . . " He stared gloomily at his right knee.

Robby's lips hung open, then he reiterated in an awed whisper, "You kissed her. Jeez."

"Yeah," Kent replied, as if unable to believe his own stupidity.

In a moment Robby recovered and asked, "That's all?"

"What do you mean, 'that's all'? That's enough!"

"Well, if that's all you did, heck, I mean, it was an honest mistake, wasn't it?"

"Of course, but I've been scared to death to talk to her ever since. I mean, what kind of a pervert kisses his sister?"

"Oh, come on, you're no pervert."

"Well, maybe not, but I feel so stupid. Trouble is, I *really* liked her, I mean, not just as a girlfriend, but as a friend. We talked about things that mattered, and I thought it was pretty great to move into a new town and find a friend like that right away. You won't believe it, but one of the things we talked about was your dad. *Our* dad, I guess I should say. Can you believe I once admitted to Chelsea that I was jealous of her for having Mr. Gardner for her dad? Pretty ironic, isn't it?"

They mulled awhile, trying to puzzle together the fragmented pieces of their lives.

Pretty soon Robby said, "What do you think would happen if you came home with me?"

Kent recoiled. "Oh, no. Nothin' doing."

"No, now wait a minute." Robby reached out persuasively. "I've got to tell you something about Chelsea. She's been totally freaked out since Dad moved out, and she's started to do all these weird things that really scare me. She hardly ever sees Erin anymore, and instead she's running around with this sleaze-woman named Merilee, and dressing in these grungy clothes, and in general hanging around with some pretty degenerate types. Last night she went to Mississippi Live with Drake Emerson."

"Drake Emerson! You mean that pothead with all the zippers?"

"That's the one. And she didn't ask first, she just took off, dressed pretty radical, and didn't get in until way past curfew. And she'd been drinking. Mom was furious. I could hear the yelling right through my bedroom door. Anyway, do you think . . . oh, shit, I don't know . . . this isn't making much sense maybe, but Chelsea liked you, too, I know she did, and maybe if you went and talked to her and told her you wanted to be her friend again . . . maybe if the three of us sort of joined forces somehow, we could get this mess straightened out."

"If I go to your house and your mother finds out, nothing's going to get straightened out. It'll only get worse."

"She's at conferences today. She wouldn't find out. And I don't think Chelsea will tell either. She's just sort of—" Robby ran out of words, blew out a breath, and took a turn at getting gloomy. "I'm going to admit it, hey. I'm scared. She's changed so much since Mom and Dad broke up. I think she's scared too, and this is the way she's showing it. Boy, I really don't understand girls, I'll tell you that much. But I thought about something else the last couple of weeks. It's about us, the three of us—

you, me, and Chelsea—and what it ought to be like. I mean, we've all got the same dad, right? So, are we going to go through the rest of our lives pretending we're not related? Or are we gonna face it and make the best of it? That's what I've been asking myself. And I've also been thinking, What about us? Why is it *all* what Mom wants all the time? What about what I want? And what Chelsea wants? And what Dad wants? Because I think he wants us to be a family again, only he's so scared and guilty that he isn't acting right. And I don't know for sure what you want, but if it's to get to know us, well, maybe we could start today, with Chelsea in on it too. What do you say?"

Kent didn't know what to say. He sat spread-kneed with his hands resting in the V of his legs, amazed by this conversation.

"You think Chelsea would talk to me?"

"Why not? If it's been bugging you about kissing her, it's probably been bugging her too, and she'll be glad to put it behind her."

"And you're sure your mom won't come home?"

"Not for another hour and a half or so. Conferences don't end until six o'clock, and Dad is really strict about all the teachers staying till the very end."

"What about him?"

"Naw, he stays in the building as long as it's open. And besides, I told you, he doesn't come home much anymore."

Kent considered less than five seconds before swinging his long leg off the bench. "Let's go."

The two of them closed their lockers and left together.

Kent had finally gotten a car of his own. He followed Robby, parked at the foot of the driveway, and approached the house.

"Man, is old Chels gonna be surprised," Robby said, and smiled as he led Kent inside.

Chelsea was nowhere on the first floor, so Robby said, "Come on," and led Kent upstairs. He knocked on her closed bedroom door and she snapped, "What?"

"Can I open this?"

"What do you want?"

"I've got somebody here who wants to talk to you. Can I open this?"

"I don't care! Open it!"

He turned the knob, gave the door a push, and let it swing back on its own. The room was meticulously clean. Chelsea was sitting on the floor folding clothes and putting stacks of socks on the neatly made bed. Her hair was clean and wet, trailing down in natural curls, and she wore an oversized blue sweat suit with thick white socks on her feet. Her face was scrubbed free of all makeup.

"So, who did you drag home?" she asked acidly.

He stepped back and Kent took his place in the doorway. "It's me."

Her hands stalled, matching a pair of socks. Horror flattened her expression, followed immediately by a blush.

"What are *you* doing here?"

He stood in her doorway feeling like an awkward oaf, but hiding it as best he could. She saw only a relaxed young man who looked not at all daunted by facing her squarely in her bedroom as Robby faded away and disappeared behind his own bedroom door.

"I hear you got grounded," Kent said.

"Yes, I did. For drinking and staying out past curfew."

"That doesn't sound like something you'd do."

"Well, I did." She folded the socks and put them on the bed, a touch of arrogance in the tilt of her eyebrows.

"Robby says you're rebelling against this whole mess involving me and your family. Is that true?"

She found two more socks and poured her attention on them. "I suppose it is. I hadn't really analyzed it."

"That's a good way to spoil a nice kid."

"Since when did you and Robby get so buddy-buddy?"

"We just talked today in the locker room. I told him what happened between you and me."

"About the kiss!" She looked up, horrified. "Oh, my God, how could you!"

He went into the room and sat down Indian fashion on the floor facing her, with a pile of unfolded laundry between them. "Listen, Chelsea, none of us are exactly children, but I think you and I have been acting pretty childish about it. Robby and I think it's time we all started to get to know each other, and we can't do that until we forget about that stupid kiss. After all, what was it but a nice little gesture that we liked each other? I can forget it if you can, and move on from there."

"But you told my brother!"

"He actually took it quite well, and acted pretty levelheaded about it, much more than you and I did."

"But he'll tease me."

"No, I don't think so. He wants us all to be friends, and to try to get your mom and dad to see straight about this whole thing. He thinks that if the three of us present a united front, we might be able to get your mom to believe that there's nothing between my mom and your dad. What do you think?"

"Is there?" She had stopped folding clothes again. Her blush had faded as she met his matter-of-fact gaze.

"No. I'd know it if there was."

"Are you sure?"

"Yes, I'm sure."

"Would she tell my mother that?"

"Tell her?"

"Yes, come over here and tell her."

"I don't know."

"Because that's the only way I can think of to convince my mother to let my dad come back home—if your mother gets right in my mother's face and says she's not having an affair with Daddy."

Kent looked staggered. "Wow, that's some radical idea!"

"It would work, wouldn't it?" She threw her elbows into the air and bumped her temples with the heels of her hands. "What am I saying? You don't even *know* my mother! How do you know if it would work? But I think it would, if we could get your mom to agree. What is she like?"

335

He gave it some thought. "She's a pretty reasonable woman. And I think she feels bad that your parents broke up because we came here. She never meant for that to happen."

"So she'd do it?"

"We could ask."

"Right now?" When he didn't respond, she rushed on. "It's Saturday. She isn't working, is she?"

"She works at home on Saturdays . . . but I thought you were grounded."

Chelsea clambered to her feet, excited. "You don't think I'm going to let a little thing like that keep me from trying to get my parents back together, do you?" She stepped over his knee on her way to Robby's room, and Kent pivoted on his backside, watching her disappear around the doorway.

"Hey, Chelsea, wait!"

She stuck her head back in. "I've *been* waiting since the first week of school and nothing has made my mother come to her senses yet. I'm not waiting any longer. *Robbeee!*" She flung open his door without asking. "I have an idea, Robby!"

They took both cars and arrived in Kent's driveway less than fifteen minutes later. When they got out of the cars Chelsea looked up at the house and breathed, "Gee, is *this* where you live?"

"My room is that one up there." He pointed. "And that one is my mother's." Her light was on. "She's home."

While they advanced toward the house, Chelsea kept thinking, Gosh, he's really my brother! How incredible to imagine that if things went the way she hoped, they'd be able to have a relationship in the future.

Inside, everything was new and fresh and beautifully coordinated. Kent pointed to a brass coat tree in the entry and said, "You can hang up your jackets, if you want." Then he raised his voice and called, "Mother?"

Her voice drifted down from above. "Hi, honey, be right there! I think we should go out for supper tonight and celebrate. I solved one of my two big problems with the electronic switch today, and you had such a great school conference yesterday that . . . Oh!" She appeared at a railing half a level above them. "I didn't know you'd brought friends."

She stood looking down while they looked up.

"They're more than friends, Mom. They're my sister and brother."

"Oh!" she exclaimed softly, one hand fluttering to her heart.

"May I bring them up and introduce them?"

Monica recovered admirably, dropping her hand and letting it ride the railing as she moved toward them. "Of course."

"Come on up," Kent invited.

They followed and were met at the mouth of the steps by the woman who appeared as flummoxed by this sudden introduction as they were.

"Mom, I'd like you to meet Chelsea and Robby Gardner."

"Hello," she said, and shook each of their hands.

"You have a beautiful house," Chelsea told her, scanning it slowly.

"Thank you," Monica said, a little at a loss, looking to her son for help.

"Well . . ." She gave a tense chuckle. "This is just so . . . so unexpected."

"I know. I'm sorry we didn't give you any warning, Mom, but it sort of happened that way. I ran into Robby in the locker room, and he and I got to talking, and there were things I needed to say to Chelsea, and we all decided it was time we got to know each other, and I went over to their house, and . . . well, here we are. But . . ." He turned to Chelsea. "There's something special we'd like to talk to you about. Do you want to ask her or should I?"

Before she could answer, Monica interrupted, "Please, children . . . come on in, let's sit down. Let me turn on a couple of lights here and . . ." She busied herself snapping on lamps in the living room, and as it sprang to life, the teenagers found seats on the ivory sofa with its array of loose pastel cushions. "May I get you anything to drink? A soda? Mineral water?"

"No thanks," they said in unison, and finally she found a perch, choosing a chair that situated them on three sides of a square, with a glass-topped table between them. They exchanged glances above a ceramic sea gull that stood on one brass leg.

"So," Monica said. "You've formed some sort of truce at last."

"Yes," Chelsea replied, for Monica ended up looking straight into her eyes. She considered Robby next, studying him overtly, satisfying her curiosity without trying to hide the fact.

"It's a curious moment for me," she said candidly, "seeing you for the first time, knowing that you're Kent's half siblings. You'll have to forgive me if I seem a bit rattled. I am."

"I guess we are too." Chelsea spoke for all of them, running her gaze past the two boys as if seeking their approval to act as their spokesperson.

"You've been together all day then?" Monica asked.

"No, just an hour or so. The boys a little longer."

"Well, I can see that everybody's a little tense here, waiting for my reaction." She settled her gaze on Kent. "I've been trying to prepare myself for the day this would happen, but never quite managed to do so. However, let me put everybody at ease by stating right from the outset that I believe this had to happen, and that it's a good thing it did." She spoke to Robby and Chelsea, who sat side by side on the sofa. "When I first got here and discovered that Tom lived here and was the principal at Kent's school, I felt quite threatened. Maybe I thought I'd lose Kent if Tom found out. On second thought, there's no maybe about it—that was the case. But Kent made me realize that it was unfair of me to try to withhold anything more from him about his father, or to try to keep them separated. In time I came to realize that the same was true regarding you."

Again she shifted her gaze to Kent. It rested on him lovingly. "He's an only child, and that can be a lonely row to hoe." To Robby and Chelsea, "Your existence, while coming as a shock to us, could turn out to be a gift that we weren't exactly expecting to find in this life. Especially Kent. I've spent a lot of time since we moved back here looking into his future, imagining the days when I grow old, and he's left alone. Yes, he'll have a wife someday—I hope—and children. But you"—she paused—"his sister and brother . . . you two will be the gift that I couldn't give him. So rest easy. I'm not going to throw a tantrum, or give you the cold shoulder because you've come here unannounced. Quite the opposite, in fact. I think it was high time we met."

They all relaxed then, sank back against the cushions, and the kids exchanged quick glances of relief.

Kent said, "You know, I think I will have something to drink after all. Anybody else?"

While he was getting the drinks, Monica visited with the other two, and only when they all had glasses in their hands did she settle back, cross her knees, and ask, "So what was it you came here to ask me?"

Chelsea and Kent exchanged a glance that said, *You first.*

"Well?" Monica tilted her head. "Who's going to tell me?"

"I guess I will," Kent said, pulling forward to the edge of his chair.

"No, let me," Chelsea interrupted. "She's my mother, and it was my idea."

Monica could see the girl's face had grown blotchy with nervousness. She was gripping her glass with both hands.

"First I have to know something," Chelsea began, "and it's pretty hard to ask."

Out of the blue, Robby spoke up. "I'm part of this too. I'll ask. Ms. Arens, we need to know the truth—if you're having an affair with our dad."

"An af—" Monica's stunned surprise was unmistakable. "An affair with your dad? Heavens no!"

Robby's breath escaped in a whistle. His shoulders wilted. "Wow, that's a relief."

Chelsea took over, rushing ahead nonstop so she wouldn't chicken out halfway through. "You see, my mother thinks you are, and she's asked him to move out of the house, and he's living with my grandpa, and our family is just going all to pot because of it, and there's only one thing I can think of to get my mother to screw her head on straight, and that's if you'd come over to our house and tell her right to her face that you and Daddy aren't doing anything together besides talking about Kent! I mean, I understand that you've probably got to do that now and then.

After all, he is both of your sons—I mean, a son to both of you—and it's just like with us three"—she waved a hand taking in her two brothers—"we're related and there's no sense pretending we're not. Like Kent said, we've been acting pretty childish about some of it, and so has my mother, but if you'd just come over to our house—please!—and tell her that she's breaking up our family for nothing, maybe she'll take Daddy back and everything will be right again. Will you?"

Chelsea's eyebrows were elevated, her face so radiant with hope that Monica couldn't help being touched by her courage. Nevertheless, as the only official adult of the group, she had to make them explore the risks.

"Your mother might not appreciate me invading her domain."

"But you don't understand! My mother's had her way in all of this right from the beginning, and nobody's been able to stop her. And she's wrong! She's dead wrong!"

Monica considered, then turned to her son. "Kent?"

"I'm with Chelsea. I think it's worth a try."

"You don't feel it might jeopardize your future relationship with Tom?"

"He's just one of the three. I've got to consider Chelsea and Robby, too."

"So you want me to do this?"

"Yes, Mom, I do."

"And you, Robby?"

"We just can't think of anything else, Mrs. Arens."

She pressed a hand to her heart, sucked in a pronounced breath, and let her eyelids close for a moment. "Whew!" she exclaimed, opening them. "The thought of it scares me to death. What if it backfires? What if she just gets angrier with him?"

The three kids looked back and forth at one another. Nobody had an answer. Their faces had gone from hopeful to glum.

"Well, listen, I'll tell you what." Monica set her glass down and curled forward. "I'll do what you ask, with two conditions. First, that I don't speak to your mother in your house. Any way you cut it, that would be invading her territory, and she's bound to take offense. And second, that the two of us are alone when I do it. Agreed?"

Robby and Chelsea consulted with their eyes and replied in unison, "Agreed." Chelsea added, "But will you do it now? Tonight? Because then maybe Dad can move back in over the weekend, if it works. 'Cause, you see, he's planning to move into an apartment tomorrow, which Mom doesn't even know yet, I don't think, but he told us. That's one of the reasons I'm grounded."

"You're grounded?" Monica repeated, trying to keep up with the tale.

"Oh, that's another whole story, but I got so upset when I found out my dad was going to rent an apartment that I did something pretty stupid, and they found out about it and I got grounded, so I'm supposed to be at home right this minute, and if you don't come over there and talk to Mom, I'm really going to be in hot water when she gets there and finds out I disobeyed her again."

Monica touched her forehead. "This is getting to be too much for me. Is your mother at home now?"

"She will be pretty soon . . ." Chelsea checked her watch. "Right after six, when conferences are over."

Monica rose. "Then let's wait until six and go over there, and I can wait out on the street in my car and you two can go inside and ask her to come out and talk to me. How's that?"

"What about Kent?"

"Kent stays here. We don't need her spying him hanging around to add insult to injury. If you want to spring him on her, you do that later when I'm not around and she's gotten used to the idea of taking your dad back."

"That okay with you, Kent?" Robby asked.

"Sure. We can talk later on the phone."

Shortly after six, they all went down the steps to the entry and began getting on coats and jackets. Monica opened a side door leading to the garage and said, "I'll back my car out and follow you two."

A moment later the power lifter rumbled through the wall, raising the garage door. The three young people stood in the foyer, wanting to reach out to one another, afraid it was too soon, each of them wishing one of the others would do it first.

"Well, good luck," Kent said.

"Thanks," Robby said.

"Yeah, thanks," Chelsea added.

"Mom will do a good job, don't worry."

On the other side of the service door the car door slammed and the engine started.

"Well, listen, I'll talk to you later, okay?"

"Yeah, sure."

There in the vestibule of this warm house where understanding was at last beginning, they hovered on the brink of caring, their common genes urging them to break the bonds that had kept them apart for too many years already. It flashed through their minds to ask, *Would it be okay if I hugged you?* but shyness overcame them.

"I wish . . ." Kent said, and stopped himself.

"Yeah, I know," Chelsea said, sharing his thought. "But it's not too late, is it?"

"Heck no," Robby said, "it's not too late. We're just beginning."

Then one of them smiled. And another one smiled. And soon all three were smiling. . . then laughing. . . and the boys pitched together first, and maybe a few tears threatened their eyes, for they couldn't have spoken at that moment if their lives had been threatened. They broke apart, and Chelsea and Kent's hug was more cautious. But it happened, and it healed, and it opened doors to beautiful vistas of future possibilities.

"Good luck," Kent whispered at Chelsea's ear just before releasing her.

"Thanks."

Then he opened the door and stood with his hands in his jeans pockets, the cold air rushing into the house around him, caring little about it or the chill on his skin, watching as his brother and sister got into the car and waved, then led his mother away down the street. He didn't go back inside until he heard Robby's light tap on the horn. His own hand remained lifted in farewell long after either Robby or Chelsea could possibly see it.

Eighteen

C laire had agreed to meet Tom in his office at six o'clock, and as she
approached he was already locking up.

"So how did your day go?" she asked in her gravelly rasp.

He withdrew his key and turned around. "Sounds like it's a bad one
this time."

"Just awful." She touched the hollow of her throat, then wrapped her
arms around the stack of conference materials she was carrying.

"Did you put some honey in your tea?"

"Any more and I'll start buzzing and growing wings."

They walked to the main door, and he hit the clattery metal handle
with his hips, letting her precede him into the night. "Not the best day to
have to go home and ream out one of the kids."

"Is that what we're going to do?" Claire asked. "Ream her out?"

"I don't know. I haven't been able to decide how to handle it."

"Neither have I." Their footsteps matched as they strode side by side
to their cars. They'd faced moments like this before, when instinct had
failed them and left them searching for the best way to handle their

children. Through so many years they'd managed to muddle through and find ways that worked for all four of them.

"First of all I think we have to talk to her and let her get her feelings out," Tom said.

"Yes, I suppose so."

"She's going to blame us, you know."

"Yes, I know."

"And she's right. It's largely our fault."

"Yes, I know that too."

Early dark had fallen, the temperature had dropped, and the wind had kicked up. The empty halyard was making the flagpole ring. Their cars were parked at two different sides of the building. They stopped on the sidewalk in front of Tom's car.

"Claire, about John Handelman . . ."

She turned and looked up at him. "Please, Tom, I can't handle it right now. I've got to get this thing with Chelsea out of the way first. Maybe later tonight, after we've talked to her, you and I could go someplace quiet and talk."

Hope took hold of his heart. "Could we make that a definite date?"

"Yes, if I have any voice left to talk with."

He stood holding his car keys, the wind flapping his coattails and batting his hair while all within him wished for an end to this separation. "All right. So, I'll follow you home, okay?"

"Okay."

She began to move toward her car.

"Claire?" he called after her.

She stopped and turned, surprised to find a hint of a grin on his face.

"I know your throat hurts, but it sounds sexy as hell that way."

He got into his car, leaving her to watch with a faint smile before she turned and moved down the sidewalk away from him.

When they reached home the children's car was gone from the driveway. Claire pulled into the garage and Tom left his car outside. She waited, and as he approached they both felt the peculiarity of changed routine—for years he had parked in the garage beside her, where the empty stall looked nearly as sad as his half of the bed.

They went into the house together through the family room as they'd done so many times before. Lights were on there and in the kitchen but the house was silent. Claire set her conference materials on the kitchen counter and hung up her coat in the front hall closet while Tom stopped at the kitchen sink to get a drink. She welcomed the sound of the cabinet door thumping closed and the water running, as she went to the bottom of the stairs, and called, "Chelsea?"

No answer.

"Chelsea?" she called a little louder, stretching her neck.

She muttered under her breath and started upstairs. Both of the kids' bedroom doors were open, their lights on. Pausing in Chelsea's doorway, she found the room freshly cleaned, some stacks of clean socks and underwear on the crisply made bed, and the remainder of the unfolded laundry in a pile on the floor. Most days Claire would have assumed Chelsea was somewhere else in the house, but today the empty room set her feet flying. She tore around the corner into Robby's empty room.

"Robby?"

A brief hesitation beat, then she was barreling down the steps, calling, "Tom, are the kids down there anywhere?" Her heart began clubbing.

He appeared at the bottom of the stairs, looking up. "No. Aren't they up there?"

"No. Their bedroom lights are on, and Chelsea left half a load of unfolded laundry in the middle of her bedroom floor."

"What!" He scowled and headed up the stairs while Claire headed down.

"Tom, she was grounded! She wouldn't leave the house, and neither would Robby, without leaving a note!" He took the steps two at a time and shot past her. She watched his coattails disappear into one bedroom, then the other, before he returned and charged down to the main level, throwing a question over his shoulder.

"Did they say anything about evening plans?"

"No, nothing." She followed him to the kitchen, where he opened the basement door and looked down into the darkness. Next he went into the family room and stood for a long time looking worried, searching the room in slow motion, as if for a dropped earring.

"Well, they're not here," he said, returning to the kitchen. "Maybe they went out to get something to eat."

"Not without leaving a note. They knew conferences were done at six. They'd have left a note. And besides, when I say grounded, I mean grounded. I just don't believe Chelsea would have defied my orders."

"There's probably a perfectly logical explanation."

She knew Tom well: he was downplaying his anxiety to keep her from panicking.

"Tom . . ." she said uncertainly.

He turned away, probably to hide his face, but gave himself away by wrapping one fist around the other and cracking his knuckles. While he was pretending to appear calm, he was glancing out the front window hoping to see the Nova drive in.

"Tom, I'm worried . . . what if they—"

He spun to face her. "There's nothing to be worried about, Claire. You mustn't jump to conclusions."

"But she left laundry half folded, and lights on all over the house. If you could have seen how she was dressed last night, you'd know what kind of state of mind she's in."

They faced each other, needing to assure and be reassured as in the past, each of them hesitant to make the first move. But the force of habit—if not need—finally grew too much for them.

"Claire," he said, and made the first move.

And she made the second.

Suddenly she was in his arms, in that comforting harbor where love buoyed and made the dire less dire. There were no kisses, only clinging and the exchanging of strength with Claire caught firmly against the canvas texture of his coat collar and the sturdy bone of his jaw. Gripping each other with their hearts racing, they stood in the kitchen, which had never seemed like home without him, whose forlorn table had been surrounded by a scattered group, never a family, since he'd been absent from it. For moments they simply clung and felt the first frayed threads of their relationship begin to mend. Their hearts wallowed partly in fear for their children and partly in hope for themselves, touching once again after all these long weeks.

Their daughter, the peacemaker, had tried to bring about this disarmament and thought she had failed, so where had she run and with whom?

"I failed her, Tom," Claire whispered with a catch in her voice.

"No, Claire, no," he soothed. "This is no time for blaming yourself. What we have to do now is find her, and Robby too." He set her back from him and held her by both arms. "Do you have any idea where they might be?"

"No, Tom, I've been trying to think but I . . ."

At that very moment lights came sweeping into the driveway and a car tore in at breakneck speed. It careened to a stop behind Tom's just as he reached the window to peer out. "Oh, thank God, they're home. Looks like they've brought somebody else though . . . there are two cars." Another vehicle had pulled up at the foot of the driveway and stopped. The exterior garage lights sent a ray of teal blue flame along a ridge of paint on the side of the second vehicle. "What the hell?" Tom mumbled, frowning.

"Who is it?"

"I'm not sure, but I think it's Kent."

Tom dropped the curtain as car doors thudded and voices sounded, muffled through the wall. A moment later Robby and Chelsea barged into the house and stood breathlessly, confronting their parents in the brightly lit kitchen.

"Where have you been?" Tom shouted.

Instead of answering him, Chelsea keyed on Claire. "Talking with somebody we think you ought to talk to, Mom."

"Who?" Claire asked.

Chelsea pleaded, "Just come outside with us, please, Mom."

"Who's out there?"

Robby stepped in, exasperation honing a sharp edge on his voice. "Will you for *once* in your life just give over control and do what we ask, Mother?"

Nonplussed, Claire stared at her son. Then at her daughter. The room held a static silence before Chelsea begged, much gentler than Robby, with her heart in each word, "We want you to put on your coat and go outside. There's somebody waiting at the end of the driveway. Will you do that for us, Mom?"

"Who is it?"

With a hint of tears in her eyes, Chelsea appealed to her father. "Dad, would you make her do it? Please? Because we're running out of ideas, and this is our last one."

Tom turned to Claire, puzzled but willing to encourage her to do whatever the children wanted, because he too felt she needed to consider their feelings more if their marriage was to go forward and their family thrive. And since it was Kent out there, she needed to strike some sort of truce with him, didn't she? Because Tom had every intention of seeing him on a regular basis and being a father to him from now on.

"Claire?" he said simply.

From the somber appeal in his eyes, she turned to the hope in her children's, realizing from their intensity that their request held great import for all of them, and that this was not the time to take them to task for defying rules. If she and Tom were to patch things up, whatever awaited her outside seemed a step she must take in that direction.

"All right," she said, and saw the collective wilting of shoulders before she retrieved her coat and, without one word of repudiation, went outside.

The garage lights laid a golden path down the driveway and lit the side of the blue Lexus. *No*, Claire thought. *Please, I can't do this!* But she made her feet carry her past the two parked cars toward the automobile whose very glint of blue had struck anger and jealousy into her whenever she'd seen it these past two months.

When Claire was halfway down the driveway, the driver's door opened and someone got out. Monica Arens emerged and stood waiting, studying Claire over the sunroof.

Claire halted fifteen feet away.

"Please don't go back in," Monica said.

"I wasn't expecting it to be you. I was expecting your son."

"I know. I'm sorry if this is a shock. Could we talk?"

Insecurity reared up and caught Claire in its unkind grip: this woman had been intimate with Tom one week before their wedding. He had gotten her pregnant when Claire was already pregnant by him, and that fact still had the power to cow Claire. But she remembered the pleading on her children's and Tom's faces as they asked her to see this through. The future of her family rested squarely with her.

"Yes. I guess it's time, isn't it?"

"Would you like to get in my car? It's warmer in there."

No, Claire really would not like to, but she acceded. "All right," she said, and she got in.

Inside, the dash lights created a faint aquamarine intimacy. Claire felt trapped and terrified, facing Monica Arens, prepared to dislike her while forced to hide it.

Monica said, "I wouldn't have chosen to do this in my car, but the children insisted. I thought it would be much better if we met on neutral territory, but . . . as I said, the choice wasn't mine."

"No, this . . . this is fine."

"I'm not sure what they told you in there."

"Nothing. They just said someone was waiting outside who wanted to talk to me."

"I *am* sorry to spring this on you. I'm sure it was a shock when you saw me get out of the car."

Claire released a nervous scrape of laughter. "Yes, I think you could say that." Her tortured tenor seemed pronounced in the confines of the car.

"Well, let me begin by explaining that our children came to me today and asked me to do this. All our children—yours and mine."

"Together?" Claire retorted in surprise.

"Yes, together. It seems that they had a meeting of the minds and decided they have to make the best of being brothers and sister, and that the sooner they get to know each other, the better. They spent part of the afternoon together here at your house. I don't know whether you're aware of that or not."

"No," Claire said, the word scarcely leaving her throat. "I . . . I didn't know any of this."

"Well, after they left here, they came to my house and appealed to me to come and talk to you, and they wanted me to do it here. I'll admit, I balked at the idea, but they were very sincere and very persuasive, so here I am, no happier about it than you are. But I'm here just the same."

Claire was surprised by the woman's candor. Some of her defenses crumbled as she realized Monica's feelings were much the same as hers.

Monica took a deep breath and continued. "I guess this would be easiest if I came right out and told you that I know about your separation from Tom. I know that the two of you have been living apart since shortly after I came to town."

In the sub-light, Claire felt herself blushing: never had her jeopardized marriage seemed like a greater blight on her pride than when admitting it to this woman.

"Yes, that's true, but we're going to start counseling next week."

"That's good. But when you do you should know exactly how things stand between Tom and me. There's absolutely nothing between us, and you've got to believe that. The truth is, there never was. The night we went to bed together was a one-night stand, plain and simple. I have no excuses for it, and neither does he. But if you let the past or anything you suppose is happening between us *now* stand in the way of your marriage, you're making the biggest mistake of your life."

Relief hit Claire like a giant breaker. She was still tumbling in its backwash when Monica rushed on. "You can ask me anything you want about the times I've seen and talked to Tom since we moved back here, and I'll answer you absolutely truthfully. What do you want to know? If I ever saw him? I did. Where? At my house, which was absolutely an arbitrary choice. All we ever did was talk about Kent and what was best for everyone involved."

Claire's heart was hammering so hard the top of her head was palpitating, but she seized the opportunity to clear up a detail that had stuck in her craw ever since she'd been told about it. "My neighbor said she saw you with him in a parked car in front of a restaurant right around the time school started."

"Yes, she did. It was another one of those days when we were caught in the exceedingly emotional tangle of trying to decide whether or not everyone should be told about Kent. Maybe we weren't wise to meet there, but at the time we just fumbled through it, doing whatever we could to figure out how to deal with the mess we'd created. If you want to blame someone, you can blame me. I made a major mistake years ago by choosing not to tell Tom that I was pregnant or that Kent had been born. Now, in the years since, we've all been enlightened, and we know that it's not just the woman's prerogative to decide whether or not a man has rights to his child when one is born out of wedlock. But in those days these things were often kept a secret, and a lot of fathers never had the choice about what part they'd play in their children's rearing. I was wrong. Let me say it again, and ask your forgiveness along with Tom's and Kent's. If I hadn't hidden the truth, this breakup between you and Tom never would have happened, and your family would still be together."

Tears sprang into Claire's eyes. Abashed at the idea of Monica detecting them, she turned her face to the passenger window. "I don't know what I expected when I saw you standing beside the car, but I guess there was still a part of me that thought maybe you were going to . . . to tell me that . . . well, that you and Tom were in love and that I . . . I should set him free."

"No, never." Monica reached over and lightly touched Claire's coat sleeve, bringing her face around. "Please believe me. If I loved him that's exactly what I'd be saying, because that's what I'm like. I don't back down from anything." She removed her hand and sat sideways in her seat, studying Claire's profile against the dimly lit square of window behind her.

"There's something else I need to say, and this is the hardest part of all. I'm saying it for two reasons—because you need to hear it and because I need to say it after all these years." She paused a beat before continuing: "That night, the night of Tom's bachelor party, what we did was wrong. I knew it then and I'm admitting it now. Just don't let it carry too much weight, after all these years. I know that's a big order, but there's a lot at stake here. Try to realize that he was young and disillusioned and under a great deal of stress, having to get married. But I'll tell you something you probably never knew before. When I moved back here, the first time Tom came to my house—the *only* time he came there—he told me how much he loves you and that since he's been married to you, every year of his life has gotten better and better." Monica's voice faded to a sincere whisper. "Your husband loves you very much, Mrs. Gardner. I think you've broken his heart by forcing this separation. You have two very beautiful children, who want their mother and father together so badly. Won't you please take him back and beat the odds?"

Claire lifted her tear-filled eyes to Monica, who went on with her appeal.

"There are so many families breaking up today, and so many single-parent families like mine. I really don't have to tell you that, working in the school the way you do. But even though I have nothing to apologize for as far as my parenting is concerned, I realize that families like yours are still the best kind—a mother and a father with kids they've raised together. That remains the true American dream, but it's becoming obsolete. If I had the history you do with Tom, and two beautiful children, and all those good years behind me, I'd fight to keep my husband, not throw him away. There. I've stated my case. Do with it what you will."

In the luminous silence that followed, the two women sat motionless, bound by this baring of souls. Claire found a tissue in her coat pocket and used it, then sat gazing at her lap, letting her emotions play out their fanciful dance—relief and gratitude and a great deal of respect for the woman beside her; hope and a huge stew of tumult as she anticipated the moment she'd walk into the house and face Tom again. Finally she released a sigh and swung to study her companion. "You know, I've always been prepared to dislike you."

"That's understandable."

"I tried to find fault with you at conferences yesterday, but I couldn't. It actually *irritated* me that I couldn't. I wanted you to be . . ." Claire shrugged. "I don't know . . . to be lacking in some way. Rude maybe, misguided or haughty, so I could criticize you, if not openly, at least to myself. Now, though, I see why Kent is the kind of boy he is."

"Thank you."

"Perhaps we should talk about him, too."

"If you want to."

"We should have at the conference and I knew it."

"But that would have muddled our parent-teacher relationship, wouldn't it?"

"Yes, but that's no excuse."

"Oh, don't be so hard on yourself. We're talking now and that's what's important."

Claire reassessed. "Actually, we did quite well yesterday, considering what was going on beneath the surface, didn't we?"

"Yes, we did." Had they been friends, this admission would have been accompanied by a grin. As it was, they knew they would never be friends. But they could be allies in a different sense.

"About Kent . . ." Claire said.

"He's understandably hard for you to accept, I realize that."

"But I must. I know that."

"Yes, for your children's sake."

"And Tom's."

"And Tom's. I know all three of the children want it, and I believe Tom does too. You probably know he's been seeing Kent since the two of you have been apart. They're trying to establish some sort of father-son relationship. But it'll take time."

"Time and cooperation from me, that's what you're saying, isn't it?"

"Mmm . . . well, yes . . . yes, it is."

Silence fell once more. At the end of it, Claire was feeling even more comfortable with Monica. "I'll tell you something I haven't even told Tom yet. I've had a lot of time to think about how I'd handle it if I ever got back together with him, and I realized that this school year is really only a very small increment of time in terms of the years we'll have in the future. Once the school year ends and Kent moves on to college, I think it'll be easier for me to be objective about him. And I won't lie to you and say that the wishes of my children don't matter, because they do. If they want to get to know their brother, who am I to stand in their way?"

"Are you saying he'd be welcome in your house?"

It took some time to come up with an answer. "Oh, Monica, you do put me on the spot."

"Then, strike that question. Take it a day at a time."

"Time . . . yes. Good old time. It really does heal, doesn't it?"

"I think it does, if you let it."

"I guess it's only fair to ask you—how did you feel about my children coming to your house?"

"Stunned. Then after I had a chance to get used to the idea, it didn't seem so threatening anymore, especially given the fact that all three kids had already decided they were going to become friends anyway, no matter what their parents said. And by the way, since you've offered me a compliment on my kid, I'll do the same for yours. They seem very nice."

"Thank you."

"So . . . it's up to you and me to smoke the proverbial peace pipe here."

"And what good will it do us not to? We'll only hurt ourselves."

"Exactly."

Claire blew out a breath: she was feeling better and better.

"What a couple of days these have been. Do you realize that just a little over twenty-four hours ago you walked up to my table in the gym with a pretty new hairdo and perky new makeup and I took one look at you and thought, *If this woman's not in love with my husband, I'll eat my grade book.*"

"What in the world does a new hairdo have to do with it?"

"It's silly. Someone told me once that you can always tell when a woman falls in love because she gets a new hairdo and starts looking prettier."

"I got a new hairdo because I needed an emotional pick-me-up. It's been pretty tense around our house too. I have to admit, it feels really good to have talked to you about all of this. Now if you'll just say you're going to go in there and patch it up with Tom, I'll go home a rather satisfied woman."

"Of course that's what I'm going to do."

"Good." For the first time Monica offered a smile. It kindled in the luster from the dash lights while her eyes rested easy on Claire.

Claire smiled too. "Thank you, Monica."

"Thank our children. They were much more courageous than me. I had to be led by them before I'd do the right thing."

It was difficult to find a parting remark. Claire put her fingers on the door handle and looked back at the other woman. "Well, here goes." She opened the door.

"Good luck."

"Thanks. And good luck to you too. I really mean that."

Their smiles took on a touch of verity now that they were parting. It struck them both that if they had met under any other circumstances, they would indeed have become very good friends, for in this short meeting they'd found much to respect in one another, a lionheartedness tempered by vulnerability, which—in both their minds—made them strong women capable of deep understanding.

"Take care," Monica said, and Claire slammed the door.

She did not watch the car pull away but turned toward her home, where the three most important people in her world waited for her to come inside and make their lives right again. Dry autumn leaves were cartwheeling across the driveway. The stars were out, and she realized that tomorrow was Halloween. She'd neglected to get a pumpkin carved and set out on the front step, nor had she dug out the skeleton wind sock that usually waved from the bare branches of the ash tree, or bought corn husks to surround the light pole the way everyone on the block did at this time of year—things she and Tom had always done together.

Well, maybe tomorrow, she thought, for tomorrow they would awaken together.

Please, Lord.

Inside, Tom was cooking supper. She stepped into the aroma of sandwiches browning on a griddle and the sound of a table being set. The moment she walked in, all motion ceased. Tom turned from the stove with a towel in his hands. The kids stalled with plates and silverware only half distributed.

Tom spoke first. "I hope it's okay that I started making some grilled-cheese sandwiches."

"Of course. It's fine."

"I couldn't find anything else in the house."

"I guess I haven't been cooking much lately. I sort of lost my heart for it."

They spoke with the breathlessness of a man and woman feeling their way, separated by an entire kitchen but locked in rapt absorption with each other. The children could have been on Mars for all the attention they received from their parents. Claire's cheeks took on spots of pink. Tom had removed his suit jacket, and through his close-fitting white shirt the sharp rack of his breathing was clearly visible. He finally flinched and cleared his throat, as if realizing how long he and Claire had been staring at each other.

"Ah . . . children . . ." He glanced at them. "Would you please excuse your mother and me for just a minute?"

"Sure," Chelsea said meekly, and very carefully set down the stack of plates.

"Sure," Robby seconded, and set down his handful of silverware.

They left the room like a pair of obedient servants, nearly tiptoeing. In their wake the kitchen remained silent but for the quiet sizzle of the sandwiches on a Silverstone griddle and the sound of two people trying to control their breathing.

Claire stood just inside the entrance from the family room, still wearing her coat. Tom waited with the stove at his back, unconsciously gripping the small terry towel.

"What did she say?" he asked at last, in a voice like that of a prize fighter who's just taken a kidney punch.

"She said, in essence, that I've been a damned fool."

He reached without looking, to drop the towel on the enamel stovetop behind him, but she was the one who did the running, straight into his arms, throwing him hard against the handle of the oven. They kissed the way immigrants kissed who had crossed oceans and prairies, endured hardships and separation to be together again. The embrace was filled with wordless promise, and the pressure of tears withheld.

When the kiss ended, she clutched him against herself, blinking hard at the ceiling while her tears made silver tracks on her face. "Oh, Tom, I'm sorry. I'm sorry."

"So am I."

"But you said it long ago, and I wouldn't believe you."

"Do you believe me now?"

"Yes! Not only do I believe you, I see how wrong I was. Dear God, I nearly tore this family apart for good."

"Oh, Claire," he whispered, and closed his eyes.

She turned to fit her forehead into the familiar cove of his jaw. "Please forgive me," she whispered while her tears wet his shirtfront.

She felt him swallow and sensed his inability to speak at that moment, having been put through a spell of fear and come through it intact.

"Please forgive me, darling," she whispered.

They embraced through a renascent stretch of silence, the house holding a still watch around them, as if this reunion were a sacrament. "I thought I'd lose everything I'd worked so hard for," he whispered, "you, the kids, our home, everything I loved. I was so scared, Claire."

"I'm so sorry I put you through that."

"The trouble was, I knew that if that happened, it would be my own fault."

"No, no, I'm just as much to blame, maybe more for not forgiving you for something that happened so long ago. Oh, Tom, I love you so much, and it's so lonely and unrewarding being as stubborn as I've been."

Their mouths joined, and he slipped his arms inside her coat to keep her, full-length, against his body. His hands took possession where they would, and hers followed suit. Several blissful minutes later Claire interrupted their idyll to murmur against his lips, "I think something's burning."

Tom's head lifted, and in one quick leap he rattled the griddle onto a cold burner. "Damn it!" He switched off the heat. Stench and smoke rose from four ruined sandwiches.

Claire peered around him and inspected the spoils. "We sure fixed them, didn't we?"

"And the refrigerator looking like everybody's gone on vacation. I don't know what we're going to eat." Twisting aside, he slung the burned sandwiches into the garbage disposal and leaned the pan against the side of the sink. All the while she clung to him like a barnacle, letting him move, but not too far.

"I have an idea," she said when he'd finished rescuing them from fire and was concentrating on her again. "Why don't we send the kids out to pick up some fast food?"

He twined his fingers low on her spine and settled her hips against his. "I have a better idea. Why don't we send the kids out for some slow food?"

She bit his chin and offered a provocative grin. "Why stop at slow food? How about a five-course dinner?"

"Well, hell, while we're at it, how about a five-course dinner at Kincaid's?"

Kincaid's was in Bloomington, about a thirty-minute ride away. It was the top-rated restaurant in the Twin Cities and required a hefty wait without reservations. Tom and Claire had been talking about going there for over three years, but hadn't made it yet.

They laughed, feeling the rhythm of their humor falling back into place.

"I suppose that would be just a little transparent, wouldn't it?" Tom conceded.

Claire shrugged. "Chelsea would grin."

"And Robby would take us up on it and it'd probably cost us about a hundred bucks."

"So how are we going to get them out of the house?"

He caught her around the neck with one arm and shifted her to his side. "Watch this." Hauling her along with him to the foot of the stairs, he raised his voice and shouted up, "Hey, kids, will you come down here?"

They appeared in record time, negotiating the steps at breakneck pace, leaping down the last two, at the foot of which their dad waited with his arm slung nonchalantly around their mom's neck.

Tom said, "Your mom and I want to be alone for a while. Any chance you'd take a bribe and go out and find yourselves some supper?"

Chelsea's eyes brightened and she looked at her brother with sheer elation all over her face. "Heck, yes!"

Robby said, "How much do we get?"

Tom let his arm slip from Claire and brandished a fist. Robby doubled over to protect his middle before the mock punch landed.

"You little bloodsucker," Tom teased. "I told your mom this would cost us money."

"Well, heck, I wasn't born yesterday, Dad. I can tell a vulnerable guy when I see one, and I know when to bleed him for all he's worth."

Tom pulled out his wallet and gave the kids thirty dollars. "Tell you what. Go out and get some supper, then find a movie somewhere. We don't want you back here until at least ten o'clock . . . agreed?"

"Sure, Dad."

"Sure, Dad." Chelsea glanced dubiously at her mother. "But I thought I was grounded."

Claire told her, "We'll talk about it later, after Dad and I have a chance to talk, okay?"

Chelsea nodded meekly.

Claire kissed Chelsea's cheek, hugged Robby, then the kids left.

The moment the door slammed, the kitchen grew quiet. The smell of the burned cheese sandwiches lingered in the air. Claire and Tom faced each other with flushed cheeks.

He asked, point-blank, "What do you want to do first, talk or go to bed?"

She wanted to go to bed. Lord, she had not wanted him this badly since the forced abstinence of their first dating days. But now that they were alone, she was terrified of the ground they still needed to cover between sex and reconciliation.

"I'll leave it up to you," she answered. "I think I'm going to cry when we talk, though—just so you know."

He remained where he was, his face still highly colored though he banked his desires and posed questions first. "There's only one thing I want to know. What did you do with John Handelman?"

"I kissed him. Once. That's all."

"All right," he said, questioning her no further. "Then it's behind us. Forgotten."

"Even though I still have to get through another three weeks of play practice with him?"

"I trust you."

"I trust you too," she replied. "I'm sorry it took so long for me to realize it."

"Monica told you there's nothing between us?"

"Yes, and much more—that there never was. She also said that the first time she talked to you about Kent, you told her that every year we were married just got better and better."

"It's true. Up until this year."

"Can you understand what it did to me though, finding out about Kent? How it undermined my security?"

"Yes, Claire, I can. No matter what you thought, I was never insensitive to your hurt, but I didn't know what I could do about it. I couldn't undo the past."

"I guess that's what I expected of you, wasn't it? Even though I knew it was impossible."

"Is that what you still expect? Because I can't. And Kent is very much a part of my plans for the future. You might as well know that right from the start. He's my son, and I plan to be there for him from now on, as his father. If you can't handle that, Claire, you'd better say so right now."

Her lips trembled as she whispered in a shaken voice, "Tom, may I please come over there and hold you? B . . . because I don't think I can get through this without your arms around me."

They each moved halfway, meeting without the abandon of earlier. She walked into his loose embrace and felt his hands curve around her waist and his head drop over her shoulder. She laid her face against his shirtfront and folded her arms up his back. The moment they touched, her tears formed. He knew it. He understood. He simply held her and let the healing continue.

They stayed that way awhile, nestling gratefully, making vows in their heads, thinking of constancy, and the past that would have to be forgiven and forgotten if they were to make it. And the future, which would include some new wrinkles.

When Claire finally spoke, her voice had calmed some. "The children were together today . . . here, in our house, all three of them. Did they tell you?"

Against her cheek she felt his heart beating wildly. "No, they didn't," he whispered.

"And afterwards at Monica's house they decided it's time they got to know each other."

He closed his eyes and fought to control a sudden sting in his eyes.

"Oh, Claire, I can't believe it," he whispered, overcome.

"If Robby and Chelsea are willing to accept him, how can I do anything less?"

"Do you mean it, Claire?" He pulled back to study her face with its luminous tear-filled eyes and shiny lips, slightly puffed from crying earlier in Monica's car.

"I'm going to try, Tom. It may take some time before I'm totally comfortable around him, but I'll do my very best, that's a promise."

He lifted both hands to push back her hair and hold her face, his thumbs resting at the crests of her cheeks. "You've given me two children of our own, and I love you for being a good mother to them, so please don't misunderstand what I'm about to say . . . but, Claire, you've never given me a greater gift than what you just said."

With her voice on the verge of breaking, she asked, "Why did it take me so long to come around to it? Why did I put our family through so much misery?"

He rested his forehead against hers. "Because you're human, and you were scared, and because love isn't perfect. We can love somebody very much and still make mistakes that hurt them."

"I'm so sorry I hurt you," she whispered.

"I'm sorry I hurt you too. The trick is to learn from what we've been through, and I think we have."

"Yes, I think so."

Gently, he kissed her forehead. The secondary issues—how to handle Chelsea, when Tom would move back home, how they would blend their future with their children's—could be dealt with later. Now there was peace to be made, love to be restored.

She whispered, "I missed you so much. This house was like a sentence without you. Mealtimes were just awful, and when the alarm clock went off and you weren't there to roll over against, and when I'd get home from school at night and know you weren't driving in behind me. And wh . . . when Chelsea started acting up. Oh, Tom, I n . . . needed you there for strength so badly, only you w . . . weren't there and I d . . . didn't understand mys . . . self . . . and . . . ."

"Shh . . . don't cry, Claire, it's over." He gathered her up hard against him, rocking her from side to side while she clung to his neck. "We're together, and that's how we're going to stay. Chelsea will be all right as soon as she sees that we're all right. She's going to come through this just fine, you just wait and see. Now come on, Claire"—he tucked her under his arm—"let's go to bed."

Climbing the stairs with him, she said, "I'm sorry I couldn't keep from crying. I've ruined our good mood."

"I think I know a way to make you happy again, and besides, we got all those tears out of the way, so from here on out it's just going to get better. Come on, take me to our own comfortable bed in our own clean house where I don't have to wonder how long it's been since the laundry was washed."

She obliged him with a chuckle and rubbed her face against his shirtfront to dry her eyes.

"I knew you couldn't last out there at your dad's permanently, but I was terrified that you'd move into an apartment of your own, and then what if you just loved it? Maybe you'd discover that it was nice not having rock music ramming through the walls, and teenagers arguing at the supper table, and junk cars needing fixing, and wives who wake you up with their blow dryers when you want to sleep an extra ten minutes in the morning."

"Are you kidding? You've just described what makes me the happiest. It's called family life, and without it I was a lost man."

"And I was a lost woman."

They had reached their bedroom. She slipped from beneath his arm to turn on a lamp while he closed the door. Then he crossed to the bed, cocked one knee onto the mattress, and fell, flipping onto his back with his arms upflung. "Ahhh . . ." he sighed, closing his eyes as he lay on the familiar softness. She studied him, stretched out, hollow-bellied, his hair dark against the spread. Days past, she had wondered what to expect when and if this moment came, and in her imagination, it was not this. She had pictured swift passion, a reclaiming in no uncertain terms. Instead, he fell back like one exhausted.

But his eyelids were twitching.

And suddenly it struck her: she had wounded him deeply by turning him away time and again. There were still amends to be made.

She removed her clothing, watching him and knowing he listened to the silken rustles of her undressing.

Naked, she went to him, dropping to one knee on the bed, bending to him with a hand on either side of his head.

"Tom," she whispered, "open your eyes."

He did, and she saw the last-minute uncertainty within them.

"Tom . . . I love you. Through all this, I never stopped loving you, never stopped wanting you . . . not even when I turned you away."

She lowered her mouth and his opened to receive it, though he lay as before, like a body washed up on a shore. She kissed his twitching eyelids, stilling them—first one, then the other—and the bridge of his nose, his temples, left and right, and the cowlick at the center of his hairline, which so reminded her of his other son. And his mouth once more, with infinite tenderness.

"No matter what," she whispered, "you must never believe it was because I didn't desire you. I was proving other things. They had nothing to do with this, Tom, nothing."

She touched him where no other woman would ever have the right to touch him, and his arms, lying lax a moment before, became instruments of possession, hauling her down where she had so missed being these past tormented weeks. From out of the past all the memories and promises they had built came back to compel, to move their hands one upon the other and bring an end to their separateness. In tangled bedding, with tangled limbs, they recommitted vows made years before, bringing back all the good, strong, wondrous sexual commitment to bond the spiritual commitment already made.

When their bodies were linked, and his eyelids no longer trembling, but open, and his insecurities no longer present, but put to rout, she moved above him, the aggressor, the seeker, the claimer of the disclaimed.

"I missed this," she said, her voice rich with passion, her motion insistent and unbroken. He closed his eyes and let his lips fall open and his fingers be webbed by hers, and his hand be pinned against the bedding.

Soon a sound issued from his throat, and his body rose one last time, as if lifted by a breaker, and shuddered within her, and his fingers folded hard upon her knuckles.

He spoke her name softly—"Claire"—and she knew she'd been forgiven. And later, he rolled her free and took her down pathways traveled many times, in their young, struggling innocence and ignorance, and their older enlightenment and certainty—pathways leading Claire to a cry, and an arching, and a following stillness, repletion for them both.

Afterward, they sighed in unison: amens at the end of a prayer. They basked in the familiarity of lazy limbs that no longer clung but lay useless, flung, slung wherever chance had landed them. Eyes closed, they lay with their breath falling softly against each other's face.

Her hand happened to be near his hair. She plucked at it a time or two, drawing it through her fingers as if knotting a thread.

Opening her eyes, she murmured, "It's so good to be here, to have it over with, to have you back."

He opened his eyes too. "I never want to go through anything like that again."

"You won't. We'll talk about everything from now on, no matter what it is that bothers us. I promise."

They lay side by side, studying each other, quiet, content.

"Someday," she said, "when we're very old, do you think we'll be able to look back at this time and laugh at our foolishness?"

He thought for a moment before answering. "No, I don't think so. What we've been through wasn't foolish. It hurt us both. There's even a chance that the hurt will never go away entirely, and we might carry a little bit of it with us forever. But if we do, it'll remind us of how close we came to losing each other and never to make the same mistakes again."

"I won't. I promise."

"I won't either."

They began growing drowsy. Outside, down the block, somebody's dog barked, so muted it could scarcely be heard through the walls. Out on Eagle Lake two old men set up their checkerboard and prepared for a long night of insulting one another. Somewhere across town a girl and boy rang the doorbell of their half brother and, when he answered, exclaimed, "It worked!" And when his mother appeared at his shoulder, "Thanks, Ms. Arens! Thanks a lot!"

On the conjugal bed, Tom's limbs gave a sudden jerk as he courted sleep.

Claire's eyes drifted open. "Honey?" she murmured.

"Hm?" His eyes remained closed.

"You aren't going to believe this, but I really liked Monica. She's a terrific woman."

Tom's eyes opened.

Claire's closed.

But her lips held the faintest smile.